Zoey tried to find the right way to suggest that it would be best if she simply went back to the airport. But she couldn't think of anything that didn't sound silly. She wasn't some nineteenth-century trembling virgin, terrified of being alone with a man. Finally, with an inward sigh, she gave up.

"Okay," she agreed with extreme reluctance. "But, you know, I can't stay long."

Tyler's mouth curved upward at the corners in an amused smile. "Don't worry, Ms. Donovan. You're perfectly safe with me."

Zoey wondered. Somehow, she suspected that no female, at least no *willing* female, was perfectly safe anywhere near Tyler Ross.

STRAIGHT FROM THE HEART

Pamela Wallace

HarperPaperbacks
A Division of HarperCollins*Publishers*

HarperPaperbacks *A Division of* HarperCollins*Publishers*
10 East 53rd Street, New York, N.Y. 10022

Cover photograph by Tom Algire/FPG International

First printing: January 1996

Printed in the United States of America

HarperPaperbacks, HarperMonogram, and colophon are trademarks of HarperCollins*Publishers*

❖ 10 9 8 7 6 5 4 3 2 1

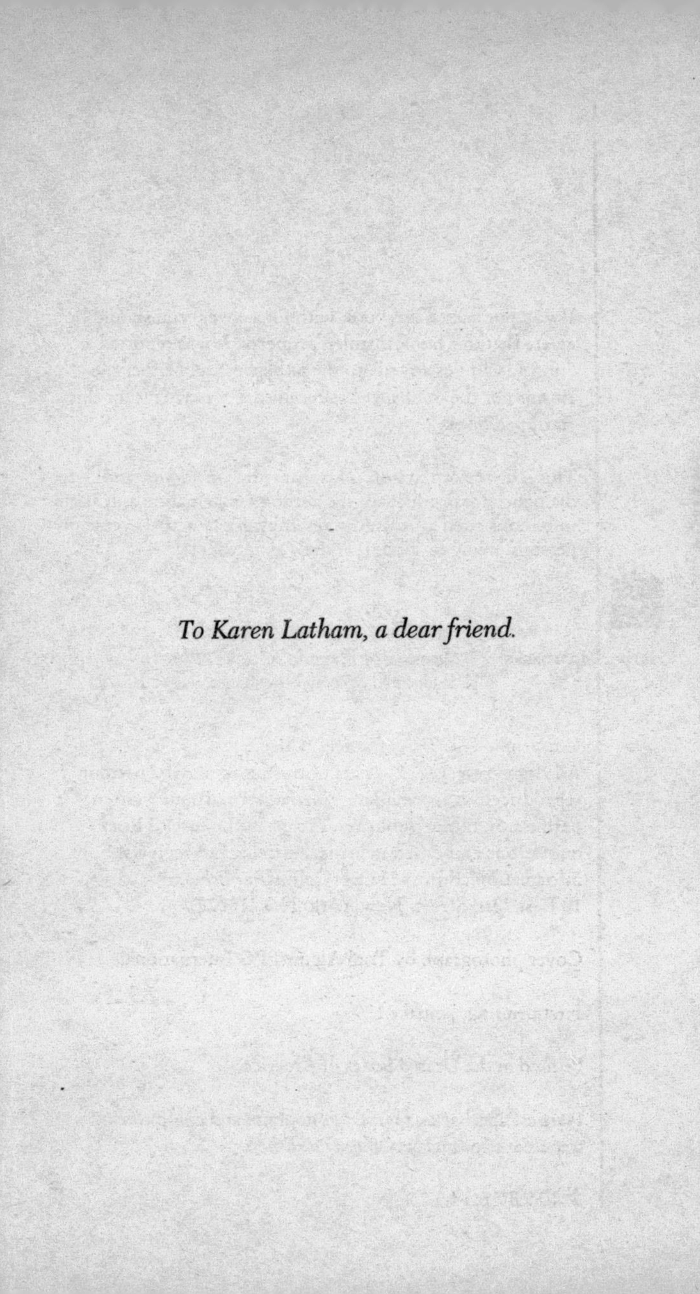

To Karen Latham, a dear friend.

Prologue

What happens when you get everything you ever wanted? You live happily ever after.

Her mother's words, a favorite refrain from Zoey Donovan's childhood, echoed in her mind as she stared out at the packed crowd of stylishly attired people in the elegant, exclusive Roget Gallery. On this glittering, glamorous night when Zoey and a handful of others were being honored as the best fine arts photographers in New York, it seemed that she had everything she'd ever wanted. Her dream of recognition and success had come true. Her stunning photographs, along with the other handpicked photographers' best work, covered the stark white walls of the large gallery. Feared critics and wealthy patrons admired her gritty black-and-white shots of New York City's back alleys, and the physical and human refuse found there. Most gratifying of all, the other photographers, most of them male and older than Zoey, accepted her as a peer.

The only missing element was her boyfriend, Brian. He was supposed to have been her escort at this elegant affair.

But, in typical fashion, he'd called at the last minute and said he had a crisis at work and couldn't make it. Zoey told herself she understood. His work was important and demanding. It didn't *really* matter if she was here alone. What mattered was that her work was being recognized. But her inner dialogue with herself rang hollow. It would have been so wonderful to have Brian share this moment with her.

The gallery owner, a rather smarmy piece of Eurotrash who went by the single name Emile, clapped his hands for attention. While the glitterati looked at him expectantly, he congratulated the photographers on their work. Holding a glass of champagne aloft, he toasted them as being the best of the best. Then, unable to resist putting in a plug for business, he announced that one of these talented photographers, Zoey Donovan, would hold her next one-woman show in this gallery the following month.

Watching Emile, Zoey could almost see dollar signs dancing in his eyes. After struggling for years, her first show at his gallery had been a huge success, bringing her a cover story in *New York* magazine and more money than she'd earned in all her previous years as a freelance photographer. Emile had told her he expected her second show to be even more successful.

She'd finally made it. She stood on the pinnacle of fame and fortune. If that didn't equal happiness, what did?

So why didn't she *feel* happy? Where did this awful, aching feeling of emptiness come from?

What's wrong with you? she asked herself sternly. *Now that you've got all you've always wanted, you don't have the sense to sit back and enjoy it.*

But, somewhere inside, a tiny voice suspiciously like that of her late, beloved great-grandmother, Gran Eileen, whispered in a lilting Irish accent, "Do you really have all you've always wanted?"

The question shook Zoey, and suddenly she felt that she couldn't bear to spend one more moment in this claustrophobic atmosphere of pretentiousness and self-congratulation.

Setting down the untouched glass of champagne that she'd been holding in order to give her hands something to do, she said a quick good-bye to a startled Emile and forced her way through the dense crowd.

Darkness had fallen over New York City when Zoey stepped out of the gallery. Nine o'clock on a hot, humid June night, and the steel gates were down over shop fronts. SoHo's cobblestoned streets were quiet and nearly deserted.

Deciding to walk home instead of catching a cab, she cut across Washington Square Park, a slender figure in a chic ivory-colored silk dress, red-gold hair curling about a heart-shaped face, gray eyes pensive behind turquoise-tinted John Lennon glasses. She passed beneath the massive, triumphal arch set grandly against the beautiful old brownstones on the perimeter of the park.

Glancing up at the sky, she saw a huge orange ball of a moon shining down on the city. Smiling to herself, she understood now why she'd thought of her dear Gran Eileen earlier. Because of her, Zoey knew this wasn't just another full moon. It was the second full moon in the same month, and that made it a blue moon.

"If you wish on a blue moon," Gran Eileen had told Zoey when she was a very little girl, "your wish is sure to come true—especially if you wish for love."

As proof, Gran Eileen had told her her own romantic story. She'd left the green hills of Connemara, a spinster at twenty, seeking a new life in America. Aboard the same ship, and also traveling in steerage, was a young man, Michael Donovan. They never spoke, only exchanged shy, wondering glances.

On the last night of the voyage, Eileen left the packed, stifling steerage and went up on deck. There was a blue moon shining that night, and she made a wish—a wish that she would find love in America.

The next day at Ellis Island, Eileen stood in line for hours, nervous, excited, and fearful. To her horror, a gruff, unsympathetic immigration official tersely informed her that, because she was an unmarried woman with no fiancé or family to guarantee her financial welfare, she wouldn't be allowed to enter the United States. Too stunned to speak, she stood there shaking, fighting back tears.

Then, to her utter amazement, Michael Donovan, who had heard the exchange, stepped forward and told the official that he would marry this girl—if she would have him. Eileen looked into his eyes, and what she saw there took her breath away. Without a word, she nodded. They were married then and there.

It had been a long and happy marriage, with a large and loving family. Remembering the story, Zoey smiled ruefully to herself. Maybe, if she wished on that blue moon, Brian would change his mind about getting married and having children. It was a crazy thought for such a modern and sophisticated young woman as she, but nothing else had seemed to work over the five frustrating years of their relationship.

Zoey stopped in her tracks and looked up at the gleaming full moon. It came to her then why she took so little pleasure in her professional success. That whispery voice of Gran's was right—it wasn't all she'd ever wanted. It was a significant part of it, but, by itself, it wasn't nearly enough.

She wanted a husband and children, a sense of connection and permanence.

Love.

Zoey had been raised with a strong sense of family, and she longed for it. The career-oriented life she'd made for herself, and her uncommitted relationship with Brian, left her feeling empty inside, as if a key ingredient were missing. That ingredient was family, and no matter how much she tried to convince herself that she was happy with the choices she'd made, she was beginning to sense that those choices weren't as fulfilling as she'd expected them to be. Especially when she was alone, as she was that night.

What good was all the recognition and success in the world if she had no one to share it with?

Feeling more than a little foolish, she gazed hopefully up at the moon and mouthed the silent words: All right, Gran, I'll trust you on this. I'll wish on this blue moon and, like you, I'll wish for love.

A soft, low sound whispered past her ear. It was the rustle of a warm summer breeze through the trees of the park, she told herself. But it sounded remarkably like the gentle sound of her great-grandmother's sigh.

1

Zoey paused at the door to her apartment and rummaged around in her large purse for her key. For the hundredth time, she told herself she needed to get a smaller purse—or a larger key ring that would be easier to find. Finally, her fingers closed around the worn rabbit's foot given to her by her mother years earlier, when she got her first car. Her mother had a bit of Gran Eileen's belief in superstitions, and she had assured Zoey the rabbit's foot would bring her luck. Zoey insisted she was far too pragmatic to believe such nonsense. But she'd never replaced the rabbit's foot.

As she opened the door, she was surprised to find the apartment in darkness. She could've sworn she'd left a light on, as she usually did. She hated walking into a dark, empty room.

Before she could reach for the switch, suddenly the lights came on in a blinding flash and a chorus of "Surprise!" nearly frightened her out of her wits.

Blinking in amazement, she stared at three of her closest

friends standing in the middle of the large loft, grinning at her. A huge banner reading Happy Birthday Zoey was strung across one wall, and colorful bouquets of helium-filled balloons were scattered around the room, which had been divided by furniture arrangements, not walls, into a living room, dining area, and kitchen. Zoey had fallen in love with the apartment for the huge windows that filled one wall and made it sunny and cheerful during daylight. It was a colorful place anyway, with deep-blue walls and silver stars painted on the white ceiling. The banner and balloons made it even more festive.

"What's the matter? Forget your birthday?" her best friend, Carla DiMaggio, a tall, thin brunette, asked with a wry smile.

Zoey knew the gaily decorated banner must have been made by Carla, a talented but so-far unsuccessful artist.

Carla went on, "I wouldn't blame you for wanting to ignore it. Now you're only *five* years from the big four-o!"

As Zoey closed the door behind her, she responded with good-natured sarcasm, "Thanks so much for reminding me. If it wasn't for you guys, I might've forgotten."

"No way," Denise Hudson responded with her characteristic giggle. "We'd never let that happen." Denise was a cute, vivacious, platinum blonde. Her high school-cheerleader image masked the sharp mind and tenacious ambition of a literary agent with one of the biggest agencies in Manhattan.

"What on earth took you so long?" Karen Cohen asked in mock anger. "Brian was supposed to hustle you out of the reception and get you back here a half-hour ago."

Zoey admitted reluctantly, "Brian couldn't make it. A crisis at work. He must've forgotten about getting me here."

Carla frowned. "I knew we couldn't count on him."

Zoey knew perfectly well that Carla wasn't Brian's biggest fan. Before Carla could launch into a tirade against him, Zoey said quickly, "If I'd known all this was waiting for me, I'd've taken a taxi home instead of walking."

Karen grinned good-naturedly. "We've been sitting in this dark apartment for half an hour. I told Carla that ten more minutes and I was gonna be into the cake whether you were here or not!"

Karen continually fought a losing battle with an extra twenty pounds that were a direct result of a terrible sweet tooth. Despite her nagging weight problem and unprepossessing looks, she was happily married to a fellow teacher at the high school where she taught English. He adored her and their three young daughters.

Unlike Karen, the other three friends were all single. Carla reveled in her independent lifestyle, dating a dizzying succession of men. Many of them would have offered commitment, but that wasn't what she was looking for; unlike Denise, who wanted desperately to get married and have children. But she could never seem to find a man who wasn't just passing through.

Zoey's boyfriend, Brian, often reassured her that he envisioned them being together for the rest of their lives. But he refused to take the next step—marriage.

Now, looking at the rich, decadent, chocolate-frosted cake proudly displayed in the middle of the glass-topped dining table, Zoey said to Karen, "Tell you what—you can take home whatever's left. I don't need the extra calories."

Karen rolled her eyes heavenward. "Oh, and like *I* do? What kind of friend are you, anyway? This is a classic example of sabotage."

"Let Alan and the girls have it."

"*If* it makes it home," Karen responded ruefully. "You know me and chocolate."

"So, are we gonna talk about this cake or are we gonna eat it?" Denise asked impatiently.

"First, the candles," Carla insisted. "We've gotta do this right. You don't turn thirty-five every day."

"Are you going to rub that in all night?" Zoey asked.

"Of course. What are friends for?"

Carla carefully placed thirty-five candles on the cake, covering the top of it. When she had finally lit every candle, the three women sang a rousing, if off-key, chorus of "Happy Birthday to You."

Zoey bent forward to blow out the mini-inferno, but Carla stopped her. "Wait! You have to make a wish."

Zoey was tempted to say she'd already done that, but she closed her eyes and repeated the wish she'd made earlier. Then she opened her eyes and blew as hard as she could. When it was clear she wasn't quite going to make it, her friends joined in and helped with the last few flickering candles.

"I'll bet I know what you wished for," Carla said. "Something to do with a commitmentphobe named Brian and a tiny box from Tiffany's."

Zoey merely gave her friend a rueful look.

"If it was me, it would involve Lucky Vanous and a box of Godiva chocolates," Karen said with a suggestive grin.

Denise responded, "Hey, don't get greedy. You've already got the kind of husband the rest of us would kill for."

"I'm married, not dead. I can still have fantasies."

While Zoey cut the cake and handed out slices, Karen poured champagne into glasses she brought from the kitchen. After a toast, Carla announced, "Time for presents!"

She picked up the boxes which were stashed behind the bright red sofa and brought them to Zoey. "Mine's the little red one. You have to open it last."

Knowing her friend's penchant for outrageous gag gifts, Zoey looked suspicious as she asked, "Why?"

Carla grinned impudently. "You'll see."

"I don't know about this," Zoey responded shaking her head. But she dutifully sat down on a chair and opened the other two gifts. There was an exquisite emerald green silk negligee from Bloomingdale's from Karen and a large bottle of Zoey's favorite perfume, *Les Must de Cartier,* from Denise.

"You guys shouldn't have been so extravagant," Zoey exclaimed, deeply touched.

She felt so fortunate to have dear friends like these. They'd met at an aerobics class ten years earlier. The class had ended after a few months, when the health club went out of business, but by then the four women had started socializing. A friendship that began with casual lunches and shopping expeditions, was gradually cemented by being there for each other in the good times and the bad: when Karen's children were born, when Carla's adored younger sister died of leukemia, when Denise was fired for not accepting her boss's sexual overtures, and when Zoey won her first photography award.

These three women, so different in so many ways, and yet so close, had become Zoey's surrogate family in New York. Observing them with deep affection as they sprawled over the sofa and chairs happily consuming cake and champagne, she thought how empty her life would be without them.

"You know," Denise pointed out in between mouthfuls of cake, "I just realized these gifts are almost more for Brian's benefit than yours."

Zoey was even more unhappy with Brian now than she'd been earlier at the reception. He'd not only failed to be there with her, he'd obviously completely forgotten about her friends' birthday plans for her. But Zoey was loyal to a fault, and she felt a need to defend him. "We'll enjoy them together," she said forcing a smile.

Turning to Carla, she asked, "*Now* can I open your gift?"

"First, a speech," Carla insisted.

Ignoring the loud groans of the others, she stood up and held her glass aloft. "A toast to our very dear friend Zoey on the occasion of her official descent into spinsterhood."

Zoey arched one eyebrow. "Oh, it's official now, is it?"

"Of course," Carla assured her gaily, adding in mock commiseration, "But not to worry. I'm here to help. The solution to your unfortunate state of spinsterhood is in that box. *Now* you can open it."

Zoey tore off the red-foil wrapping paper and found an old shoe box. Pulling off the lid, she gave Carla a questioning look when she saw what at first glance appeared to be a small, neatly folded newspaper. But when she took it out of the box and opened it up, the title said it all—*Country Connections, A Newsletter for Rural Singles*.

"What on earth . . . ?" Zoey looked at Carla in puzzlement. A huge grin was plastered across Carla's face. "It's a lonely-hearts newsletter for single people living in rural areas. It's full of ads from men because, believe it or not, there are actually more single men than women out there. Unlike in New York."

Karen said dryly, "Well, at least the odds are in your favor out there. But it's a long way to go for a date."

"Hey, they're advertising for *wives*, not a little afternoon delight," Carla pointed out. "Listen to this."

Leaning across the sofa, she took the newsletter from Zoey and read, "'Have a hundred acres and two hundred sheep. If you like sheep, and me, I'm the critter you've been lookin' for.'"

Karen and Denise roared with laughter. Zoey merely shook her head in disbelief at Carla. "Where did you find this?"

"My cousin in Des Moines. The one who keeps asking when I'm going to settle down and get married. I guess she figured New York guys weren't working out so she'd better help me look a little farther afield."

Turning the page, she went on, "Oh, listen to this! 'Looking for a marriage-minded lady who can cook, drive a tractor, and mend a fence. It helps if you look good in jeans.'"

Collapsing against the back of the chair she was sitting in, Karen wiped tears of laughter from her hazel eyes. "Hey, now we know the answer to the eternal question, Where do you find guys? They're out in the boonies!"

Forcing down the laughter that bubbled up within her, Zoey said gently, "We shouldn't be laughing at these guys. They're just looking for love."

"Yeah," Karen agreed. But her support of Zoey was

undercut by the giggle she couldn't suppress. She took another sip of champagne to cover it.

Denise's expression sobered. "You're right. Who am I to be laughing at these poor dumb hayseeds. *I've* answered singles ads, and even taken out one myself."

"You did?" Zoey asked in surprise. "Why didn't you tell us?"

Denise looked away in embarrassment. "I didn't want you guys to know I was that desperate."

"It wasn't desperate. It was . . . practical," Karen responded hesitantly, trying to be supportive.

"Well, it didn't work," Denise said tightly. "It was just more of the same kind of guys I always attract. Losers I wouldn't have on a bet. Attractive, successful guys looking for another notch on their bedpost. Needy types who'd be better off with a shrink than a date."

Suddenly losing her appetite, she set down her plate on the wooden chest that served as a coffee table and sighed heavily. "At this point, I don't know if the problem is with them or with me. All I do know is that I'm thirty-eight and I seem to keep moving further and further away from getting married and having a family. Breaking through that damn glass ceiling at work is easier than finding someone to love me, who I can love."

Zoey left the sofa and went to Denise, who sat in a chair opposite her. Kneeling down, she put her arms around her and gave her a tight hug. "Hey, it's their loss. You're the best thing that ever happened to any of those guys. And they're stupid for not recognizing it."

Denise smiled through the tears that had suddenly sprung to her eyes. "Thanks, Zoey."

Carla spoke with her usual confident bravado. "Don't worry, you'll find someone. It just takes awhile. You gotta kiss a lotta frogs, y'know, before that prince comes along."

Denise said helplessly, "I'm afraid he doesn't exist outside of those fairy tales we all read as kids."

Looking at her friends, she went on, "You all have someone—Karen has Alan, Zoey has Brian, Carla has more men than she can keep track of. I haven't been involved in a real relationship in months. And if things continue the way they've been going lately, I'm looking at another New Year's Eve without a date. You have no idea what that feels like."

Zoey felt a sharp inner pang. "Oh, yes I do," she insisted. "Last New Year's I planned a romantic dinner for two. I cooked for hours and dressed up in that little black silk slip dress Brian gave me for my birthday. He had to work late, as usual. He finally showed up at five minutes to twelve, with effusive apologies and the biggest bouquet of roses I'd ever seen. But the apologies and the roses didn't make up for the fact that I had sat here alone for hours."

"You shouldn't have waited around for him," Carla said bluntly. "You let him take you for granted."

This was a running disagreement between Carla and Zoey, and Zoey handled it as she always did—by ignoring it. Turning back to Denise, she said reassuringly, "You've got so much going for you. You'll find someone one of these days. It just takes time."

"Yeah, well, time is the critical issue," Denise replied in a tight voice. "I'm not getting any younger. My biological clock is ticking so loud it's keeping me awake at night."

Zoey had no glib response to that. She understood all too well how Denise felt. Both of her brothers were married and had children. She adored her nieces and nephews, and enjoyed being the official family photographer, taking pictures of the children that their parents' treasured. But she wondered if she would ever be photographing her own children.

Denise took a deep breath, then went on in an embarrassed rush, "So that's why I decided to be artificially inseminated. Apparently, it worked first time out. I'm pregnant."

Her friends reacted with varying degrees of stunned amazement. Karen's hazel eyes opened wide in surprise, Carla frowned with disapproval, and Zoey was flabbergasted. Quickly pulling herself together, she was the first to speak. "But . . . when?. . . why?. . . "

Denise faced her unflinchingly. "When? Last month. Why? Because I want a child so bad I can't stand it. Look, I know all the arguments against artificial insemination—it's selfish and self-indulgent, the child has to grow up without a father. And how do you answer the inevitable question, Who's my daddy?"

She paused, took a deep breath, and went on in a voice trembling with feeling, "But I'm telling you, if I get to the end of my life and all I have to show for it is a series of promotions at work, that isn't going to be enough! I want to have a *family*. And I just decided it wasn't going to happen any other way."

Karen, Carla, and Zoey exchanged confused glances. None of them knew quite how to respond. Carla got up from the sofa and walked over to the window, looking out at the view intently as if seeing it for the first time. Karen cleared her throat nervously, trying unsuccessfully to think of something, anything, to say.

Looking at her friends, Denise's expression crumpled. She let out a breath. "I hoped you guys would understand and . . . and be there for me. To tell the truth, I'm kind of scared about going through this alone."

Pulling herself together, Zoey responded with a confidence she didn't actually feel, "Of course we understand! And you won't be going through it alone. We'll be there every step of the way. Right, guys?"

Karen said quickly, "Of course. I'll put you in touch with my obstetrician. You'll love her; she's fairly young and up on all the latest trends."

Carla just looked at Denise with a flabbergasted expression. "Are you *sure* this is what you want?"

Denise gave her a weak smile. "Look, Carla, I know how you feel about kids. They tie you down, and the last thing in the world you want is to be tied down."

Carla spoke in an uncharacteristically grim tone. "If you'd grown up the oldest of five children and had to take care of them while your mother went off to work and your father was gone, having fun with his new little wife, you wouldn't want to be tied down, either."

"Maybe not," Denise said softly. "But that was *your* history, not mine. I grew up an only child, an unexpected, unwanted change-of-life baby, with parents who were too old to do much with me. When I was a little girl, I had all these dolls, and when I'd go to bed at night, I'd make sure they were all covered up with a blanket so they wouldn't be cold. All I ever wanted was someone to take care of, someone to make me feel that I wasn't alone. I think I'll be a pretty good mother, even if I have to do it on my own. Oh, God, I have so much love to give, and I want to have someone to give it to."

At the end of her emotional, heartfelt speech, Denise broke down in tears. Karen and Carla rushed to join Zoey at Denise's side and put their arms around her.

Carla said quickly, "Hey, you're gonna be a *great* mother! This is one lucky kid."

"Definitely," Karen agreed. "I think I'm a pretty good judge of mothers, and you're going to be one of the best!"

Zoey added warmly, "You bet!"

But inside she felt deeply torn. She understood all too well how desperate Denise was to have a child. And she was confident that Denise would be a wonderful mother. If ever a child was wanted, this one was. It would be deeply loved and well cared for, with all the advantages financial security could bring.

Yet, she wished there could be a father in the picture, too. She felt a profound sadness on Denise's behalf at the thought of having a child alone. It wouldn't be the same, attending Lamaze classes with a friend instead of the child's father, going through labor and delivery without a mate to share the pain and the exultation, and, as the child grew up, facing the challenges of parenthood alone.

Zoey understood that last one all too well. Her mother had been a single parent, raising three children alone. Only now, as an adult, did Zoey have a sense of how lonely and tough a job that must have been.

Zoey knew her friends well enough to sense that both Karen and Carla shared her concerns. But they'd made an immediate, unspoken agreement to give Denise unqualified support rather than criticism.

For a few minutes, the conversation revolved around baby matters—the latest thinking about what pregnant women should and shouldn't do, possible names for the baby, the best agency for nannies. Eventually, the party broke up. Karen, who had to get up early to teach, left first, taking the remainder of the cake at Zoey's insistence. She was followed closely by Carla, who had a late date with a policeman whose shift ended at eleven. Denise stayed behind, supposedly to help Zoey clean up the few dishes and utensils they'd used with the cake and champagne. But Zoey sensed she actually wanted to talk about something private that she hadn't wanted to share with Karen and Carla.

After they had finished doing the dishes in the compact kitchen area of the loft, Zoey made coffee. When it was ready, she poured two cups for herself and Denise, and they took them into the living area. Settling on the sofa, Denise nervously cleared her throat. Zoey knew she was right in thinking there was more to come. She wondered what on earth could be left to reveal. The news about Denise's pregnancy was about the biggest bombshell Zoey could imagine. Nothing else could possibly top it.

"Zoey . . . there's something I wanted to ask you, but I didn't want to do it in front of Karen and Carla."

"Okay, shoot," Zoey said easily.

"The thing is, you see, I don't have very many relatives. Just a couple of cousins I barely know. And they're a lot older than I am, anyway. So I was wondering . . . "

"Yes?" Zoey prompted when Denise hesitated and looked away.

Denise forced herself to meet Zoey's curious look. "After the baby's born, I'll need to make arrangements for someone to take care of it if anything should happen to me. I know it's a huge responsibility, and a lot to ask, but could you, that is, would you be willing to consider being my baby's godmother?"

Whatever Zoey had expected, it wasn't this. She was completely caught off guard. "But . . . don't you think Karen would be a better choice?"

Denise shook her head firmly. "No, I don't. Of course, she's a terrific mother, and she and Alan have just the perfect family. She's so kind, she'd agree to do it in a second. But the fact is, she's got her hands full with three kids of her own and a classroom full of other people's kids. And as for Carla, well . . ."

She didn't have to explain further. They both understood that Carla didn't want to have her own children, let alone someone else's.

Denise hurried on, "Like I said, I know it's a huge responsibility, and I want you to feel free to be honest and say you'd rather not do it."

"It isn't that," Zoey replied. "The truth is, I'm deeply touched at your confidence in me. But what makes you think I could do it?"

Denise smiled, her eyes warm with affection. "Because you want children as badly as I do. And you have every bit as much love to give."

A lump rose in Zoey's throat. Denise's faith in her was deeply touching, adding a new depth to their friendship. Impulsively, she hugged Denise. "Oh, Denise," her voice trembled, "I'd be honored to be your child's godmother."

Denise relaxed visibly and let out a sigh of relief. "You have no idea what that means to me," she said in a heartfelt voice. "In this whole complicated process, the only thing I really worried about was what would happen to my child if I wasn't there."

"You'll be there," Zoey reassured her. "And in the highly unlikely event you're not, *I* will be."

Denise hesitated, then went on carefully, "It's very generous of you to act like you're okay with all this."

"But I *am* okay with it. I understand how you feel, and I know you'll be a great mom."

Denise gave Zoey a penetrating look. "But you believe this child deserves a father as well as a mother. Don't you?"

Zoey looked away, unsure how to answer that without hurting Denise's feelings.

Denise went on gently, "I know why you feel that way, Zoey. And I don't blame you."

Zoey's father had abandoned the family when Zoey was eight, and she had no contact with him after that. He'd left his young wife and three small children to fend for themselves in the small town in upstate New York where both families had lived for generations. At first, Zoey's mother had assured the children they would see their father again. Cards and cheap gifts at Christmas and on their birthdays kept their hopes alive. But after only a couple of years even those inadequate attempts at maintaining a connection ended.

Devastated, Zoey retreated into the world of books, especially her favorite, *The Secret Garden.* In that lovely, safe world, she could briefly forget that her father was never coming home.

A photography class in high school began a healing process for her. A camera became both a barrier between herself and the world, and a way of looking closely at the world and trying to make sense of it. Just as, deep inside, she never stopped trying to understand why her father had abandoned her, her two younger brothers, and her mother.

That was why commitment and stability were so important to her. Because she hadn't gotten those things from the most important male in her life—her father.

All that painful past was in Zoey's mind as she met Denise's look. Her voice shook slightly as she answered honestly, "Yes, I believe that having a father is important. I know what it's like growing up without one. Having a mother who's busy all the time working hard to support a family by herself. No matter how hard she tried, and God knows no one tried harder than my mother, she couldn't be both mother and father to us. And always wondering what was wrong with me that made my father want to leave. Feeling, deep down inside, that I must just not be worth loving, or he never would've left."

Denise's golden-brown eyes softened with compassion. "Oh, Zoey, I knew it must've been hard on you, but I had no idea."

Zoey's hand went to her throat at a sudden choking sensation. The vividness of unhappy childhood memories made it hard for her to catch her breath. She forced herself to continue, "How could you? It isn't something I like to talk about, even to you, one of my closest friends. Some wounds never heal. And talking about it is like rubbing salt in them. Most of the time I try not to think of it, not to remember that last day when he came into my room and said he was going away for awhile."

She paused as a sharp stab of remembered pain shot through her. *Awhile*. For years she'd clung to that word as desperately as a drowning person clings to a life vest, telling herself it meant that someday he would return. Eventually, she accepted that "awhile" meant forever.

Taking a deep breath to steady her suddenly shaky nerves, Zoey went on in a determinedly matter-of-fact tone, "But that was me and this is you. You have the right to do what you think is best with your life. I do respect that. And I'll do everything I can to help. I just wish . . ." Her voice trailed off helplessly.

As if reading her mind, Denise said, "I think I know what you wish. That I could fall in love and get married and live happily ever after with someone who would be a wonderful father to my child."

Zoey nodded eagerly. "Oh, *yes*. I do wish that for you, Denise. And your child."

Denise looked dubious. "It's a fairy tale, Zoey. It doesn't exist. At least not for me. Not so far."

Suddenly, Zoey had a crazy thought. Taking Denise's

hand, she pulled her over to one of the huge windows that covered one of the walls of the apartment. Pointing up to the sky, she said, "Look there."

"What? It's just the moon. Okay, a full moon, but so what?"

"It's the second full moon this month. That makes it a blue moon. My great-grandmother told me that if you wish on a blue moon, your wish will come true. Especially if you wish for love."

Denise cocked her head to one side and eyed Zoey critically, as if she'd suddenly gone crazy. "I remember you telling me once that your great-grandmother also believed that you could give someone's cow the evil eye and make its milk go bad."

"All right, so it's a superstition. But what can it hurt? Go ahead. Make a wish. Wish for love."

"This is silly."

"*I* did it," Zoey admitted, not caring how foolish she looked. "Tonight, on my way home."

"*You* did it?"

"Uh-huh. And if you ever tell Karen or Carla, I'll kill you."

"But you have Brian," Denise pointed out.

"Do I? We've been together for five years, and we're not even engaged. I figured maybe this would help nudge him."

Denise laughed. "All right. What can it hurt?" Looking up at the moon, she said in a self-conscious voice, "I wish for love." Turning back to Zoey, she said, "There, are you satisfied? Now I've made a fool of myself, too."

Just then the doorbell rang. Denise grinned at Zoey. "Speak of the devil. I'll bet I know who that is. I think it's time for me to go."

As Zoey and Denise went to the door, Zoey said politely, "You don't have to rush off."

"You know damn well you don't mean that," Denise responded with a grin. "You'll want to yell at him. And then you'll want to make up. I don't need to be around for either."

She grabbed her purse from where she'd left it near the door. As Zoey opened it, revealing Brian standing on the other side, Denise said breezily, "Hi, Brian. Bye, Brian."

"Um, bye, Denise," he responded as she hurried past him.

When she was gone and Zoey had closed the door behind her, Brian said, "I like your friends. They don't hang around."

"They're also kind enough to go to the trouble of planning a surprise party for me. A party *you* were supposed to make sure I got to at the right time."

Brian slapped his forehead. "Damn! I knew there was something I was forgetting. What can I say? I'm very, *very* sorry. My mind was on other things. The McCluskey settlement fell apart at the eleventh hour, and Lewis told me if I didn't somchow put it back together before court convenes at 9:00 A.M., I shouldn't bother showing up for work."

"He didn't mean it," Zoey said coolly, unwilling to forgive Brian too quickly.

"Hey, you never know with Lewis. They don't call him the Terminator for nothing."

Walking up to Zoey, Brian, whose six-foot-two-inch frame towered over her slender, five-foot-four-inch body, stared down at her with a penitent expression. "I'm truly sorry. Is there anything I can do or say to win your forgiveness?"

Before Zoey could reply, he bent to kiss her deeply. When they finally pulled apart, he said in a husky voice, "You're not *really* mad at me, are you?"

No, Zoey had to admit to herself, she wasn't. No matter what Brian did, somehow she could never stay mad at him. It was partly his charm—and partly her need to erase any distance between them as quickly as possible.

Looking up at him, Zoey was struck yet again by how handsome he was. Thick blond hair, chocolate-brown eyes, and a narrow, patrician face. He looked exactly like what he was—a well-bred, successful member of the Eastern elite, the product of a good family and all the right schools, and a rising star in one of the biggest law firms in Manhattan.

Remembering Denise's poignant speech on being alone, Zoey told herself how lucky she was to have a boyfriend like Brian. If only he wanted to be more than just a boyfriend.

"I'm still mad," she said in a teasing voice that held not a hint of anger.

Brushing her lips again lightly with his own, Brian murmured, "Somehow, I don't think you mean that. But I won't argue with you on your birthday. And speaking of birthdays . . . "

He pulled a small package wrapped in silver foil from the pocket of his pinstripe suit and held it out to her. She hesitated for only a moment before accepting it. Then she went to the sofa and sat down. Brian sat next to her, putting his arm around her affectionately. She tore off the wrapping paper, and her eyes lit up with delicious anticipation as she saw the Tiffany's logo on the little black velvet box. A box just the right size for an engagement ring. Would it be a traditional diamond, or had Brian remembered that she preferred sapphires?

It didn't really matter, though. It could be a tin ring from a Cracker Jack box, and she would love it for its symbolism. Because it meant that at long last Brian was ready to say, "I love you and I want to spend the rest of my life with you."

Zoey glanced at Brian, who had a smug, I-just-know-you're-going-to-love-this look on his face.

She looked again at the tiny box. It held her future within it. A future of living happily ever after. Denise might have lost faith in that romantic ideal, but Zoey hadn't. Despite everything, she still believed it was possible.

With breathless anticipation, Zoey slowly opened the box.

2

Nestling on the white-satin interior of the jeweler's box were earrings. Diamond studs. At least a carat each.

Zoey's face froze in an expression of profound disappointment.

Somehow, Brian was oblivious to the fact that her reaction wasn't what he'd expected. Misinterpreting her silence for stunned pleasure, he said proudly, "I know they're extravagant, but you deserve it. Besides being your birthday, this is the anniversary of the night we met."

"Our *fifth* anniversary," Zoey said in an almost inaudible voice.

"Yeah, five years ago tonight. I looked across that restaurant, and there you were with your friends."

Zoey's voice was flat. "Celebrating my thirtieth birthday."

"Right. I made up my mind immediately to somehow finagle a date with you."

And tonight is my thirty-fifth birthday, Zoey thought dully, *and we're still just dating*. Where would they be on her fortieth birthday? Still just dating? Or would Brian even be there? By then, he might've moved on to someone he *could* make a commitment to. Zoey had seen it happen all too often. A couple was together for years, unmarried but apparently committed. Then, one day, they broke up. And a few months later, the guy was getting married to some other woman.

Brian went on reassuringly, "Don't worry about these earrings being too expensive. I'm doing very well this year. And guess what? Harrison told me in confidence that next year I'll probably make junior partner. The youngest in the firm's history. What do you think of that?"

It took a moment for her to respond. "That's just great, Brian," she finally murmured in a tight voice. Something seemed to be stuck in her throat, and she could barely get the words out.

"I told you all these late hours would pay off some day."

Zoey could only nod, not trusting herself to speak without revealing her profound disappointment.

Taking the box from her hands, Brian took the earrings from it. "Here, put them on. Let's see how great you look in them."

Slowly, Zoey took off the big gold hoops she was wearing and put on the diamond studs. Taking her hands, Brian pulled her to her feet and led her to a brightly painted oval mirror, a gift from Carla, hanging on the wall. He stood Zoey in front of it and positioned himself behind her.

Pulling back her thick, curly hair, he beamed, "See? You look stunning."

Looking at her reflection, Zoey didn't see a woman who was stunning. She saw a woman who would have traded all the diamonds in the world for a simple declaration of love and commitment. She had been waiting for five years to hear such a declaration. For the first time in all those years, she was beginning to feel that she might never hear it.

Brian nuzzled her neck and murmured, "Why don't you put on that little black dress—you know the one. We'll go out on the town. A little dancing. A lot of champagne. And then we'll come back here for the *real* celebration."

Zoey turned to face him. She knew every plane and angle of his face, every inch of his body. But she looked at him now as if seeing him for the first time. He was handsome, charming, generous. And faithful. Of that, she was certain. The kind of man her family approved of and most women would envy her for attracting. And yet, at that moment, none of those things seemed to matter. The sense of disillusionment she felt was devastating.

He cocked one eyebrow quizzically. "Well? Feel up to a little club hopping?" His arms, encircling her, tightened suggestively as he drew her closer to him. "Or shall we just stay in? It's your choice. You're the birthday girl."

She opened her mouth to answer him. But instead of the words she'd meant to say, she blurted out, "Denise is pregnant."

His dark-brown eyes widened in surprise, and he pulled back from Zoey. Clearly, he hadn't the faintest idea why she had chosen to share that information with him—or how he should respond to it. Finally, after an awkward silence, he said, "Okay, well, is this a problem? I mean, I assume it wasn't planned. Last I heard, she wasn't involved with anyone in particular."

"Oh, it was definitely planned. She had artificial insemination."

Brian visibly relaxed. "Good. I thought you might want me to represent her in a lawsuit against the father, and I'd rather not do that. Personally, I have strong feelings about women who get pregnant even though they know the guy doesn't want that responsibility."

"I can't believe you're reacting to this news like a lawyer!" Zoey snapped, finding her voice again.

"Well, I *am* a lawyer," Brian pointed out reasonably. "And I deal with that kind of problem all the time."

Zoey told herself that her anger was unfair to Brian. He barely knew Denise, and certainly didn't understand her disappointment with relationships or her desperate desire to have a child before it was too late. Zoey wanted desperately to avoid an argument over this, an argument that might go in a direction that could prove fatal to her relationship with Brian.

Adopting a less confrontational tone, she asked, "So you think what she did is a good thing?"

Brian frowned, and his voice went cold. "Of course not. I think it's stupid. But it's her problem, not mine."

Zoey couldn't bear the coldness that had crept into his tone. She needed to reach him, to make him understand. Because she wasn't really talking about Denise—she was talking about herself.

She gazed up at him imploringly. "Denise wants so much to have a child. Her life feels empty and unfulfilled without that experience. I can understand that. Can you, Brian?"

His mouth tightened in a thin line of impatience. "Zoey, we've had this discussion before."

She frowned. "No, we've begun this discussion before, but we've never quite finished it. Somehow we always get sidetracked."

A familiar, stubborn expression came over Brian's handsome face. "Look, it's your birthday; we should be having a good time instead of arguing about this stuff. There really isn't any point in carrying the argument to the bitter end."

But this time Zoey wasn't going to cave in for the sake of peace. Stepping back from him, she stood with her hands on her hips and said firmly, "Oh, I think there is. This is very important to me, Brian. I need to be clear about where we both stand on this issue."

She waited for him to respond. When he didn't, she continued in a heartfelt tone, "I *want* children. I *need* to be a mother. I need it as badly as I need to express myself through my photography."

"So photograph children," Brian quipped with a placating smile. "That way you can enjoy them, then leave them for someone else to deal with when you get tired of them."

Anger flared within her. "This isn't a joke! I'm very serious. Lately, I get misty-eyed when I see a baby in a stroller.

Or when I look through my mother's photo albums and I see myself surrounded by my brothers and cousins and aunts and uncles. The whole idea of family is important to me." She added sheepishly, "I've even started watching some of those silly family sitcoms that I used to make fun of."

Moving toward her, Brian cupped her face in his hands and forced her to look directly at him. "We've got a great life together, Zoey," he pointed out, carefully enunciating each word for added emphasis. "We both love our careers, we're free to take off on great vacations whenever we want, without being tied down to anyone. That's enough for me."

He finished in a disapproving tone, "I thought it was enough for you, too."

"It *was* enough, for awhile," Zoey agreed haltingly. "The excitement of finally succeeding after working so hard for so long, sharing it all with you, knowing you were proud of me and wanted me to focus on my career."

"I never complained about the long hours you put into your work," Brian reminded her.

Zoey pulled away from him and shook her head slowly. "No, you didn't. Because you didn't want me to turn around and complain about *your* long hours."

"It worked out well for both of us," Brian insisted.

"Yes. For awhile." Zoey's voice lowered to a poignant whisper. "But I need more than that now. I need to have a family."

"You have an idealized vision of what families are all about," Brian accused in the tough, put-your-adversary-on-the-defensive tone he used in the courtroom.

Zoey frowned. "*No*. I don't. I'm painfully aware of both the good and the bad of being part of a family. But, for me, the good far outweighs the bad."

Obviously recognizing his mistake, Brian backtracked. Nervously running his hand through his hair, he admitted, "Okay, that was an unfair accusation, and I apologize. But since you raised the issue, look at the situation with your own family. That should be enough proof that—"

"Proof!" Zoey exploded, her self-control finally snapping. "I wish you would stop talking like a lawyer and just be a human being!"

"As a lawyer, a *family law* attorney," he reminded her pointedly, "I see far too much of bitter, financially devastating breakups and emotionally shattering custody battles. I don't *ever* want to find myself in that situation. And I'm going to make damn sure I don't!"

Zoey felt as if she'd just gotten a sucker punch to the gut. "What do you mean? What are you trying to tell me, Brian?"

He hesitated, then stated flatly, "Today I made an appointment to have a vasectomy."

Zoey was stunned. Pulling out of Brian's grasp, she stared at him for a long moment. Finally, she managed to stammer, "You—you weren't going to tell me, were you?"

Brian had the grace to look slightly guilty. "I would've mentioned it eventually."

"Eventually! You know how I feel about having children. How could you make such a major decision without at least discussing it with me?"

"There was no point in discussing it. My mind was made up."

She looked at him standing there before her, this stranger whom she had thought she knew. She wondered how on earth she could have spent five long years with him, been intimate both emotionally and physically, and not realized that they wanted very different things out of life. A sick feeling churned deep within her as she realized that she didn't begin to really understand him.

Seeing the profound disillusionment in her expression, Brian hurried on, "Look, Zoey, you're overreacting to this whole thing. It's one small part of an otherwise great relationship. This is the *only* issue we disagree on."

"It's not exactly a minor issue," Zoey said in a forlorn voice.

"But look at the big picture. We share the same interests, enjoy doing the same things together—we even vote the same way. We've got everything in common, and we never argue. Except about this kid thing. We're *right* for each other, Zoey."

"I thought so, too, Brian," she said, more in sadness than anger, "but apparently we were both wrong."

Finally, he seemed to recognize the severity of their disagreement. Determined to make her understand how wrong she was, he said, "Look, we both know that in a city full of lonely people, we were lucky to find each other." Trying unsuccessfully not to sound smug, he went on, "All you have to do is look at most of your female friends to see how hard it is to find the right guy. There are a lot more single women than men out there. I'm that rare commodity, a successful, heterosexual, financially stable male."

Zoey had always been aware that Brian had a healthy ego. When her friends accused him of being conceited, she defended him, insisting that, with all he had going for him, it would be insincere of him to feign modesty. But she had never realized how overweening his ego was until that moment. Carla was right, she realized with a sinking feeling. He took her for granted. And she had let him get away with it.

Her gray eyes, normally amiable in their expression, glinted with anger. It had often been pointed out to her, especially by her mother when she was growing up, that she had an Irish temper. At that moment, it was about to explode. Her entire body was rigid and her hands were clenched at her sides.

Brian wasn't stupid. Recognizing that he'd gone a bit too far, he hastened to add, "And, of course, I know how lucky I am to have you. You're the kind of trophy girlfriend any guy would kill to have. Beautiful, bright, sexy—"

"You make us both sound like we're advertising ourselves in a meat market," Zoey said furiously. "I haven't heard you say one word about love or marriage."

"Damn it, Zoey, you know I love you!"

"Do you? I always assumed trust was part of love, and you obviously don't trust me. Otherwise you wouldn't be getting a vasectomy. What's the matter, Brian? Afraid I might be one of those women you detest who trap men into fatherhood?"

Now Brian was as angry as she. He snapped, "You're being ridiculous and you know it. I can't carry on a reasonable conversation with you when you're like this. I told you I love you, and that should be enough."

"I think you just find me awfully convenient. You sure don't love me enough to get married and have a family."

"I've made a commitment to you! And I don't intend to break that commitment! It doesn't have to involve a piece of paper!"

Suddenly, Zoey couldn't bear to stand there confronting him one more moment. She walked over to the window and looked out at the city, not really seeing it. She willed herself to calm down. Turning back to face Brian, she said carefully, "That piece of paper is called marriage, Brian. And you're terrified of it. Until this moment I didn't realize just how terrified you are of the whole idea of spending the rest of your life with one person."

Noticing the *Country Connections* newsletter lying on the table where Carla had dropped it earlier, Zoey walked over and picked it up. "And despite what you think, you're not the only game in town. This newsletter is full of men who want marriage and children."

Choosing an ad at random, she read aloud, "I'm thirty-six years old, been to college, cattle rancher, would like to get married and have children. I'm not perfect and I'm not looking for someone who is. Tyler Ross."

Brian had sat down on the sofa. Now, he leaned against the back and snorted, "Yeah, right, like you'd actually be interested in that country bumpkin."

Zoey's attempt to calm down failed. Facing Brian, she glared at him. "At least he isn't a big-city wimp, afraid of commitment!"

Brian threw up his hands in helpless frustration. "Okay, if that hick is what you want, go for it! Answer his stupid ad!

Never one to back down from a challenge, Zoey responded with equal fervor, "All right, I will!"

Going to her phone on a desk at the far end of the living area, she punched in the number on the front page of *Country Connections*. After listening to the recorded message explaining how to respond to the ad of your choice, she said, in a voice trembling with defiance, "I'd like to respond to Tyler Ross's ad—"

Before she could finish, Brian stood up and stormed out of the apartment, slamming the door behind him.

Quickly giving her name, address, and phone number, Zoey hung up the phone and stared at the door that Brian had just slammed shut. *What have I done?* she asked herself. But she knew the answer perfectly well. She had just shown Brian that she was no longer going to be taken for granted. And while there was a certain exhilaration in standing up for herself, there was also fear that he'd just walked out of her life forever. Worst of all, she'd involved a total stranger in her declaration of independence.

Now that she was beginning to calm down, Zoey realized that she'd just done something really dumb. She couldn't believe she'd actually called that silly newsletter. No matter how angry she'd been at Brian's smug conviction that she was lucky to have him, or how hurt she'd been at the thought that he didn't want her to have his child, that was no excuse.

Instinctively turning to her mother's answer to every crisis—a strong cup of tea—Zoey went into the kitchen, filled the copper teakettle with water, and turned on the burner underneath it. As she waited for the water to boil, for one panicky moment she considered calling back and canceling the call. But how do you cancel a message on voice mail? she wondered. What could she say? Ignore my message, I'm a silly female who got carried away by anger at my boyfriend and decided to use you to bring him down a peg?

And, to be honest, it wasn't that simple. The truth was she was stunned by the realization that, on some fundamental level, Brian didn't trust her not to get pregnant without his permission. And, even more painful, his refusal to make a commitment and dislike of the whole notion of parenthood was carved in stone. Not to be argued with.

With a few brief but painfully clear words, he had shattered the dream Zoey had for their future together.

She couldn't call *Country Connections* back and leave *that* message on Tyler Ross's voice mail.

She would have given anything to be able to take back that thoughtless, impulsive act. But it couldn't be taken back. It was recorded live and in the heat of the moment.

Zoey sighed heavily, more angry at herself now than she'd been at Brian only moments earlier. But there was simply nothing to be done about it. She told herself the men in the newsletter probably got a lot of calls, and hers would just be one of many to Tyler Ross. After all, there were undoubtedly many desperate women who didn't care that those men lived far from civilization and couldn't offer much in the way of sophistication or intelligence or culture.

And Zoey hadn't exactly made herself sound eager or interested. She had made a point of saying that she lived in New York City. Surely a rancher in Wyoming wouldn't be interested in someone that far away. He would realize that she wasn't exactly the kind of woman who would know how to mend a fence or drive a tractor.

As the teakettle began to whistle, Zoey, desperate for reassurance, told herself it was highly unlikely she would hear from Tyler Ross.

3

A fiery red ball of morning sun rose over the valley of Jackson Hole, Wyoming. Across an achingly beautiful alpine meadow dotted with colorful wildflowers and bordered by tall spruce and pine trees, the magnificent, snow-capped Teton Range mountains rose up majestically, almost seeming to pierce the pristine blue sky. It was utterly silent save for the occasional high-pitched sound of birds calling to each other.

In a shallow stream that ran along the edge of the meadow, an elk and her baby, born that spring, stood drinking deeply of the cold, clear water. Suddenly, the elk's head shot up at the warning sound of a low, distant rumbling. Stepping out of the stream, she trotted away, closely followed by her calf.

Hidden among the trees that ringed the meadow, Tyler Ross sat astride his chestnut cutting horse, Dolly. He sat on the horse easily, confidently, as at home in the saddle as city people were behind the wheel of a car. At thirty-six, Tyler had the lean ranginess and crinkly-eyed, direct stare of a quintessential country boy. He was handsome enough, in a rugged kind of way, to pose for an ad for Ralph Lauren. Which he would never do, because he felt designer labels were only for people insecure enough to pay big bucks to slap someone else's name on their behind.

He listened intently for a moment, then turned to his companion, who was also on horseback. His voice was husky with excitement. "They're coming, Jesse."

Jesse Sayres, a slight, wizened, older man with thinning gray hair and gray stubble on his heavily creased face, nodded laconically. "Yup." Then, knowing it was useless but unable to resist, he asked, "Sure you wantter do this, Ty?"

Tyler grinned engagingly. "You always ask me that, and the answer's always the same."

Jesse shook his head and muttered under his breath, "Damn fool young 'un."

Tyler heard him but wasn't offended. He'd grown up with Jesse, who had been the only permanent hired hand to live on the Tyler Ranch for as long as Tyler could remember. Next to his father, who had died when Tyler was twenty, there had never been any man Tyler respected more. Jesse hadn't made it past the sixth grade, and he had little knowledge of, or interest in, the world outside the forty-eight-mile long, six-mile-wide Jackson "Hole," or valley, where he'd been born and raised. But he knew everything there was to know about horses and ranching and surviving in the wilderness. More importantly, he had an unswerving loyalty to the people he cared for, and an innate sense of integrity that made him a far better man than most of the better-educated, more successful men Tyler had met.

Tyler valued Jesse's opinion of him and wished he could make the older man understand why he was about to do what he was about to do. But he knew Jesse couldn't—or wouldn't—understand. He wasn't even sure *he* understood. He only knew it was something he had to do.

Suddenly, he went rigid in the saddle and pointed to the far side of the meadow. "Here they come!"

There was a heavy, mounting rumble. From a thick stand of trees burst a small band of wild horses—mustangs—led by a big Appaloosa stallion. The stallion was magnificent—nostrils flaring, mane flying, iron muscles rippling. The soft dawn light shone on his black coat and white rump with its tiny black spots.

The band of mares, yearlings, and foals following him was a heart-stopping spectacle. There were bays, blacks, chestnuts, pintos, palominos—all glossy, muscular, spirited, and free. A striking mosaic of colors racing across the meadow as if they owned it. Their flanks gleamed, their muscles flexed, their manes rose and fell in time to the rhythmic pounding of their unshod hooves. Surefooted, totally unrestrained, they seemed to run for the sheer joy of running.

The mustangs were a vibrant expression of complete and total wildness. Watching them, Tyler's rugged face was lit by a fierce joy he never felt at any other time. Something deep within him responded to the primal nature of these untamed animals.

Digging his spurs into his horse's flanks, he tore out of the trees and raced to intercept the stallion. Jesse followed obediently. He might think Tyler was a damn fool, but he would follow him into hell itself if Tyler asked him.

Grabbing the lariat curled over the pommel of his saddle, Tyler twirled it expertly above his head for a moment. Then, carefully gauging the distance between himself and the stallion, he let the rope go. It flew gracefully through the air and settled around the stallion's massive neck. Tyler pulled Dolly up abruptly, bringing the stallion to a rearing, snorting halt. As the stallion tried to shake off the restraining rope, Dolly backed up, keeping the rope taut. Dolly was a well-trained cutting horse. She wouldn't let the stallion fight his way out of the lasso.

Jumping off Dolly, Tyler strode toward the stallion and dragged a rope halter over his tossing head. Leaping onto the horse's bare back, he threw off the lasso and pressed his muscular legs tight against the stallion's heaving flanks. Then he said impudently, "All right, let's go dancin'."

Freed from the restraining rope, the stallion tore off, bucking and kicking. A moment later, Tyler was unceremoniously dumped onto the ground. The stallion shook off the irritating rope halter, then sped away in the direction his band had disappeared.

Riding up, Jesse stared down at Tyler, who was brushing himself off and slightly favoring a bruised left leg. "Why don't'cha just take the damn animal to the corral and break him proper?"

"Nope. I don't want to tame him. I just want to prove I can ride him—once."

"Never happen," Jesse said matter-of-factly.

Tyler merely grinned. "We'll see."

They rode their horses back to the pickup they'd left at the end of a dirt road that petered out a few miles from the meadow. After loading the horses into the trailer attached to the pickup, they got in and started back toward the ranch house. Tyler was already beginning to feel sore from his abrupt landing on the hard ground, and a long soak in a hot bath sounded real good.

His thoughts were interrupted by the ringing of the car phone. There was only one person who would be calling him in the pickup, and he knew who it was before he answered.

"Hi, Laurie."

"Tyler Franklin Ross, you went after that stupid horse again, didn't you?"

"'Morning to you, too, sis," Tyler responded easily.

There was a long sigh on the other end of the line, then Laurie went on in a gentler tone, "Listen, you got *another* call at *Country Connections*. This one's a woman from New York City of all places."

"Uh-huh," Tyler said with a complete lack of interest.

"When on earth are you going to call one of these women?" Laurie demanded.

"Sometime," Tyler answered evasively.

"*Sometime* never seems to come around, little brother."

Tyler snapped, "Remember whose idea this was, Laurie."

She shot back, "Oh, I remember, all right. And I remember you agreed to meet at least *one* of them before crawling back into your shell."

"Right—*one*. And then you agreed to stop pestering me."

"Well, you haven't lived up to your part of the bargain, so I'm not going to stop pestering you."

"All right, damn it, I'll get it over with. I'll get back to one of them."

"Which one?" Laurie asked eagerly. "The one from Laramie, who sounded so nice? Or maybe the one from Denver, who left such a cute message? I know Denver's kinda far away, but . . ."

"You'll see," Tyler answered cryptically. "Just remember our deal. I meet *one* of them, and then you stop playing Cupid. *Forever*." And with that he hung up the phone.

Sitting beside Tyler on the seat of the pickup, Jesse gave him a knowing look. "You got that sparkle of deviltry in your eye, like you had when you was a kid and was about to get into mischief. What're you up to, Ty?"

Tyler shrugged. "Oh, nothing much. Just getting a pesky sister off my back." But his wry grin belied the innocence of his words.

Zoey and Carla left the SoHo restaurant where Carla worked as a hostess and headed toward Zoey's apartment a scant two blocks away. It was a stifling, hot day, humid and muggy the way the city always seemed to be in the middle of summer. Both wore bright-colored, loose-fitting, gauzy dresses that bared their arms and swung loosely around their ankles, but they were still uncomfortably warm. Sweat glistened on their pale skin. The humidity made Zoey's hair even curlier than usual, and Carla's even straighter.

"*Then* what did you do?" Carla asked, her dark eyes wide with interest.

"I picked up the phone and called *Country Connections*," Zoey responded ruefully. "I actually answered one of those dumb ads. I can't believe I did it. It was so stupid!"

Carla whooped with delight. "Good for you! What ad did you answer?"

"I don't remember. Tyler something from Montana or Wyoming or somewhere. Anyway, it doesn't matter. What matters is that Brian stormed out slamming the door behind him. That was four days ago, and I haven't heard a word from him."

Carla reached out to grab Zoey's arm, stopping her in the middle of the packed sidewalk. As people maneuvered around them like a stream parting around a rock, Carla said firmly, "Listen to me. You did the right thing."

Zoey groaned. "Oh, right, calling some cowboy halfway across the country was a real smart thing to do. I'm sure that's exactly what Dr. Joyce Brothers would recommend as a mature way to deal with a problem in a relationship."

"You stood up to Brian. And, I might add, it's about damn time. He's kept you dangling for years. I'm glad you finally said this fish is letting go of the hook."

Zoey resumed walking, shaking her head in frustration. "You don't understand . . . "

"Oh, yes, I do," Carla insisted. "You've been so afraid of losing Brian you let him treat you like a hotel, some place he can check in and out of whenever he feels like it. You're just the local Holiday Inn, as far as he's concerned."

"That's not fair," Zoey responded feeling defensive anger rise within her. "Brian's a terrific guy. He's got so much going for him. He's hardworking and successful and smart and—"

"And he has the upper hand in your relationship," Carla responded tartly. "Everything revolves around *his* schedule. Everything you do is designed to meet *his* needs."

"That's an exaggeration, Carla," Zoey said absently. Her

photographer's eye was caught by passing vignettes she would dearly love to capture on film: a homeless man leaning against a doorway, a fresh flower incongruously tucked into the buttonhole of his tattered jacket; a teenage couple, both with bright-orange, spiked hair, both wearing black leather vests and torn jeans, walking arm in arm, looking like a mirror image of each other.

Carla's dark eyebrows rose questioningly. "Oh? When was the last time *you* picked the movie you saw together? When was the last time he took off work early to attend some function with you? Or, to put it another way, when was the last time he attended a function with you that wasn't related to his job? He even missed your reception the other night."

"He had a crisis at work," Zoey argued halfheartedly.

"Hey, there's *always* a crisis at work."

Zoey's mouth tightened in an unhappy line. Carla was right, but she'd be damned if she'd admit it. Instead, she said in a soft voice that betrayed her vulnerability, "But you know that if I let him go there'll be dozens of women waiting in line to snap him up."

"Yeah, because all they care about is that he comes in the right package. The high-powered career, the debonair looks, the prominent family."

"That isn't why I love him," Zoey insisted.

Carla sighed in agreement. "I know. Somehow, he's got your heart wrapped around his little finger. But what you've got to understand is that if you really want him, you're not going to get him by being *too* available. If *you* don't value yourself, *he* won't."

They had reached Zoey's building. Stopping in the lobby, Zoey took a thick wad of mail from her mailbox and idly leafed through the stack of bills, junk mail, and magazines as they took the elevator to her loft.

Carla went on, "I've known a lot of guys like Brian. If they think you're chasing them, they put on their track shoes and they're gone in a cloud of dust. But if they're unsure of you, if you hold back, and especially if they think you may be interested in someone else, then they're eager to make a commitment. A man never wants a woman more than when he thinks another man might want her."

"You mean play hard to get," Zoey said with obvious disapproval.

"Hey, it's more effective than playing easy to get."

Zoey frowned. "I'm not playing."

"Well, Brian is, and he's winning the game."

Zoey unlocked the door to her loft and Carla followed her in.

"Trying to make him jealous by responding to a singles ad from a cowboy definitely isn't the answer," Zoey responded tersely.

"Oh, well, you're probably never gonna hear from that guy anyway," Carla said with breezy confidence. "Don't worry about him."

Suddenly, Zoey stopped dead in the middle of the apartment. "Oh my God," she whispered, letting the mail fall to the floor, except for one envelope.

"What? What is it?"

Zoey held out the envelope to Carla. Taking it, Carla noticed the postmark—Jackson Hole, Wyoming. She grinned wickedly. "Well, what do you know. Who'd've thought—"

Zoey interrupted her by grabbing the envelope and ripping it open. Dread was written all over her face and her eyes narrowed in dismay. As she read the enclosed letter, she murmured disjointedly, "Pleased to get your response to my ad . . . like the sound of your voice . . . thousand-acre cattle ranch . . . love to show you my place . . . enclosing a ticket . . ."

She stopped, looked in the envelope once more, and pulled out an airline ticket. Carla grabbed it from her and looked at it eagerly. "Round trip to Jackson Hole. First class," she pointed out approvingly.

Taking back the ticket, Zoey shoved it into the envelope,

along with the letter. Walking over to her desk, she threw the envelope down on it. "It doesn't matter if he's sending his private Lear jet. Of course I'm not going."

Following right behind, Carla grabbed her arm. "Wait a minute. There's no of course about it."

"Oh, now, hold on," Zoey said in amazement. "You're not for a minute suggesting I should actually go out there and meet this guy!"

"Why not?" Carla asked simply.

"Why not?" Zoey sputtered. After a moment, she repeated, "Why not? Because it's the most ridiculous idea you've ever had, and you've had some pretty ridiculous ideas."

"I'm an artist unappreciated in my time," Carla said automatically, her standard complaint. Then she went on with a suggestive grin, "Look at it this way—it would make Brian stop taking you for granted."

"I'm not going to use some poor, innocent man to make Brian jealous. It's completely unfair to this guy."

"Do you think it's fair to return his ticket with a Thanks, but no thanks? That will really hurt his ego."

"Carla, I know that where men are concerned you tend to have a show-no-mercy philosophy," Zoey said bluntly, "but I don't want to hurt this guy's feelings by pretending an interest that I don't feel."

"If you're truly concerned about his feelings, you'll go to meet him." Before Zoey could respond, Carla hurried on, "Now stop and think about it. Right now he thinks he's interested in you. But that's only because he doesn't know you."

Zoey shook her head slowly. "Gee, thanks. You're doing wonders for my ego." She headed toward the kitchen, thinking she really needed a cup of tea.

"I mean," Carla explained carefully, "that the unknown is always more intriguing than the known. If you meet him, and he sees how different the two of you are, he'll lose interest. But at least that way you'll let him be the one to do the rejecting. And that will be much kinder to him than rejecting him sight unseen."

Zoey automatically opened her mouth to retort, then stopped. To her surprise, she was unable to think of a good counterargument. After roughly twenty years of dating, she knew from painful personal experience that it always felt better to be the one doing the rejecting than the one being rejected. And Carla was probably right that, as soon as this Tyler Ross met her and saw how different they were, he would completely lose interest in her. Whatever he was looking for, she was sure it wasn't a New York career woman.

Recognizing her advantage, Carla pressed it. "Let him have the upper hand. Just like you do with Brian," she couldn't resist adding.

Zoey poured water into the copper teakettle and turned on the burner beneath it. Then she set out two cups and saucers on the white tile counter. Turning back to Carla, she gave her a thoughtful look. "You've never really liked Brian. Why are you trying so hard to talk me into doing something crazy just to pique his interest?"

"Because I know you so well. Unlike me, you're a one-man kind of woman, and you've decided Brian's the man. So, because you're my best friend in the whole world and I want you to be happy, I'm trying to help you get what you want."

Carla was right, Zoey knew. Unlike Carla, Zoey wasn't interested in seeing how many men she could get to fall in love with her. She wanted one man's love—Brian's.

She couldn't believe that she was actually considering taking Carla's suggestion and going through with this. But that was exactly what she was doing.

The teakettle whistled, indicating the water was boiling. As she poured the hot water into the cups and added tea bags, Zoey said in a hesitant voice, "But I couldn't let him pay my way out there. I don't know what his financial situation is. Maybe he could barely scrape together the money for a first-class ticket."

"He owns a thousand-acre ranch, for Chrissakes," Carla pointed out.

"That doesn't necessarily mean he's well off financially," Zoey threw back over her shoulder as she carried her cup into the living area.

Picking up her cup and following Zoey, Carla said reasonably, "So, fine, give him back the ticket and buy your own." She added teasingly, "You can afford it now that you're a rich and famous photographer."

Zoey threw herself on her bright red sofa and leaned her head against the back of it. Staring at the ceiling, she said with a heavy sigh, "I can't believe I'm seriously considering this."

Carla kicked off her sandals and curled up in the big, overstuffed red-and-white-striped chair facing the sofa. "Neither can I, frankly. You're normally much too uptight to do something this wild and adventurous."

"I am *not* uptight."

"Compared to me, you are."

"Madonna is uptight compared to you," Zoey said with a wry grin.

At that moment, the phone on the desk rang. Zoey rose quickly and hurried over to answer it. "Hello?" Her voice softened as she said, "Brian . . . hi." Her entire demeanor changed and she visibly relaxed, as if abruptly shedding a ton of tension.

Ignoring Carla's grimace, she went on, "Tonight? I'd love it." After listening for a moment, she finished, "I've missed you, too. Bye."

When she hung up, her mouth curved in a big smile and her gray eyes were alight with excitement. She threw herself onto the sofa and grinned at Carla. "He's sorry we had a fight, and he wants to make it up by taking me out to a belated birthday dinner at the River Cafe. I can't imagine what he had to do to get reservations on such short notice."

"Uh-huh," Carla responded unenthusiastically.

"Oh, Carla, come on, be happy for me," Zoey begged.

"Everything's going to be all right. We're going to work out our differences and—and—"

"And get married and have kids and live happily ever after," Carla finished for her in a tone that suggested she didn't believe it for a minute.

Zoey hesitated. "Well . . . hopefully," she said slowly, her desperate desire to believe this dream could come true warring with the knowledge that it was just that—a dream.

Sipping her tea, she went on determinedly, "Anyway, obviously he thought it over and realized how inconsiderate it was to make a major decision about a vasectomy without discussing it with me. So we'll talk and find a way to reach some kind of compromise."

Even as she said the words, she felt an old, familiar, disturbing memory—of when she was a child, reassuring herself that her father *would* come back someday.

"How do you compromise on marriage and children?" Carla asked pointedly. "Either you're married, or you're not. Either you have kids, or you don't."

"I don't know. But . . . Look, the important thing is, he called." She jumped up and headed toward her bedroom. "Come and help me decide what to wear tonight and how to fix my hair. I want to look irresistible."

"It will take more than your sexiest dress and a good hair day to make Brian stop taking you for granted," Carla muttered under her breath.

Zoey heard her but didn't respond. She wasn't going to let Carla ruin her happy, hopeful mood. It was fragile enough without Carla's cynical attitude.

Zoey and Brian sat on the outdoor patio at the River Cafe. From its waterfront perch on the Brooklyn side of the East River, the restaurant had a superb view of the Manhattan skyline. A cool breeze from the river softened the hot summer night and sent wispy tendrils of hair brushing against Zoey's cheeks.

Not wanting any reminders of her disastrous birthday, Zoey had decided against wearing the little black dress that Brian liked so much. Instead, she had chosen a gold-lace number that brought out the gold highlights in her copper-colored hair. The look in Brian's eyes when he picked her up confirmed she'd made the right choice.

She'd also made a point of wearing the diamond-stud earrings he'd given her, an act he noted with approval.

Brian had clearly made a special effort as well. He had slicked back his dark blond hair and wore his best suit, a light gray, double-breasted Armani. He looked like he belonged on the cover of *GQ*. Zoey was aware of other women casting covert, interested glances at Brian.

While they drank a fine Chardonnay and ate a delicious meal of succulent prawns and baby vegetables, they talked about Zoey's upcoming show at the gallery and Brian's latest case. They laughed at shared jokes and held hands across the small table. It should have been magical, Zoey thought. But somehow it wasn't, because in the back of her mind was the knowledge that at some point they would have to address the issue that had kept them apart for the past several days.

After dinner, they lingered over coffee. Zoey had stopped talking, and Brian carried on an easy monologue about the office, his work, his friends, and family.

"Henry invited us out to his place in the Hamptons for the Fourth of July," he said, referring to one of the senior partners whom Zoey had met at various office parties over the years. "I told him we'd love to come." He added belatedly, "I hope that's all right with you."

"Of course," Zoey agreed automatically. It didn't matter to her what they did on the Fourth. What mattered was when—or if—Brian would bring up the subject of the vasectomy. If he didn't, then she would have to, because she couldn't pretend that the issue was resolved when it definitely wasn't. But she was extremely nervous about doing so. She desperately wanted to preserve the pleasant evening they were sharing, and didn't want to shatter their tenuous rapprochement.

When Brian suggested they go to the Rainbow Room for a little dancing, Zoey eagerly agreed. She knew she was being a coward, grasping at a further delay in raising the difficult issue of the vasectomy, and she wondered if Brian was feeling the same, looking for ways to postpone the inevitable.

As they danced at the glamorous nightspot, with its art deco glitz and stunning view of Manhattan, Zoey waited for Brian to bring up the subject she was certain was on both their minds. Finally, long after midnight, they left the Rainbow Room and went back to her apartment.

As Brian took her key from her and opened the door, Zoey thought, *Now he'll talk about it. He'll begin by saying, "About that argument the other night," and he'll apologize and say that he understands how I feel. And after thinking it over, he's decided not to get the vasectomy after all.*

In her fantasy, she imagined him going on to say that maybe it was time for them to get married. Maybe even have children. At least one. She wanted three, but she would settle for one.

But as they stood in her kitchen together while she made coffee, he didn't say those things. Instead, he chuckled lightly and said, "Boy, that was a dumb fight we had the other night, wasn't it?"

Zoey looked at him but didn't respond. Appearing to be focused on pouring the coffee into big, black porcelain mugs, she held her breath, hoping against hope.

He continued with a rueful grin, "I still can't believe you called that hayseed."

She gritted her teeth. "That *hayseed* wants to meet me. He even sent a plane ticket."

Brian's smug look dissolved into startled surprise. "You're kidding! You heard from him?"

She nodded. "Today."

"Look, Zoey, this isn't funny anymore."

"No," she agreed, handing him a cup of coffee, "it isn't."

He accepted the mug and took a sip without really tasting it. "All right, then stop being so ridiculous. You were just trying to make me jealous, and you know it."

Zoey set her mug down on the counter and sighed heavily. "I'm not sure what I was trying to do, Brian. The one thing I am sure of is that we have a serious difference of opinion. And it doesn't have to do with some rancher in Wyoming. It has to do with *us*."

He set his mug down next to hers so hard that some of the coffee splashed onto the tile. "This is about my plans to get a vasectomy," he stated flatly.

"Yes. And what that says about our relationship."

His chocolate-brown eyes narrowed in anger. "Our relationship was just fine until you decided to disagree about one little decision I made."

By now, any superficial pretense of accord between them was shattered. Shocked by his insensitive and inaccurate choice of words, Zoey responded passionately, "It isn't about one *little* decision! It's about what that decision says about how you feel about me! Whether or not you trust me! And the ramifications of it, in terms of marriage and children!"

Placing her hands on Brian's chest, she looked up at him, her eyes glistening with tears. "Brian, *please*, can't we talk about this before you make an irrevocable choice?"

"It's *my* choice, Zoey. And I've made it."

She let her hands drop to her side and fought back the tears that threatened to spill from her eyes.

Brian went on in a slightly more conciliatory tone, "I don't want children. As for marriage, who knows? Maybe someday. I just don't know how I feel about it yet."

Zoey whispered, "I know how I feel about it. Even that guy who wrote to me knows how he feels about it."

The sculpted planes of Brian's face hardened in anger. Making a determined effort to control that anger, he said with a shaky laugh, "Come on, Zoey, you and I both know you're not interested in anyone else."

"Then why am I flying to Wyoming tomorrow to meet him?" As soon as the words were out of her mouth, she couldn't believe she'd said them. She had completely surprised herself, as well as Brian.

"I'm not going to play these stupid games," Brian snapped. "When you come to your senses, call me."

And with that, he left. This time he didn't even slam the door.

4

Denise, the only one of Zoey's close friends who owned a car, drove her to the airport early on the morning of July 1st. As Denise maneuvered her little red Mazda Miata convertible through the heavy morning traffic heading toward Kennedy Airport, Zoey asked how she was feeling.

"Awful," Denise answered with a grimace. "I have morning *and* evening sickness, I'm actually losing weight instead of gaining, and I have to carry around a pack of saltine crackers with me. They're the only things that stave off the nausea. I can't tell you how many times I've had to run out in the middle of a meeting and pray that I make it to the bathroom in time." She finished with a long sigh, "I'm not at all sure it's worth it."

Zoey said reassuringly, "Oh, I think you are."

Denise smiled. "You're right. I *am* sure."

"So, have you started decorating a nursery yet?"

"No. I don't want to really get into decorating or buying baby things until I'm well into the second trimester. You know—in case something goes wrong."

Her voice shook on those last words, and Zoey realized how scared Denise must be about being pregnant for the first time, at thirty-eight.

Denise went on, "But I have to admit I did buy one thing—the most adorable little pale blue donkey. When you wind it up, its little head moves up and down and it plays 'The Donkey Serenade.' I put it in the bedroom that's going to be the nursery."

Zoey grinned. "Blue, huh? So you want a boy?"

"It isn't that I *want* a boy. But the thing is, I think it's going to be a boy. I don't know why. I just *feel* it." Glancing briefly at Zoey, then returning her gaze to the road, she finished, "You think I'm crazy, don't you?"

Zoey responded, "No, you're not crazy. I think you already feel a bond with this child."

"I think I do. And it isn't like any feeling I've ever had in my life. It's amazing."

Listening to Denise, Zoey felt a sharp pang of envy. She couldn't agree with Denise's decision to have a child without benefit of marriage, or at least a father somewhere in the picture, but she could strongly relate to Denise's desire to have a child.

Oh, Brian, she thought miserably, *why don't you feel that way, too?*

They had reached the airport. Denise pulled her little car up to the passenger loading curb and asked, "So when will you be back?"

"Day after tomorrow," Zoey answered promptly. Getting out of the car, she pulled her overnight bag and ever-present camera case from the trunk.

"You're not taking much," Denise commented.

"I'm not staying out there any longer than necessary," Zoey replied. "I figure I'll have dinner with this guy tonight, spend a little time on his ranch tomorrow, and by tomorrow night he'll realize how mismatched we are. He'll be relieved when I say I have to be back here for some Fourth of July party."

At the mention of the Fourth, Zoey remembered Brian

and his plans for them. Plans that were obviously canceled now. Her determination not to think about him or worry about the future—if any—of their relationship dissolved. She felt a profound sadness wash over her. She couldn't lose him, she just couldn't. Somehow, when she got back, she would have to find a way to bridge the gulf between them.

Reaching over to hug Denise, she said, "Thanks for the ride."

"Zoey, may I give you some advice?"

"Sure," Zoey answered absently, checking her watch and noting with disappointment that she had plenty of time to get to her flight.

"Try to meet this guy with an open mind. Don't judge him before you even get to know him. You might be pleasantly surprised."

"No way. He's probably a nice enough guy, but he is what he is, and I am what I am, and we are definitely *not* what each other is looking for."

"You're absolutely sure of that?"

"Absolutely."

Denise smiled enigmatically. "Well . . . if you're sure."

Before Zoey could respond, Denise went on breezily, "Call me if you need a ride when you get back." And with a quick wave good-bye she was gone.

Hoisting her camera bag and small overnight bag, Zoey turned reluctantly toward the concourse.

A thin spiral of smoke rose into the warm summer air, and the pungent odor of burning hair filled Tyler's nostrils. Lifting the branding iron from the calf and jumping back, Tyler waited as Jesse shook his lariat loose from its neck. The terrified animal lurched to its feet, bawling loudly. Jesse opened the corral gate and shooed the calf through it and into the pasture beyond, where other calves were recovering from the branding.

"Tyler!"

Looking up, Tyler saw his older sister, Laurie, striding toward the corral, irritation evident in every tight line of her face. At forty-one, she was five years older than Tyler. Their mother had died when Tyler was six, and, as far back as he could remember, Laurie had been more a mother than a sister to him. She'd taught him how to tie his shoelaces, made him clean his room, and helped him with his school work. When he began dating, she sat him down and told him the biological facts of life, in case he'd somehow missed learning them in school. She told him in no uncertain terms that he'd better show enough concern for girls not to get one pregnant. Because if that did happen, it was every bit as much *his* responsibility, and *his* problem, as the girl's.

When Laurie married at eighteen, instead of moving out and establishing her own home she persuaded her husband that they should live with her father for awhile. She said it was for financial reasons, until they could save enough money to buy their own home, but Tyler knew the truth. At thirteen, she felt he was too young to be left with just their father. Andrew Ross was a decent, caring man, but he didn't know the first thing about creating a warm, loving home for a child. He'd depended on his wife to do that, and after she died he let Laurie take on what he saw as "woman stuff."

At five-feet-eleven-inches tall, Tyler towered over the five-foot-two-inch Laurie, but she could still put the fear of God in him, especially when she was angry, as she clearly was now.

Stopping at the corral fence, she glared at Tyler, her blue eyes a mirror of his own. "Do you realize what time it is?"

"Nope, but I'm sure you're gonna tell me," he replied with an impudent grin.

Behind him, he heard Jesse smother a laugh.

"That woman from New York City will be arriving at the airport in exactly one hour, and it takes the better part of an hour to get there—so what're you doing out here?"

"Can't you tell? I'm branding calves. For some reason,

they won't brand themselves. Although I'll bet if *you* told 'em to do it, they'd sure give it a try."

Jesse chuckled out loud, but his laughter was cut short by Laurie's furious glare. An instant later, she turned her attention back to Tyler. "Listen here, Ty, you get in that house and get cleaned up and get to the airport. Do you want to be late?"

I don't want to go at all, he thought but didn't say so out loud. Reluctantly, he hung his rope over a fence post and started toward the house. Laurie called after him, "And wear something nice. Put on that tie I got you for Christmas."

"I'm not wearing a damn tie," he called back over his shoulder. "This isn't a wedding or a funeral." Although, he thought, it sure felt like the latter.

In his bedroom, he stripped off his dusty clothes and stepped into the shower. After barely rinsing off his lean, hard body, he stepped out again and quickly dressed in the clothes that were his usual working attire—jeans and a chambray shirt. Without even glancing in the mirror, he briefly ran a comb through his thick, damp hair.

As he left the room, his gaze inevitably went to the silver-framed photograph on the dresser. In the photo, a younger Tyler, wearing a black tuxedo, stood next to a lovely girl in a wedding gown, with flaxen hair and golden-brown eyes. Her face was sweet without being vapid. There was something in the mischievous twinkle in her eyes that suggested a young woman of spirit and humor.

Sarah.

Looking at her, Tyler felt the old familiar lump in his throat. He wondered if he would ever be able to look at that picture without feeling a terrible emptiness inside and, far worse than the emptiness, a gut-wrenching guilt. *Never*, he thought. He would never get over those feelings.

In Tyler's mind, Sarah had been the most beautiful bride imaginable. In the photograph, they smiled lovingly at each other, a young couple looking forward to a long and happy future together. Neither had any way of knowing that the children they'd expected to have as soon as possible after the wedding would never live—and that Sarah would tragically die young.

Because of me, he thought miserably. *Damn it, because of me . . .*

Unable to bear those thoughts a moment longer, he hurried out of the room.

As he got into his pickup, Laurie came up to the open window for one last word. "If you have time, you might stop and pick up some flowers to give her. She'd like that."

He gave her a look that clearly said he wasn't bothering with any flowers.

Laurie shook her head in helpless frustration. "You're not gonna give this woman a chance, are you?"

"Look, I'm fulfilling my end of this damn fool bargain. I'm meeting one of the women who replied to the ad *you* placed. Now you live up to your part of the deal and leave me alone."

"That's why you picked this woman, isn't it?" Laurie asked, understanding finally dawning. "Someone from so far away, someone you know won't work out."

"Look, she'll take one look at this place, realize she'll never fit in here, and leave. She's not—"

"Not what? Sarah?"

Tyler didn't answer.

Laurie went on gently. "Give her a chance, Ty. She's come all this way."

Without responding, he turned the key in the ignition and drove off. In his rearview mirror, he saw Laurie standing there staring after him, her hands on her hips, frowning in frustration. If she was unhappy with his lack of enthusiasm, it was her own fault, he told himself firmly. This was her idea, not his. He just wanted to get the damn thing over with and get on with his life. There was no room in that life for any woman, especially one from New York City.

* * *

Zoey's plane landed at the small airport outside Jackson, Wyoming, three hours after leaving New York. She let all the other passengers move past her before finally leaving her seat and making her way slowly down the aisle. As she stepped out onto the small platform at the top of the steps, she paused for a quick glance at her surroundings.

They took her breath away. She'd heard Jackson Hole was beautiful, but she hadn't expected *this*. The air was fresh and sweet. A blazing summer sun shone down from a cloudless blue sky more vast and empty than any sky she could ever remember seeing. In the distance, across a gray-green sagebrush plain, the fabled Teton Range mountains towered abruptly from the valley floor. They were so awesome, they almost didn't appear real.

Zoey felt something stirring within her, something she'd never felt before. She'd grown up in a small town in upstate New York and couldn't wait to get out of there and experience the bright lights and excitement of New York City. Save for a brief trip to Los Angeles with Brian once, she'd never been out West, had never imagined it would hold any appeal for her. She knew now how wrong she was. She responded instinctively to this magnificent place and couldn't wait to take out her camera and start shooting.

"Um, miss . . ." the stewardess standing just behind Zoey said, reminding her that everyone else had descended the stairs and was making their way into the small airport.

Clutching the camera bag and overnight bag that she hadn't bothered to check in New York, Zoey made her way with great reluctance down the steps, across the tarmac, and into the building.

A milling crowd, nothing like the dense, packed crowds at Kennedy Airport, greeted arriving passengers. Zoey stood just inside the doorway, looking around helplessly. Until this moment, it hadn't occurred to her that she had no idea what Tyler Ross looked like. Many of the ads in *Country*

Connections included photos, but some, like Tyler's, didn't. She hadn't described herself, either, so neither of them had the foggiest notion of what the other looked like.

She thought she'd never felt more awkward, uncomfortable, and embarrassed in her whole life. Carla and Denise were both dead wrong. She never should've come. As bad as it would've been to reject Tyler Ross without meeting him, this was worse. If she'd simply returned his ticket with a brief note explaining that she'd changed her mind, or suddenly met someone else, or even that she was dying, she would've felt guilty, but she would've gotten over it. Standing here now, feeling like an idiot, waiting to meet a total stranger whom she couldn't possibly have anything in common with was sheer torture. At that moment, she would have given anything to be anywhere else.

Suddenly, she saw a man approaching her. He looked to be in his mid-thirties and was the stereotypical portrait of a rancher, wearing stained bib overalls and a cap with the word "Coors" on the bill. He had a massive beer belly straining the overalls and was desperately in need of a shave.

Zoey's heart sank. *Oh my God*, she thought miserably, *it's even worse than I imagined*. She remembered the words in the ad—"I'm not perfect, and I'm not looking for someone who is."

She held her breath as the man came closer. To her profound relief, he kept right on walking, passing her by with hardly a glance. Turning to watch him, Zoey saw him go up to an elderly woman, possibly his grandmother, and give her a big hug. Then the two of them walked away chattering happily.

Zoey let out the breath she'd been holding and turned back to scan the now-dwindling crowd. Most of the people had met the passengers they'd come to greet and were headed out the front doors toward the parking lot. But one man walked slowly toward Zoey, his long legs striding effortlessly across the room. Without knowing anything about Tyler Ross save for his age, somehow Zoey knew this must be him. As she watched him close the distance between them, she felt a tightness in the pit of her stomach and a curious breathlessness.

Whatever she'd expected, it was nothing like the man standing before her now, hands shoved casually in the pockets of form-fitting jeans. A face only slightly too rugged to be considered conventionally handsome. Blue eyes as clear and intense as the Wyoming sky. Thick, golden-brown hair curling over the collar of a chambray shirt that was open at the throat, the sleeves rolled up to his elbows. Tall and lean. Tanned and muscled. Exuding an aura of uncomplicated maleness.

Looking up at him, Zoey suddenly felt like a little girl. Small and vulnerable and shy. She had no idea what it was about him that made her feel that way. He was tall, but not nearly as tall as Brian. Strong without being overpowering.

Different men in her life had brought out various aspects of her personality—uninhibited passion, tenderness, anger, and love. But none had ever made her feel this way. Her cheeks were warm and she knew she was blushing, but she couldn't seem to help it.

"Zoey Donovan?" he asked in a husky voice.

"Y-yes," she replied, furious at herself for the nervous catch in her voice.

"I'm Tyler Ross."

"Oh." She hesitated, then went on, "Pleased to meet you."

He nodded. "Pleased to meet you, too."

There was an awkward silence. Finally, Tyler reached out to take Zoey's overnight bag and, gesturing toward the front of the building, said, "My pickup's just outside."

A pickup. Of course, Zoey thought. Probably old and dirty. She wished she'd worn the jeans in her bag instead of a black skirt that would show every bit of dirt it came into contact with.

But the pickup was a surprise—fairly new, clean, with a surprisingly comfortable interior and a state-of-the-art stereo radio and CD system. *All the better to listen to Garth Brooks*, she told herself, clinging stubbornly to her stereotypical assumptions. But when Tyler turned on the ignition and the radio automatically came on, it was tuned to a jazz station playing classic Miles Davis.

Reaching over, Tyler turned it off, then said, "I thought you might want to stay at the Snow King Lodge. It's about the nicest place around here."

"Fine," Zoey murmured. She didn't really care where she stayed. She just wanted to leave as soon as possible.

"It's close to downtown, if you want to do some shopping or anything. Jackson isn't all that big."

"Fine," she repeated realizing she sounded like a broken record. As a photographer, she'd learned to talk to total strangers, often in difficult circumstances. She never was at a loss for words as she persuaded them to let her take their picture. But somehow she couldn't think of a single intelligent thing to say to this man.

She concentrated on the scenery, which was magnificent. On the way to the small town of Jackson, they passed through some of the most impressive countryside Zoey had ever seen. Across the sagebrush flats and the low, rolling hills, the incredible Tetons formed a constant backdrop. She felt tiny and insignificant as she looked out at this Big Sky country with its vastness and silence. As they passed an elk refuge and she saw hundreds of elk grazing in the huge fenced pasture, again she wished she could pull out her camera and start shooting. And then, to her amazement, she saw a real, honest-to-God buffalo grazing alone.

She gasped with delight. "Look!" she blurted out.

Following her gaze, Tyler said matter-of-factly, "It's just a single buffalo. Some of the local ranchers raise them. There are whole herds of them around here, especially in Yellowstone." He went on carefully, "'Course, I don't know if you'll have time to get over there."

No, she realized, she wouldn't, and was surprised at the hint of disappointment she felt.

They soon reached the small town of Jackson. It struck

Zoey, who had grown used to the dense crowds and hectic pace of a big city, as being the quintessential idyllic small town of our collective imagination. Jackson was nestled against the green foothills that sloped up to the low mountains west of the town. Interspersed among the thick stands of trees on those hills were bare areas that would be ski runs in the winter.

The town was composed primarily of single-story wooden buildings with a strong Western-style architecture, and there was a classic, two-lane Main Street. But, along with the usual drugstores and hardware stores found on every small-town Main Street, there were, surprisingly, designer boutiques as well. Ralph Lauren had come to Jackson. The local multiplex theater was playing an award-winning European film among the usual American fare. Zoey realized she would have to revise her opinion of this place as an uncultured, unsophisticated outpost.

In the center of town there was a small park, a kind of town square. At the four corners of the park were unusual arches composed of antlers. Elderly people sat on the worn wooden benches watching children play, and mothers gossiped on the edge of the playground. The atmosphere was warm and friendly, the pace slow. Zoey was caught off guard by her attraction to it.

Tyler parked in front of the lodge, a charmingly rustic-modern building overlooking a broad, rolling meadow and, in the distance, the ever-present Teton Range. Zoey followed Tyler into the lobby and up to the reservations desk.

The pretty young reservations clerk gave Tyler a decidedly flirtatious smile. Suddenly, it occurred to Zoey that a man as attractive as Tyler Ross must surely have his pick of women in a small town like Jackson. Why on earth had he bothered to advertise for a wife?

The clerk's voice held a none-too-subtle invitation as she said, "Why, Tyler, it's sure good to see you. It's been way too long since you stopped by."

Tyler's response was polite but cool. "Nice to see you, too,

Amy." Then he went straight to the point. "I need a room for a, um, friend visiting from out of town."

Amy gave Zoey a calculating look that was far less friendly than the one she'd given Tyler. "I wish I could help your *friend*, Tyler, but we're full up. Every last room is booked, and there are a half-dozen people on a waiting list."

This clearly came as a surprise to Tyler. He said, "But I thought you wouldn't be full until the weekend."

"Normally we wouldn't be, but there's a convention in town. Three thousand insurance adjusters. Every last room in the whole dang place is taken. I don't know what to suggest for your *friend* here."

Zoey felt a sinking sensation followed by a sudden surge of hope. Maybe this would give her a good excuse to drive right back to the airport and catch the next flight to New York. As Tyler thanked the desk clerk and Zoey followed him out of the lobby, she was trying to figure out exactly how to phrase her retreat. Perhaps she could say, "This is so disappointing, but I guess there's nothing to be done about it. Maybe I can come back another time."

They got back into the pickup. Before Zoey could speak, Tyler said tersely, "I should've made a reservation for you ahead of time. Sorry about that."

To her surprise, Zoey found herself responding, "It's all right."

"If it's okay with you, I'll take you on out to my ranch just outside of town." At her dismayed look, he added quickly, "My sister, Laurie, and her daughter, Cheryl, live with me. We'll be well chaperoned."

There was a hint of wry humor in those last words.

Zoey tried to find the right way to suggest that it would be best if she simply went right back to the airport, but she couldn't think of anything that didn't sound silly. She wasn't some nineteenth-century trembling virgin terrified of being alone with a man. Finally, with an inward sigh, she gave up.

"Okay," she agreed with extreme reluctance. She added pointedly, "But, you know, I can't stay long."

Tyler's mouth curved upward at the corners in a hint of an amused smile. "Don't worry, Ms. Donovan. You're perfectly safe with me."

Am I? Zoey wondered. Somehow, she suspected that no female, at least no *willing* female, was perfectly safe anywhere near Tyler Ross.

Traffic was light on the two-lane road heading north from Jackson. They were in the real countryside now, where unfenced grazing land stretched up to the forests at the base of the mountains. They came up behind a slow-moving livestock truck, and Tyler started to pass it. But when he saw what it was hauling, his expression changed dramatically. His piercing blue eyes glinted with silvery shards of anger and his hands gripped the steering wheel so hard his knuckles turned white.

"Damn!" he swore under his breath.

To Zoey's astonishment, he began trying to run the livestock truck off the road. Zoey desperately gripped the door handle with one hand and the dashboard with the other as Tyler repeatedly swerved to within inches of the truck. In a matter of moments, he succeeded in forcing the truck into a shallow gully beside the road.

Pulling a baseball bat from behind the seat of his pickup, Tyler threw open his door, got out, and stormed over to the livestock truck. The driver and his sidekick seemed to know Tyler and to wisely want no part of him. They locked the doors of the cab.

Tyler ordered them out and, when they didn't budge, he swung the bat and shattered the windshield. Flying glass quickly produced the truck crew. Moving to the rear of the truck, Tyler threw open the gates and snapped at the two frightened men, "Cut 'em loose!"

The men did as they were ordered, and a moment later a half-dozen wild horses, looking terrified but eager to be free, came pounding down the ramp. Bunching up, they galloped off across the range, heading toward the safety of the forests along the wide Snake River.

"You tell Jamison who did it!" Tyler shouted at the two men.

Getting back into the pickup, he said matter-of-factly to Zoey, "Sorry about that. Wild mustangs—those boys were going to sell 'em for meat. It's illegal. They know I don't put up with it."

Zoey stared at him, stunned speechless as he pulled back onto the road and headed toward his ranch.

5

Tyler turned off the main highway onto a single-lane paved road heading toward the mountains. After driving for a couple of miles, they rounded a bend and came upon a ranch house and a surrounding cluster of outbuildings. The setting was breathtakingly lovely, an oasis of pastoral beauty. Lush-green fenced pastures stretched to the edge of the foothills. The landscape, with a shallow stream running through it, was dotted with magnificent trees—aspen, fir, spruce, and pine. And, as in every other part of the Jackson "hole," or valley, in the distance the snowcapped Tetons dominated everything.

With her vivid imagination, Zoey could sense what it must have been like when the first Ross arrived here and decided to claim this particular piece of land for his own. It had everything necessary to survive and prosper—fresh water, abundant grazing land, plenty of game in the foothills, and timber in the mountains. This was a place where someone could put down roots that would last for generations. There was an aura of permanence and stability such as Zoey hadn't felt since she was a child and her father was still with them in their small town in upstate New York.

The ranch house, built of peeled pine logs silvered now with age, was larger than Zoey had expected—two stories, with a broad veranda across the front and a balcony running along the second story. The wood-and-stone house looked as if it had been there for a hundred years and would still be there in another hundred.

Noticing Zoey's look of surprise, Tyler explained with undisguised pride, "My great-grandfather, Joshua Ross, built it before the turn of the century. He hauled the rocks up from the riverbed. It's been modernized somewhat since then, of course, and I've done a bit of carpentry work to it myself. But it's basically the same as it was a hundred years ago."

Those were the first words Tyler had spoken since the frightening incident with the mustangs in the livestock truck. Zoey was amazed at how calm he sounded now. It was hard to reconcile this apparently reasonable, quiet-spoken man with the furious, baseball bat–wielding vigilante who had taken it upon himself to liberate horses belonging to someone else.

She tried to imagine Brian losing control like that, but knew that it would never happen. Brian prided himself on always being in control because that guaranteed him the upper hand in any situation. Occasionally slamming a door was the closest he would allow himself to come to expressing anger.

Remembering the incident, Zoey corrected herself. Tyler hadn't been merely venting anger in an irresponsible manner. He'd been filled with a righteous fury on behalf of those horses. Such concern—such *passion*—was frightening, but also intriguing.

Zoey wondered who Jamison was, and why there was clearly a feud between him and Tyler. Somehow, she sensed it wouldn't be a good idea to ask Tyler about the mysterious Jamison.

As Zoey stepped out of the pickup, she saw two women come out onto the porch. One appeared to be in her middle forties, the other in her late teens or early twenties. Zoey thought that a decent haircut and the right makeup would take ten years off the older woman's appearance. With her shoulder-length hair pulled back in a plain ponytail and her face devoid of makeup, wearing faded jeans and a pink cotton blouse, she obviously made no effort with her appearance. The younger woman, clearly her daughter, was a vision of what her mother must have been like when she was young. Her long, glossy hair hung halfway down her back and subtle makeup highlighted a naturally pretty face.

Zoey didn't have to be introduced to the women to know they must be Tyler's sister and niece. The family resemblance—golden-brown hair, ice-blue eyes and high cheekbones—was pronounced.

The older woman came down the porch steps followed by her daughter, who stared with undisguised curiosity at Zoey. Extending her hand, the woman said with real warmth, "Welcome to our home, Ms. Donovan. I'm Tyler's sister, Laurie Graham, and this is my daughter, Cheryl."

"Pleased to meet you, ma'am," Cheryl said politely.

Zoey forced a smile. "How do you do, Mrs. Graham. Cheryl."

Laurie went on, "We didn't think we'd get to meet you until dinner tonight."

Tyler came around the pickup carrying Zoey's bags. "The lodge was full up," he explained tersely. "Some damn convention's taken every room in town."

"That's all right," Laurie responded easily "we've got plenty of room. And as a house guest, we'll get to visit with you more than if you were staying in town. That'll be real nice." She turned to Tyler. "Won't it, Ty?"

Tyler didn't immediately agree. For a moment, there seemed to be an unspoken but powerful tug-of-war going on between him and Laurie. Finally, as if conceding defeat, Tyler said with an utter lack of feeling, "Real nice."

Then he climbed the steps, crossed the porch, and went into the house.

Damn it, Zoey thought angrily. If Tyler hadn't wanted her here, and he clearly didn't, why had he invited her?

Placing a hand lightly on Zoey's shoulder, Laurie said, "Come on, I'll show you to your room. Then you can take a few minutes to freshen up. You must be tired out from that long flight. Imagine, coming all the way from New York City. I've never been there, but I've always wanted to go. I hope you'll tell me all about it."

With Laurie prattling on in a friendly way and Cheryl still eyeing Zoey curiously, Zoey allowed herself to be led into the house.

The interior was open and spacious, dominated by a huge stone fireplace that took up much of one wall. Zoey suspected that at some point walls had been knocked down to create a large great room out of several smaller ones. Colorful Native American rugs were scattered over highly polished oak floors, and the furniture was covered in chocolate-colored corduroy, a practical choice for ranch life, Zoey realized. Heavy wooden beams ran across the tall ceiling. The atmosphere was unpretentious and comfortable.

She was impressed by the artwork on the walls. The watercolor paintings appeared to be local scenes, and whoever had chosen them had a good eye. One particular painting of the mountains on a stormy day would have fetched thousands in a SoHo gallery, Zoey guessed.

Turning to Laurie, she said, "This is stunning. Is it a local artist?"

"Yes, a young man who lives over at Laramie. I got this when he was just starting out, before he'd even had his first show. He's become extremely popular. I can't afford his work now."

"Did you choose all the artwork here?" Zoey asked moving across the room to study another painting, this one of a stand of aspens.

"Mmm-hmm. Do you like it?"

"Oh, yes. You've got great taste."

Laurie beamed. "Thanks, Zoey. Oh—do you mind if I call you that? Ms. Donovan just seems so formal."

"No, that's fine."

"And please call me Laurie. 'Mrs. Graham' makes me feel even older than I am."

"Do you paint?" Zoey asked.

"Heavens no. I can't even draw a straight line. But I love art. I've taken a few night classes in art appreciation and history at the local junior college. I'd love to study it more, but there's not a lot of opportunity here. Or time."

"I imagine you're pretty busy with the ranch."

"Oh, Tyler takes real good care of the ranch," Laurie responded with an affectionate smile toward her brother, who waited impatiently at the foot of the stairs, "but I have a full-time job."

"In town?" Zoey asked.

"No, right here. I work out of an office here in the house. I do customer service for a big telecommunications company based in Denver. I've got a computer and a modem, and that's all it takes nowadays."

Tyler waited for the women to precede him up the stairs. As they climbed the stairs, Laurie asked questions about New York—what part of the city Zoey lived in, and what she did for a living. When Zoey mentioned that she was a photographer, Cheryl spoke up for the first time.

"Really? Oh, Mom, do you think—"

But Laurie interrupted her daughter quickly. "Hush, Cheryl, don't you dare ask her that."

"Ask me what?" Zoey asked as Laurie led her into a large corner bedroom with windows looking out toward the mountains.

Before Laurie could respond, Cheryl said in a rush, "It's just that I'm getting married next week, and the photographer came down with chicken pox. Can you believe it? At his age! He got it from his little boy. And with all the weddings going on at this time of year, *nobody's* available. It looks like Chuck and I will be lucky to have some of those instant Polaroids his dad likes to take."

Laurie was clearly mortified by her daughter's presumptuousness. "Cheryl, we've barely met Zoey. We can't ask her to do something like that."

Tyler added firmly, "And besides, Ms. Donovan won't be here then."

"Oh," Cheryl said in a small, disappointed voice.

Feeling sorry for her, Zoey responded, "Actually, I'd be more than happy to help you out, but I'm afraid your uncle's right. I can only stay a couple of days."

Laurie gave Zoey a startled look. Obviously, she'd expected a longer visit. She turned to Tyler and glared at him in silent reproach.

Ignoring his sister's pointed look, Tyler said to Zoey, "Well, I've got some work to do before dinner. I'll leave you to get settled in."

Laurie gave him a sharp look. Apparently realizing he was being less than hospitable toward his guest, he added without enthusiasm, "If you'd like to join me, I'll be in the corral out front." And he was gone.

Cheryl followed, saying forlornly, "I guess I'd better get back on the phone and try to find a photographer."

Alone with Zoey, Laurie said in embarrassment, "I apologize for my daughter."

"No need. I can imagine how panic-stricken she must be feeling right now."

"You have no idea. We've been planning this wedding for months, and of course it's real important to Cheryl that everything go smoothly. We just found out about the photographer last night, and she's been a nervous wreck since then."

"I meant it, you know," Zoey said kindly. "I'd be happy to do it if I was going to be here. But I can't stay that long. I—I have to get back to New York for—for business."

Laurie gave her a shrewd look that instantly dispelled

Zoey's assumption that she was a simple country woman. "It's all right, Zoey, you don't have to explain. I think I can understand how you must be feeling right now. Coming to a strange place and meeting a total stranger, and all."

Zoey didn't respond, but she felt guilt wash through her. Laurie couldn't begin to understand because she didn't know the real truth.

Laurie went on, "I'll let you settle in. There's a bathroom down the hall to the right. When you're ready, come on down. I'll be in the kitchen getting dinner started."

"Okay."

At the doorway, Laurie paused and said, "I know Tyler must seem kind of, well, reserved. That's just his way. When you get to know him better, you'll understand. But I want you to know, we're all real glad you came."

And with that, she was gone, closing the door behind her.

Alone in the pleasantly decorated room with its flowered wallpaper in pale blue and pink, and white lace curtains at the windows, Zoey felt even guiltier than she had before. She sat down on the edge of the big, old four-poster bed and sighed heavily. How could she mislead these perfectly nice people? Back in New York, the choice to go through with meeting Tyler had seemed to be the lesser of two evils. Now, she suspected that she'd only made matters worse by coming here under false pretenses.

The only mitigating circumstance seemed to be Tyler's apparent lack of interest in her. At least she didn't have to worry about disappointing him by leaving as quickly as possible. Though she realized she was being utterly contrary, she couldn't help but be both confused and insulted by his disinterest. Well, the sooner she got out of there, the better.

After unpacking and changing into jeans and a T-shirt, Zoey went downstairs and found the kitchen at the back of the house. It was a wonderfully cozy room, with a small stone fireplace that was a miniature version of the massive one in the living room. An old, round oak table, highly polished but deeply scarred, sat near the fireplace. In a Manhattan antiques shop it would be considered an expensive "find." Here, it was simply another piece of furniture that had undoubtedly been handed down through the generations.

A delicious aroma of something baking in the oven filled the room. Zoey's stomach growled in response, and she was surprised to realize that, despite her nervousness, she was very hungry.

Laurie sat at the table snapping fresh green beans into smaller pieces and dropping them into a bowl. She smiled as Zoey came in. "There's coffee on the stove. Help yourself."

"Thanks," Zoey responded. A thick brown mug sat on the countertop near the stove. She filled it with coffee, added cream and sugar from bowls set out for that purpose, then joined Laurie at the table. "Can I help?" she asked.

"No, thanks. Everything's just about done. The roast's in the oven, along with potatoes and carrots. I'll just steam these green beans right before the roast beef is ready."

Suddenly, a worried frown appeared on her plain face. "You *do* eat meat, don't you? I mean, you're not a vegetarian or anything?"

Zoey smiled, amused at Laurie's assumption that New Yorkers would automatically have different eating habits. But then, she realized ruefully, she had made similar assumptions about these people. She said easily, "No, I'm not a vegetarian. Roast beef sounds great."

"It's just that, being from New York City and all, I thought maybe you might not care for the kind of food we eat here."

"It's true that a lot of New Yorkers seem to just graze. But some of us do eat meat," Zoey replied with a grin.

Laurie's plain face lit up with eager interest. "Tell me about New York. Where you go, what you do. I've always wanted to go there, but I've never been able to. When I was growing up here, I dreamed about maybe going away to college at an Ivy League school. I used to read *Seventeen* magazine and see those models in their preppy clothes, posing on campuses like Sarah Lawrence or Bryn Mawr. It seemed so different from here. So exciting."

Zoey talked easily of her life in the city, answering Laurie's eager questions with detailed descriptions of her favorite places in Manhattan—the boutiques, art galleries, restaurants, latest plays, and "in" clubs. Laurie took it all in with a wistful look that made Zoey wish she could show it all to her personally.

"If you ever get to New York, I'd be happy to show you around," Zoey said sincerely. It would be fun, she thought, to show Laurie a bit of excitement.

Laurie sighed and shook her head. "Thanks, that's real sweet of you. But I don't think I'll be going anywhere for a long time. Pete—he's my husband—doesn't like big cities."

"Will I be meeting Pete?" Zoey asked sipping the strong, hot coffee.

"I'm not sure," Laurie answered evasively. She explained, "He's on the rodeo circuit and I don't expect him back for a few days."

The way Laurie avoided Zoey's gaze as she discussed Pete suggested that theirs was less than a wonderful marriage.

Zoey found herself feeling sorry for Laurie, a woman growing old before her time, a woman who was far too bright and creative for the limited life she was living, a woman who was probably a wonderful mother but was about to lose her only child to marriage. How would Laurie deal with the empty-nest syndrome? Zoey wondered. Would she simply live out her life waiting for her husband to return from the rodeo circuit and taking care of her bachelor brother? To Zoey, it was a very sad and limited picture.

Thinking of Tyler reminded Zoey that she knew almost nothing about him. While she insisted that she had no interest in him, no matter how attractive he might be, she couldn't help but be a little curious. She said slowly, trying to sound casual, "You know, Laurie, I know very little about Tyler. Except what he wrote in his ad, and that didn't tell me much."

Laurie gave her a knowing smile. "I'll bet he didn't exactly talk your ear off on the ride home from the airport."

"No," Zoey agreed.

"Tyler and I are the exact opposite that way. He's definitely a man of few words, and I'll chatter on forever if someone doesn't shut me up."

"Has he ever been married?" Zoey asked trying not to sound too interested in the answer.

Laurie raised an eyebrow. "He didn't even tell you that much about himself?"

Zoey shook her head.

Laurie went on, "He's a widower. His wife, Sarah, died three years ago. Asthma, you know. It was real sad. She was so young."

That explained a great deal, Zoey thought soberly. For all his strength and sheer bullheadness, Tyler had an enormously sad quality about him. "They didn't have children?"

"N-no," Laurie answered hesitantly.

Zoey sensed that somehow that innocent question had touched on a highly sensitive subject, but she told herself it would be impolite to probe. Instead, she said, "Frankly, I'm surprised he would advertise in something like *Country Connections*. I mean, he's rather attractive, and I would think he'd be considered quite a catch."

Laurie rose and took the bowl of green beans over to the counter. Setting the bowl aside, she rinsed off her hands in the sink and dried them on a dish towel hanging from a hook nearby. "The problem is, there aren't that many single women in these parts," she explained as she stood by the sink. "In a rural area like this, most people get married right out of high school, like Pete and I did. Or right out of college, like Tyler and Sarah. Men stay to work the farms and ranches, but the women who don't marry young either move to the city to work or go away to college and never return.

So, unlike what I hear about the rest of the country, there are actually more single men than women in rural areas."

Coming from a city like New York, where attractive single men like Brian were literally worth their weight in gold, Zoey was amazed. Maybe, she thought guiltily, she and her friends shouldn't have been so quick to laugh at *Country Connections*.

Zoey said carefully, "Still, it must be rather awkward advertising for a wife. I know I certainly felt awkward answering your brother's ad." She couldn't explain the whole reason why she felt so awkward.

Laurie dismissed this consideration with a wave of her hand. "Oh, it's just a modern version of an old practice. Settlers in colonial times imported brides from Europe. And frontiersmen advertised in East Coast newspapers for mail-order brides. I guess people have always been willing to cross a lot of miles in their search for love and companionship."

Eyeing Zoey thoughtfully, Laurie went on, "You should understand. After all, you responded to Tyler's ad."

Zoey felt like the most dishonest person on the face of the earth. *That's it,* she told herself miserably, *I'm getting out of here as quickly as possible.*

When Laurie suggested Zoey might want to join Tyler, Zoey reluctantly left.

Stepping onto the front porch, Zoey drew in an awed breath. The gigantic Teton Range mountains, charging at the sky, were stunning every time she saw them. To live in that towering presence would surely affect one's whole outlook on life. Idly, she wondered if that helped to explain the enigmatic Tyler.

Pots of brilliant-red geraniums brightened the length of the porch, and a hedge of multi-colored peonies edged the lawn contained by a rail fence. At each end of the house, placed as though not to interfere with the view of the mountains, were two towering pine trees.

The air was crisp and pleasant, with sunlight reflecting off the snowy Tetons. Hands in her jeans pockets, Zoey strolled around the house toward the sound of voices. Across the yard, she saw a pole-fenced corral attached to a large log barn. The voices she'd heard were Tyler's and Jesse's. They were both on horseback, maneuvering an obviously fractious and uncooperative young bull.

Wishing she'd brought her camera, Zoey decided it would be interesting to take a closer look at an animal she'd never seen in real life before. If the scene looked promising, she'd get her camera and take a few pictures of ranch life before catching a late-afternoon flight back to New York in two days.

Walking up to the corral, she leaned against the railing and smiled politely at Tyler. "Hi."

He nodded, barely glancing at her.

She thought how confident he looked on his horse, one hand grasping the reins, the other holding on to a loosely coiled lariat. The battered Stetson he wore shaded his face from the bright summer sun, giving him a slightly enigmatic look. He was a mystery, all right, Zoey thought. She felt a twinge of regret at the knowledge that she wouldn't have an opportunity to get past his defenses and unravel that mystery.

"So . . . what're you doing with the bull?" Zoey asked trying to make conversation and painfully aware that she sounded like a city slicker who didn't know anything.

With a disdainful look, Tyler gestured toward a small wooden pen barely wide enough to hold one animal. It opened off the corral only a few feet from Zoey. Casually looping his lariat in his hand, he answered, "Trying to get him into that pen so he can be vaccinated."

Turning away from Zoey, he kicked his horse's flanks and headed toward the bull. One man on each side of the animal, he and Jesse worked seamlessly together to guide the bull toward the chute, eventually forcing the reluctant creature into it.

"Get the vaccine," Tyler called to Jesse. "I'll shut him in."

Jesse dismounted and headed toward the barn.

"I can do it," Zoey said easily. And before Tyler could

respond, she climbed through the bars of the corral and hurried over to the gate.

Suddenly aware that the gate was open, the bull turned and charged toward freedom. He came to a rushing stop a few terrifying feet from Zoey. His baleful eyes glared at her as he tossed his head, then lowered his horns. She knew what that meant from movies she'd seen. With a sick feeling in the pit of her stomach, she realized she was in real danger.

"Oh, my God!" The words came out in a terrified whisper. Turning to flee, Zoey stumbled and fell just as the bull pawed the ground, bellowing and sending a swirl of dust into the air.

Tyler was there before she could react to the expected charge of the bull. He rode between her and the furious animal, shouting and waving his lariat. Confused, the bull stopped in mid-charge, his massive head swinging uncertainly from Tyler to Zoey.

Jesse leaped the fence, an electric cattle prod in one hand. He jabbed the bull with the prod so that it gave a startled bellow. All the aggression melted from the bull's attitude and he trotted almost meekly back into the pen. Jesse quickly shot the bolt on the gate.

Tyler dismounted and went to Zoey, who had shakily pulled herself to her feet. She stood utterly still, nearly paralyzed with fear.

"Damn it!" he shouted. "Don't you know anything?! You never go up to a bull on foot!"

"I didn't realize—" she began in a trembling voice.

"You might've been killed!"

Looking into Tyler's furious countenance, Zoey felt tears welling up in her eyes. She desperately wanted not to make a fool of herself in front of him, but she couldn't help herself. Tears began trickling down her cheeks, which were still white with shock, and she began to shake uncontrollably. She knew she was about to collapse.

As her knees began to buckle, Tyler grabbed her and held

her against him. As she looked up into his face, only inches from her own, what she saw in his eyes astonished her. Beyond the anger, she saw profound fear for her safety. It was unexpected—and deeply touching.

As she leaned against that broad, hard chest and felt strong arms holding her up, she had the strangest sense of déjà vu. Where did this feeling of complete and utter security come from? she wondered. And then she remembered. This was how she'd felt when she was a very little girl and her father had hugged her tight.

"Are you all right?" Jesse asked running up to them.

Zoey whispered, "Yes." Then, more loudly, "I'm all right."

"Sure, thanks to Tyler. If he hadn't acted so quick, that bull would'a made mincemeat outta you."

"It's all right, Jesse," Tyler cut in. Slowly letting go of Zoey, he went on, "I think you'd better go back to the house and lie down for a bit."

Jesse nodded agreement. "You bet. You've had quite a scare, miss." He couldn't resist adding, "Jest try to be a little more careful, as all. You don't know your way around a ranch."

Feeling that she'd made a complete fool of herself, Zoey murmured, "All right," then turned and walked with as much dignity as she could muster back to the house.

When she was out of earshot, Jesse said with a shake of his head, "Now there's a woman without a lick of sense."

Tyler said nothing. Jesse was right, of course, he thought. And yet it wasn't Zoey's total lack of common sense that bothered him. It was the way he'd felt as he held her in his arms. A wave of protectiveness had washed over him and, for an instant, he hadn't wanted to let her go.

The sooner she leaves, the better, he thought, more angry at himself now than he'd been at her only a moment earlier.

° ° °

Dinner that evening was strained. Tyler was quiet. Jesse didn't say much, either. He merely flashed curious looks from Tyler to Zoey and back again. Fortunately, Cheryl and Laurie kept up a running dialogue about the wedding preparations, interspersed by questions from Zoey.

While Zoey tried to concentrate on descriptions of the bridesmaids' dresses ("the sweetest shade of pink") and flowers ("I went with pure white. You just can't beat tradition"), she was all-too-aware that she and Tyler were the focus of attention. Laurie, Cheryl, and Jesse watched them avidly, clearly waiting to see romance unfold.

Cheryl, who was madly in love with her fiancé and seemed to see everything through a romantic haze, was especially intrigued. She kept looking from her uncle to the woman who'd come all the way from New York to meet him, as if waiting for a page from a Danielle Steele novel to come to life.

Instead of romance, what unfolded was disaster. As Tyler became drawn into the conversation and he and Zoey began to exchange opinions about everything from politics to entertainment, it became clear they were total opposites. She was a democrat, he was a republican. She listened to Howard Stern, he listened to Rush Limbaugh.

Trying to get onto safer ground, she started talking about her upcoming show. "The photographs are all pictures of various types of refuse, both material and human," she explained proudly.

Tyler frowned. "If that's so, the New York art world must be a playground for idiots."

Stung, Zoey shot back, "You're obviously an expert on idiocy."

Things went rapidly downhill from there.

Claiming exhaustion from her trip, Zoey retired to her room immediately after dinner. She told herself she wouldn't wait until the day after tomorrow to leave. Somehow, she would come up with an excuse to leave the very next day.

Downstairs, Laurie turned on Tyler as soon as Jesse and Cheryl left them drinking coffee in the living room. "That was inexcusable!"

"What?" he asked, feigning ignorance.

"Don't you 'what' me, Tyler! You were downright rude to that poor woman!"

"I was just carrying on a conversation. Would you prefer I didn't speak to her?"

"Of course not! But you went out of your way to be disagreeable. All that talk about Rush Limbaugh. You don't even agree with him most of the time. You were just trying to yank her chain."

"Laurie, I told you she doesn't belong here. I think she feels it, too. She isn't any more interested in me than I am in her."

He didn't add that he couldn't imagine ever being seriously interested in any woman again. He had been supremely fortunate once and had found the one woman who was absolutely perfect for him. He couldn't imagine such a thing ever happening again. Lightning didn't strike twice.

Laurie was silent for a long moment. Then she said with studied casualness, "Don't you think she's pretty?"

"I don't know. I didn't really notice. She's not bad, I guess."

Laurie smiled triumphantly. "Then there's hope yet. That's the first time you've admitted you find a woman besides Sarah attractive."

"I didn't say she was attractive," Tyler insisted stubbornly.

"No, but you didn't say she's dog meat, either, and for you that's really something."

Tyler tried to think of a retort, but somehow none came to mind. Frowning, he turned and went upstairs to his room.

It was well past midnight, and the house was silent. Zoey knew everyone must be sound asleep. Ranchers kept early hours. But, try as she might, she couldn't fall asleep. She was still angry at Tyler, whom she was starting to refer to in her mind as that pigheaded, arrogant cowboy.

Finally, after tossing and turning for an hour, Zoey got out of bed and stepped out onto the veranda. The night breeze was restless, matching her unsettled frame of mind. She looked out into the inky blackness at the mountains in the distance, barely visible in the pale light of a moon half-obscured by clouds.

Down the hall, Tyler awoke abruptly in a sweat, his bare chest damp and his hair plastered against his head. For a moment, he felt the sharp stab of the old, remembered pain as he lay in the double bed that seemed far too large and empty without Sarah sharing it.

The nightmare was the same one that had tormented him for three years. He was trying to hold on to Sarah, but something was pulling her away from him. He felt her slip through his fingers, then she was gone, looking back at him helplessly, leaving him with an overwhelming feeling of guilt.

For a moment, his body trembled. He forced the trembling to stop. When he felt in control once more, he flung off the sheet and blanket, got up from the bed, and strode, half-naked in pajama bottoms, to the French window that opened out onto the balcony. He'd left it open, as he always did in the summer, to catch the cool night breeze. Standing there, he inhaled the fresh air, feeling the welcome sensation of the night breeze against his bare skin.

He had no idea how late it was, but he knew it couldn't be close to dawn yet. There was no telltale streak of silver on the horizon that presaged sunrise. Surely it must be the dead of night.

As always, he told himself that the nightmare was just that—a bad dream. Eventually, the recurring nightmare must stop. It couldn't go on forever.

Hearing a sound, he looked toward the far end of the balcony. Someone else couldn't sleep, either, he realized. He saw Zoey leaning over the balcony railing. She was looking out at the mountains, oblivious to the fact that he was watching.

Her hair was disheveled around her shoulders, as if she, too, had slept restlessly. She wore a thin cotton shirt that stopped just above her knees. With the light from her bedroom shining behind her, silhouetting her body, her high, round breasts and gently rounded hips were evident.

She was exquisitely lovely, in a way she hadn't appeared to be earlier, when her demeanor toward him had been so cool. To his surprise, Tyler felt desire stir deep within him. He'd felt attraction toward other women, had even slept with a couple of them who understood he could only offer his body and not his heart. But those experiences had been mere releases of physical tension compared to the feeling that swept over him now, a desire as fierce as it was disturbing and unwanted.

He imagined pulling that nightshirt over her head, slowly, carefully, savoring the pleasure of seeing her naked, then kissing her, at first gently, but with increasing pressure.

But this situation didn't allow for desire, seduction, satiation. He'd gotten Zoey here under false pretenses, using her to get a well-meaning but irritating sister off his back. The moment he met Zoey at the airport, he began to realize how unfair he was being. That was why he'd been so unfriendly. He wanted her to dislike him so that she would be eager to leave.

He started to step back into his room, when he heard a sound drift over from the end of the balcony. Straining to listen, he realized Zoey was speaking softly to herself, whispered words that seemed to hold a world of feeling: "I should never have come. What have I done?"

Suddenly, she turned from the railing at the veranda, her arms wrapped around her as if she were cold. Tyler watched as she went back into her room, shutting the French door behind her.

What had she meant? he wondered. He was caught off guard by the depth of curiosity and unexpected desire he felt toward this unwanted, irritating woman. Trying to shake it off, he went back to bed. But it was a long time before he finally fell into a fitful sleep.

6

Zoey awoke at eight o'clock exhausted and wishing she could lie in bed for awhile longer. But she assumed ranchers rose early, and knew she'd probably already missed breakfast. Her stomach growled hungrily at the thought of a hearty ranch breakfast. In New York, she would have skipped the meal entirely, save for one cup of hot, black coffee. But somehow—maybe it was the crisp, clean air—she felt ravenous here. She hurriedly threw on jeans and a T-shirt, then went down the hall to the bathroom.

As she splashed water on her face, then brushed her teeth, she tried to think of a polite excuse to leave that day. Perhaps, she thought, she could call back to New York and while on the phone pretend there was an emergency that required her immediate attention. An ill relative? A problem with her upcoming show? A friend in trouble?

She knew that Tyler, and probably Laurie for that matter, would see right through any excuse she could come up with, but it didn't matter. Tyler clearly didn't want her there anyway, and Laurie was merely an interested bystander with no real stake in a possible relationship between Tyler and Zoey.

Deciding that a fictitious problem with her upcoming show would be the best excuse, Zoey made up her mind to place the call to New York as soon as possible.

Downstairs, she went into the kitchen and found Cheryl sitting at the table, still in her robe, checking off items on a list that Zoey assumed had to do with her upcoming wedding. There was a pot of coffee on the stove, and Zoey smelled a wonderful aroma of bacon and eggs.

Cheryl said a cheerful good morning, then explained that her mother had left Zoey's breakfast warming in the oven. Urging Zoey to sit down at the table, Cheryl waited on her, pouring her a cup of coffee and taking her plate from the oven and placing it on the woven rattan placemat in front of her. The plate was piled high with scrambled eggs, several strips of bacon, and two homemade biscuits.

As Cheryl bustled around, getting a napkin and silverware and generally being a good hostess, Zoey apologized for oversleeping.

"Oh, that's all right," Cheryl reassured her. "Mom had to get to her computer, and Uncle Tyler always starts working early, but there was no need for you to get up at the crack of dawn." As she joined Zoey at the table, she yawned tiredly. "Actually, I just got up myself. I was over at Chuck's house last night and got back kinda late."

Meeting Zoey's look, she blushed prettily.

"So, tell me about Chuck," Zoey said encouragingly.

Cheryl didn't need much encouragement to talk about her fiancé as she joined Zoey at the table. Her face lit up as she said in a rush, "Well, his full name is Charles Edward Carter and that means I'm gonna be Cheryl Carter, which has a nice ring to it, I think, don't you? He's a little bit older than I am, twenty-six, and that's good, because men are real immature until they hit about twenty-five or so, don't you think?"

Zoey nodded agreement. Actually, she thought men were pretty immature until at least thirty, but she wasn't going to tell Cheryl that.

Cheryl continued, beaming with pride, "He's a real sensible kinda guy. Hard working and steady and all. His truck's paid for, and he owns a lot just outside town that he an' his dad are gonna build us a house on. His dad's a contractor, and Chuck's in business with him. He has all kinds of ideas about expanding the business. There's a lot of opportunities, y'know, what with a lot of folks moving in here from California and other places."

Zoey suspected that Cheryl could go on forever talking about Chuck. Trying to steer the conversation in a different direction, she asked, "And what do you do? Are you in college?"

Cheryl shook her head. "Nope. Mom *really* wanted me to go, but I wasn't interested. I always knew what I wanted to do, from the time I was a little girl."

"And what's that?" Zoey asked taking a big bite of creamy scrambled eggs and crisp bacon.

"Work with kids. I'm a teacher's aide at a daycare center in town. I just *love* it. They're real sweet. The only thing better will be havin' my own. As soon as the house is built, in a year or so, me an' Chuck are gonna start a family."

"That soon, huh?" Zoey commented biting into a flaky biscuit oozing with butter.

"There's no reason to wait. I'm an only child, and Chuck's only got one sister, who's ten years older. So neither of us came from a big family, and we both want that." Eyeing Zoey curiously, she went on, "How about you, Ms. Donovan? What's your family like?"

"I have two younger brothers."

"That must've been fun, growing up together."

Thinking of Skipper and Andy, who had been cute but extremely rambunctious little boys, Zoey said with a wry grin, "It was never dull. They used to spy on me when I'd come home from dates. One time they actually dropped a water balloon on my date's head from their upstairs bedroom window. He was the quarterback on the football team, and I'd been waiting for months for him to notice me and ask me out. I wanted to kill them."

Cheryl chuckled. "I'll bet." Then she went on, "Are you close now?"

Zoey nodded. "Oh, yes. Unfortunately, we don't get together much, except for holidays. They still live in our hometown in upstate New York, and it's a long drive from Manhattan, where I live. But every once in awhile the phone will ring and it will be one of them, just calling to see how I'm doing. They worry about me, being in the big, bad city. It's an odd reversal of roles, since I was used to being the one taking care of them."

"Oh, it sounds wonderful," Cheryl said with a sigh. "I always wanted brothers and sisters. That's why Chuck and I are gonna have a whole passel of kids."

Looking at Cheryl, Zoey felt a tiny twinge of jealousy. Cheryl was young and in love and about to embark on the adventure of marriage. With or without a photographer, it was obviously a happy event.

Zoey remembered a cynical comment Denise had made recently as she and Zoey passed a group of young, twenty-something women walking in Central Park. "Their futures are still ahead of them. They haven't yet made the choices that will ruin their lives."

Zoey had given Denise a startled look of dismay. Her friend had shrugged and said, "Just kidding." But Zoey sensed that she meant every bittersweet word. As Denise approached forty, she was beginning to look back on her life and regret some of the critical decisions she'd made, especially the choice to focus so intently on a high-powered career at the expense of a personal life.

Will I feel the same way in a few years? Zoey wondered. God, she hoped not.

Blissfully unaware of Zoey's pensiveness, the talkative Cheryl went on, "I'm not working right now. I had enough vacation time so I could take a week off before the wedding and another week off for the honeymoon."

"Where are you and Chuck going for your honeymoon?"

"Oh, just up to a cabin his parents have in the mountains. It's nothing fancy, but it's in the most beautiful spot you can imagine, and we'll be all alone. That's what really matters on a honeymoon, right?"

"Right," Zoey agreed with a smile. She didn't volunteer her own fantasy of the perfect honeymoon—renting a tiny Caribbean island for just her and her husband. She'd read about such places in travel magazines and couldn't imagine anything more romantic. Thinking of Brian and his reluctance to get married, Zoey felt pessimistic about her chances of ever making that fantasy come true.

"Well, I'd better go on up and get dressed," Cheryl said. "I've got a million things to do to get ready for the wedding. And number one on the list is finding a photographer."

When Cheryl had gone, Zoey finished the breakfast, which was delicious, and indulged in a second cup of steaming black coffee.

"Good morning."

Zoey looked up to find Laurie standing in the kitchen doorway smiling at her.

Zoey returned the smile. "Good morning to you, too."

"Did you sleep okay?"

"Yes," Zoey lied.

"Good, because I came to ask if you feel up to going out and seeing something of the ranch. Tyler and Jesse have to round up some strays and brand them, and I thought we could pack a lunch and make a picnic out of it."

"Can you take time away from work?" Zoey asked trying to make it sound as if it was concern for Laurie's schedule and not her own reluctance that prompted the question.

"Oh, sure. I won't take off all day, just a couple of hours. I'll work a little later tonight to make up for it. What do you say? It would give you a chance to see the place up close. We're pretty proud of it."

"I don't think Ms. Donovan's up to it."

Tyler stood in the open doorway that led from the kitchen to the outdoors. Coming in and closing the screen door behind him, he went on, "She'll probably want to just take it easy after her long flight yesterday. Not to mention that run-in with the bull."

Zoey was stung to the quick. She'd allowed herself to appear weak, and now Tyler was treating her as if that's all she was.

"What run-in?" Laurie asked worriedly.

"It was nothing," Zoey insisted. She glared at Tyler, silently daring him to contradict her. When he didn't say anything, she turned back to Laurie. "I'd love to see the ranch."

Laurie looked from Tyler to Zoey, clearly wondering what was going on between them, but she thought better of probing into a subject that apparently neither wanted to get into further. "Okay," she said slowly. "Let's go, then."

The setting was glorious, and Zoey was glad she'd brought her camera. They built a fire to heat up the branding irons at one end of a narrow canyon with a shallow stream running through it. Smoke from the fire drifted upward, a thin ribbon against the pristine blue sky.

The canyon was dotted with bright patches of flowers—lavender, purple, and white—that turned gracefully in the summer breeze. A host of white butterflies hovered above the flowers, gleaming in the sunlight. It was quiet, peaceful, idyllic. Everything that Zoey's life in New York wasn't. She hadn't expected to be drawn to this. She had expected to find it boring. Instead, she felt layers of big-city stress melt away, to be replaced by a feeling of relaxation that she hadn't known in a long, long time.

Tyler and Jesse unloaded their saddled horses from the horse trailer, then rode off to round up unbranded calves.

Laurie explained to Zoey that they would bring the calves into the small, rustic corral in a nearby grove of aspen trees. Cheryl had remained at home to deal with the never-ending wedding preparations, especially the desperate, last-minute search for a photographer.

Beneath the lightly fluttering shade of the aspens, Zoey helped Laurie set up a small folding table and chairs. She covered the table with a red-and-white-checked cloth while Laurie unpacked the cold lunch—fried chicken, potato salad, biscuits from breakfast, and juicy red apples. There was a big thermos of coffee, and a pitcher of tart lemonade.

By the time they'd finished setting up and sat down to relax with glasses of lemonade, the men had returned driving a small bunch of bawling calves. Fascinated, Zoey watched as they expertly maneuvered the calves into the corral. She grabbed her camera. This time, she was cautious in her approach to the corral full of milling calves. Tyler was too busy to pay much attention to her, and Jesse was busy building up the fire to heat branding irons.

While they went about their business, Zoey got what she knew would be great shots of Tyler and Jesse working with the frightened animals. Pleased with herself, she hurried back to the table to reload the camera.

She watched Laurie bustling around the table. "Hold it for a second," she ordered, going into her professional-photographer mode. "I want to get some shots of you."

Laurie's hands flew up to cover her face. "Oh, no, I hate having my picture taken."

"Just relax. I promise it won't hurt," Zoey responded with a reassuring smile. "I'll bet you never get your picture taken. Your husband would probably love a current one to take with him when he's out on the rodeo circuit."

Laurie had dropped her hands and reluctantly faced the camera, but she grimaced at Zoey's suggestion. "Pete isn't the kind to carry my picture around."

"How do you know until you give him one?"

"I know Pete. We've been married since we were both eighteen."

Her expression was pensive, almost regretful. "Pete never wanted to do anything but rodeo. While Cheryl was growing up, I didn't want to be on the road." She sighed. "It's a hard, lonely life for rodeo wives."

Zoey had no idea how to respond to the implicit sadness in Laurie's words. So she did what she'd learned to do so well. She took refuge behind her camera, telling Laurie how to pose, searching for just the right angle to flatter her.

Despite her protests, Laurie didn't turn away. Zoey wished she were in a studio with a hairstylist and makeup artist. Laurie would never be a beauty, but the Ross family clearly had good bone structure, and Laurie had the potential to be much more attractive than she seemed at the moment.

Zoey knew Laurie was uncomfortable, so she took only a few shots. When she had what she thought would be some interesting ones, she said, "Okay. All done. That was pretty painless, wasn't it?"

Laurie grimaced. "For the person on the other side of the camera, maybe." Then she continued, "There are some lovely places down the creek. While we're waiting for the men to finish the branding, maybe you'd like to take some photographs there."

Zoey agreed enthusiastically. The whole area was so beautiful she wanted to take it home with her, if only on film. She remembered with a guilty start that she hadn't made that fake phone call to New York.

They walked along the creek, listening to the musical flow of the water. Zoey got shot after exquisite shot of wildflowers, trees, and the creek itself. When she finally ran out of film, she and Laurie sat down on the grassy bank of the creek and talked. Ever since learning that Tyler was a widower, Zoey had been curious about his late wife—and why he hadn't remarried. Now, she asked tentatively, "I don't mean to pry, but do you mind telling me about Tyler's wife?"

Laurie's expression was open, unguarded. "Not at all. I was real fond of Sarah. It's good to talk about her. That way, she's still with us, at least in our memories."

"What was she like?"

Laurie pulled her knees up to her chest and wrapped her arms around them. "Well, I'll have to go way back to answer that. You see, Tyler met Sarah Jamison in high school."

"Jamison?" Zoey interrupted, recognizing the name Tyler had thrown out at the men driving the livestock truck the day before.

"Yeah. Why?"

"It's just that I heard Tyler mention the name to—to someone after he picked me up at the airport."

"Not in a good way, I'll bet," Laurie said matter-of-factly.

"No," Zoey admitted. "I got the impression there's some kind of feud between them. Something to do with horses."

"I suppose you might say that. There's sure a lot of bad feeling between them."

"Why?"

Laurie hesitated, and for a moment Zoey was afraid she wouldn't answer. Suddenly, Zoey felt a strong need to understand this intensely personal, and deeply unhappy, aspect of Tyler's life.

To her relief, Laurie went on, "You'd have to know the whole story to understand the disagreement between Ty and Hank Jamison."

Sitting opposite Laurie, Zoey leaned forward, eager to unravel this mystery. "What is the disagreement, exactly?"

"Supposedly it's about the mustangs. You see, there are a lot of wild horses roaming around this area, descendants of horses brought in originally by the Spanish explorers, then those belonging to the Indians. Some folks, like Tyler, believe the mustangs should be protected and allowed to run free, just as they've done for hundreds of years. But a lot of folks, especially big ranchers like Jamison, see them as competition for grazing land. They want to get rid of them, and keep all the grazing land for their cattle."

"But that isn't the whole story," Zoey guessed.

"No, it isn't. That's just the tip of the iceberg. As I said, Tyler and Sarah met in high school. It was like something out of a movie—love at first sight. I've never seen two people more perfect for each other. They were truly like two halves of the same heart. They completed each other, somehow."

Listening to Laurie describe Tyler's relationship with Sarah, Zoey thought of her own relationship with Brian. Did they complete each other? She'd thought so . . . until a few days ago.

She felt a sharp stab of envy toward Sarah, who had been so deeply loved by Tyler. Zoey had never experienced that kind of love from a man. Facing the hard truth about her relationship with Brian, she wondered if she ever would. What must it feel like to know you were totally and devotedly loved? she wondered. It must be wonderful.

"I don't think either of 'em ever looked at another person after that," Laurie went on. "Even when Ty went away to the University of Wyoming, he came home as often as possible to see her. And he didn't really date anyone else, at least not seriously."

"Sarah didn't want to go with him to college?"

"I'm not sure what she wanted to do. But her father didn't want her to go, and she wouldn't leave him all alone. He was a widower, you see, and she was his only child. Anyway, Sarah stayed on the ranch with her dad, and waited for Tyler to graduate and come home. One week after he graduated, they were married."

"How did her father feel about that?"

"Oh, I think he realized she was bound to leave at some point." Laurie smiled dryly. "'Course, no man was good enough for his little girl. But he liked Tyler as well as most. At least, in those days."

"What happened?" Zoey pressed.

Laurie sighed, and her expression grew profoundly sad. "Looking back on it now, I see that we all should've been prepared for what happened. On their wedding day, there was an omen."

"An omen?"

Laurie explained, "Sarah had to be rushed to the emergency room at the hospital the morning of their wedding. She'd had asthma real bad all her life, and that morning she had an attack. The doctor told her to postpone the wedding for a few days, but she wouldn't hear of it. She got one of those shots she had to take sometimes, and a few hours later was walking down the aisle of the church."

"So she was ill," Zoey said as understanding dawned.

"Mostly she was okay," Laurie insisted, "as long as she took her medication and didn't try to do anything too strenuous. But the thing is, she wasn't supposed to have children. Apparently, if you have asthma bad enough, going through pregnancy and childbirth can be life-threatening."

"Did Tyler know this?"

Laurie shook her head. "No. None of us did, at the time. Except for her dad. He knew a lot more about her condition than anyone else. It wasn't something she liked to talk about. She hated the way it kept her from doing some things she wanted to do. And, besides, Sarah knew how much Tyler wanted a family, and I think she was afraid his feelings for her wouldn't be the same if she didn't give him children. She should've trusted him more. He wouldn't have let that stand in their way."

When Laurie hesitated, Zoey said gently, "I suppose she got pregnant."

"Yes." Laurie's voice was small and helpless with remembered tragedy. "Finally, after ten years of marriage, she got pregnant. Tyler was more thrilled than I've ever seen him in his life. Even happier than he was on his wedding day. When people would ask him what he wanted, a boy or a girl, he'd say—" Laurie hesitated, swallowed hard, then forced herself to go on, "He'd say, 'I don't care what it is, as long as both Sarah and the baby are all right.' But there was no real worry in his voice. Nowadays, people don't worry much about childbirth."

Some people do, Zoey thought remembering Denise's fear of giving birth for the first time at thirty-eight. Sarah's tragic story made Zoey realize that Denise wasn't being paranoid. She made a mental note to herself to do everything she could to help Denise through her pregnancy. Her friend shouldn't have to face those very real fears alone.

Zoey said thoughtfully, "She must have wanted a child very badly. Not just for Tyler, but for herself." At that moment, she felt an entirely unexpected kinship with this woman she'd never known. She could understand how Sarah would have wanted to have a child so badly that she'd be willing to risk her health.

Laurie nodded unhappily. "She sure did. She talked about naming it after her late mother if it was a girl, and our late dad if it was a boy. But she shouldn't've done it. No matter how badly she wanted to give Tyler a child, she shouldn't've done it. She knew better. I guess she must've persuaded herself that somehow it would be all right, despite what the doctor said."

Her voice lowered to a whisper. "We'll never know. She died suddenly, in her seventh month of pregnancy."

"And the baby?"

Laurie's blue eyes glistened with unshed tears. "It was a tiny, perfect little girl. She only survived a few hours."

Zoey felt her heart constrict with sympathy for Tyler. To have lost his wife and his child at the same time must have been unbearable. How could he ever recover from such a tragedy? How could he go on to rebuild his life?

As if sensing Zoey's thoughts, Laurie continued pensively, "Tyler was devastated, of course. It was like pulling a blind down over a window and never opening it again. He wouldn't show his feelings, though. Out here, men are told to 'cowboy up,' to never show how hurt they are. Our father was a fine man, but he bought into all that macho stuff, and he passed it on to Tyler."

Zoey felt a deep inner pang of outrage on Tyler's behalf. "But why does Jamison hate Tyler? It wasn't his fault Sarah died."

"According to him, it was. He said Tyler must've known about the seriousness of Sarah's condition. He accused Tyler of wanting a child, especially a son and heir, bad enough that he put Sarah at risk."

"Did Tyler try to tell him the truth?"

"Once, right after the funeral. He went over to Jamison's ranch. The old man pointed a gun at him and told him if he didn't get off his property in one minute, he'd shoot him." Laurie finished, "That was four years ago. Since then, they've been at war. On the surface, the conflict is about the horses. But it's really about poor Sarah."

"Having his father-in-law blame him for Sarah's death must make Tyler's guilt even greater," Zoey said feeling even sadder for him.

Laurie's expression was poignant as she reached out to lightly trail her hand in the cool water of the creek. "It does, for sure." She looked at Zoey helplessly. "The fact is, unless Tyler is able to stop feeling guilty, he'll just quietly drown in it eventually."

"I take it he hasn't moved on to another relationship."

"No. Not unless you count a few dates with women he couldn't care less about. I know it sounds terrible to say this, but they're just a convenience, if you know what I mean."

Zoey knew exactly what she meant. She'd begun to wonder if that was all she was to Brian—a convenience. The thought was a painful and bitter one. Forcing it aside, she focused on Tyler again—and was more confused than ever. "Then why," she asked, "did he place that ad in *Country Connections*? It's obvious from his reaction to me that he isn't looking for a relationship, let alone marriage."

To Zoey's surprise, a profoundly guilty look crossed Laurie's face. There was a long moment of awkward silence before she finally said awkwardly, "The thing is—" She stopped, then went on in a rush, "Oh, hell, I'd best come clean. The truth is, Tyler didn't place that ad, *I* did. He didn't know anything about it until it was a done deal."

"What?" Zoey was stunned at the revelation, though she quickly realized it explained Tyler's less-than-friendly treatment of her. Now she understood why the man who'd asked her to come all the way out there to meet him had seemed so uninterested once she arrived.

Laurie hurried on in a rush of self-justification, "You have to understand, it's for his own good. Tyler needs to come alive again, and I thought this might be just the jolt he needed to make him realize he didn't die when Sarah and their baby did."

"But why on earth did he go along with it?" Zoey asked in amazement. From what she'd seen of Tyler Ross, she couldn't imagine him letting anyone, even his own sister, pressure him into doing something he didn't want to do.

"He didn't want to, at first," Laurie admitted. "He was furious with me, and we had a big blowup over it. But, you see, lately I've been trying to set Tyler up with some nice single women. They're hard to find around here, but there *are* a few. It really irritates him when I do that, so we made a deal. He'd meet one woman who responded to the ad, and I'd get off his back forever."

Suddenly, it all fell into place. Instinctively, Zoey sensed that Tyler had chosen her because she lived far away, in a big city, and wasn't likely to be the kind of woman who would trade her sophisticated lifestyle for life in the country. He was *using* her, she thought furiously. But before she could let her righteous indignation explode into anger, she remembered that *she* was using *him*. Her anger subsided in the face of massive guilt. But it was still there.

Laurie was watching Zoey worriedly. "Are you mad at me? I wouldn't blame you if you were. Honestly, I was just trying to help Tyler. He can be a real pain in the ass sometimes, but he's my brother and I love him. You probably don't think that's a good enough excuse for being dishonest, and you're right, of course."

"Oh, Laurie, I'm not mad at you." *I'm mad at Tyler*, Zoey thought irritably. She went on calmly, "I understand your feelings of protectiveness toward him. I have two younger brothers of my own. And though there were many times I wanted to strangle them when they were growing up, I'd do anything to help them."

Laurie let out a huge sigh of relief. "I am *so* glad to hear you say that. You have no idea how guilty I've been feeling ever since you showed up under false pretenses."

Zoey had the uncomfortable thought that Laurie had no idea just how false those pretenses were.

Laurie said, "We'd better be getting back. They're probably done with the branding by now."

They rose and started walking back toward the camp in the distance. Laurie continued with a sigh of relief, "It feels so good to get it off my chest. Now, we can start off on the right foot, and see what happens with you and Tyler."

"Wait a minute, Laurie, you understand that Tyler isn't interested in me."

"Maybe not. Then again, maybe he could be."

"I'm not what he's looking for," Zoey insisted adamantly. *If he's even looking,* she thought.

"How do you know that?"

"Look, I'm nothing like Sarah."

Laurie eyed her thoughtfully. "No, in most ways you're not. She was a product of her upbringing, content to be a housewife and spend her whole life in the place where she was born and raised. But you've got her spirit. Sarah was no sweet, submissive little woman standing by her man no matter what. She gave as good as she got. Just as I expect you do."

"I'm definitely not what Tyler wants," Zoey insisted with absolute conviction. She politely refrained from saying that he definitely wasn't what she wanted, either.

Laurie grinned. "Hey, Tyler doesn't know what he wants. When he finally figures it out, he might be kind of surprised. Sometimes what you're looking for doesn't come in the package you're expecting."

Zoey started to retort, then stopped when she remembered what Carla had said about Brian coming in the right package. It was a beautifully wrapped package, but inside it was empty. Maybe, she thought reluctantly, Laurie had a point.

Then she gave herself a mental shake. If there was one thing that was perfectly clear, it was that she and Tyler were definitely not right for each other.

7

By the time Laurie and Zoey got back to the camp, the branding was done. The last of the calves was gone and the branding iron fire had been carefully extinguished. The four of them—Laurie, Zoey, Tyler, and Jesse—ate a quiet lunch. After her frank conversation with Zoey earlier, Laurie seemed to have little left to say. While Tyler and Jesse discussed ranch matters, Zoey cast covert glances at Tyler. Now that she knew so much more about him, she found him even more fascinating and attractive. He had seemed reserved, with a passion to protect the mustangs but without passionate feelings for anything or anyone else. Now, Zoey knew better. His feelings ran so deep he had to keep them firmly hidden.

Not that any of this mattered, she told herself sternly. She needed to get out of this situation as quickly as possible. But as she tried to decide exactly how to handle the phone call that would be her excuse to return to New York, she felt a twinge of regret.

When lunch was over, the two men helped load the folding table and chairs, dishes, and leftover food into the pickup Zoey and Laurie had driven in. Zoey was about to get into the pickup when Laurie stopped her.

"Wait a minute. I've got a great idea."

The sly expression in her bright-blue eyes warned Zoey that something was up.

Avoiding Zoey's questioning look, Laurie turned to Tyler. "It's only a half-hour ride back to the ranch. Wouldn't it be nice if Zoey could ride back with you? That way she could see the place in a way she can't from the road."

She'd put Tyler on the spot. He glanced uncomfortably at Zoey. "Oh, I don't think—"

Before he could finish, Laurie said to Zoey, "You don't have to be an experienced rider. Jesse's old mare is as easy to sit as a rocking chair."

Feeling somehow compelled to show that she wasn't totally inept, Zoey automatically responded, "Actually, I know how to ride. I ride every Sunday in Central Park."

Tyler looked dubious. "Central Park." The words were laden with unspoken disdain, as if riding in a park wasn't the real thing.

"I'm quite good," Zoey insisted, annoyed at his attitude.

"On a paved trail, maybe," Tyler said tersely. "This is rough ground out here."

Laurie frowned. "Oh, for heaven's sake, Ty, you make it sound like you'll be crossing the Continental Divide. It's an easy ride back, and you know it."

Zoey's immediate impulse to salvage her pride and defend her ability as a rider gave way to the recognition that she was on the wrong side of this debate. She hastened to say, "Maybe Tyler's right. I should probably go back in the pickup with you, Laurie. Although," she couldn't resist adding stubbornly, "I'm sure I could handle the ride."

"Then that settles it," Laurie said, abruptly ending the discussion. When Zoey opened her mouth to argue, Laurie said brightly, "Just think of the pictures you can take." She turned to Jesse. "Hop in."

Jesse looked from Laurie to Tyler and back again. Clearly, he had no idea what to do. Finally, he just shook his head and got in the pickup.

But Tyler wasn't about to give up. "Laurie, this isn't a good idea."

Laurie smiled sweetly at her brother. "I think it's a real fine idea." Then, nodding at both Tyler and Zoey, she said, "See you back at the ranch. But don't hurry. Take your time."

She started the pickup and a moment later was gone in a swirl of dust.

When the truck had disappeared beyond the trees, Zoey and Tyler looked at each other blankly for a moment. Then Tyler shrugged and said with a complete lack of enthusiasm, "All right, let's saddle up."

As he headed toward the horses, tethered to a nearby tree, their saddles lying on the ground nearby, he threw a comment over his shoulder, "You do know how to saddle a horse, don't you?"

"*Yes*," Zoey snapped.

Without waiting for him to help, she settled the blanket on Jesse's horse, then hefted the saddle onto its back. She wouldn't reveal to Tyler that she was used to riding English style; the Western saddle felt heavy and cumbersome. She cinched it up tight, but not too tight, then slipped the bridle over the mare's head. Untying the rope tethering the horse to the tree, she coiled it and hung it from the pommel of the saddle.

With a brief, smug glance at Tyler, as if to say, "See, I told you I can handle this," she put her left foot in the stirrup and swung up onto the horse. Almost. She was in mid-air when the saddle slipped and she fell to the hard ground, landing solidly on her behind.

In the background, she heard Tyler's husky laugh, which he made no attempt to conceal.

Embarrassed beyond belief, Zoey quickly jumped up and brushed off her sore bottom. Glaring at Tyler, she said with righteous indignation, "I cinched it tight. There must be something wrong with the saddle."

Walking over to her, Tyler said with a grin that was at once maddening and surprisingly appealing, "It's not the saddle. It's the horse. She's a wily old thing. She sucked in enough air to make her belly bigger so you'd think you were cinching it tight, but you weren't. Then she let it out, and the strap was loose."

The saddle hung below the mare's stomach. Pushing it onto her back, Tyler cinched it tighter, then waited for the mare to breathe. He cinched it even tighter and stepped back. "There you go," he told her with a smug grin. "It should be okay now."

"You *knew* this would happen!" Zoey exploded. "You just wanted to see me make a fool of myself!" Pent-up humiliation from the fiasco with the bull, and now this—falling on her ass in front of Tyler—filled her with embarrassed rage.

"Hey, you're the one who claimed to know how to saddle a horse," Tyler insisted in a perfectly reasonable tone. "I would've done it for you, but you seemed to feel you had something to prove."

She wasn't buying his innocent act for a moment. Standing there glaring at him, her hands on her hips, she couldn't contain her exasperation. "You're enjoying seeing me look like a fish out of water, aren't you? You're having a real good time at my expense. Well, let me tell you something, Tyler Ross, you've behaved like a total jerk since the moment we met, and I've had enough! I'm going back to New York on the next available flight!"

His look of thinly-veiled amusement dissolved. He said quietly, but with conviction, "Maybe that's where you belong."

"You're damn right it is!"

"I'm sure you're used to a whole lot more excitement in the city. All this," he gestured at the surroundings, "must seem pretty boring." He finished sarcastically, "At least you'll have some amusing stories to tell your sophisticated friends."

"Of course, we're all just a bunch of superficial, insensitive—"

Before Zoey could finish, Tyler raised a hand to shush her. "Listen!"

She stood there silently, wondering what on earth he was getting at. She didn't hear a thing. He listened intently for a moment, his brows furrowed and his blue eyes narrowed, straining to hear something that eluded Zoey.

Then she heard it—a low, mounting rumble in the distance.

Grabbing the mare's reins, Tyler quickly tied them to the tree, then yelled at Zoey, "Come on!"

Taking her hand, he led her toward a large, sloping rock nearby.

"What on earth—" she began. But, before she could finish, he'd pulled her onto the rock with him.

"Here they come!" he shouted.

The rumble grew into an almost deafening roar of pounding hooves, and an instant later a herd of wild mustangs came racing down the narrow canyon.

It was the most stunning spectacle Zoey had ever seen, and it took her breath away. The pathetic group of half-starved horses Tyler had liberated from the livestock trailer the day before was nothing compared to these magnificent animals. They seemed to run for the sheer joy of running, sure in their movement, restrained by nothing.

The sight of the horses flying in single purpose across the unbroken ground, led by a beautiful Appaloosa stallion, was an expression of pure freedom and sheer wild spirit, as glorious an expression of wildness as Zoey could imagine existing in this domesticated land. And it awakened something primal in her, something she'd never felt before and couldn't begin to identify.

Zoey looked at Tyler and saw that his expression was transformed. She knew that what she saw in his eyes was a mirror of her own feeling of awe.

"Now I understand why you fight for them," she said softly, her anger toward him completely gone.

He sighed, nodded, and said, almost to himself, "There's nothing more beautiful on this earth than a herd of wild horses thundering across open ground. They're all just wild at heart. The way people should be."

Then, as if realizing he'd allowed Zoey to see a glimpse of his soul and regretted it, he went on in a gruff tone, "We'd better be getting back."

When they reached their waiting horses, Zoey eyed the deceptively placid mare with mistrust. Looking at Tyler, she asked pointedly, "Does this one have any other tricks I should be aware of?"

"Nope. Except, of course, when she goes right up to a fence and tries to brush you off. Or when she heads for a low tree limb, looking to knock you off."

Zoey eyed him skeptically. "Anything else?"

"Nope, that's about it. Other than that, she's a good little cutting horse."

Zoey looked doubtful. "Yeah, right."

Tyler added teasingly, "But even if she weren't, I'm sure you could handle her. Being an experienced rider and all."

Instead of getting her back up over the good-natured teasing, Zoey took it in stride. The atmosphere between them had lightened. Zoey was no longer angry. Tyler was still reserved, but now there was a distinct thaw in that cool self-possession. Zoey knew where the change came from—they had shared a momentary connection as they watched the mustangs. Now they were no longer total strangers, but two people who had shared the same intense feeling.

As they got on the horses, Tyler gave Zoey a thoughtful look.

"What is it?" she asked, curious about his thoughts.

"When I first met you, I wondered if your red hair was natural. Now I think it must be, 'cause you've sure got a red-head's temper." The observation was softened by a slight upturn at the corners of his mouth.

To her embarrassment, Zoey found herself blushing—something she hadn't done in years. She lowered her gaze, unable to meet Tyler's look. "Okay, I admit I get carried away sometimes. My mother calls it my Irish temper."

He responded easily, "Don't worry, Ms. Donovan. I can handle it."

She forced herself to look at him and saw a mischievous twinkle in his piercing blue eyes. "Think so, huh?"

"Yup."

And with that he kicked his horse into a trot. Zoey followed right behind. When they'd gone a short ways, she said to herself, "Damn, I wish I'd gotten some shots of those horses." Then, kicking her mare forward so that they rode abreast, she asked Tyler to tell her about the mustangs.

His expression grew sober. "It's a miracle they survive, they're threatened by so many things. Starvation in winter. Natural predators like mountain lions. Being rounded up and killed or sold to slaughterhouses by cattle ranchers who see them as competition for public grazing land."

Zoey didn't admit that she knew all about one of those ranchers—Tyler's ex-father-in-law, Hank Jamison. Instead, she said, "You're obviously a preservationist."

"Definitely. To me, the mustangs are a living symbol of the Old West. I've set up my ranch to be a refuge for any that wander onto it."

"I imagine running a refuge for them can get to be expensive," she observed.

He gave a noncommittal reply, but she sensed that it was, indeed, a financial struggle for him, and she reminded herself that she needed to give Laurie the ticket Tyler had sent her. She'd bought her own ticket, intending to return his. She knew better than to try to give it to Tyler himself, though. He was a proud man, and his pride wouldn't let him accept it.

Gathering her courage, Zoey risked his ire by daring to ask about the confrontation of the previous day. "Those horses you set free yesterday," she began haltingly, "you said they were going to a slaughterhouse?"

He nodded grimly. "Those boys driving the truck work on the Jamison ranch. Hank rounds up all the mustangs he can catch and sends them off to the slaughterhouse. It's illegal, but he's rich enough and politically connected enough to get away with it, as long as he doesn't call attention to it."

"So that's why they didn't come and arrest you for attacking the truck," Zoey said frankly. "They didn't want to have to explain what they were hauling."

Tyler glanced at her. Once again, there was a hint of humor as he said, "Worried about me winding up in jail, were you, Ms. Donovan?"

She met his look and struggled not to blush again. "Not especially. I'm sure you can take care of yourself."

"Damn straight," he replied. Without looking at her, he asked, "Think you could handle something a little faster than a walk?"

"Oh, I think I could manage to stay in the saddle."

"All right, then let's go."

Tyler kicked his horse into a trot, and Zoey did the same. They were silent for the remainder of the ride back to the ranch, but, unlike the atmosphere on the ride in from the airport the day before, this was a companionable silence.

When they reached the barn a half-hour later, Jesse was waiting to take care of the horses. The expression of surprise on his grizzled face as Zoey came trotting up suggested that he wasn't entirely sure she would make it. When she dismounted, she felt a stiffness in her legs and a soreness in her derriere from her unceremonious fall earlier. A hot bath was called for as soon as possible.

Tyler and Zoey handed their horses' reins to Jesse, who led both animals into the barn. As they started toward the house, Tyler spoke in a carefully cool tone, "I imagine you've just about seen enough of Jackson Hole and will be glad to get back to New York. There's a flight out this evening. If we hurry, you can just about make it."

Zoey felt a pang of disappointment that she knew was completely illogical. Only a few minutes earlier, she'd been insisting she couldn't wait to go home. Now, she felt extreme reluctance to leave this beautiful place. She refused to admit, even in the privacy of her own thoughts, that Tyler himself played any part in that reluctance. It would be best to leave, she told herself firmly. And the sooner the better.

As they reached the front porch, Laurie stepped outside and said to Zoey, "You got a phone call from New York while we were out. I took down the name and number from the answering machine."

It must be Carla, Zoey thought, surprised. Carla was the only one who had the number. Zoey had given it to her in case of emergency. She wondered why on earth Carla would be calling, and immediately felt a rush of concern for Denise. Had something—possibly a miscarriage—happened? That was the only reason Zoey could imagine Carla calling.

"Who was it?" she asked though she was certain she knew the answer.

"Someone named Brian Morgan," Laurie said with barely suppressed curiosity.

Zoey stopped dead in her tracks. Beside her, Tyler halted, flashing her a surprised look. Zoey felt guilt wash over her as she was unexpectedly confronted by the lie that had brought her there.

Mustering all her emotional resources, she managed to say in a voice that sounded nearly normal, "Oh? He's, um, my attorney. There must be a business problem he needs to discuss with me."

Obviously reassured by this explanation, Laurie said, "You can take it in my office, if you want. It's more private there. I'll show you where it's at."

But Tyler didn't follow as Zoey walked toward the house. Turning back toward the barn, he called back over his shoulder, "I've got things to do."

Laurie led Zoey to a small room at the back of the house that she explained had been a sewing room once upon a time. Now it was an impressively arranged home office, with a computer, printer, modem, fax machine, and copy machine. A phone sat on the wide metal desk.

"I'll just go into the kitchen and make some tea," Laurie said. "Join me when you're through."

Zoey sat down at the desk and stared at the phone for a long moment. A turbulent mixture of emotions roiled through her—amazement that Brian had called, a tenuous hope that it meant he was ready to say the words she needed to hear, and a curious reluctance to talk to him.

Come on, stop being an idiot, she told herself. She let out the breath she'd been holding, picked up the phone, and dialed Brian's private office number. It was only six o'clock New York time, and even if Zoey hadn't seen the number Laurie wrote down, she would have known he was still at work.

The phone rang once, and he answered immediately. Zoey felt a brief thrill of pleasure at the knowledge that Brian was eager for her call.

"Brian, it's me," she said simply.

"*Zoey.*" The familiar voice was tight with suppressed irritation.

She realized that if she'd expected a warm response, she wasn't going to get it.

Before she could speak, Brian went on, "Where are you calling from?"

Zoey hesitated, reluctant to answer the blunt question. But there was no way to avoid it. She said evasively, "From the ranch where I'm staying."

"*Whose* ranch?" he demanded in his best attack-lawyer mode. Zoey had never seen Brian in action in the courtroom, but she was beginning to sense just how good a lawyer he was. He'd certainly put her on the defensive.

"It's outside Jackson Hole."

"Who does it belong to?"

She sighed and gave in. "Tyler Ross."

There was a momentary silence on Brian's end, then he said matter-of-factly, "The cowboy whose ad you answered."

"He isn't a cowboy, he's a rancher," Zoey retorted, somehow feeling the need to stand up for Tyler.

"What the hell are you doing staying at his place?" Brian exploded.

"His sister and niece live with him. We're well chaperoned."

"Oh, well, that certainly makes everything all right." Brian's tone was snide in the extreme.

Zoey suddenly realized something she'd never noticed before. Anger brought out a pettiness in Brian that was distinctly unattractive.

Recognizing that this call wasn't going the way she'd hoped, Zoey said with a sigh, "Look, Brian, there doesn't seem to be much point in this conversation, so I'm going to hang up now."

"Wait a minute, damn it! Zoey, you've carried our stupid argument too far. You're making a fool of yourself."

"Am I? I'm not the one who called, Brian. *You* are. And if you don't have anything civil to say, I'm not going to talk to you." She felt a rush of adrenaline and realized that standing up for herself felt pretty darn good.

"Zoey, I'm ordering you to return immediately!"

Astounded, she gripped the receiver so hard her knuckles turned white. "You're *what*?"

"I'm telling you to get back here at once. I've been as patient as I'm capable of being."

"Well, you're just going to have to learn to be more patient, Brian, because I'm not coming back until I'm damn good and ready." She started to hang up, then added as a final coup de grace, "And don't you ever *order* me to do anything again!"

She slammed down the receiver with a satisfying thud.

Zoey sat there for a few seconds, shaking with anger. How dare he? The nerve of the man. Who did he think he was, anyway? He would be extremely lucky if she ever deigned to speak to him again.

But, in the midst of her anger, she realized she had just burned her bridges behind her. And, while it made a lovely flame, it presented very real problems. Only an hour earlier, she'd told Tyler in no uncertain terms she was returning to New York immediately. Now, she couldn't go straight back. If she did, she'd look like a beaten dog crawling home with her tail between her legs. Brian would assume she'd caved in and he'd never let her forget it. Somehow, without meaning to, she'd just committed herself to remaining in Jackson Hole, at least for a few more days.

Her first thought was that now she could photograph the mustangs. She was eager to capture them on film. Already, the seeds of an idea were beginning to take shape in her mind. A plan for her next show—all about the wild horses.

Then she remembered that there were no hotel rooms to be had in the area. She would have to swallow her pride and see if Tyler and Laurie would let her stay there. Somehow, that didn't seem as unpalatable as swallowing her pride and following Brian's orders.

Squaring her shoulders determinedly, she got up and went into the kitchen. Cheryl was sitting at the table with her unending list of wedding preparations. Laurie was standing at the counter pouring a kettleful of hot water into a plain, white china teapot. She smiled at Zoey as she came into the room.

"Did your call go okay?" she asked politely.

Zoey forced a thin smile. "Fine." Then, before she could lose her courage, she went on awkwardly, "Would you mind, that is, would it be okay, I mean, if it's no trouble—"

"What?" Laurie asked with a hint of impatience at Zoey's rambling.

Zoey took a deep breath and plunged in. "May I stay here for a few days?"

Laurie looked confused. "Of course. I assumed you were. That's the plan, isn't it?"

"Right. It's just—I didn't want to wear out my welcome."

Laurie gave her a look of genuine warmth. "Oh, Zoey, we're so pleased to have you here. I hope you'll be able to stay long enough to come to Cheryl's wedding."

Zoey looked at Cheryl, who had a transparent, hopeful expression on her face. "I'd love to come to it. And I'd be happy to be your photographer, if you'd like."

"If I'd like!" Cheryl exclaimed. Jumping up, she grabbed Zoey and hugged her. "Oh, Ms. Donovan, I hope you don't mind, but I just can't thank you enough. I had just given up on finding anyone, and Chuck's dad's Polaroids were beginning to look better and better."

Laurie protested, "Zoey, you don't have to do this, you know."

"I know," Zoey said with a grin, feeling unaccountably happy, "but I want to. It will be my gift to Cheryl and Chuck."

She didn't add that the young couple was getting an award-winning photographer who, even if she were willing to do a wedding, would have charged a fee of several thousand dollars.

"So when is the wedding exactly?" she asked Cheryl sitting back down at the table.

"Saturday."

Zoey nodded thoughtfully. "Well, that gives us three days to decide what kind of pictures you'd like."

"I've got some ideas," Cheryl said eagerly. "Maybe I could have Chuck come over for dinner tonight and we could talk about it." She turned to Laurie. "Okay, Mom?"

Laurie nodded. "Sure."

"I've gotta go call him right away. He won't believe it. He just won't believe it." She hurried out of the kitchen, practically walking on air.

Joining Zoey at the table, Laurie handed her a cup of tea and sat down opposite her. "You're very generous to do this for Cheryl."

"It's my pleasure."

Laurie gave Zoey a curious look. "Earlier you said you couldn't stay that long. Did that phone call change your mind?"

"You might say that," Zoey answered carefully. "I thought

I needed to get back to New York, but now it seems there's no reason to hurry back."

"I'm glad," Laurie said simply.

At that moment, Tyler came into the kitchen. Looking at Zoey, he said, "I brought the pickup around front. Are you ready to go? We'll need to hurry if we're going to get to the airport in time to catch that flight."

Before Zoey could respond, Laurie said brightly, "Zoey's going to stay after all, Ty. Isn't that good news?"

Tyler looked stunned. It was all Zoey could do not to grin at his obvious surprise and discomfiture. His eyes met hers, locked, and held them for a long moment. She felt a curious breathlessness and wondered why her heart suddenly felt as if it were in her throat.

"When did this happen?" he finally managed to ask.

"I just discovered I didn't need to hurry back after all," she managed to reply.

"I see," he said. But it was clear he didn't see at all. He went on, "So how long will we be enjoying your company, Ms. Donovan?"

"Until Cheryl's wedding. I'll be leaving right after that."

"Zoey's going to photograph the wedding," Laurie explained proudly.

"Really." The single word held a world of meaning.

There was a moment of awkward silence when no one seemed to know what to say, then Tyler asked, with a hint of dry humor, "Well, Ms. Donovan, considering the way your visit's gone so far, do you think you can survive a longer stay?"

"Oh, I think so, Mr. Ross. The question is, can you?"

His ice-blue eyes met her cool gray ones. "I can survive anything, Ms. Donovan." The unspoken addendum was, *Even you.* Then he turned and strode out of the kitchen.

8

Zoey sat on the chocolate-colored corduroy sofa in the living room flipping through bridal magazines with Cheryl and Chuck. Laurie sat nearby, occasionally refilling everyone's after-dinner coffee and glancing at the pictures, offering her opinion as mother of the bride. Jesse and Tyler had disappeared the minute dinner was over, muttering something about work to do in the barn. Clearly, the two men were uninterested in wedding talk.

"That's kind of a nice picture," Chuck commented pointing to a casually posed bride and groom in an outdoor wedding setting.

Zoey had liked Chuck immediately. He was rather unprepossessing-looking, with mousy brown hair and a face that was a bit too round and full to be considered cute, let alone handsome. His stocky build was toughened by the hard physical labor of construction, although he didn't have the muscular physique of many of the construction workers Zoey passed on building sites on the streets of Manhattan.

However, his plain countenance was honest and open, his

manner easygoing. Cheryl had been right about him—he seemed a steady sort. And, most importantly, he adored her. It was almost embarrassingly evident every time he looked at her with his lovesick-puppy expression. Cheryl was a very pretty girl with an appealing personality to match, and Zoey knew Chuck must feel enormously lucky to have won her over what had undoubtedly been many other suitors.

Zoey remembered something her mother had said once—it's best if the man loves the woman just a little bit more than she loves him. That way he's more likely to remain in the marriage. Because, normally, it's easier for men to walk away than for women to do so. The bittersweet comment had sprung from her own unhappy experience, Zoey knew. Now, looking at Cheryl and Chuck, Zoey sensed that Cheryl genuinely loved him, but her feelings were a bit more practical than his more romantic ones. And that was probably a good omen for the success of their marriage.

"I like that picture, too," Cheryl said agreeing with Chuck.

"I get the feeling you two want casual photos, as opposed to stiffly formal ones," Zoey observed.

Both Cheryl and Chuck nodded enthusiastically. "Oh, yeah," they said in unison.

Chuck added, "It's gonna be bad enough bein' in a monkey suit, without havin' to stand around like some dang model or somethin' for hours an' hours."

Realizing he might've just put his foot in his mouth, he hastened to add, "Not that it's not worth it, of course."

Cheryl gave her fiancé an indulgent look. "Don't worry, honey, I understand. You're a lot more comfortable in jeans. I promise you, this is the only time in our whole life I'll ask you to dress up."

"It's okay. You're worth it," Chuck responded, eliciting a smile of delight from Cheryl.

Zoey was both amused and touched by this mushy expression of young love. Glancing at Laurie, she was surprised to see a mixture of emotions play across her face as she watched her daughter and soon-to-be son-in-law. There was pride in her lovely young daughter. And a warm acceptance of Chuck. But something sad, as well. As if watching them being so happy together were a poignant reminder of . . . what? Zoey wondered. The disappointment of her own marriage?

And yet she hadn't shown anything other than total support for Cheryl's decision to marry at twenty-one instead of going to college as Laurie had wished. Thinking of her own mother's well-intentioned but irritating attempts to tell Zoey how to live her life, she thought what a wise mother Laurie was. Whether or not she agreed with Cheryl's decision to marry so young, she accepted that Cheryl would undoubtedly do as she pleased.

Cheryl interrupted Zoey's thoughts. "So what kind of pictures will you take?"

"Unfortunately, there will have to be *some* formal poses, especially of the entire wedding party." In response to Cheryl and Chuck's look of dismay, she hastened to add reassuringly, "But not too many, I promise. I'll get them over with as quickly as possible. Then I'll just take a lot of candid shots. If the photographer knows what he's doing, those are always the best."

"How do you know when to take pictures?" Chuck asked, a hint of nervousness in his voice.

Zoey sensed that he was concerned about having to constantly look over his shoulder to check if he was being "caught" by the photographer. "Don't worry," she said easily, "I won't be looming over you two the whole time. I know you need your space, especially before the ceremony. But to answer your question, I have a good sense of which moments are important to capture. I wouldn't be a professional photographer if I didn't. You see, photography is like a memory box, and you want to store the most precious memories in it so that when they fade, and even disappear from your mind, they're still captured on film and you can have them forever."

Cheryl and Chuck both glowed with pleasure at this metaphor.

Laurie and Zoey exchanged a warm look. Then Laurie said in a polite but firm tone, "We need to talk about paying you."

Zoey interrupted quickly, "I told you this is my wedding gift. It's the best one I could possibly give. Much better than another toaster."

For a moment, Laurie looked as if she might argue. Then, giving in gracefully, she said in a heartfelt tone, "It's wonderful of you to do this for us, Zoey. We're very glad you're here."

To her surprise, Zoey realized she felt the same way—she was glad she was there, too. She was stunned at this unexpected turn of events. She'd arrived in Jackson Hole just a little more than twenty-four hours earlier with only one thought uppermost in her mind—how soon she could turn around and fly right back to New York. Now, as she sat in this cozy room with these thoroughly nice people who had opened their home and their hearts to her, she felt more content than she had in years. She really wanted to stay for awhile.

Until she remembered Tyler. He hadn't wanted her there. And even though his initial resistance had mellowed, Zoey knew damn well he still didn't want her there. She felt a vague twinge of the hurt of rejection at that knowledge. Immediately, she told herself not to be stupid. After all, it was Brian she cared about, not Tyler. And, while she was still angry at Brian's domineering attitude during their phone conversation, the fact that he'd called at all revealed how much he cared for her. She clung to that knowledge, telling herself it meant there was hope for them after all.

At that moment, from outside came the sound of a car pulling up in the driveway and the loud honking of a horn, as if announcing someone's arrival. Cheryl's face lit up with excitement. "Daddy's home!" she exclaimed. Jumping up, she tore out of the room, followed closely by Chuck.

Laurie didn't get up, Zoey noticed. She remained in her chair, her hands clasping her cup of coffee, her expression enigmatic.

Zoey had a sudden vision of what the years had been like for this family—Cheryl as a little girl, then a teenager, and finally a young woman, missing her daddy, thrilled every time he would return—Laurie having to cope by herself much of the time, almost like a single parent—both of them missing terribly the most important man in their lives.

It was a poignant picture that touched Zoey's heart—and made her respect Laurie all the more.

A moment later, Chuck, Cheryl, and her father came into the room. Cheryl stayed close to her father and smiled up at him adoringly. Pete was much as Zoey had expected—forty-ish but looking older because his skin was tanned to a leathery appearance by so much time spent outdoors. He wore faded jeans and a plaid shirt studded with brass buttons. His close-cropped, salt-and-pepper hair was beginning to recede from a narrow forehead. He wasn't much taller than Laurie, probably no more than five-six or so, with a thin, wiry body.

In his strong, even features there were traces of the decidedly handsome young man he'd probably once been, and a remnant of charm in the sparkle in his blue-green eyes. Zoey could understand why Laurie had fallen in love with him and married at the tender age of eighteen. But he hadn't aged well. If it was true that at twenty you have the face you were born with but at forty the face you deserve, then Pete didn't deserve much.

Going up to Laurie, Pete bent to give her a light kiss on the cheek. Laurie turned her face up to his, but didn't seem to really look at him.

"Hi, sugar," he said in a lazy drawl. "Sorry I'm so late gettin' home, but things came up. You know how it is."

Laurie said evenly, "Yes, I know how it is."

The words were neutral, there was no telltale inflection of anger or pain. Yet Zoey sensed both emotions were there in abundance.

Gesturing toward Zoey, Laurie said, "This is Zoey Donovan. Zoey, my husband, Pete."

"She came all the way from New York," Cheryl offered excitedly. "And she's gonna be our photographer at the wedding."

"That's real nice," Pete responded with a clear lack of interest. "Pleased to meet you, miss."

Zoey murmured a polite response. She was struck by Pete's singular lack of curiosity about what on earth someone from New York was doing there.

Laurie had gone into the kitchen and returned with a cup of coffee for Pete. Taking it, he settled into a big easy chair that almost seemed to have his stamp on it. Now Zoey understood why no one had sat there earlier. It was Pete's chair. Period.

Cheryl eagerly questioned her father about the rodeos he'd competed in. Chuck sat quietly while Cheryl focused on her father. Somehow, Zoey sensed that Chuck wasn't nearly as fond of his future father-in-law as he was of his future mother-in-law.

Pete rambled on about every competition he'd entered, from roping calves to riding bucking broncos. He skimmed over the ones where he didn't shine, offering self-serving excuses for his poor showing, and went on at length about the competitions where he'd come in second or third. He didn't seem to have won any, confirming Zoey's suspicion that Laurie was the financial support of the family.

As Pete went on and on about himself, it didn't seem to occur to him to ask about his daughter's upcoming wedding. Or to show an interest in Chuck's business. Or to have any curiosity about Zoey. He was clearly a man who was totally caught up in himself and his own interests.

There was something extremely immature about him. Oddly enough, next to Pete, the much younger Chuck seemed the more mature and dependable man. Zoey gave Cheryl mental kudos for having the good sense to choose a man with the qualities her father lacked.

Feeling that she needed to give the family some time to themselves for their reunion, Zoey announced she was going outside for some fresh air before turning in. Laurie advised her to take a sweater because evenings could be chilly, even in summer. Cheryl, caught up in her father, barely noticed Zoey was leaving.

Zoey ran up to her room to get her denim jacket, then went outside. As soon as she stepped out onto the porch, she was glad she'd taken Laurie's advice. While the day had been downright hot, it had cooled down considerably with nightfall, and there was a brisk breeze rustling through the trees.

Having no idea where to go, Zoey set off aimlessly. As she passed the barn, she saw a campfire burning just on the other side of it. Drawn by the inviting warmth of the fire, she walked over to it. She wasn't surprised to see Tyler standing near the fire. In fact, she'd expected to see him tending it. While she didn't want to admit it, even to herself, that was a big part of the reason she'd decided to head in that direction.

Silhouetted by the dancing flames of the small fire, he was a lean figure, his hands shoved into the pockets of his jeans, his shoulders slightly hunched against the chill of the night.

"Hi," she murmured, startling him. He'd been so lost in thought he hadn't heard her walk up.

He looked at her blankly for a moment, almost as if he'd forgotten who she was. She wondered what he'd been thinking about so intently that he'd lost all sense of his surroundings.

"Hi," he finally said in response.

For want of anything better to say, Zoey offered, "Your brother-in-law just arrived."

"I know."

Obviously, Tyler had no interest in talking to Pete. Zoey

wondered if he disliked his brother-in-law and guessed that he probably did. From what she was learning about Tyler, she suspected he didn't have much use for a man like Pete, who would frequently abandon his family and return at his convenience. She was struck by the harsh irony of life—Tyler had tragically lost the family he cared about so deeply. Pete had a wonderful family, but didn't value them. Life, Zoey thought, not for the first time, was terribly unfair.

Recognizing that she'd exhausted any conversation potential regarding Pete, Zoey looked upward, turning her attention to the sky. She marveled at the vastness of the heavens in this part of the world. Millions of stars could be seen with crystal clarity. In New York, she was lucky to see a few stars shining through the murky Manhattan atmosphere. Here, the universe seemed to be laid out for all to see and admire. She felt tiny and insignificant, and yet somehow more aware of the importance of life, including her own. In a place like this, a place of natural beauty and spirituality, it was somehow easier to be in touch with one's true self, without the distractions of the noise and bustle of a city.

Following her gaze, Tyler said, "Do you see those seven little stars in a group?"

Zoey's eyes followed his pointing finger and found the constellation. In response to her questioning look, Tyler went on, "That's the Pleiades. The Kiowas have a legend about those stars. Would you like to hear it?"

Zoey nodded, and he continued, "Some Kiowas were camped by a stream in a place where there were lots of bears. Seven little girls were playing some distance from the village when suddenly some bears began chasing them. Just as the bears were about to catch them, the frightened girls jumped on a rock. One of the girls cried to the rock, 'Take pity on us. Save us.' The rock heard the child's plea and began to push itself up out of the ground, raising the girls out of the reach of the bears, up into the sky. They're still up there, seven little stars in a group. Seven beautiful little girls."

When Tyler finished the charming story and lapsed into silence, Zoey wondered if he was thinking of his own baby daughter, whose fragile hold on life had lasted such a short time, and, if so, what he was feeling. She couldn't ask; it was far too personal a question.

"What a lovely story," she breathed. "How do you know it?"

"My great-grandmother was a Kiowa. Unlike most of the white settlers who came here, my great-grandfather respected the Indians and their ways. Many of their legends have been passed down through the generations of my family."

"My great-grandmother was from Ireland," Zoey offered.

The firm line of Tyler's mouth curved upward slightly in the barest hint of a smile. "Another people who were badly treated," he observed. Then he added, "So that explains your Irish temper."

"I come by it honestly," Zoey said dryly.

Changing the subject abruptly, Tyler bent to add wood to the fire as he said, "It's good of you to photograph Cheryl's wedding. It means a lot to her."

"I'm happy to do it."

Instead of making deprecating comments about her work as he'd done over dinner the night before, he responded simply, "I'm sure you're a very good photographer."

Just then, a strange, sad sound moaned in the air.

"Wind music," Tyler explained as Zoey glanced around nervously. "It's a common phenomenon out here. Nothing to be afraid of."

"I'm not afraid," she insisted automatically.

Now he was openly smiling at her. "Does living in New York City make you so touchy?"

"Possibly. What's your excuse?" she shot back teasingly.

The smile turned into a broad grin, and Zoey was struck by how incredibly appealing he was when his expression was lightened by humor. She'd found him surprisingly attractive when they first met. Now she realized he was actually quite handsome.

Watch it, she told herself firmly. *It's time to say goodnight.*

To Tyler, she said, "I think I'll turn in now."

As she started to walk away, she heard him say gently, "Goodnight, Zoey."

Looking back at him over her shoulder, she responded, "Goodnight, Tyler," and walked quickly back toward the house, almost feeling as if she were running away.

The next morning, Zoey and Laurie went into Jackson to do some shopping, since Zoey hadn't brought enough clothes for an extended visit. They hit the Ralph Lauren boutique first, because the country style of his clothes seemed especially appropriate for Wyoming. Zoey bought some jeans and shirts and a sweater for the cool nights.

Then she and Laurie moved on to a shoe store. If she was going to do any real riding, she needed boots, not the Reeboks she'd worn on the short ride with Tyler the day before. She didn't say anything to Laurie about her plans, but she intended to ride out, find the herd of mustangs, and photograph them.

When the shopping for essentials was completed, they started looking for a dress for Zoey to wear to the wedding. Nothing seemed right. Zoey's personal style was bohemian. She was given to wearing casual, wildly colorful clothes that were perfectly acceptable in her role as a photographer in New York, but were unacceptable for a formal wedding in a rural, country church. She accepted that she needed to dress in a slightly more conservative style than she was used to, but she couldn't bring herself to buy any of the dresses Laurie suggested. They were . . . conservative. And if there was one thing Zoey prided herself on *not* being, it was conservative.

She had just about given up hope of finding anything that wouldn't shock the other people at the wedding and that she could stand to wear when she found the perfect thing in a tiny boutique. The owner, an escapee from Los Angeles crime and smog, had brought with her a casual yet stylish Southern California taste in fashion. The mid-calf-length dress that caught Zoey's eye was of a soft golden color, somewhere between cream and butter-yellow, in a fluid fabric. Sleeveless, it had a feminine touch of lace at the deep-vee neckline. The instant she saw it hanging in the window, Zoey decided that she had to have it. When she tried it on a moment later, she was enormously relieved to discover that it fit perfectly.

As Zoey and Laurie left the boutique, Zoey said with an exhausted sigh, "I'm glad that's over. I hate shopping."

Laurie shot her a surprised look. "You do? Even in New York? I'd think it would be so much fun to go shopping there."

"I'm just not into clothes. All my creativity goes into my work, and I don't care what I throw on my back, as long as it's not too conventional."

She started to add that the only really nice clothes in her closet had been purchased by Brian, who was very conscious of how she looked when she was with him. Fortunately, she caught herself in time. Mentioning a boyfriend would sound rather odd under the circumstances.

Laurie didn't seem to notice Zoey's hesitation. She went on, "I know you wouldn't think so judging by how I dress, but I love clothes. I just don't have the money, or a good enough excuse, to shop for anything other than good old jeans."

"You'll have to come to New York for a visit some time," Zoey offered. "There are some wonderful little boutiques in SoHo. And you can get some really unique things from corner flea markets."

Laurie's face lit up as it always did when Zoey talked about New York. "Oh, it sounds so fun."

"So, when you get your next vacation, come," Zoey said encouragingly. "You can stay at my place. All it would cost is plane fare and a little spending money."

"It's sweet of you to invite me. I'll think about it."

But Zoey knew that, much as Laurie might like to do it, she wouldn't. She felt sad for Laurie, tied down to a life that was clearly not fulfilling, unable or unwilling to make a major change in that life.

Deciding it might be a good idea to change the subject, Zoey said, "I'm thirsty. Why don't we find some place to park ourselves and get something to drink."

"I know just the place," Laurie responded. "A little sidewalk cafe on Main Street."

Five minutes later, they were sitting at a small, round table sipping iced tea and watching the parade of humanity—locals and tourists. They chatted casually, commenting on some of the unwise fashion choices passing by, discovering a mutual love of chocolate and a loathing of politics. It was a beautiful day, warm but not hot, with not a cloud in the pristine-blue sky.

After their third refill of tea, they decided it was probably time to return to the ranch. Laurie had to get back to work. They had just paid the bill and were starting to leave when Laurie stopped abruptly. Following her gaze, Zoey saw a man walking down the opposite side of the street. He saw Laurie, but averted his glance and kept walking.

Laurie's expression was deeply troubled. She whispered, "That's Hank Jamison."

"I guessed as much," Zoey admitted.

"Lord, I wish he could stop hating so much," Laurie said fervently. "It's not good for him. And it's so destructive for Tyler."

"Maybe someday he'll see things differently," Zoey said with more hope than conviction.

Laurie shook her head. "Hank's the most stubborn man in the whole valley. Next to Tyler," she couldn't resist adding. "Knowing Hank, hell will freeze over before he changes his mind. Come on."

They walked on. But the incident had cast a pall over what had been a wonderful morning.

* * *

Late that night, Zoey was once again tossing and turning, unable to sleep. Finally giving up the futile effort, she decided some hot milk might help. It had been her mother's remedy for sleeplessness when Zoey was growing up, and it always seemed to work. Even on the long, dark nights shortly after her father left, when she was too frightened to sleep because the house had seemed so much safer when he was there.

Throwing on the white chenille robe Laurie had loaned her, Zoey padded softly down the stairs and turned in the direction of the kitchen. Just before she reached the doorway from the living room into the kitchen, she heard voices. Angry ones.

"I'm here for the wedding, what more do you want?" Pete demanded.

"I want you to stick around for awhile," Laurie begged. "Why do you have to rush off that very night?"

"Because I have to be in Laramie the next day."

"You could skip the Laramie rodeo."

"Skip it!" he exploded. "That's a dumb idea."

"Why? Because you don't want to miss the rodeo—or because there's a woman waiting there for you?"

"Now, don't start that. You know better."

"I know it wouldn't be the first time." The heartache and humiliation in Laurie's voice were painful for Zoey to hear.

Pete insisted, "I got a real shot at winning some big money there, and you're asking me to skip it!?"

"Oh, Pete, you say that about every rodeo, and it never happens. It hasn't happened in a long time. You're not as young as you used to be. You're up against kids half your age."

"Oh, well, that's real fine, talkin' me down like this! You never did believe in me, Laurie. If you had supported me more, I would'a gone a damn sight farther."

Laurie's voice held an unexpected hint of steel as she

responded, "I believed in you when you didn't believe in yourself. I supported you, financially and emotionally. Never once did I ask you to consider what I wanted or needed. All I ever hoped for in return was that you would love me. But you can't even give me that, can you?"

"There's no reasoning with you when you're like this," Pete snapped. "It's no wonder I don't wanna come home more. I'm sleeping in the bunkhouse."

An instant later, Zoey heard the sound of the back door opening and closing, immediately followed by the sound of Laurie's muffled sobs. For a moment, Zoey stood there, unsure about what to do. Should she tiptoe quietly back up to bed and pretend she hadn't overheard this unhappy exchange? Or should she go to Laurie and try to comfort her? She wasn't sure which course of action was the right one. She only knew she couldn't bear to hear Laurie crying.

Stepping into the kitchen, Zoey said softly, "Laurie?"

Laurie's head shot up, then she quickly looked away in embarrassment, wiping her eyes with the back of her hand. "Zoey, what're you doing up this late?"

Zoey sat down at the table. "I couldn't sleep. I thought some hot milk might help. I didn't mean to eavesdrop."

"It's okay," Laurie responded in an exhausted voice. "You would'a seen soon enough how it is between me and Pete. Our marriage has been an empty shell for years. The only reason I stuck by him was for Cheryl's sake. I didn't want her to have to go through divorce."

"Oh, Laurie, I'm so sorry. Is there anything I can do to help?"

Laurie forced a weak smile. "Afraid not. Unless you can turn a sorry excuse for a husband into a good one."

Zoey said gently, "If I had a magic wand, I'd do just that." She reached out and squeezed Laurie's hand. "Do you want to talk about it? My friends tell me I've got a real good shoulder for crying on."

Laurie sighed heavily. "Oh, I don't know that there's any point in going over it. What is, is."

She was silent for a moment, lost in bittersweet reverie. Then she said, more to herself than Zoey, "The thing is, I never expected it to turn out like this. Pete was the only boy I ever dated. I was crazy in love with him from the first moment I laid eyes on him. We got married one week after high school graduation, and I thought I was the luckiest girl in the whole state of Wyoming."

"You were very young. There was no way you could've seen what was coming."

"It was okay at first," Laurie insisted. "When I went with Pete on the rodeo circuit we had a lot of fun. Then Cheryl came along, and I wanted her to have a more stable life. So I started staying here on the ranch while he went off rodeoing, and I got a job. Actually, I didn't have much choice. We needed the money. Pete never did earn much on the circuit." She finished, "From then on he wasn't what you'd call a real involved husband or father."

"But Cheryl adores him," Zoey commented matter-of-factly.

"Oh, yeah." There was a bitter edge to Laurie's voice. "I've never done anything to make her think less of him. It was tough enough on her, having to say good-bye to her daddy all the time. She would've been crushed to realize he wasn't really the hero she needed to believe he was."

Zoey knew all too well how important it was for little girls, and boys for that matter, to look up to their fathers as heroes. Her admiration for Laurie grew. She'd put her own feelings aside and handled a difficult situation with unselfish grace.

Just as her own mother had done, Zoey realized. Growing up, she'd taken her mother's strength and courage for granted. It wasn't until she was grown, and had endured her own disappointments in relationships, that she realized how much restraint and generosity of spirit it took for her mother to refrain from criticizing the man who had abandoned her and their children.

Now, looking at Laurie, Zoey said with deep admiration,

"You made a lot of sacrifices for Cheryl, and I admire you for it. But she's leaving now. Maybe it's time to start thinking about yourself."

"You mean divorce," Laurie responded bluntly.

"Perhaps. Or maybe asking Pete to go for marriage counseling."

Laurie gave a bitter little laugh at that suggestion. "Oh, Zoey, I know you folks in New York probably do that as naturally as you go to the doctor. But most men out here figure if they've got a problem they should handle it themselves. Pete is definitely one of those men."

The two women sat in silence for a long moment. Then Laurie said wistfully, "When I was growing up, before I fell so hard for Pete and couldn't think about anything else, I used to dream of going to college, living in a big city, pursuing some exciting career. But it's too late for that now."

Zoey responded adamantly, "Have you heard the saying that it's never too late to become what you might have been? I believe it."

"But I'm *forty-one*," Laurie said miserably.

"Hey, a lot of women your age are going back to college. There are even reentry programs to help them do just that."

Laurie's expression brightened a little. "You're kidding. Really?"

"Really. Look, I don't want to encourage you to leave your marriage, but I do want to encourage you to not give up on your dreams just yet."

Laurie shook her head negatively. "Dreams are for the young. I've made my bed, and I've got to lie in it."

Zoey felt frustrated on Laurie's behalf, but knew better than to press the issue. However, there was one question Zoey couldn't resist asking, though it was rather pointed. "Considering your own situation, why are you so eager to see Tyler remarry? I mean, your own marriage isn't exactly a glowing testimonial to the institution."

"You have the right to ask that, I guess, seeing as how I got you out here in kind of a dishonest way." Laurie leaned forward and looked intently at Zoey, as if desperate to make her understand. "The thing is, despite the impression you've gotten of Tyler as being, well, difficult, there's a real decent guy underneath that stubborn, willful exterior. He's the kind of man who can love someone fully and deeply, with passion and commitment."

"Something Pete can't do," Zoey commented bluntly.

Laurie didn't argue. "You're right. Pete can't do it. But Tyler can. He did, with Sarah. He loved her the way every woman needs to be loved, deserves to be loved. I don't want the tragedy of her death and the death of their baby to destroy Tyler's ability to love that way again."

Zoey was silent for a moment thinking about what Laurie had said. Instinctively, she knew it was true. Tyler was a very rare man indeed.

Laurie looked hopefully at Zoey. "That's why I was so pleased to see what kind of woman you turned out to be. A woman who deserves a man like Tyler."

Zoey's guilt at misrepresenting herself to these people could no longer be ignored. There was a sour taste in her mouth as she took a deep breath and, avoiding Laurie's eyes, plunged in. "Look, there's something you need to know. You're not the only one who's been less than honest in this situation. The fact is—"

She hesitated, then finished in a guilty rush, "I've got a boyfriend back in New York. He's the guy who called yesterday. He's been reluctant to make a commitment, and we had an argument about it and, well, I answered Tyler's ad to make him jealous. That's the only reason I'm here."

She forced herself to meet Laurie's gaze and was surprised to see her smiling. "Oh, Zoey, don't you think I suspected something of the sort? I mean, I didn't know the details, of course, but I knew that guy wasn't your lawyer. And I knew the minute I met you that whatever the reason why you'd answered the ad I placed for Tyler, it wasn't because you were really interested in being a mail-order bride for a Wyoming rancher."

Zoey was flabbergasted. "But you didn't say anything."

"Of course not. It wouldn't've been polite. Besides, by the time you and Tyler came back from that ride together, I knew that somehow your attitude had changed."

"That was just because I had enjoyed the magnificent scenery, and the ride was very pleasant, and-and all," Zoey stammered awkwardly.

Laurie smiled and nodded. "Sure. Whatever you say."

Zoey sighed in exasperation. "Look, Laurie, I just told you I have a boyfriend. A serious, long-term relationship."

"Does he feel as deeply about you as Tyler felt about Sarah?" Laurie asked pointedly.

Zoey opened her mouth to retort, "Of course he does," but somehow she couldn't say the words. She didn't believe them. And she knew Laurie wouldn't, either.

"More importantly, do you care about him that deeply?" Laurie pressed.

Feeling distinctly uncomfortable at the question, Zoey insisted, "That's not the issue here."

Laurie raised one eyebrow quizzically. "Isn't it?"

When Zoey had no ready answer, Laurie went on gently, "I'll make you that warm milk now. Then we can both try to get some sleep."

But, as Laurie got up and moved toward the refrigerator, Zoey knew it would take a lot more than a glass of warm milk to calm the disturbing feelings raging within her.

9

On the morning of the Fourth of July, Zoey came down late to breakfast. She was surprised to find everyone—Laurie, Cheryl, Tyler, Jesse, and even Chuck—sitting around the breakfast table, waiting for her. Only Pete was absent. She thought no one seemed to miss him.

"Good morning," Laurie said brightly.

The only hint of the previous night's trauma was a tired look around her eyes. Zoey assumed that, over all the unhappy years of her marriage, Laurie had learned to put scenes like that behind her and get on with what needed to be done. She wasn't a woman who would crumple under pressure.

"You just made it," Tyler chimed in with a mischievous glint in his blue eyes. "We were about to leave without you."

"Oh, Uncle Ty, we were not," Cheryl corrected him.

As she sat down and accepted the cup of coffee Laurie offered, Zoey noticed that they were all a bit more dressed up than usual. Cheryl wore a bright-red sundress, Laurie was in knit slacks and matching top in a lovely shade of turquoise. The three men wore new jeans and freshly ironed shirts. Tyler's shirt was the clear blue of the Wyoming sky, and it made his eyes look even more intense.

Remembering their tête-à-tête over the campfire the night before, Zoey felt that somehow their relationship had altered slightly. When he'd called her by her first name instead of the formal and impersonal "Ms. Donovan," it signaled a distinct thaw.

"Are we going somewhere?" she asked.

"Oh, dear, I forgot to tell you," Laurie said, her hands flying to her face in dismay.

"Tell me what?"

"About the Fourth of July celebration in town," Cheryl answered, too impatient to wait for her mother to explain. "There's a parade."

"Which we're gonna miss if we don't get a move on," Jesse interrupted tersely.

Ignoring him, Cheryl went on eagerly, "And a picnic in the park and baseball and a dance. And, of course, fireworks," she finished happily.

"It's just about the biggest thing in Jackson all year," Laurie added. "And a whole lot of fun. I really think you'll enjoy it."

Looking down at her new jeans and peach-colored T-shirt, Zoey asked, "Am I dressed up enough? Maybe I should change."

"You look just fine, miss," Jesse insisted in an impatient tone. "Let's go." And he was up and out of the kitchen before Zoey could respond.

"Jesse's right," Laurie said, "you look just fine. But you might want to grab a jacket for tonight."

"All right. I'll be right back."

As she hurried out of the kitchen, she heard Tyler say to Laurie, " Chuck and I will go on into town with Jesse. We'll meet you ladies there."

Zoey, Laurie, and Cheryl drove into Jackson in Laurie's pickup, which was older and a bit more battered than

Tyler's, but immaculate. The radio was playing rousing country-and-western music. It was a warm, clear, gloriously beautiful summer day, and the scenery was magnificent. Zoey felt energized, eager to experience the full range of events in a small-town Fourth of July celebration. Surely it would be a far cry from the Fourth of July celebration Brian had invited her to in the Hamptons.

"You're really gonna enjoy this," Laurie said with a smile and a brief glance at Zoey before returning her gaze to the road.

"Daddy's gonna be in the parade," Cheryl announced proudly. "He rides in it every year."

Laurie didn't add anything to Cheryl's comment, but her smile faded.

Remembering the argument she'd overheard the night before, Zoey found herself feeling irate on Laurie's behalf. While Laurie worked hard and struggled to support the family, Pete was off playing cowboy. And not always alone, if Laurie was right. Zoey wondered what Laurie got out of such an unhappy, unequal relationship that made it worthwhile. From Zoey's perspective, it seemed to be very little. It must be extremely important to Laurie to keep the family together, no matter how unfair the situation was to her.

Thinking of the fairness issue reminded Zoey of her relationship with Brian's and Carla's insistence that Brian didn't consider Zoey's feelings and needs. When they were together, they enjoyed each other's company and rarely disagreed about anything. That had been enough to keep her from being dissatisfied. Zoey rarely questioned Brian's workaholism, that severely limited the amount of time they could spend together, or the fact that they seemed to always end up doing what Brian wanted to do, especially if it involved his job in some way.

Carla was right, Zoey reluctantly admitted now. Brian talked as if he supported her career, but he rarely took the time to show that support. Yet he expected her to be by his side at social functions involving his work, and she'd been happy to do so. Their relationship had proceeded smoothly precisely because Zoey asked for so little in return. Now that she was finally asking Brian to consider her feelings and needs, especially about marriage and children, the ugly truth about the imbalance in their relationship was becoming apparent.

Just as with Laurie and Pete, Zoey's relationship with Brian met his needs perfectly, but gave her very little in return. The only difference, and it was a big one, was that Zoey never had to worry about whether Brian was faithful. He had a very traditional code of conduct, and fidelity was part of that code. Unfortunately, consideration of Zoey's feelings and willingness to make a permanent commitment didn't seem to be part of it.

Looking at Laurie concentrating on driving the pickup toward Jackson, Zoey thought how similar they were in spite of their superficial differences in background and lifestyle. Both needed something critical from the men in their lives, something those men seemed unable, or unwilling, to give. Laurie's poignant words to Pete the night before—"All I ever hoped for in return was that you would love me"—were burned in Zoey's memory. The sadness she felt for Laurie was for herself, too. It could have been her saying those words. Like Pete, Brian wouldn't have an adequate response.

Why did women give so much, Zoey wondered, and accept so little in return? It couldn't be simply that they were raised to do it. It had to go deeper than that. Some deeply ingrained instinct to nurture, to give all they had to give, to share the deepest part of themselves—and to hope against hope that the men they loved would do the same.

Freud had asked, "What do women want?" Thinking about Laurie and Pete and her own relationship with Brian, Zoey felt she knew the answer. It was amazingly simple. Women wanted to know in their hearts they were loved and appreciated. To feel it so surely that there was absolutely no question. To look into their lovers' eyes and feel that they might drown in the love they saw there.

As Gran Eileen had done when she had looked into the eyes of a stranger and found love, Zoey thought. For the first time since she'd heard that story as a very little girl, she understood why her grandmother had taken that amazing leap of faith in marrying a man she barely knew—she knew in her heart that he loved her.

Looking at Laurie sitting next to her on the hard bench seat with its cracked and torn Naugahyde upholstery, Zoey wanted to say to her, "You deserve so much more. Don't settle for so little." But she couldn't make such a personal statement to someone she'd known only a short time. Laurie would be deeply embarrassed.

And besides, Zoey thought unhappily, Laurie wasn't the only one those words applied to. Zoey might just as well say them to herself.

They arrived in Jackson a good half-hour before the parade was due to start to find the wooden sidewalks of Main Street already packed with people. After driving around for several minutes, Laurie finally found a parking place a couple of blocks off Main Street. When they had made their way back to the main thoroughfare, they found Tyler and Chuck, who had reserved a space for them near the street. Jesse had gone off to talk to friends who would be riding in the parade.

Zoey looked at the crowd lining Main Street and was amazed at the size of it. Surely everyone in Jackson was there, along with tourists and summer visitors. In this idyllic small town, something as old-fashioned as a Fourth of July parade was still a big deal.

She felt a patriotic stirring in her heart. As a jaded New Yorker, she was taken aback by her response to the scene. It was so very Norman Rockwell, and she knew when she described it to her sophisticated friends they would make fun of it. She could just hear Carla. "A *parade*? How quaint." Somehow, she didn't want to think of Carla's derisive response.

As always, she'd brought her camera. And, as always, she took refuge from disturbing feelings by hiding behind the lens. She began shooting pictures of excited children perched on their father's shoulders or burrowing through the crowd to get a better view, people waving tiny red-white-and-blue flags, and uniformed sheriff's deputies mounted on horses.

When Tyler wasn't looking, she took a few quick shots of him. Through the eye of the camera, she was able to look at him more closely than she did normally, when she tended to avoid looking at him directly. His face had quickly become familiar—the straight nose, high cheekbones, firm mouth, and strong chin. But she saw things she hadn't noticed before—a small, jagged scar on his chin, white against the deep tan of his complexion; tiny lines at the corners of his eyes, especially pronounced when he squinted against the glare of the sun; a touch of gray at his temples. And, in the deep vee where his shirt was unbuttoned at his throat, a glimpse of curling, golden-brown hair.

As always, the eye of the camera saw more than just the physical. Somehow, the essence of what Zoey was photographing came through in a way it didn't when seen with the naked eye. Tyler's essence was thoroughly male, strong without being domineering, and extremely self-contained. This was a man who would reveal no more of himself than was absolutely necessary. That thought only made Zoey all the more curious about him.

Intently focused on getting the most deeply probing shots, she was so startled when he turned and stared straight into the camera that she nearly dropped it. Reaching out, he gently but firmly lowered the camera. Without saying a word, he made it clear he didn't want his privacy invaded. Zoey's cheeks burned with embarrassment at having been caught trying to capture him on film.

At that moment, the parade began, and Zoey aimed her camera at it. But the shots she got of splendidly attired riders and beautifully groomed horses, gaily decorated floats, and energetic marching bands didn't hold nearly the fascination for her that Tyler had.

Toward the end of the parade, after Boy and Girl Scout troops had marched past and local dignitaries were driven by in convertibles, a group of horsemen appeared. Pete was riding a beautiful buckskin quarterhorse. Zoey assumed it was the horse he used in some of his rodeo competitions. He was dressed to the teeth, polished silver gleaming on his hatband and at his belt buckle. He looked thoroughly pleased with himself, and flashed a cocky grin at the crowd—especially at the attractive women.

Cheryl gazed at her father adoringly. To his little girl, he was a white knight on a steed. Zoey understood that feeling all too well. Unlike Cheryl, she had long since had to accept the death of her fantasy about her father. She felt torn between hoping Cheryl could hold on to her fantasy and knowing that it was probably impossible.

Glancing at Laurie, Zoey saw that she had a heartrendingly wistful expression, as if she wished that Pete's dazzling smile were for her alone, as it must once have been, years and years ago.

After the short but colorful parade was over, the crowd dispersed. Some people returned home, but many made their way to the park in the center of town, where families began laying out picnics. Zoey helped Laurie and Cheryl unpack the two large picnic baskets they'd brought with them. She was glad to see that Chuck helped as well. That boded well for their marriage. Jesse hadn't returned, and Zoey assumed he was off with his buddies from the parade, probably downing a few beers in one of the more down-to-earth bars in town.

Tyler had disappeared immediately after the parade without saying a word to Laurie, who didn't seem concerned. Zoey could only assume Laurie knew what her brother was up to.

Her curiosity was satisfied when Tyler returned and said everything was all set for the softball game after everyone had had a chance to eat.

"Who are the teams?" Zoey asked with an interest that surprised everyone.

"Basically, the ranchers in the surrounding area are on one team, and the townspeople are on the other," Tyler answered. "Technically speaking, I guess Chuck should be on the town team, but because of Cheryl, he plays on my team. We're pretty flexible about the whole thing. Anyone who wants to play, can."

"You're the captain?"

"Yeah. And Fred Cooper, who runs the drugstore, is the captain of the town team." Tyler couldn't resist bragging a bit. "My team usually wins. None of us are exactly professional athletes, but working hard outdoors keeps us in better shape than the town guys."

Turning to Chuck, Tyler said, "I want you to play shortstop this year."

Chuck looked dismayed. "Shortstop? What happened to Alvie Hicks?"

"He's home with a busted ankle."

"But—"

"Don't worry, you can handle it," Tyler assured him.

As they all filled paper plates with the fried chicken, potato salad, and fruit that seemed to be standard picnic fare, Zoey asked with studied casualness, "Do women play?"

Tyler snorted. "'Course not." Then, realizing he'd been less than politically correct and remembering this was a New York woman he was talking to, he hastened to add, "I mean, not that there's anything wrong with that, of course. If a woman wanted to play, she could. But no one ever does. Want to play, that is."

He was smart enough to recognize that he wasn't doing a great job of extricating himself from the hole he'd dug. Giving up, he concentrated on eating, studiously avoiding Zoey's eyes. When he had finished, he said to Chuck, "Come on, we've got to get together with everybody for the pre-game strategy session."

Chuck, who had to wolf down his last few mouthfuls of

food, hurried off with Tyler in the direction of the baseball diamond in the center of the park. Cheryl trailed after Chuck, eager to provide moral support for him.

Watching Tyler walk away, Zoey had a wild thought. She tried to dismiss it, but it was persistent. After all, he'd been so arrogantly male about the very idea of women playing in the game. Finally, she turned to Laurie. "Can you point out Fred Cooper to me?"

"Sure. He's that red-haired guy in the white T-shirt with the Cooper's Drugs logo over there by the diamond." She eyed Zoey thoughtfully. "Why?"

Zoey flashed a sly grin. "Because I want to teach your brother a lesson."

"Zoey Donovan, what do you have up your sleeve?" Laurie asked with a twinkle in her eye, as if she'd already guessed.

"You'll see."

Zoey made a beeline for Fred Cooper. They spoke in low tones for a few minutes. At first, he shook his head vehemently. Then he looked surprised, intrigued, and, finally, he grinned and nodded. As Zoey made her way back to the sidelines, she passed Tyler. He eyed her curiously, but she merely gave the briefest polite nod.

The game began, and it was hard-fought. Tyler's team led from the beginning, but in the seventh inning the townsmen made a determined comeback. By the top of the ninth, the townsmen were ahead by one. The crowd watching the game was thoroughly enjoying it, punctuating each play with whistles, applause, and boos where appropriate. This was more suspense than they'd seen in this annual competition in a long time.

Tyler's team was batting, and Fred Cooper's team was taking the field when he made a surprise announcement. Their pitcher was being replaced by a newcomer—Ms. Zoey Donovan from New York City. As Zoey walked to the pitcher's mound, a glove on her right hand, Tyler stared at her in complete amazement. She felt thoroughly pleased at the knowledge that she'd succeeded in catching him totally off guard.

Hurrying over to Fred Cooper, Tyler demanded, "What the hell do you think you're doing?"

"Just bringing in a relief pitcher. No rule against that, is there?" was the bland reply.

"No, but—"

"But what?"

"This is ridiculous!"

"We'll see about that," Fred said smugly. "Now, do you want to finish the game or do you want to kick dirt and complain?"

Tyler's mouth tightened in a disapproving line. "All right, if you want to blow the game, that's your choice."

Turning on his heel, he marched back toward his teammates on the bench. He spoke to them in a low voice, and several of the men chuckled.

The first man at bat was Chuck. He looked helplessly at Cheryl in the crowd as if to say, "I'm sorry that I have to humiliate your houseguest, but I've got no choice." Zoey had been carefully watching each of the players on Tyler's team throughout the game, gauging their strengths and weaknesses. She knew Chuck had a problem with fastballs. Her first pitch was a fastball, and it was a strike. Chuck looked surprised, but not worried. The second pitch was even faster, and it, too, was a strike.

A murmur of excitement went through the crowd, and Cheryl began to look worried for her fiancé. Now, Chuck took the situation seriously. He gripped the bat hard, waiting expectantly for another fastball. So Zoey threw a slowball. Chuck swung hard and missed by a mile, striking out. He looked thoroughly embarrassed as he headed back toward the bench.

The next batter fared slightly better. He got a hit off Zoey. Unfortunately, it was a pop fly easily caught by the shortstop.

Both batters had been right-handers who'd had a hard time dealing with a southpaw pitcher.

Now, the crowd watched as excitedly as if they were watching the final game of the World Series. When Tyler walked slowly up to the plate, there were shouts of, "Go get her, Tyler!" and "You can do it!" He was easily the best player on his team, and the hopes of his teammates and their supporters were riding on his athletic prowess.

He stared intently at Zoey, but she wasn't about to be intimidated by him. Her first pitch was a ball. So was her second. But she didn't panic. She knew her ability, knew how to marshall it when necessary. Her third pitch was a strike. The fourth a foul ball, and a second strike. The next pitch was another ball. In classic fashion, the entire game was riding on the final pitch of the last inning.

Then, as the crowd held its breath, Tyler pointed to the center of the field, mimicking Babe Ruth's famous gesture. Zoey couldn't help laughing along with the crowd. The man's confidence was amazing.

She wound up and let the ball fly. Unlike the fastballs and slowballs she'd been pitching to Tyler, this was something special she'd been saving for just this situation—a curveball. Tyler swung hard and missed. Strike three! End of game. Fred Cooper's beleaguered townsmen had finally won one.

The crowd let out a roar, punctuated by an especially vocal response from the women. Zoey's teammates surrounded her on the mound, hoisting her onto their shoulders and parading her around the diamond. She felt as exhilarated as if she'd won a real game in the bigs.

When the men finally let her down, she came face to face with Tyler. To his credit, he was gracious in defeat. He shook Fred's hand, congratulating him on a well-deserved victory. Then he turned to Zoey. "You've played this game before, haven't you?" he commented dryly.

"Yup," she admitted gleefully. "My father was a baseball fanatic who saw to it that I was the first girl on my local Little League team." She didn't add that she'd continued playing after he left home, hoping that when he returned he would be proud of how good she'd become.

"And you've played some since then," Tyler observed.

"A bit in college," she said feigning modesty. "We only came in fourth in the state women's softball finals. And, of course, there's the team I play on with other photographers in New York. It's just for fun. All the proceeds go to charity."

Tyler shook his head slowly. "Remind me never to underestimate you again, Ms. Donovan."

Her gray eyes glinted like quicksilver. "Oh, I will, Mr. Ross."

It was early evening, and the heat of the day was lessening. A soft summer breeze rustled through the trees in the park. A bandstand had been set up at one end, with a portable dance floor ringed by lights. Shortly, a country-and-western band began to play. People packed up the remains of their picnics and made their way over to the bandstand.

Cheryl and Chuck were among the first to start dancing to the energetic music. Watching from the sidelines, Zoey was amazed at the intricate steps of the line dances, and even more amazed at the fact that everyone seemed to know how to do them without a misstep. Though there were clubs in Manhattan where line dancing was done, Zoey had never gone to one. She was completely caught off guard when a young man asked her to dance. Shaking her head, she explained, "I don't know how."

"That's all right, ma'am, you'll pick it up real quick," he assured her with an encouraging grin. "Just follow me. By the way, my name's Mel."

For a moment, she hesitated, feeling awkward and embarrassed. Why not? she asked herself throwing caution to the wind. She let him lead her into the throng of dancers. It was confusing at first, and she felt that she was making a fool of herself. But no one seemed to care, least of all her partner, who patiently showed her the steps. Gradually, she began to get the hang of it, and in a few minutes she was energetically doing the "Boot Scootin' Boogie" with everyone else.

It was more fun than she could remember having in a long, long time. *How staid I've become,* she thought. *Carla's right; I need to be more adventurous.*

Whirling around the dance floor, she caught a glimpse of Tyler watching her from the sidelines. His expression was, as always, difficult to read. He must be quite a poker player, she thought. As Mel put his hands on Zoey's hips to guide her in a difficult step, she glanced again in Tyler's direction. To her surprise, she detected a hint of something entirely new in his expression. If she didn't know better, she would have described it as jealousy.

A rousing version of "If I Could Make a Livin' Out of Lovin' You" left her exhilarated but exhausted. Excusing herself from Mel, she started to head back through the throng of dancers toward the sidelines. Suddenly, Tyler was there standing before her. He looked down at her with just a hint of a smile curving the corners of his mouth and asked politely, "May I have this dance?"

Zoey was caught totally off guard. She could make the excuse that she was out of breath after that last rousing dance, but she realized the band was playing a slow song. Before she could say a word, Tyler took her in his arms. He pulled her toward him until their bodies were barely brushing against each other. One hand held hers gently but firmly, fingers intertwined, while the other pressed against the small of her back.

Zoey's breath caught in her throat and for a moment she forgot to breathe. Then she exhaled slowly as she relaxed against him. Instead of feeling awkward, it seemed the most natural thing in the world to be in his arms. She was struck by his intense physicality. His touch was sure and strong, yet tender. She had never felt more secure, as if while she was next to him he were shielding her from all the terrors of the world.

As with most of the songs the band was playing, Zoey was unfamiliar with this one. It was called "Tonight I Climbed the Wall." Listening to the bittersweet lyrics about a man swallowing his pride and "climbing the wall" separating him and his lover, she was struck by their sensitivity. It was the exact opposite of all her stereotypical assumptions that country-and-western music was about "good-hearted women and good-timin' men."

It occurred to her that the words were especially relevant to her and Tyler. From the first moment they met, there had been a wall between them. A wall built of prejudgments and sharply conflicting cultures, vastly different lifestyles and romantic histories. A wall made almost insurmountable by dishonesty on the part of each of them. Neither had intended to do anything more than dismiss the other as quickly as possible. Neither had any intention of attempting to bridge the gulf between them.

Until now. Forcing herself to look up at Tyler, Zoey saw her own budding attraction mirrored in his eyes. Without saying a word, she knew they were thinking the same thing. Could they climb the wall separating them? And, if they did, what would they find on the other side?

Their lips were a hair's breadth apart. Zoey was certain that, if her face remained tilted up to his and she closed her eyes, he would bridge that infinitesimal yet vast distance between them and kiss her. And she knew that if he kissed her, she would respond in a way that would shake her to her very bones.

Should I surrender? she wondered. A tiny voice inside whispered, *Yes. Oh, yes.*

Her eyelids began to lower almost of their own volition. She knew she that in a moment she would feel his firm lips on her trembling ones.

The music stopped. The song was over. And instead of moving immediately into another song, the singer announced that the band was taking a break.

For an endless moment, Zoey and Tyler stood there, reluctant to break the connection between them. Then his fingers, entwined with hers, relaxed, his hand at her back fell away, and he stepped back. The magic of the previous moment dissolved in the reality of people leaving the dance floor, talking, laughing.

They looked at each other. Neither spoke. But each knew how close they'd come to climbing the wall between them.

Without a word, they made their way toward Chuck and Cheryl waiting at the picnic table. They were immediately joined by a pensive-looking Laurie. Zoey hadn't wanted to comment on Pete's conspicuous absence from the picnic, the softball game, and now the dance, but Laurie's expression of distraction and thinly disguised disappointment was eloquent. Wherever Pete was, he wasn't with his wife.

Darkness had fallen. "It's time for the fireworks," Cheryl announced to Zoey. Confident in Chuck's devotion to her, she was blissfully unaware of her mother's unhappiness—or was trying very hard to maintain a facade of normality. Zoey wasn't sure which was actually the case.

They spread out blankets on the grass, and Zoey put on the denim jacket she'd brought. With nightfall, the temperature had fallen and the cool of the evening had turned to chill. For an hour, they sat, watching fireworks brilliantly light up the vast black sky in bursts of red, blue, white, and green.

Sneaking glances at Tyler, Zoey marveled at the thought that she'd never known a man quite like him. She knew she would never meet anyone quite like him ever again. And she felt a sinking sensation as she realized that, when she left this beautiful place, she would step out of his life forever.

Suddenly, she shivered. Pulling her knees up to her chest, she wrapped her arms around them, hugging herself to keep warm. She told herself it was the chill night breeze, but her heart knew it was something else entirely.

Watching Zoey's delight at the colorful fireworks, Tyler sensed the shy, vulnerable girl beneath the mature woman's independent, sophisticated facade. He'd only known her a few days, yet already he realized how greatly he'd misjudged her when they'd first met. She was a continual surprise. A sometimes-infuriating, often-delightful one.

And she was so very lovely. Her red-gold curls gleamed softly in the moonlight, inviting him to run his fingers through them. He longed to caress her pale skin, as soft and fair as his was dark and rough. Her slender body had felt so fragile in his arms when they'd danced. Yet it had felt so right.

The dance had been a revelation to him. One that had shaken him to his very core. He hadn't danced with anyone since the last time he danced with Sarah, at a neighbor's wedding only weeks before her death. He hadn't expected another woman to feel natural in his arms in the way that Sarah had. Yet Zoey had felt as if she belonged there. It amazed him that her small hand could fit so perfectly in his, that her body could mold so perfectly to his.

With each movement of their bodies while they danced, he'd felt he was moving away from Sarah's memory, away from a past that he treasured, and toward an unknown future. He resisted that future, even while he was powerfully drawn to it. Now, he felt profoundly torn between a pain he'd learned to live with and the first stirrings of something remarkably like joy.

Casting covert glances at Zoey, he thought of how she'd turned his unhappy but settled life upside down. And they hadn't even so much as kissed. He was immensely grateful that damned song had ended when it did, because if it had gone on a moment longer, they would have kissed. Who knew what would have happened then?

10

The Chapel of the Transfiguration was a small log church built in 1925. Above the altar, a large picture window framed the magnificent Tetons. Trees in shades of green ranging from nearly gray to the deepest emerald covered the lower portion of the range, and the tops of the granite peaks were white with snow. Zoey was transfixed by the simple beauty of the rustic place of worship.

"It's an Episcopal church, but people of all faiths are welcome," Laurie explained to Zoey as the two women stood in the center aisle. Laurie had just finished hanging huge white-satin bows at the end of each aisle, while Zoey checked out the best angles for photographing the wedding ceremony.

"It's magnificent," she breathed. "No altar piece in any of the great cathedrals can match this view."

Laurie beamed. "I know. I can't imagine a more wonderful setting for a young couple to start out their lives together."

"Were you and Pete married here?" Zoey asked hoping

the question wouldn't upset Laurie. Zoey had awakened in the middle of the night to the sound of a pickup driving into the front yard of the ranch house and knew it must be Pete finally dragging himself home. When everyone had left on their wedding errands that morning, Pete hadn't been in sight. Zoey assumed he was sleeping off the good time he'd had the night before.

Laurie didn't seem unduly bothered by the question. She shook her head and explained, "We eloped. Ran off to Reno, got married in one of those tacky little pink-plastic wedding chapels, spent the night, then came home the next day."

Zoey knew she was treading on sensitive ground, but she couldn't help asking, "You didn't want to get married here, in this beautiful place?"

Laurie's expression turned guarded, as it often did when Pete was the subject of the conversation. But a poignant wistfulness was apparent behind the guardedness. "I would've liked it, I guess. But Pete didn't want to wait, and it seemed very romantic to go dashing off like that."

Zoey didn't miss the emphasis on "seemed."

Smiling determinedly, Laurie went on, "But Tyler and Sarah were married here. I had so much fun planning their wedding. Since Sarah didn't have a mother to help her with the arrangements, she let me kind of take over. I got to do all the things I hadn't done when I got married."

"I imagine it was a beautiful wedding," Zoey said gently, guessing at the hurt Laurie was hiding.

"Oh, yes. It was in the early summer. The wildflowers were in bloom, and everything was so green. Sarah was a talented seamstress, and she made her dress and the bridesmaids' dresses. It was quite a sight, let me tell you. Sarah had wonderful taste. Simple but elegant, you know what I mean?"

Zoey nodded encouragingly, and Laurie continued, "She was such a beautiful bride. And Tyler was a handsome groom. They were so very much in love . . . "

Laurie's voice trailed off sadly and she looked away.

Zoey felt an incredible pain on Tyler's behalf. Only a few years ago, he'd stood in this church and married the woman he loved deeply. Now he would have to stand here again and watch his niece be married. Until that moment, Zoey hadn't realized the terrible significance of this event. For Tyler, it must be a day of profoundly mixed emotions.

Laurie turned back to Zoey and, as if sensing her thoughts, said softly, "There are significant memories here for all of us. Some of them happy, some terribly sad. Tyler and I were baptized here. Our mother's funeral was held here, as was Sarah's. But in this special place, if nowhere else, there is a sense of the continuity of life. I don't know how you believe, Zoey, but I believe in a hereafter. I'm certain we will all meet again."

Zoey had no idea what to say to Laurie's heartfelt expression of religious belief. She hadn't been raised in a particular church, and throughout her life had focused on material matters, not spiritual ones. She asked curiously, "Does Tyler share your religious beliefs?"

Laurie sighed heavily. "He used to. But I'm not sure he believes in anything anymore."

The two women were silent for a moment, then Laurie forced a smile. "Come on, this is no time for maudlin conversation." Looking around at the beautifully decorated church, with two large stands of white carnations at the altar and the white bows on each aisle, she said, "I'm done here. Now we have to get ready for the wedding. If everything doesn't go absolutely according to clockwork, I'll never hear the end of it from Cheryl."

Zoey returned her smile. "You're right. We'd better get dressed. I want to get the formal shots done before the ceremony."

Because the chapel was so small and didn't have a dressing room, the bridal party was getting ready at the home of a bridesmaid who lived nearby. Laurie and Zoey arrived at the small frame house to find a scene of controlled chaos. The groomsmen, strapping young men dressed in formal black tuxedoes, were lolling about the living room while the four bridesmaids were getting dressed in pink chiffon gowns in a back bedroom. The girls, all in their early twenties and all friends of Cheryl from childhood, laughed and chattered excitedly and squeezed in together to share the one bathroom and mirror.

"This lipstick is the worst. Can I borrow yours?"

"Sure, but give it back; I'll need it later."

"I knew I needed to lose another five pounds. I can barely breathe in this dress."

"I don't know why I have to walk with Jimmy. I don't even like him."

"Because you two are the tallest. That's how it works."

"I heard the guys are doing something special to Chuck's pickup."

"Well, it better not be something dumb."

"Remember that stink bomb Gary tied to the back of Cliff's car at his wedding?"

"That was so juvenile. Marlene was really pissed off, and I don't blame her."

When Cheryl noticed her mother and Zoey standing in the doorway taking in the chaotic scene, she said, "It's about time, Mom. I was getting worried. You only have an hour to get dressed before we have to start taking pictures."

Laurie smiled indulgently at her daughter. "Oh, I think that will be plenty of time. I don't require quite as much preparation time as you do."

Cheryl had the glow of anticipation special to all truly happy brides. She was already dressed, her makeup was flawless, and one of the bridesmaids, who was a hairstylist, was putting the final touches on her elaborate upswept hairdo. Cheryl was a bit more overdone than would have been considered fashionable in New York and her dress had a few more ruffles and flounces than Zoey would have liked, but she looked lovely.

Zoey quickly changed out of her jeans and into the simple, butter-yellow dress she'd bought in Jackson. She put on the pearl stud earrings she'd borrowed from Laurie, ran a comb through her unruly curls, applied a modicum of makeup, and was ready.

Laurie had slipped on a lavender linen dress that was simply cut but flattering to her petite figure. She pulled her shoulder-length hair back with a velvet ribbon, applied a dash of lipstick, and announced she was ready.

Cheryl eyed her mother critically. "Oh, Mom, for once in your life let yourself go. Look a little glamorous."

Laurie frowned. Much as she loved her daughter and wanted this day to be perfect for her, she didn't want to be anything other than who she was. "I don't feel comfortable in a lot of makeup," she stated flatly, "and my hair's too straight to stay up in an elaborate style. It would just fall down halfway through the ceremony."

Recognizing that mother and daughter were about to clash, Zoey decided a little diplomacy was called for. She said to Laurie, "You know, one of the many jobs I had at the beginning of my career was working as an assistant to a fashion photographer. I learned a lot about doing makeup and hair. Would you mind if I made a few little suggestions?"

Laurie looked reluctant. "Well . . . I guess not. I just don't want to end up looking like Tammy Faye Bakker."

Zoey chuckled. "Not to worry. One of the things that job taught me is that it's important to let the real you shine through."

Turning to the bridesmaid who was a hairstylist, Zoey asked, "Do you think you could give Cheryl's mom a quick pageboy cut, just below chin length?"

The girl nodded enthusiastically. "Oh, sure. It would only take ten or fifteen minutes, and it would look super." As Laurie opened her mouth to protest, the girl went on, "It would really bring out your pretty blue eyes and take at least five years off your age."

"Five years?" Laurie asked doubtfully.

"Maybe ten," the bridesmaid responded in a bit of hyperbole that Zoey decided not to correct.

"All right," Laurie agreed hesitantly. "Just don't cut it *too* short."

Fifteen minutes later, her hair was done and everyone agreed it looked fabulous. Zoey had given the hairstylist some direction as to how to feather it around Laurie's face to soften the rather severe look of straight hair.

"See? With this cut it doesn't matter how straight it is," Zoey pointed out. "And now that it's not so heavy, it will hold a curl better, too. Now for the makeup."

Laurie flashed her a nervous look. "Don't worry," Zoey assured her, "no false eyelashes. And no clown cheeks."

Some subtly applied blusher, Zoey's own soft-peach lipstick, light-brown shadow on her eyelids, and sparingly applied brown mascara brought out Laurie's innate good looks. When she gazed into the mirror, she was surprised and pleased at the transformation that the new hairstyle and expertly applied makeup had wrought. She smiled happily. "I don't believe it. I look like a different person."

"Mom, you look gorgeous!" Cheryl said, and the other girls hastened to agree with her.

Laurie turned to Zoey and said in a heartfelt voice, "Thank you. I haven't felt this pretty in a long time."

Zoey shrugged. "Hey, I just let the real you shine through."

Cheryl couldn't resist suggesting, "Maybe just a little more mascara. And a touch more blusher."

"No!" Laurie and Zoey said in unison, then laughed together.

"Trust me on this," Zoey said to Cheryl. "Your mom looks perfect just the way she is. She'll be beautiful in the photos. Speaking of which, we'd better get to the church and take care of them before the guests start arriving."

Outside the church, Tyler and Jesse had finished setting up the marquee tent, tables, and chairs where the reception would be held following the ceremony. While Zoey took shots of everyone else, the two men hurried to the bridesmaid's house and changed. Tyler returned wearing a dark suit, but Jesse was in a white shirt and jeans. Nothing could get him into a suit, not even for Cheryl's wedding.

Cheryl was beginning to wonder out loud what was keeping her father when Pete finally showed up at the last minute. He looked quite handsome in his tux, and Cheryl's eyes glowed as she posed with him. But as Zoey photographed them, she was all too aware that Laurie's expression wasn't nearly so happy as she stood next to her husband.

Then the guests began to arrive, and the bridal party dispersed. In the crowd of about fifty guests, Zoey recognized some of the people she'd met at the celebration the day before, including Fred Cooper. He thanked her profusely for helping them win the game and asked hopefully if she might be back next year. Casting a quick, covert glance at Tyler, she murmured, "Probably not."

"Too bad," he responded looking disappointed.

At last it was time for the ceremony to begin. The guests took their seats, the organist began to play "We've Only Just Begun," and the wedding party moved down the short aisle. It went as smoothly as anyone, even the bride, could have possibly hoped. The five-year-old flower girl and ring bearer, who were the groom's twin niece and nephew, looked adorable and behaved with a maturity far beyond their years. The bridesmaids and groomsmen looked wonderful. And when Cheryl finally came down the aisle on her father's arm, she was the perfect image of a beautiful bride.

Waiting for her at the altar, Chuck gazed at her with all the love in the world evident in his misty eyes.

Zoey remained standing unobtrusively in the background getting shots of everyone but focusing on Cheryl and Chuck. When the music stopped and the minister began to speak, she put down her camera. She wouldn't pick it up again until the ceremony ended. Then she would get shots of Cheryl and Chuck walking triumphantly down the aisle together.

Zoey hadn't attended a wedding in a long time. As she

watched this one unfold, she felt a sharp stab of envy that she tried unsuccessfully to suppress. Once more, she was forced to confront the hard truth that Brian didn't love her in the way the shy, devoted Chuck loved Cheryl. She despaired of ever standing before an altar with Brian and exchanging vows of love and fidelity.

With great reluctance, she accepted the inevitability of something she'd known since shortly after arriving in Jackson Hole—when she returned to New York, she would have to break off with Brian once and for all. Coming out here had somehow clarified things for her. She knew what she wanted and needed, and knew that Brian couldn't, or wouldn't, give it to her. She couldn't go back to their old, uncommitted relationship. It just wasn't enough.

It occurred to her that, in his own mind, Brian might have already written her off. If so, it was for the best. That way, she wouldn't have to face him again and feel the pain of looking into his eyes and not finding the love she so desperately wanted to see.

From her position at the rear of the church, she saw Tyler sitting in the front pew watching the ceremony. In his dark suit, he looked surprisingly sophisticated. Very different from his usual image of a jeans-clad cowboy. Unlike Brian, he wasn't handsome in a *GQ*-cover-model sort of way. He was simply ruggedly male. To Zoey, that made him a great deal more attractive.

He seemed to be listening respectfully to the service, but Zoey sensed he must be thinking of his own wedding here—and of Sarah. *What a bittersweet moment this must be for Tyler,* she thought feeling terribly sad for him. Much as it must hurt, he handled it like everything else, with a quiet strength and dignity.

Laurie said he had loved deeply once. Could he ever do so again? Zoey wondered pensively. Probably not, she thought with an inward sigh. Surely that kind of love only came once in a lifetime. And not even that often to those who were unlucky.

Immediately, she berated herself for such pointless musing. Tyler wasn't looking for anyone, and he certainly wasn't looking for anyone like her. Zoey would be gone in the next day or so, as soon as she'd managed to photograph the wild mustangs. If she ever thought of Tyler again, it would only be with a sense of embarrassment and chagrin that she'd tried to use him to make Brian jealous. What a stupid, childish way to behave, she thought, angry at herself.

Surely Tyler would never give her another thought once she was gone.

As the minister, a gray-haired man with a stentorian voice, spoke of honoring and cherishing each other, Tyler's attention wandered. He hadn't set foot in this church since Sarah's funeral. He tried hard not to think of that terrible day. Instead, he forced his thoughts back to their wedding and a happier time.

That proved even more painful. Poignant memories washed over him. Tyler had never loved her more, and had never been happier. He'd confidently assumed that a long and fulfilling life lay ahead of them. Only a few years later, on the worst day of his life, Sarah collapsed and never regained consciousness. That day, Tyler learned that life is viciously unpredictable.

He felt his heart constrict with the memory of so much love and joy and tragedy. Tears came to his eyes, but, as always, he fought them back. Looking at him, his blue eyes glistening with unshed tears, most of the guests assumed he was carried away by the emotion of seeing his only niece get married. But sitting next to him, Laurie glanced at his face and knew better. Unobtrusively taking his hand, she squeezed it hard and whispered, "I know."

He met her look of compassion and felt enormous gratitude toward the big sister who'd been there for him since he was a small child, even when she was hardly more than a child herself.

Tyler was pulled out of his reverie as Cheryl and Chuck each said, "I do." As they exchanged rings, the sun was setting in a blaze of glory through the big picture window behind them. The blue sky had turned deep purple, the scattered clouds were orange, pink, and gold. Both Cheryl and Chuck seemed bathed in the golden glow of the setting sun. Against that magnificent backdrop, Chuck took Cheryl in his arms and kissed her briefly but passionately, and the ceremony was over.

And not a moment too soon, as far as Tyler was concerned. He desperately wanted to get out of that church and away from the painful memories that overwhelmed him.

Under the huge tent outside the church, people sipped champagne and punch, partook in the bountiful buffet, and listened to the sedate music of the Jackson String Quartet. Cheryl had been determined that her wedding would be elegant rather than raucous, and it was. The setting, with strings of fairy lights illuminating the tent and the Tetons looming in the background bathed in moonlight, was incredibly lovely and romantic.

While Chuck and Cheryl mingled with the wedding guests, Zoey got wonderful, candid shots of them. When it came time to cut the cake, she made certain she captured the obligatory moment as they fed each other a bite of cake.

Confident that she'd gotten enough pictures for a dozen wedding albums, she put down her camera and treated herself to a glass of champagne. She'd just finished it and was thinking about raiding the buffet when Laurie came up to her. As mother of the bride, Laurie had been surrounded by well-wishers since the ceremony had ended. This was the first chance she and Zoey had had to speak.

"So what do you think?" she asked anxiously. "Will the pictures be any good?"

"They'll be wonderful," Zoey assured her. "I got some great shots. And Cheryl and Chuck are very photogenic."

Laurie breathed a sigh of relief. "Thank God. After everything that happened, having a photographer, then not having one, and finally having you volunteer at the last minute, I was afraid something else would go wrong."

"I think you'll find it hard to choose which one to put on the mantel, if I do say so myself."

Laurie gave her a profoundly grateful look. "Oh, Zoey, I don't know what we would've done without you."

"It's my pleasure. Really."

Her eyes followed Laurie's to Chuck and Cheryl, who were talking to Chuck's proud-looking parents. "I think they'll be very happy together," Zoey said sincerely.

"Oh, I think so, too," Laurie agreed quickly. "Of course, you can never know about these things, but they truly love each other and they want the same things out of life. That's important."

Zoey silently and ruefully agreed. Wanting the same things out of life—like marriage and children—were critical to a successful relationship.

"Come on, I want to introduce you to someone," Laurie said suddenly as if she'd just remembered it. "I've been meaning to do it all evening, but it's been so hectic."

She led Zoey over to an elderly woman sitting in a wheelchair. The woman had a thick white shawl wrapped around her to ward off the chill of the night. She looked to be at least in her eighties, possibly even in her nineties. Her white hair was thin and wispy, her pale skin like parchment. But her dark eyes were bright and alert, and there was something in her expression that reminded Zoey of her Gran Eileen. By the time Zoey had known her, Gran Eileen had been about the same age as this lady.

"Mrs. Simpson, I'd like you to meet someone." Laurie spoke in a slightly louder voice than usual. "This is Zoey Donovan, and she's come all the way from New York City."

"How do you do, Mrs. Simpson," Zoey said politely.

The elderly woman gave her a warm smile. "I do pretty well for my age, young lady. And yourself?"

"Oh, I'm fine, thank you."

"All the way from New York City, you say? My mother came from there."

"Did she?" Zoey asked wondering why on earth Laurie had wanted her to meet this woman.

"She did, indeed. Before the turn of the century. Came on the train, and it took four days to get here. At one point the train was robbed—actually robbed, can you believe it? And you know who the robbers were?"

Zoey rose to the bait. "I can't imagine. Who were they?"

"Butch Cassidy and the Hole in the Wall gang." She chuckled, and her dark eyes were alight with amusement. "My mother said Butch was very polite as he asked everyone to hand over their valuables."

"Why don't you tell Zoey what brought your mother here," Laurie prompted.

Mrs. Simpson smiled a remarkably engaging smile. "She came to be married. She was a mail-order bride, you see."

Zoey flashed a wry look at Laurie. "I see," she said slowly.

"My father was a farmer here. He'd homesteaded a place back in '84 and was doing quite well for himself. But he was lonely. So he advertised in a New York newspaper for a wife. He wrote that he wanted someone who was brave enough to have an adventure. My mother answered the advertisement. She wrote that she'd never had an adventure and didn't want to grow old and die without ever experiencing one. So he sent her a train ticket, and, one week after she arrived, they were married."

"One week, hmm? A short engagement," Zoey commented, speaking to Mrs. Simpson but looking straight at Laurie.

"My mother always said you don't need a long engagement unless you know you're not really right for each other but you're afraid to admit it."

Zoey said politely, "Your mother sounds like a remarkable woman, Mrs. Simpson."

The elderly woman's smile was warm with affection and pride. "Oh, she was, Miss Donovan. She was married for seventy years and bore eight children." Her expression sobered. "There were hard times, of course. Farming is never easy, and there was that terrible Depression. Along the way three of the children died. But at the end of her life, my mother said that she would do it all over again just the same, if she could, because life with my father had been an adventure, just as he'd promised."

"A fascinating story," Zoey said diplomatically.

Just then, Mrs. Simpson's middle-aged daughter came to get her, saying that she was sorry they couldn't stay till the end of the party, but it was past her mother's bedtime.

As the woman wheeled her mother away, Zoey gave Laurie a shrewd look. "What was that all about?"

Laurie feigned innocence. "What do you mean? The Simpsons are our closest neighbors, and I just thought you'd be interested in meeting one of the oldest citizens of Jackson Hole."

"Mmm-hmm," Zoey murmured.

"She has wonderful old photographs of her parents, including their wedding photo. You might be interested in looking at them some time—you being a photographer and all."

"*Laurie*," Zoey began firmly, intending to straighten her out about a few things. Before she could continue, she noticed that Laurie was no longer looking at her, but staring off into the distance. Following her gaze, Zoey saw Pete getting into his pickup in the nearby paved parking area.

"Excuse me," Laurie said distractedly, then hurried after Pete.

Her back to Zoey, she spoke to him through the open window of the pickup. Zoey couldn't hear what they were saying, but she could easily imagine what was going on. Pete was leaving his daughter's wedding before the bride and groom had even left. And he'd tried to sneak off without letting Laurie know.

Laurie gripped the open window, speaking in a low, urgent tone to Pete. He listened impatiently for a moment, then spoke sharply. Zoey could hear his slightly raised voice but couldn't make out the words. But his tone was crystal clear. He was angry. Turning away from Laurie, he started the car and drove off without looking back.

Laurie had stepped back slightly from the pickup when Pete turned on the ignition. She stood there for a moment, hands hanging limply at her sides, her expression helpless.

Zoey debated whether to go to her. She knew it would be better for Laurie's pride to think that no one had seen the humiliating exchange, but she wished she could comfort her. Glancing to the side, she saw that Cheryl had witnessed her father's departure. The expression on her face was very revealing. There was profound pity for her mother. Before Zoey could move, Cheryl hurried to Laurie's side and placed an arm around her shoulders. Mother and daughter walked off together.

So Cheryl does know what a jerk her father is, Zoey thought in surprise. She'd just assumed Cheryl's love for her father was blind. The girl was more perceptive than Zoey had given her credit for being. Zoey felt immense sympathy for Cheryl. She knew all too well what it was like to have to face the fact that your father isn't the hero you need to believe he is. But at least this meant that Laurie wasn't alone.

Suddenly, Zoey felt the need to get away from the laughing, happy crowd and be by herself. The situation with Pete had brought her own painful feelings about her father to the surface. She needed some solitude, if only for a few minutes, to pull herself together and push those unhappy memories back down deep inside, where she tried to keep them.

Assuming the chapel would be empty, she went inside. Even though it was deserted and silent, the atmosphere was serene and peaceful. It was exactly what she needed, Zoey thought, sinking down into a darkened side pew and staring out through the large window behind the altar. Though it was dark outside, the moon was shining, and she could make out the outline of the Tetons in the distance.

Zoey closed her eyes and willed herself to relax, to let go of the painful feelings that haunted her. Suddenly, she felt utterly exhausted. It had been a long day. And although it had been a happy one, it had also been more than a bit stressful.

Just as she was beginning to feel more at peace, she heard a sound. Opening her eyes, she saw Tyler standing before the altar and looking out through the window. He hadn't seen her and clearly assumed he was alone in the chapel. For once, his expression was open, unguarded, and what Zoey saw there tore at her heart. This was a man whose soul was in agony.

She knew she must speak, must let him know he was observed, but she felt like a voyeur. She would have given anything to be able to steal away and grant him the privacy he so clearly needed. She stood up slowly, murmuring in an infinitely gentle voice, "I'm sorry."

Whirling around, he glared at her as if she'd purposefully sneaked up on him.

"I was just sitting here, resting," she explained quickly. "I-I guess you didn't see me."

The anger that had flashed in his eyes dissolved. "No, I didn't." Then, before she could figure out how to make a graceful exit, he asked tersely, "What are you sorry about?"

Without stopping to censor herself, Zoey said honestly, "I'm sorry about your wife and baby. I know their funeral was held here."

His entire body stiffened, and for a moment he looked as if he would tell her it was none of her business. To her surprise, his guard came down just a little, and he said in a husky voice, "Yes. There were two caskets, my wife's and one for our daughter."

He shook his head slowly in disbelief. "It was so small, it didn't look real. She was so tiny, you see. In the hospital, they let me touch her briefly, while she was in the incubator. Her hand closed around my little finger, barely reaching around it. It was more like a doll's hand, than a real baby's. But she held on tight for an instant, and I knew . . . "

He finished in a hoarse whisper, "I knew she was fighting to live. And I wanted to help her, to give her my strength. But I couldn't . . . any more than I could help Sarah . . . "

His blue eyes met Zoey's gray ones. Laurie had told Zoey that when Sarah and the baby died Tyler had reacted as if a shutter had closed over his eyes and never opened again. But now, for an instant, the shutter was open, and Zoey could see into his mind and heart. What she saw was more touching than she could possibly have imagined. This was a man who had survived devastating loss only by the sheer force of his powerful will. But it had taken a terrible toll.

Her heart melted as she looked at him. She wanted to take him in her arms, as if he were a wounded child, and whisper, "It's all right. Don't be afraid. It's all right."

He said wonderingly, "I don't know why I told you that. I've never talked to anyone about it."

"I'm glad you did," she said in a voice that was infinitely tender and compassionate.

At that moment, there was a magical communion between them. A communion of shared feeling, of love and loss and a fragile hope of healing. For an instant, there was no wall between them. They were simply two people who had let down all the barriers.

Tyler closed his eyes and, when he looked at Zoey again, the shutter was down. The connection was broken.

"The reception is nearly over," he said matter-of-factly. "Cheryl and Chuck are about to leave. We'd better rejoin the others."

Zoey felt as if someone had thrown cold water on her. She hesitated, then, not knowing what else to do, turned and headed toward the door. Tyler waited while Zoey walked ahead of him down the aisle that Cheryl and Chuck had strode down so triumphantly only a couple of hours earlier.

Zoey felt bereft, as if for an instant she'd held something precious that had slipped out of her grasp. But she knew that something remarkable had just happened. And no matter how hard Tyler might try to deny it, to himself as well as to her, things had changed subtly yet profoundly between them. The wall he'd so carefully built around his heart was beginning to crumble, brick by brick.

11

Zoey was beginning to get used to ranch life and its early hours. She awoke early the next morning and lay in bed for awhile, thinking about the night before. So much had happened, from the emotional high of Cheryl's and Chuck's wedding ceremony, to the heartache of Pete's callous abandonment of Laurie. But, what had touched Zoey most deeply, was her brief, poignant conversation with Tyler in the chapel.

She went over every nuance of word and gesture and look, examining it as closely as she might examine a subject through her photography. But this time there had been no camera to provide a barrier between her and her feelings. The profound emotions she'd felt toward Tyler—immense compassion for his pain, an attraction so intense as to almost be physically painful—had been right there on the surface. Not deeply buried, as she tried to bury all her most vulnerable feelings.

It all came down to this—Tyler had loved deeply once, in a way that Zoey now recognized she had never done. Could he love that deeply again? No, she answered, probably not. How could anyone put that kind of love behind him and go on to someone new? But *if* he could, a tiny, persistent voice asked, if he could, then could he love someone like Zoey? And could she love him?

Running away from that dangerous question as if from a frightening apparition, Zoey bounded out of bed. After quickly dressing, she went down to Laurie's empty office to return the call from Carla that had come in the night before.

Carla answered on the first ring as if she'd been waiting by the phone. Zoey had barely said hello before Carla launched into a spirited diatribe. "Zoey! What are you still doing out there? You were supposed to be back for the Fourth. What on earth's going on? Did Brian call you? Don't be mad at me, he practically forced me to give him the number—"

"Carla!" Zoey interrupted sternly. "If you'll be quiet for a second, I'll answer your questions."

Carla took a deep breath, then went on in a calmer tone, "All right, first things first. Did Brian call?"

"Yes."

"Are you mad at me for giving him the number there?"

"No."

"What did he say?"

"He ordered me to come back—"

"*Ordered* you?!" Carla screeched into the phone.

Zoey went on calmly, "Yes, but I basically told him I don't follow orders. So I decided to stay for awhile longer, to teach him a lesson."

"Good for you, girl! I don't believe it. He actually *ordered* you. The jerk."

"Look, Carla, it's not important. I don't expect to see Brian again."

There was a thoughtful silence on Carla's end. Then she asked perceptively, "So, what does Tyler Ross look like, anyway?"

Zoey hesitated. "He's . . . attractive, I guess. Not that it matters."

"Uh-huh. I get it. We're talking Mel Gibson, with maybe a little Harrison Ford thrown in?"

"Hold it, you're jumping to conclusions. Tyler has *nothing* to do with my decision about Brian," Zoey insisted, trying to convince herself as well as Carla.

"Oh, right," Carla said, her voice dripping sarcasm. "You just *happened* to decide to dump your boyfriend of five years after a few days with this cowboy. But he has nothing to do with it."

"I thought you wanted me to break off with Brian," Zoey pointed out defensively.

"Hey, don't get me wrong, Zoey, I'm thrilled you're finally taking off your blinders where he's concerned. I'm just real curious about this Tyler Ross. After all, you could've decided to dump Brian and come right back. But you didn't. You're still out there, in the boondocks."

"I'm here for a practical reason," Zoey insisted.

"Does that reason look real good in tight jeans?" Carla asked mischievously.

Zoey's patience was running out. "Carla, I know this is hard for you, but try to get your mind off sex for a minute, okay?"

"Whatever you say, girl," Carla answered blithely.

Zoey forced her irritation aside and explained carefully, "The thing is, there are these horses. Wild mustangs. And they're not like anything you can possibly imagine. They're, well, they're just magnificent. And I want to photograph them. I *have* to photograph them."

"Horses. Sure."

"Carla!"

"What did I say?" Carla demanded feigning righteous indignation. "I'm agreeing with you."

"Anyway, I'm going to photograph them today, or tomorrow at the latest, and then I'm hopping on the next plane home."

"Really?"

"Really." Even as Zoey made the flat statement, she felt a deep unhappiness at the thought that in just a day or two she would be leaving this beautiful place. And Tyler.

A heavy sigh of disappointment came through the line. "So there's nothing going on with you and this cowboy?"

"N-no," Zoey stuttered.

"You don't sound real sure of that."

"Carla, I'm going to hang up now. But before I do, tell me one thing. How's Denise?"

"Fine. That is, if someone who throws up twice a day can be considered fine."

"Give her my best. And tell her I'll let her know when to pick me up at the airport."

"Okay."

"Good-bye, Carla," Zoey said firmly and she hung up the phone before Carla could ask any more awkward questions.

Zoey went into the kitchen and was pleased to see that she'd finally made it down to breakfast while everyone else was still there. Everyone except Cheryl, of course, who was off on her honeymoon in the mountains. Tyler and Jesse were sitting at the table finishing breakfast. Laurie was at the range pouring a cup of coffee from the pot that always seemed to be warming there.

"Good morning," Zoey said with forced cheerfulness.

"Morning," Tyler and Jesse responded. Tyler didn't quite meet her eyes. She sensed he felt uncomfortable about their brief but revealing conversation in the chapel the night before. In the harsh light of day, he was undoubtedly regretting letting his feelings show. She felt more than a little uncomfortable herself, but was determined not to give in to it.

Tyler turned to Jesse and said, "We'd better get the fence repaired. If that bull pushes hard enough, he could get through it. If he doesn't realize it now, he'll figure it out soon enough."

Jesse nodded briefly. "Yup."

"Let's get to it, then," Tyler said, and they left.

Zoey sat down at the table and studied Laurie with concern. She wasn't her usual cheerful self, and she looked tired and drawn, as if she hadn't slept well the night before. Zoey knew it wasn't just a result of the inevitable letdown following all the excitement of the wedding. She was undoubtedly depressed about Pete and his abrupt departure.

"What would you like for breakfast?" Laurie asked. "I can make bacon and eggs, or pancakes. There are no biscuits, though. Somehow I didn't get around to making any."

"Why don't you let me make breakfast," Zoey offered.

"Oh, no, you're a guest. And besides, I love to cook," Laurie insisted.

"Actually, I'd just like a cup of coffee," Zoey replied.

"That's all?"

"I'm not very hungry."

Laurie nodded in sympathy as she poured a cup of coffee for Zoey and handed it to her. "I know what you mean. I'm not very hungry, either. I guess I'm still tired from yesterday. It was a long day." She sat down heavily at the table and slowly sipped her own coffee.

"It was a beautiful wedding," Zoey said sincerely. "The most beautiful I think I've ever seen."

Laurie's expression brightened perceptibly. "Yes, it did turn out well, didn't it. I'm so glad for Cheryl's sake. As her mother, it was the last thing I could do for her before she starts her own separate life."

"I imagine you'll miss her," Zoey volunteered.

"Yes," Laurie admitted with a sigh. "*Very* much. Ever since she was born my life has revolved around her—taking care of her, making sure she had what she needed, worrying about her. Would she do okay in school? Would the boy she liked like her back?"

She gave Zoey a faint smile. "When you have a child someday, you'll see—they just take over your life. Everything else is a distant second, in terms of being a priority."

Zoey didn't respond. This wasn't the time to get into a

discussion with Laurie about her fears that she might never have children.

Laurie looked wistful as she continued, "It's going to feel strange, not having Cheryl to focus on. For so long, my days were defined by her schedule—meeting her at the bus stop, putting her to bed at night, getting her to 4-H Club meetings and school dances, waiting up till she was home from dates. Now, all I have to think about is myself. I haven't done that in a long, long time. It feels strange."

"You know," Zoey offered, "this could actually be a great opportunity for you."

Laurie looked at her with a puzzled expression. "How do you mean?"

"You've been a *wonderful* mother, Laurie. I can see it in your close relationship with Cheryl. She's turned out just great—a sweet, level-headed young woman with a real sense of direction in her life. But your job with her is done. Now, you can devote all your time and energy to yourself. Figure out what *you* want, and go for it."

Laurie's expression was rueful. "That's easier said than done. I'm not some kid with my future ahead of me."

Zoey leaned forward and spoke intently. "Listen to me, Laurie. You're a relatively young woman. You've still got half your life to live. The first half was spent taking care of others—Tyler, Cheryl, Pete. Why don't you spend the second half taking care of yourself?"

Laurie frowned. "I don't know. It seems selfish to only think of myself."

Zoey smiled encouragingly. "That's because you haven't had a lot of experience at it. I'll bet you can't remember a time when you didn't have to put someone else's needs first."

Laurie nodded in agreement. "That's true."

"There are a lot of years stretching out ahead of you, and you can make them very fulfilling ones, if you choose. It's all up to you."

Laurie looked uncertain but intrigued. "I wouldn't even know how to begin."

"Begin by taking a vacation and visiting me in New York. It's something you've always wanted to do." Zoey finished meaningfully, "Who knows where things may go from there?"

Her unspoken thought was that maybe, if Laurie got away from Jackson Hole and out of her normal routine, she would find the courage to make positive changes in her life—like leaving a bad marriage.

Laurie said, with real gratitude in her voice, "It's sweet of you to keep inviting me. I do appreciate it."

"I mean it, you know. Think about it. Don't just forget about it once I'm gone."

Laurie looked sad. "Now that the wedding's over, you'll be leaving soon, won't you?"

"I'm afraid so," Zoey admitted reluctantly. "It's time to go home. I never intended to stay this long. There's only one thing left to do."

"What's that?"

"Photograph the mustangs. I didn't tell you, but after you and Jesse left the other day, Tyler and I saw them. Oh, Laurie, they were so—" She stopped, at a loss for words. Finally, she said inadequately, "They were unlike anything I've ever seen. I *have* to photograph them. *If* Tyler will help me find them."

"He'll do it," Laurie said confidently. "I'll see to it. I have to admit, I don't share Tyler's crazy devotion to those horses, but if they'll keep you here awhile longer, then they're good for something."

She reached across the table to pat Zoey's hand. "You've become a good friend practically overnight. I'll miss you." She added pointedly, "We all will."

"I'm not sure about *all* of you," Zoey responded dryly.

Before Laurie could argue, they heard the sound of a car driving up to the front of the house. "I wonder who that could be," Laurie said getting up from the table. "I'm not expecting anyone, and we live too far out of town for casual visitors."

Zoey followed her out to the front porch and saw a standard, government-issue white sedan with Bureau of Land Management painted on the door. Two men stood near the car talking to Tyler, who faced them with evident dislike. One of the men, Zoey was surprised to see, was Hank Jamison, Tyler's ex-father-in-law.

"Uh-oh," Laurie said under her breath.

"What is it?" Zoey asked with concern.

"I don't know. But if Hank's actually setting foot on our land, it can't be good."

The officious-looking, middle-aged man with Jamison introduced himself to Tyler as Greg Goodwin. "I'm the new district manager with the BLM. I've come to notify you there's going to be a helicopter gather of mustangs in our local management area tomorrow for the Adopt-A-Horse Program."

"I see," Tyler said tightly. "And what exactly are you going to do with these horses?"

"They'll be put up for adoption, of course."

"Of course," Tyler repeated tightly. "And if a lot of those people who are supposedly adopting them for pets at $150 a head turn around and sell them to slaughterhouses for $1,000 a head, you don't give a damn, do you?"

Goodwin's pale countenance turned red with anger. "That's uncalled for, Ross! We need to do these roundups and adoptions to protect the range from overgrazing."

"To protect it for politically connected ranchers like Jamison, you mean," Tyler shot back, his expression grim. "You don't care what happens to the mustangs, as long as you get them off the range."

"I don't have to stand here and take this slander from you, Ross. I just came to notify you of the roundup."

"Why?" Tyler demanded.

"Because according to Mr. Jamison here, who's on our advisory board, you've interfered with these gathers in the past. I'm warning you not to try that this time."

Tyler glared at Jamison, and his voice was tight with

barely repressed anger. "Having you on the advisory board is like asking the fox to guard the henhouse! This is all part of your plan to get rid of the mustangs!"

Jamison was a big, strong, thoroughly intimidating-looking man. He gave Tyler a look that would have shriveled a lesser man. But, when he spoke, his voice was rigidly controlled. "Those horses are useless. You can let 'em run all over your land if you want, but there are better things to do with public land."

"Like providing more grazing land for your Trinity Ranch herd," Tyler replied scathingly.

Jamison didn't bother to deny the accusation. "Just stay out of our way tomorrow, Tyler—or pay the consequences," he finished in a thinly veiled threat.

Undeterred by the threat, Tyler responded, "Just remember, any horses on my land are off-limits."

Goodwin looked as if he wanted to respond, but when he looked at Tyler he thought better of it. With a curt nod, he got back in the car, followed by Jamison. A moment later, they were gone.

Tyler turned on his heel and headed quickly toward the barn.

"Oh, dear," Laurie murmured worriedly.

"What is it?" Zoey asked.

"I know what Tyler's gonna do. And there isn't a damn thing I can do to stop him."

Shaking her head, she turned and went back inside the house.

Zoey hesitated for only a moment before hurrying to the barn. She found Tyler saddling his horse.

"What are you going to do?" she asked without preamble.

He didn't look at her as he pulled the strap up tight. "I can't save all the mustangs in the management area. But if I can locate my herd today, then go out early tomorrow and drive them onto my land, they'll be safe. At least for now."

"I want to go with you," Zoey said determinedly.

"No," he responded automatically.

"Yes."

He turned to face her. "Why?"

"To photograph them. I've been wanting to do that since I saw them."

"Go up in the helicopter with Goodwin," Tyler said harshly. "You'll get some great shots of terrified mustangs being forced into a trap. Or driven to their death. You could probably get a lot of money for those pictures. Hell, they'll beat pictures of garbage any day."

"Stop it!" Zoey shouted trembling with anger. "Don't you dare put me in Goodwin's league! You know me better than that!"

Tyler's blue eyes blazed. "No, I don't! I don't know you at all, lady!"

"Well, you would if you'd give me a chance!"

Zoey stopped abruptly, realizing she'd just said more than she'd intended.

Tyler looked at her with a startled expression.

She forced herself to calm down and said evenly, "Look, I know you're mad as hell at Goodwin and Jamison. And you're worried about the mustangs. But none of that is my fault. So don't dump your misplaced anger on *me*."

Tyler stood there rigidly for a moment. Zoey held her breath, waiting for him to respond. Finally, his shoulders relaxed slightly, as did his grip on the reins. "You're right. I'm sorry."

Zoey could hardly believe it. She hadn't expected such abrupt and total capitulation. *You're right. I'm sorry.* Words that any woman would kill to hear from a man.

"Oh," she said in a small voice, unsure of how to respond.

Then she remembered another insult he'd casually thrown into the argument. "And don't you dare put down my work," she added. "I'm damn good at what I do."

If she was hoping for a second apology, she didn't get it. He asked tersely, "Why do you want to photograph the mustangs?"

"Because it's what I do," she answered simply. "I take pictures of things that have meaning for me. And I try to do it in such a way that the pictures will have meaning for the people who look at them."

"The mustangs mean something to you?" Tyler asked warily.

"Yes. Just as they mean something to you. I can't explain it or put it into words that would make sense. It's easier for me to say what I feel through my camera. But look at it this way—my photographs will make other people see what magnificent animals they are—maybe even help make a difference in how they're treated."

He stood there for a moment, clearly weighing how to respond. Zoey made up her mind that, no matter what Tyler said, she was going to photograph the mustangs. Even if she had to go out and find them by herself.

Finally, he said, "I don't know where they are, exactly. I could ride all day, and not find them. Most likely get back late tonight. It will be a long, hard day in the saddle. No ride in the park," he finished pointedly.

"I can handle it," she replied confidently.

He stared at her for a moment, then nodded slowly. "All right. Get your jacket; you'll need it this evening. And ask Laurie to throw together some food real quick."

Zoey raced back to the ranch house, gave Laurie the message about the food, then ran up to her bedroom to grab her jacket and her camera. Five minutes later, she was back in the barn with a tinfoil-wrapped package of sandwiches, a thermos of coffee, and some bottled water. Tyler had saddled her horse, a young roan mare with just enough spirit to not be boring to ride.

"Isn't Jesse coming?" Zoey asked as they set off.

"He's got work that needs to be done here. Besides, it doesn't take two of us to find the herd."

They rode for three hours before finally stopping to water the horses at a shallow stream. When Zoey dismounted, her derriere was already beginning to throb. Riding for an hour every Sunday on the paved trails of Central Park was nothing like this hard trot over rugged terrain. But Zoey wasn't about to complain. She didn't want Tyler to regret letting her accompany him. Still, she wished fervently they would find the herd soon.

As they stood by the stream while the horses drank deeply of the cool, clear water, Zoey listened to the murmur of water over the stones in the rocky creek bed. Red-winged blackbirds scolded from the willows and cottonwoods lining the banks. It was another hot, clear day, as all the days had been so far since she'd arrived in Jackson Hole. Once again, Zoey thought what an idyllic place this was. A place she would be leaving very soon. She felt a sharp stab of regret that had even more to do with the man standing beside her.

Then, in the distance, she heard a faint, sad *coo . . . coo . . . ahcoo.*

"What is that?" she asked Tyler, who was staring off into the distance lost in thought. Pulled out of his reverie, he answered, "A mourning dove."

"It sounds so plaintive."

"That's why it's called a mourning dove," Tyler responded. Then he added pensively, "Sometimes, especially if you're alone out here, it's the loneliest sound imaginable."

"What is it in mourning for?" Zoey asked watching his expression, searching for something she couldn't quite identify.

Tyler looked away, then shook his head. "Who knows?" He said tersely, "We'd better be going."

They rode for another hour, still without seeing any signs of the horses. They had long since left Tyler's ranch and were now on public land. Zoey was beginning to feel that she was seeing every square inch of Wyoming from horseback. Just when she thought her sore behind couldn't take any more, Tyler suggested they stop for lunch. She eagerly agreed.

They stopped at a place where a small spring bubbled up from underground amidst some boulders. "This is a natural hot spring," Tyler explained as they dismounted and tied the horses to a cottonwood tree.

"Is the water actually warm?" Zoey asked in surprise.

He nodded. "Feel it."

Going over to the spring, she bent down and ran her fingers through the water. The temperature was nearly as high as a hot tub. "This feels wonderful!" she exclaimed.

"It's nice in the fall, when the weather's brisk, to come out here and take a dip," Tyler said. "The contrast of the hot water and cold air is exhilarating."

Zoey could only imagine how great it would feel to soak her sore behind in that warm water.

Tyler had spread a small blanket on the ground and unwrapped the simple lunch Laurie had prepared. Zoey joined him, and couldn't suppress a groan as her sore bottom hit the ground.

To her dismay, Tyler grinned knowingly at her. "Feeling a little sore?"

"Just a little," she admitted with great reluctance.

He eyed her thoughtfully for a moment, then said, "Tell you what. We could both use a break. Go ahead and soak for a few minutes."

The prospect of sitting in that warm water was deliciously appealing. Then her spirits sank. "But I didn't bring a swimsuit," she pointed out.

There was a mischievous upturn to the corners of his firm mouth. "I wouldn't've thought a big-city woman like yourself would be so provincial."

"Well, I am," she shot back, irritated that he found her modesty so amusing.

"You mean to tell me, you and your friends don't go skinny-dipping in each other's hot tubs?"

He was really putting her on now, she knew. She gave him a scathing look. "No, we don't. And stop making fun of me."

He chuckled. "Tell you what, Zoey. There's another hot spring on the other side of those rocks. You take this one, I'll take that one, and we'll both get to relax for a few minutes—without offending each other's tender sensibilities," he finished dryly.

"All right," she agreed.

They ate quickly, then Tyler disappeared behind the boulders to his pool, and Zoey went to hers. She quickly stripped off her clothes and stepped into the shallow pool. Gently lowering herself into the hot water, she thought nothing in her life had ever felt so good. Her body relaxed, the muted throbbing in her bottom ceased, and she felt as though she wanted to stay there forever.

Closing her eyes, she let the summer sun beat down on her and the hot water swirl around her. As she sat there, she inevitably thought of Tyler, only a few yards away. To her dismay, she found herself picturing him in her mind sitting in the pool of hot, swirling water, naked. It was a disturbing image. She felt herself flush, and knew it wasn't from the warm water beating against her skin.

She called out, "Tyler!"

"What?" came the reply.

"Just checking."

She heard his husky laughter. "What's the matter, Zoey? Afraid I drowned, leaving you out here in the wilderness all by yourself?"

"*No.*"

Somehow, she wanted to keep him talking, to maintain the connection. "May I ask you something?"

"Depends on the question."

She heard a wariness in his voice and knew he was steeling himself for a personal inquiry. She asked, "What did you major in at Wyoming State?"

"Why on earth do you want to know that?"

"I'm curious. Humor me. It's not exactly restricted information."

"You're a strange lady, Zoey Donovan."

She didn't respond. After a moment, he answered, "English lit. Poetry, mainly."

"Poetry?" she asked in amazement.

"You weren't expecting that, were you?"

"No," she admitted.

"You expected maybe ag science, or something equally rustic."

"Of course not. It's just—" She stopped. He was absolutely right.

Sensing her chagrin, he went on good-naturedly, "It's all right. Now we're even for my crack about your photography."

She smiled to herself. Tyler Ross was an astonishing man.

"What kind of poetry do you like?" she asked.

He didn't answer immediately, and she knew he was debating what to say. Taste in poetry revealed a great deal about a person, and Tyler was reluctant to reveal any more about himself than was absolutely necessary.

Finally, he said slowly, his voice low and husky, "There's one poem, I forget the title, but the poet's name is Michael Blake. There's a line in it about a creature who is unbowed, whose eyes are 'full of God.' I liked that. I liked it a lot."

"It's beautiful," Zoey whispered.

Tyler went on, "It reminds me of the mustangs. Especially this one stallion, the Appaloosa who leads the herd."

"He's magnificent," Zoey agreed remembering the black Appaloosa she'd glimpsed for a brief, unforgettable moment the second day she was there.

Tyler went on, "You didn't get much of a look at him. But if you could see him up close, look into his eyes, you'd see what I mean."

She prayed she'd have the opportunity to see the stallion again. Not just because she wanted to photograph him, along with the other mustangs, but because she wanted to see what Tyler meant, to feel what he felt.

As if suddenly remembering why they were out there, Tyler said, "We're gonna have to leave in a minute. You might want to get out and dry off in the sun before getting dressed."

Zoey sighed in disappointment. She didn't want to leave. She wanted to sit in that soothing, hot spring and carry on this detached yet intimate conversation with Tyler forever. It took all her self-discipline to force herself to stand up and step out of the pool.

As she did so, she caught a glimpse of Tyler through a narrow opening in the boulders. He stood up, and water poured in tiny rivulets down his body. Zoey's breath caught in her throat at the sight of his lean, bronzed figure. Taut muscles rippled beneath glistening, wet skin. His broad chest tapered to narrow hips and long, sinewy thighs. His wet hair was swept back from his face and plastered against his head. The hard planes and angles of his face were even more pronounced than usual. Toughness was written in every rugged line of his body.

He started to turn, and Zoey quickly stepped back so that he wouldn't catch her staring at him. Without waiting to completely dry off, she hurriedly dressed. By the time Tyler came around the boulders, she was untying her horse.

"I'm ready," she said in a voice that sounded surprisingly normal considering the feelings raging inside her. She felt like an adolescent in the throes of her first experience with desire, and, no matter how much she told herself that Tyler was hardly the first attractive man she'd ever seen, she couldn't recall any other man who had affected her like this. Not even Brian in the beginning of their relationship, when she'd fallen in love with him.

Unaware of Zoey's inner turmoil, Tyler untied his own horse and mounted. He rode slightly ahead of her, as he'd done all day, since he knew in which direction to go and she didn't. Now, she was glad she was behind him, afraid her face would betray feelings she didn't want to begin to acknowledge to herself, let alone to Tyler.

An hour later, just as Zoey was beginning to despair of ever finding the mustangs, they came upon them grazing near a watering hole.

"Where there's water, there's mustangs," Tyler murmured in a low voice.

The roughly two dozen horses stood like statues in knee-high-to-a-colt sagebrush. Zoey was amazed by the range of colors—black, brown, white, red, pinto, and palomino. Mares, foals, and yearlings. And, off to one side standing guard, the black Appaloosa stallion, head up, nostrils sniffing the wind for telltale scents of predators.

"Can we get closer?" Zoey asked in a whisper.

"Not unless we want to scare them off."

When she had seen them run by a few days earlier, Zoey had thought they appeared to be like any other horse. Now, as she took out her camera, attached the telephoto lens, and looked at the herd through it, she saw distinctions. Long manes. Clipped ears. Muddy hides. Coarse heads and compact bodies adapted to winter survival in a harsh climate.

Restless spirits, they hovered like a heat wave over the grassy plain.

Turning the camera on the stallion, Zoey saw him arch his neck and prance protectively around his herd. Focusing on his head, she saw obsidian eyes in cavernous sockets, always watchful. Eyes "full of God," Tyler had quoted. Words so true, it took her breath away.

Mesmerized by their untamed beauty, Zoey took photograph after photograph. Foals nursing from mares, yearlings playfully nudging each other, colts and fillies lying in the warm sun, sleeping, their mothers hovering nearby. For the first time in years, Zoey found herself emotionally caught up in her work without giving any thought to what a gallery owner or critic might think of it. She felt a deep-seated sense of exhilaration, a joy in what she was doing without regard to commercial potential.

When something—some distant sound or scent—spooked them and they took off in a dust-trailing gallop toward a distant stand of sheltering trees, she captured that as well.

And then, seemingly in an instant, they were gone.

Zoey felt bereft and, like a child, wanted to call them back.

Tyler had taken out a topographical map and was marking their location on it. He put it away in his saddlebag, then looked at Zoey. For an instant, their eyes met and locked. She whispered in a voice ragged with worry, "Will they be all right?"

"They will if I have anything to say about it," Tyler insisted, his eyes hard, his mouth set in a tight line.

"Why would anyone want to destroy them?" Zoey asked knowing it was a futile question.

"Greed," Tyler snapped. Then, he said in a less angry voice, "We'd better be heading back. It'll be dark soon."

They rode back toward the ranch in silence, each caught up in his own thoughts. Zoey had decided she would go with Tyler the next day and help him drive the horses onto his range. She didn't say anything because she wasn't sure how he would react. She'd simply show up as he was leaving in the morning and announce that she was going.

In the Western sky the sun had slipped into a bank of clouds, setting them ablaze with color. The air was cooling and a breeze came up, bringing with it the scent of pine trees. In the gathering dusk, the Western thunderheads turned gold and coral above the Tetons. It was a breathtakingly spectacular scene. Zoey noted it dispassionately, almost oblivious to the beauty around her, because she was consumed with concern for the mustangs.

They'd been trotting at a good pace trying to make it back to the ranch house before dark, when suddenly Tyler pulled up and exclaimed harshly, "Son of a bitch!" Zoey reined in her horse and followed his grim gaze. Her eyes widened in horror, and what she saw sickened her.

12

Lying on the ground was a dead mare, her body battered and chewed up. Standing helplessly next to its mother was a spindly legged foal, no more than a few days old. It was so thin its ribs showed through its dull coat.

"Oh, my God," Zoey breathed fighting back the nausea rising within her.

Dismounting, Tyler handed Zoey his reins, then walked over to the foal, averting his eyes from the mare. Nothing could be done for that poor animal. The foal skittered away nervously, but was too weak to run. Murmuring reassuringly to the foal in the gentlest voice Zoey had ever heard from a man, he picked it up in his arms and carried it back to his horse.

He handed it to Zoey to hold while he mounted his horse, then took it from her, laying it across the saddle.

"Poor baby," Zoey said in a shaky voice as they set off again, tears stinging her eyes. "What will you do with it?" she asked Tyler.

"Take it back with us. Bottle feed it. Hope it'll make it."

"Do you think it'll be all right?" Zoey asked anxiously, hoping for reassurance.

"I don't know. Sometimes they make it, sometimes they don't." As the colt struggled in Tyler's strong arms, he allowed himself a hopeful smile. "This little guy seems like a fighter. Maybe he'll make it."

"What happened to his mother?"

His expression hardened. "She probably died as a direct result of the government's management program."

"You mean the Adopt-A-Horse Program?" Zoey asked in amazement.

"Exactly. Oh, I know it sounds good when you read about it in the newspaper. Wild horses collected in periodical roundups, processed by the BLM, and placed for adoption. Most of the time it works out, and the horses find homes. But that's because they take only the more desirable, younger horses. Bad-tempered, older stallions and less-attractive, older mares are turned back out onto the range. Mares like that one often get caught in the vicious fighting between the disproportionate number of studs over the mares, and their bodies litter the range."

Zoey was outraged. "But that's terrible! Why does the Bureau of Land Management allow it?"

"Maybe because they want them to die. It's one way of taking care of the problem the mustangs represent. They clash with ranchers for grazing land."

Zoey said furiously, "But it's so vicious. There must be a more humane way of dealing with them."

"They're not looking for humane methods. They're looking for effective ones," Tyler said bitterly.

He was silent for a moment, then he went on, "Ancient people worshiped these animals. Now they're hunted and killed for dog food. Or to be the daily special in some fancy European restaurant. Well, not *my* herd. Not tomorrow, anyway."

Zoey felt a profound respect for Tyler. He had deep-seated convictions and the courage to fight for them. His values, his moral convictions, were based on bedrock, not on the shifting sands of situational ethics, like so many of the people she knew in New York.

Looking at him gently but firmly cradling the pitifully weak foal in front of him, Zoey thought that the safest place in the world must be in Tyler's arms.

Night had fallen by the time they arrived at the ranch house. Laurie had been anxiously waiting for them, and hurried out to join them in the barn, along with Jesse, who took their horses and began unsaddling them.

"I was getting worried," Laurie admitted, anxiety written all over her drawn face. Then, noticing the foal, she exclaimed, "Oh, dear, not another little orphan!"

"Afraid so," Tyler answered.

He took the foal to a box stall and called back over his shoulder, "I'll need a bottle, Laurie."

"You got it," she responded and hurried back to the house.

A few minutes later, she returned with a large bottle filled with a milky liquid. Laurie and Zoey leaned over the side of the stall and watched while Tyler tried to get the foal to suck the nipple. At first, the foal shied away from the bottle. Zoey watched, taut with fear that he would be too weak and too frightened to drink. Tyler squirted some of the liquid into the foal's mouth. The foal swallowed automatically, then leaned forward for more. In a moment, he was enthusiastically pulling at the nipple.

Zoey watched, entranced, as Tyler fed the entire bottle to the foal. She had never seen a man be so gentle with a small, helpless thing. Remembering her initial view of Tyler as arrogant and hard, she couldn't help smiling to herself. In the chapel, she'd begun to see a whole other aspect of his character, the vulnerable man beneath the gruff facade. And on this remarkable day, he'd lowered the barriers even more, to reveal a surprisingly sensitive nature.

But it was also a decidedly passionate nature, and that passion was at times disturbing, at other times exciting.

When the foal had finished the bottle, he collapsed, exhausted, onto a pile of straw in the corner of the stall. "That'll keep him for awhile," Tyler said tiredly. "I'll come back out again in a couple of hours and give him some more." He looked at Laurie. "Can you feed him tomorrow?"

"Of course. Don't worry, I'll take good care of the little guy. Now, come in and have some dinner," Laurie urged. "It's all ready."

After a hearty dinner of chicken and dumplings, Tyler outlined the plan for the next day. He told Jesse he would need his help in rounding up the herd and bringing it onto his land. Jesse didn't argue; he merely nodded in agreement.

When Zoey announced that she was going with them, Jesse looked surprised and entirely disapproving. Tyler tried to talk Zoey out of what he called her wrongheaded determination to accompany them on what might prove to be a difficult trek. It wouldn't be easy to herd the mustangs onto his land. It could even by dangerous. But she was adamant. She had been deeply touched by the mustangs and was determined to help.

At one point, Jesse shook his head in frustration and said to Zoey, "You're as damned stubborn as he is," gesturing toward Tyler.

She grinned. "I'll take that as a compliment. I imagine there aren't many people who can match Tyler for stubbornness."

Jesse threw up his hands. "I give up. I'm goin' to bed. Sunup's gonna come early tomorrow."

When he had gone, Laurie said that she, too, was turning in. "I'll get up early to make breakfast," she told Tyler.

"Don't bother; we won't be hungry that early. Especially after such a late dinner tonight."

"Well, at least let me pack a big lunch for you."

"We won't need it, Laurie. If all goes well, we'll be back before lunchtime. Now that I know where the herd is, it won't take long to find them tomorrow," he said confidently.

Laurie looked worried. "Be careful, Ty."

"Aren't I always?" he asked with a disarming grin.

"*Never*. You are *never* careful," Laurie insisted.

Turning to Zoey, she said ruefully, "I don't suppose there's any hope of talking you out of this foolishness?"

"Nope," Zoey responded realizing she was beginning to sound like a Wyoming native.

Laurie sighed and shook her head. "You're both crazy."

When she was gone, Zoey and Tyler were left alone at the round oak table. They sat in surprisingly companionable silence, sipping the last of their after-dinner coffee. Finally, Tyler yawned and stretched and said, "I'm going to bed. Jesse's right; sunup will come early."

"I'd better go, too," Zoey agreed. "I'm still not used to getting up that early."

"You don't have to," he began, but she interrupted him.

"Don't start. My mind's made up. And don't think about sneaking out early without me. I'll just follow you, and probably get lost, and it'll all be your fault."

He grinned. "You probably would, at that."

They walked through the house and up the stairs together, Tyler turning off lights as they went. His bedroom was farther down the hall than Zoey's, and he paused at her door. He looked at her intently, as if he wanted to say something but couldn't quite bring himself to do so. She stood there looking up at him, suddenly aware of how quiet and still the house was with only the two of them still up.

"Yes?" she said, unaware that she'd spoken in a breathless whisper.

His blue eyes bore into her gray ones and his expression was intense but unreadable. "You don't understand how dangerous it could be tomorrow. We'll be going at a full-out gallop some of the time. Horses can trip and fall. The herd could turn unexpectedly, and you could be swallowed up in it. Don't go, Zoey. Stay here with Laurie, where it's safe."

She had wondered what it was she saw in those piercing blue eyes. Now she knew. It was a raw, gut-wrenching fear for her safety. A fear that went even deeper than Tyler wanted to acknowledge. She was immensely moved.

Instead of stubbornly arguing, as she'd done earlier, she tried to be sensible and reassuring. "Despite what you may think, I'm not foolhardy. I value my life too much to put myself in any real danger. I'll follow behind you and Jesse, staying out of your way. I know you'll have enough to worry about without worrying about me. So I won't be stupid and do anything that will make a problem for you. If I get too close to a risky situation, just tell me to back off, and I will."

"You'll do as I say?" he asked, clearly not believing her.

"Yes, because I know you're concerned for my safety."

He responded reluctantly, "All right. But I still wish you'd stay."

"I want to get more photographs of the mustangs. And I want to help you and Jesse, if I can. But I won't knowingly put my life in danger to do it. No picture is worth that."

"I wish I could trust you," Tyler said slowly.

"You can," Zoey said, realizing as she spoke that she meant a great deal more by those two simple words than she'd originally intended to suggest.

For a moment, he stood there, so close she could feel his warm breath on her face, could almost hear the beating of his heart. She held her breath, waiting for whatever was about to happen, wanting it, whatever it might be.

Then, dimly, in the distance, came the mournful howl of a coyote. The plaintive sound shattered the fragile moment. Tyler sighed and pulled back. Zoey let out the breath she'd been holding.

Without saying a word, he turned and headed down the hall toward his room. As Zoey went into her own room, firmly closing the door behind her, she knew that the wall was still there between them.

* * *

An hour later, Zoey lay in bed, unable to fall asleep. She was physically exhausted from the long, hard day spent in the saddle and emotionally drained from all that she'd experienced, yet she couldn't stop her mind from racing.

Zoey punched her pillow in frustration, then tried to close her eyes and relax. But it was no good. There was no way she could fall asleep.

Finally, she threw off the covers, got up, and walked out to the balcony. She looked out at the night sky studded with billions of stars. God, it was glorious. She would miss it when she returned to New York and the smoggy, hazy Manhattan sky.

A tiny pinpoint of light moved across the front yard toward the barn. It was a flashlight, she realized. Straining to see in the darkness, she made out a familiar tall, lean outline—Tyler. He disappeared into the barn. Probably going to give the foal his midnight feeding, Zoey knew.

Without giving herself time to think twice, she decided to join him. As she threw on her robe, she told herself she just wanted to check on the foal. She wouldn't be able to fall asleep until she'd assured herself he was all right. The fact that Tyler was out there had nothing to do with it.

Yeah, right. She could almost hear Carla's sarcastic response.

A moment later, Zoey opened the barn door and crept inside. The huge barn was dark save for an electric lantern hanging from a hook near the box stall where the foal lay. Moving toward the light, Zoey peered over the tall side of the stall and saw Tyler feeding the foal. It was sucking on the bottle as greedily as it had done only a couple of hours earlier.

Glancing up, Tyler started with surprise when he saw Zoey.

"Sorry," she apologized for startling him. "I just wanted to see how he was doing."

Tyler smiled. "As you can see, his appetite's healthy. And his breathing's stronger. I think he may make it."

"Good," Zoey said with real relief. She watched in silence for a moment, then asked curiously, "What will you name him?"

"I don't know. Hadn't thought of that. Why don't you choose a name," he offered.

Zoey was thrilled. "You mean it? I can choose?"

Tyler nodded. "As long as it's not dumb."

She bristled. "I would never choose a dumb name."

"Okay. So what do you have in mind?"

She thought hard for a moment. "Well, he's such a pretty reddish-brown color. What about Red?"

Tyler considered the suggestion. "Not bad." He nodded slowly. "Okay, Red it is."

Zoey beamed. "All right."

Watching Tyler caring for the foal, Zoey suddenly had an image of him as a little boy growing up surrounded by animals, roaming the nearly limitless expanse of the ranch, experiencing a kind of freedom she could only imagine.

"What are you thinking? he asked.

She realized he'd been watching her, too, even though he hadn't seemed to be.

She answered slowly, "I was just thinking how different our lives have been."

He frowned. "You mean because you live in a sophisticated, cultured environment and I live in the middle of nowhere."

A few days ago that's exactly what she would have meant. But not now. She hastened to explain, "No, not at all. I was just thinking that you must've grown up with so much freedom. You were probably riding as soon as you could walk."

"Sooner," he corrected her with a hint of a smile, his irritation dissolving.

"Exactly. Whereas I grew up in a small house in a small town, where there were always people around and it was impossible to ever find any solitude. And the only animals I ever knew were dogs and cats."

He looked at her curiously. "Why did you want to be alone?"

She shrugged, trying to minimize the significance of her words. "Oh, just to have time to think without always being interrupted."

"Ah, I see. A loner, were you?" Tyler teased.

"No way, not with two pesky little brothers always invading my space."

His blue eyes twinkled mischievously. "I can identify with them. *I* was the pesky little brother always invading Laurie's space."

"Well, on behalf of big sisters everywhere, I want you to know that you guys were a real pain in the ass."

Tyler chuckled. "I think all of us little brothers knew that—and didn't give a damn."

They were silent for a moment, then, to Zoey's surprise, Tyler repeated his earlier question. "Why did you want to be alone?"

She answered evasively, "I told you—to think about things."

"What things?"

She knew she couldn't put him off with a humorous response. She explained slowly, not quite meeting his look, "I was trying to make sense of life."

"What didn't make sense about it?" he pressed.

She couldn't avoid it any longer. Forcing herself to look at him, she said, "I didn't understand why one day my father was coming home from work, bringing me treats and saying he loved me, and the next day he was gone."

"He died?" Tyler asked automatically.

She shook her head. "No. He just . . . left."

"And you never saw him again?"

Again, she shook her head. But this time she didn't trust herself to speak.

Tyler said in a genuinely mystified voice, "I'll never understand how anyone can walk away from a child."

"Maybe it's easy if the child isn't all that lovable," Zoey replied in a barely audible voice.

But Tyler had heard her. He said sharply, "Stop it. Don't

do that to yourself. Whatever the reason for your father leaving, it had to do with *his* shortcomings, not yours."

Zoey looked away, embarrassed at having revealed her deepest insecurity.

After a moment, Tyler went on more gently, "I'm sorry. I didn't mean to sound so harsh. It's just, when you said that, it reminded me of when my mother died. For a long time, I thought somehow it must've been my fault. It was a terrible burden for a little kid to bear, and it took me years to get over it. I don't want you to feel that way. Okay?"

Finally, she looked at him again. "Okay," she whispered.

After a moment, he said thoughtfully, "Maybe we have more in common than I thought, both of us growing up without a parent."

"It sucks," Zoey said bluntly.

Tyler smiled grimly. "Big time," he agreed.

They looked at each other, feeling a connection that bridged the gulf between them. At that moment, it didn't matter what their differences were. All that mattered was that both understood exactly what it felt like to experience a terrible abandonment when they were very young and vulnerable.

The foal had finished the bottle. Reluctantly turning away from Zoey, Tyler set the empty bottle on a nearby ledge. Then he stepped out of the stall, closing the door firmly behind him. Facing Zoey, he eyed her intently for a moment.

Suddenly, she was very aware of her intimate attire. She told herself not to be silly, the T-shirt and chenille robe weren't nearly as provocative as the sexy negligee she'd gotten as a gift on her birthday. But the way Tyler was looking at her, she felt that she might as well have been wearing something that revealing.

It was cold in the barn, even with her robe on, and she hugged herself tightly.

Noticing this, Tyler motioned toward an old Indian blanket hanging over the side of the stall. "Wrap that around you. It'll keep out the cold."

The blanket was frayed at the edges, the once-bright colors badly faded. But it was well made, thick and heavy.

"The workmanship is beautiful," Zoey observed looking closely at the blanket, trying desperately to focus on anything other than Tyler.

"My great-grandmother made it," Tyler said with great pride.

She looked up at him. "Really? So it's a family heirloom."

"Passed down from generation to generation. In the house, there are other blankets she made, in better shape than this one. It's always been out here in the barn."

"Did you know your great-grandmother?" Zoey asked.

Tyler shook his head. "Unfortunately, no. She died when my father was a baby. But she left a vivid legacy—the blankets she made and the stories she told of her people's traditions."

"You mean legends like the one about the Pleiades?" Zoey asked remembering the fable Tyler had told her as they'd stood over a campfire together shortly after she arrived.

"Yes. And stories about her people's traditions. For instance, the bride price."

"Bride price. What's that?" Zoey asked in a breathless voice that sounded strangely unlike her own.

"A young man courting a young woman would take a horse to her teepee. If she accepted the horse—the price of her hand in marriage—they would be married."

"And if she said no?" Zoey asked teasingly.

"Well, at least he still had his horse," Tyler quipped.

Zoey laughed nervously. Then she asked in a soft voice, "What other traditions did she pass on?"

He hesitated, then began slowly, "There's a tradition about a blanket—"

"*This* blanket?"

"Any blanket, but it could be that one. When a young man would approach a young woman he was attracted to, if she liked him, she would open the blanket she was wearing, and invite him to share it. Then she would wrap it around the two of them together."

Tyler looked at Zoey intently, his blue eyes dancing with sly humor—and something more.

Zoey looked right back at him, her gaze unwavering.

Then he hugged himself and said with mock innocence, "It's mighty cold tonight."

She hesitated for one long, breathless moment. Everything hung in the balance. Past and future. Fear and desire. The world seemed to stop, and there wasn't a sound, not even the usual night sounds of owls calling, wind rustling through the trees, and horses neighing softly.

Zoey looked into those piercing blue eyes and suddenly her fears dissolved. This was Tyler. In his arms, she knew she had absolutely nothing to fear. Slowly, she opened the blanket.

13

He stepped forward, pressing his body against hers. She wrapped the blanket tightly around the two of them, and they kissed. For Zoey, it was a feeling of coming home again. For Tyler, it was a crumbling of the barriers to feeling and emotion.

His kiss was infinitely gentle at first, but it quickly became hard, possessive, passionate. His lips crushed hers, his tongue sought hers. It was as if he had been as starved as the foal and wanted to devour her. She never dreamed she could elicit such hunger in a man. Her body arched against his, her hands released their grip on the blanket, letting it fall to the ground, and she clung to him, responding with all her being.

She was borne away on a tide of desire so fierce it made anything she'd ever felt before seem like a pale imitation of passion. Tyler's kiss sent her senses reeling, left her knees weak, and made her heart race. Nothing, *nothing* in Zoey's life had prepared her for the impact of this moment. The tiny area of her mind still capable of thought registered the realization that this was how it should be when a man and a woman came together. Not tentative, but with absolute certainty. There would be a time for gentleness later. Now was a time for need and response to that need.

My God, Zoey thought as she drowned in Tyler's kiss. *My God.*

The kiss seemed to last an eternity. When Tyler finally pulled away, his hands cupped Zoey's face and he stared down at her as if seeing her for the first time. She gave a great shuddering sigh as he released her body from his possession. Slowly opening her eyes, she looked up into his.

Whether it was wise or foolish, right or wrong to give in to what she felt for this man, she knew only that there was no other way to find out if she could reach his heart, and to learn if what she felt for him was merely a powerful but passing attraction—or love.

He undressed her quickly, letting his fingers linger only for a fleeting, tantalizing moment at each newly exposed area of her body. The robe fell to the ground, then the T-shirt. Picking up his great-grandmother's blanket, Tyler led Zoey to a small mound of hay in a corner of the barn. He threw the blanket onto it. As he quickly undressed, Zoey lay down on the blanket and waited.

When he lay beside her, his fingers caressed the tight curls at the nape of her neck. With the other hand, he traced the smooth indentation at her waist and the gentle flare of her hips. Finally, he let his hand rest on the curve of her thigh.

"Oh, Tyler," Zoey whispered, her voice hoarse with desire.

His hand resting on her thigh moved up to flatten against her bare stomach. Her flesh, highly sensitive to his touch, tingled. The tightly curled tendril of desire that had lain deep within her since seeing him naked at the hot springs began to unfurl.

He stared at her wonderingly. "You feel so soft, so small and helpless. I'm afraid you'll break."

She smiled seductively. "Don't worry, love. I promise you, I'm not breakable."

"I've wanted to touch you like this since the first night you were here."

She glowed at the heady realization that he wanted her as much as she wanted him.

He rained tiny kisses down her throat and across her breasts. The gentle yet tantalizing gesture sent small shivers down her spine.

Her body arched invitingly against him. It was an instinctive reaction. She was no longer capable of thought. She could only respond automatically to his every touch, his every movement.

"Please," she whispered.

Then he kissed her eyes, her lips, her throat. He pulled her even tighter against him, so that her breasts pressed against his hard chest, her stomach against his stomach, their legs entwined.

Her first thought was how perfectly their bodies fit together. Then how hard and powerful he felt. Then how different were the textures of their skin.

Her every nerve ending was alive now, tingling with anticipation.

It had been so long since Tyler had felt this way. It went beyond need. It was . . . His mind groped for the means to express what he felt, stopping short of one word—love. He wanted to possess Zoey body and soul, to call her heart his own.

"Zoey, *my* Zoey," he murmured, his lips brushing her hair.

"Yours, Tyler. Only yours."

His body clamored for release from the almost-unbearable pressure of the passion he felt for her. It took all his considerable strength of will not to take her immediately. For her sake, he forced himself to still the clamor. For her sake, he forced himself to proceed with infinite patience, because his own satisfaction wasn't enough. He wanted it to be everything for her that it was for him.

"Tyler?" There was a questioning note in her dusky voice.

Looking down into her eyes, he could read the strain of almost unbearable passion in them. Her full mouth quivered, her gray eyes glinted quicksilver with desire.

"You're so beautiful," he whispered.

That delicious rosebud mouth curved almost imperceptibly in a smile of happiness. "Tell me that you want me, Tyler."

"I want you more than words can say," he answered, almost against his will.

Then her eyes opened wide in surprised pleasure as his fingertips began to explore the quivering inside of her thighs. Her legs flowered open in response to his irresistible touch. Her body seemed to melt beneath his hand, to become lighter than air.

She ran her fingers lightly over his body, wanting to feel every hard inch of it. Then she gripped his back, pulling him against her. He moved his body over hers, and her arms moved downward to encircle his waist. She kissed him softly, then with growing need.

He couldn't wait any longer. His hardness met her welcoming softness, and he was enveloped in it. Their bodies moved together in exquisite rhythm. It had been so long since Tyler had felt at one with another human being. The feeling of being part of this woman shattered his terrible isolation.

He heard her call his name over and over again. Then he sensed a tightening deep within her that seemed to flow from her being into his, erasing all barriers between them, crossing all boundaries. They clung to each other as all consciousness slipped beneath the dark surface of desire and fulfillment.

It was a long time before Zoey could think clearly again. Her first coherent thought was a simple one—the question she'd asked herself as he stepped into her arms had been answered.

Not just desire. Love.

Against all expectations, she had fallen in love with Tyler

Ross. And, unless she was completely mistaken, he had fallen equally in love with her.

She felt his warm, damp body next to hers. Felt his breath on her cheek, his arm lying gently across her breasts. An utterly feminine smile of contentment softened her mouth and lit her eyes.

So this is what love feels like, she thought in wonderment. *How could I have ever mistaken anything else for this feeling?*

Then a tiny flicker of uncertainty crossed her face. Had Tyler been as deeply affected by their lovemaking as she was? Emotionally as well as physically? Surely what she felt in her heart couldn't be a one-sided thing. He must feel it, too. But what if he didn't? What if she was just like the other women Laurie had mentioned—convenient?

She would have given anything to be a mind reader at that moment. If only he would tell her what he was thinking, share his feelings with her.

She had shared her deepest self with him, and she thought he'd done the same. Doors had opened between them, a connection was made, and something greater than their two individual selves had been created. If only for a fleeting moment.

Zoey had felt connected to Tyler as strongly as anything she'd ever felt. All her boundaries melted as she allowed herself to become completely vulnerable. Surely it had been the same for Tyler. Their souls had touched. That *must* be love.

She turned to face him, and their eyes met. She held her breath, waiting expectantly. His first words were more important than anything he might say later, when he'd had time to compose his thoughts and devise a calculated response.

Would those first words be an expression of love, or merely satisfaction with a mutual exchange of pleasure?

"Thank you," he whispered. "For making me feel again."

She wanted to cry with relief and happiness.

Then his expression changed from warmth to something she couldn't quite identify. Pulling away, he began to get dressed.

"Don't do this," she pleaded. "Don't break the connection we've made."

He turned back to her, and now she clearly saw guilt in his countenance. "It's not you, Zoey. It's me, when I think how I got you out here under false pretenses, letting you think I was looking for a wife when the truth was I didn't want anything to do with you." He shook his head, angry at himself. "I used you to get Laurie off my back. I was a complete jerk."

Without thinking, she blurted out, "It's okay, I was doing the same thing. I was using you to make my boyfriend jealous . . . "

Her words trailed off as she saw the stunned look on his face and belatedly realized this was no way to break such a hard, unexpected truth to him.

His voice, so warm only an instant earlier, was cold. "What do you mean?"

She would have given anything to take back that rushed, awkward confession, but it was too late. There was no going back. She had to tell him everything and hope he would understand. And forgive. Just as she was more than willing to forgive him for being less than honest initially.

"I-I've been dating someone for-for awhile. It was quite serious, but he wouldn't make a commitment. We argued about it, and-and I ended up answering your ad."

With each word, his expression hardened even more. She could feel herself digging her own grave, but had absolutely no idea how to extricate herself. Even if she could have thought of a plausible lie, she could no longer do that. They *had* to be honest with each other. If they didn't have the truth, then they had nothing.

"I didn't know you then," she whispered unhappily.

"And that made it all right to use me?" he demanded. Every ounce of feeling he'd had for her only a moment earlier seemed gone.

"No, it didn't make it all right! As soon as I met you, I felt terrible. I felt so guilty that I wanted to leave right away. Then, when I stayed, I wanted to tell you the truth, but I didn't know how."

"That's who called the other day, isn't it?" Tyler said suddenly putting it all together. "Did your little plan work? Is Brian jealous?"

"I don't know! I don't care about him!"

"My, your affections are fleeting, aren't they?"

"No!" Now Zoey was furious, too. "And, anyway, who are you to accuse me of anything? You used me, too. At least I'm willing to forgive you."

"That's real big of you," Tyler snapped.

He'd dressed, and now he pulled on his boots. Feeling intensely uncomfortable and vulnerable in her nakedness, Zoey threw on her robe. She wrapped her arms around herself to still the trembling of her body.

She and Tyler stood facing each other.

"Tell me something, Ms. Donovan," Tyler said, his eyes ice-cold and his voice even harder than it had been when he'd argued with Jamison and Goodwin earlier that day. "Was fucking me part of the plan? Were you gonna share that little tidbit with your boyfriend?

She slapped him. She'd never slapped anyone in her life, but her hand seemed to fly out automatically and connect hard with his face. It left an ugly red mark that was nothing compared to the ugliness she felt inside at his cruel accusation.

The violent, unthinking action stunned both of them. Suddenly, as Tyler and Zoey stood there glaring at each other, she realized the truth.

She said slowly, "This isn't about Brian, or even whether or not I was honest. It's about Sarah."

Tyler's expression was more pained than when she'd slapped him. "*Don't*," he whispered.

"I know it hurts," she said with infinite tenderness, "but we have to talk about it. We have to talk about Sarah."

Tyler said flatly, "Sarah would never have lied to me."

Without saying another word, he turned on his heel and strode out of the barn.

Zoey watched him leave, aware there was absolutely nothing she could say or do to stop him. Feeling her heart break and knowing that, without Tyler's love, it would never heal.

14

Zoey slept fitfully and was up and dressed while it was still dark. Now, through the bedroom window, she gazed out at the most magnificent sunrise she had ever seen. Wispy clouds tinged with gold and orange drifted across a deep-lavender sky. Sunup. Time to go after the mustangs. And time to face Tyler.

During the long, wakeful hours of the dark and dreary night, she'd tried desperately to think of some way of reaching him, of getting past his anger and disappointment, and making him understand that she hadn't meant to hurt him, that she loved him.

When had it happened? she wondered. When they made love the night before? No, before that. She wouldn't have made love to Tyler if she hadn't already fallen in love with him. Was it when she saw him at the hot springs and felt so drawn to him she could barely catch her breath? No, earlier still.

And then she knew the exact moment when she'd realized she was in love with this man, though she hadn't acknowledged it at the time. They were standing in the chapel and he was talking about his baby daughter's heartbreaking struggle to live and his futile wish that he could have given her his strength.

In that place of worship, their souls touched. It had only lasted for a moment. Then, frightened by the vulnerability they had each revealed, the masks were back up again, and they turned away from each other. But, in that instant, when Tyler had allowed himself to trust Zoey enough to reveal himself to her, she had fallen deeply, irrevocably in love with him.

And he had fallen in love with her. But he wouldn't let himself love her because he saw it as a betrayal of Sarah's memory and what he had felt for her. Oh, he probably wasn't consciously aware of it, Zoey knew. He told himself Zoey's dishonesty came between them. But she knew better. That was just a convenient excuse to once more bury himself emotionally in the past.

Looking out at the ever-lightening sky, Zoey realized she'd come full circle. She was back where she'd been off and on during the long, sleepless night. The same question haunted her—how to get Tyler to forgive her. And, more importantly, how to get him to let go of the past and move toward the future. A future that Zoey hoped desperately would include her.

She had wished on a blue moon and to her amazement had found love. But finding it and keeping it were separate challenges.

As she went downstairs, she steeled herself for her initial confrontation with Tyler. Even before their argument last night, he hadn't wanted her to go with him and Jesse. He would be all the more adamant about it now. But, as Jesse had recognized, Zoey was just as stubborn as Tyler. She was going with them. Even if she had to follow behind.

The kitchen was empty, but the perennial pot of coffee was warming on the stove, so Zoey knew Laurie must be up. Buttoning her denim jacket against the early morning chill and hoisting the strap of her camera bag onto her shoulder, Zoey made her way toward the barn. As she expected, she found Laurie, Tyler, and Jesse there. Laurie was cupping a mug of coffee in her hands to warm them and watching with obvious disapproval as Tyler and Jesse saddled their horses.

"We should be back by noon," Tyler was saying to Laurie.

His sister didn't respond.

When Zoey came in, Tyler glanced up at her and frowned in surprise and irritation. Obviously, he hadn't expected, nor wanted, Zoey to show up after what had happened between them the night before.

There was so much Zoey wanted to say to him. That she understood why the mustangs meant so much to him. That she knew he related to them because he, too, was an untamed spirit. And, most poignantly, that part of his determination to save them stemmed from his inability to save his wife and child.

But she couldn't say any of those things to him. Instead, before he could tell her to get the hell out of there, Zoey said flatly, "I'm going, too."

Tyler turned back to his horse and threw over his shoulder in a deceptively calm voice, "No, you're not."

"You can't stop me." To prove it, Zoey went over to the horse she'd ridden the day before and began saddling it.

Laurie watched her intently, clearly aware that something had changed, and not for the better, between Tyler and Zoey.

As Zoey saddled her horse, she went on, "I said I won't get in the way, and I meant it. But I'm going. I'm going to photograph the mustangs. And I'm going to help you and Jesse in any way I can."

"You can't help," Tyler insisted in a hard tone that brooked no argument.

Jesse didn't say anything, but he nodded agreement.

Laurie asked with concern evident in her look and her voice, "Zoey, are you sure?"

Zoey's horse was saddled now. She swung up into the saddle and repeated stubbornly, "I'm going."

Both Laurie and Jesse looked to Tyler to respond. To their surprise, he didn't say a word. Mounting his horse, he said tersely to Jesse, "Let's go."

Without a backward glance at Zoey, he rode out of the barn. Jesse followed right behind, with Zoey a few yards back. Laurie watched them leave, worry etched in every line of her face.

They rode in the same direction that Tyler and Zoey had gone the day before. But this time they knew exactly where to locate the herd, and they made a beeline for that spot. By the time dawn had turned to full daylight, they found the herd grazing near a stream not far from the watering hole where they'd been on the previous day. They stopped far enough away so that the horses wouldn't hear them, and they made certain they stayed downwind of the herd.

Not once had Tyler turned and looked at Zoey. He occasionally threw a brief comment at Jesse, but he behaved as if Zoey didn't exist. Jesse took his cue from Tyler and didn't speak to Zoey, either. But he did periodically look back to make sure she wasn't lagging behind and in danger of getting lost.

Tyler and Jesse consulted each other as to the best way to drive the herd back to Tyler's land. As they talked in low tones, Zoey took out her camera and got several more shots of the horses. Seeing them again, in all their magnificence, she found herself praying they could be saved. If anyone could do it, she knew Tyler could. Despite the unhappiness between them, she had an enormous respect for his strength and determination.

Finally, for the first time since they'd set out, Tyler turned and faced Zoey. He said in a whisper, "We're going to drive them back this way. Ride up onto that rise over there, and stay there until the herd is past you. Whatever happens, don't get caught up in it. Got it?"

Zoey nodded. She didn't mind his hard tone, understanding that he was only trying to make sure she would be safe.

She headed toward the slight rise in the distance while Tyler and Jesse split up and circled the herd from opposite sides. Waving their lariats in the air and whooping and hollering, they got the herd's attention. Before the stallion could gather the herd and head it in another direction, the two men had startled the mustangs into running toward the ranch.

As the horses ran past her, Zoey got shot after shot of them. When they were well away, she put away her camera and began following, making certain she kept a safe distance between herself and the herd. She had meant it when she told Tyler she didn't intend to get in the way. She knew he had enough to deal with without having to look out for her.

They were all going at a slow gallop—the herd, Tyler, Jesse, and Zoey. This kind of hard riding over unfamiliar terrain took all her concentration, and she was a little nervous. But it was going well. The herd was rapidly heading toward Tyler's land. At this rate, in only a few minutes they would be on safe ground.

And then it happened. One minute there was no sound but the pounding of the mustangs' hooves on the hard ground, and the next there was an ominous whirring noise in the distance that grew louder as it came closer. Pulling up, Zoey looked around in fear and confusion. Then she saw it—a helicopter with Bureau of Land Management written on its side. A vicious bird of prey, it swooped down low over the herd, turning the terrified animals and sending them into a dust-roiling, full-out gallop in a different direction.

Zoey watched as Tyler and Jesse tried desperately to turn the herd. But they couldn't. They were swallowed up by the pell-mell rush toward a box canyon.

As they got closer to the canyon, Zoey saw that a fence trap had been erected there. A moment later, the horses were in the trap and came to a shuddering halt. The horses were rearing and squealing, pacing and head-butting, milling around like an outlaw gang holed up in some open-air jail cell.

The helicopter landed nearby, and the BLM manager, Greg Goodwin, got out and headed toward the trap.

In the distance, Zoey saw a huge livestock trailer heading across a rough dirt road toward the trap. Soon, it had arrived. Zoey wasn't at all surprised to see Hank Jamison step out and head toward Goodwin.

Zoey's gaze immediately went to Tyler. He and Jesse were on the periphery of the trap and clearly had no idea what to do. Zoey felt a tight knot in the pit of her stomach. It was over. They'd lost. The horses hadn't been saved. And Tyler, she knew, would never forgive himself.

She saw him lean over and say something to Jesse, then dismount. Jesse took his horse's reins while Tyler, carrying his lariat and a rope halter, quickly headed toward the Appaloosa stallion. Zoey watched as Tyler roped the stallion, then threw the halter over his head. A moment later, he'd swung up onto the stallion. The furious, terrified animal bucked and kicked, but Tyler stayed on, his legs gripping the horse's flanks.

And then Zoey understood. Tyler knew there was only one way to get the confused and frightened herd out of the trap. They would automatically follow the lead of the stallion.

After a minute of violent bucking, with the stallion arching his back and kicking out with his legs, he began to tire. As the bucking subsided, Tyler headed the stallion away from the trap and toward his land, leading the herd behind him. Jesse hurried after them with Tyler's horse.

Zoey heard Goodwin shout an obscenity, then rush back toward the helicopter. Jamison merely stared in impotent fury as the herd disappeared in the distance.

Before Jamison could get back in the truck, Zoey rode over to him. Dismounting, she confronted him.

"Wait!" she shouted as he opened the door to the truck. He turned and looked at her as if she were crazy. She knew she might well be. But Zoey sensed he held the key to Tyler's salvation. Laurie had said she didn't think Tyler would ever stop blaming himself for Sarah's death as long as Jamison blamed him. Zoey had to try to get through to him.

"You've got to stop punishing Tyler for Sarah's death," Zoey began without preamble.

Jamison was thoroughly confused. "Who the hell are you?" he demanded.

He was an intimidating bear of a man, but Zoey refused to back down. "I'm . . . a friend of Tyler's."

As soon as she gave the vague identification, his eyes narrowed thoughtfully, and she could tell he remembered seeing her at the ranch house. His frown deepened. Any friend of Tyler's was no one Hank Jamison wanted to know. Turning his back on Zoey, he started to get in the truck.

"Damn it, listen to me!" Zoey shouted. "Tyler didn't know how bad her asthma was! He didn't know that pregnancy could kill her!"

Jamison turned to face her again. Now his expression was even more angry. If Zoey hadn't been desperate to help Tyler, she would have cowered in the face of such fury.

"I don't know who you are, young lady, and I don't give a damn about you! But I'm warning you—don't say another word about my daughter!"

Forcing herself not to tremble before him, Zoey took a deep breath to steady her voice and went on, "Sarah ignored her doctor's warnings and got pregnant because she wanted more than anything to have a child. For herself and for Tyler."

"He didn't care about Sarah!" Jamison roared. "He made her do something he knew was dangerous!"

Zoey shook her head slowly. "No. Tyler would have never knowingly put her in danger. He loved her too much. And she loved him so much that she wanted to give him what he wanted most—a child." She hesitated, then asked in a gentle voice, "Haven't you ever loved someone that much?

When Jamison didn't answer, Zoey went on, "I think you have. I think you loved your daughter that much. And that's why you blame Tyler and feed on your rage toward him. Because it's less painful to feel anger than to accept your unbearable sense of loss."

Jamison's eyes glistened with unshed tears. He said in a hoarse voice, "You don't know anything about it."

Zoey responded in a helpless whisper, "I know how much Sarah loved Tyler because that's how much I love him. And I know he could love me, if he could only forgive himself for her death. But he can't do that as long as you blame him. Please," she begged, "please stop hating him. He doesn't deserve it."

She knew it was hopeless. There was no way to reason with this bitter man. Still, she held her breath, waiting for his response, hoping against hope that he could look into his heart and find forgiveness rather than blame.

But he didn't speak. He simply turned his back on Zoey and got into the truck. Through the open window, she heard him order the driver to leave.

She knew she couldn't stand there and let herself fall apart. Forcing back the tears that stung her eyes, she mounted her horse and set off in the direction Tyler had gone with the herd.

Urging her horse into a full gallop, she eventually caught up with the herd. She was on slightly higher ground, and she saw them below her, Tyler still on the stallion, the herd following, and Jesse bringing up the rear.

Above them, the helicopter swooped low and tried to turn the herd. But Tyler, exhibiting consummate horsemanship, evaded the craft's every maneuver leaping over gullies, sending sprays of water high into the air as they splashed through shallow streams, racing through a thick stand of trees, the horses a blur of red, black, brown, and white.

Tyler, whipped by branches, barely avoided being knocked off the stallion.

And then, the brink. A near-vertical incline. In a seemingly impossible, death-defying move, Tyler and the stallion leapt out into space. Man and horse sailed down the fall line, with the sure-footed mustangs following close behind.

And all the while the helicopter continued diving at the horses.

Just when it looked to Zoey as if the helicopter might succeed in turning the herd, they reached the narrow canyon on Tyler's land where Zoey had first seen the herd, and the helicopter had to pull up abruptly to avoid slamming into the canyon walls.

The helicopter circled for a moment, and Zoey could sense Goodwin's frustration. Finally, accepting defeat, it turned and flew away.

Zoey wanted to shout for joy. But the thrill of victory died within her as she saw the stallion stumble and fall. Horse and rider went down. The herd parted around the fallen stallion and continued on down the canyon.

With a sickening feeling in the pit of her stomach, Zoey urged her horse down the hillside toward Tyler, who was pulling himself to his feet. Next to him, the stallion struggled to rise but couldn't. One foreleg dangled uselessly, and the animal screamed in pain.

Jesse got to him first. Zoey saw Jesse hesitate, then pull his rifle from its sheath. He held it out to Tyler. Tyler just looked at him for a moment, then, with extreme reluctance, accepted the rifle.

As long as she lived, Zoey knew she would never forget the look on Tyler's face as, for one awful moment, he agonized over what he must do. Then, knowing there was no choice, he cocked the rifle, took careful aim, and fired.

It only took one shot. The stallion's cries of agony were silenced. His body lay deathly still.

Tyler stood there staring helplessly at the magnificent animal he'd worshiped as Zoey came riding up. She jumped off her horse and hurried over to him.

Seeing his expression of utter devastation, she felt heartsick for him. "Oh, my God, I'm so sorry," she said reaching out toward him.

He jerked away from her as if he couldn't bear her touch. It was worse than a slap in the face to Zoey. "Please," she whispered, "don't shut me out. Let me in."

"Go back to the ranch!" he ordered, his voice harsh.

"Tyler—"

"I don't want you here! Go away!"

She died inside. The very core of her being shriveled up and died. Turning away, she stumbled back to her horse, mounted it, and rode off as fast as she could go.

She was oblivious to the half-hour ride to the ranch. Her horse automatically headed for home, and suddenly they were there. Zoey awoke to consciousness, as if from a dream, and had no recollection of how they'd gotten there. Doing what must be done, she went through the motions of unsaddling the horse, walking it for a few minutes to allow it to cool down, then turning it loose in the corral.

Then, still operating on autopilot, she walked toward the house. Only then did she notice the car in the driveway. A car with rental agency plates. Uninterested, she barely registered the fact as she opened the front door and entered the house.

And immediately came to a dead halt.

Sitting in the living room were an immensely uncomfortable-looking Laurie—and Brian. Both of them rose as Zoey came into the room.

"Hello, Zoey," Brian said politely. His voice lacked its usual confident tone.

Laurie cleared her throat nervously and explained, "Your, um, friend, just arrived. I told him you'd be back soon and invited him to wait. Did-did everything go okay?"

Zoey nodded, unable, for the moment, to speak.

"Where's Tyler?" Laurie asked, the two simple words heavy with questions and implications.

Zoey said in a voice that sounded as if it came from someone else, "He and Jesse are with the herd. I came on ahead."

"Why don't I go make some coffee?" Laurie said trying unsuccessfully to sound casual, as if this were a perfectly normal social situation.

She hurried from the room, and Zoey knew that the coffee was just an excuse to let the two of them have some time alone. Time to sort out a sticky situation.

Before Zoey could speak, Brian said quickly, as if repeating a well-rehearsed speech, "I know I have no right to be here. I have no rights at all where you're concerned. I relinquished them, if I ever even had them to begin with, when I didn't do what I needed to do to keep you in New York."

"Brian," Zoey began in a tired voice, wanting to stop his apology.

But he interrupted eagerly, "No, let me finish. Please." Walking over to her, he put his hands on her shoulders and looked down at her. "I've done a lot of thinking over the past few days. At first I didn't really believe you'd leave. Then when you did, I was sure you'd turn around and come right back. I thought you were just trying to make me jealous, you see."

I was, Zoey thought dully. *Not that it matters now. Nothing matters now.*

Brian frowned and shook his head slowly. "I was a damn fool, Zoey. I thought you were playing games. It took me much too long to realize you were perfectly serious, and that I might very well lose you. Maybe not to this guy, but to someone, someday."

She couldn't meet his look. Pulling away, she collapsed onto the sofa, feeling more physically and emotionally exhausted than she'd ever felt in her life.

Sitting beside her, Brian finished in a heartfelt voice, "I love you, Zoey. I've missed you more than words can say. I want to do whatever I have to do to keep you with me always."

She looked up at him then, unsure if he meant what she thought he meant.

He smiled the brilliant, dazzling smile that had won her heart five years earlier. "I'm asking you to marry me," he said.

She was utterly silent for a moment. Then, she said slowly, "But what about children?"

"I'm willing to have *one*, if that's all right with you. I honestly don't think our hectic work schedules will accommodate a larger family. Do you?"

No, she thought. *Probably not.*

He waited, and, when she didn't respond, he went on uncertainly, "Well, what do you say? Will you marry me?"

She'd waited five long years to hear those words. It was what she'd wanted more than anything. Not only did he want to marry her, he was willing to have children. *One* child, she corrected herself. Well, that was better than none at all, she thought.

Looking at Brian, Zoey was surprised to see how nervous he was. Normally cool and confident, now he was genuinely worried that she wouldn't accept his belated proposal. His vulnerability made him infinitely more appealing than his bravado had ever done.

"I love you," he repeated. "I never realized how much I loved you, until you were gone. My life is empty without you. Please say you'll marry me."

What happens when you get everything you ever wanted? You live happily ever after.

The old refrain echoed in Zoey's confused, unhappy mind. She told herself this was what she wanted—to marry Brian, to have a family together.

And besides, a vicious little voice deep inside her said, *Tyler doesn't want you.*

He would have turned to Sarah for comfort after being forced to kill the thing he loved, the stallion. But he didn't turn to Zoey. Sarah had belonged there. Zoey didn't.

She looked at Brian. "I'll marry you," she said.

His handsome face lit up with relief and joy. As he took her in his arms and hugged her tightly, she told herself they would live happily ever after.

A few minutes later, Zoey had packed her few belongings and Brian had carried them to the car. While he waited behind the driver's seat, Zoey stood on the porch saying good-bye to Laurie. It was much harder than she'd realized it would be. In only a week, they'd become good friends, and Zoey had come to care deeply for the kind, sad Laurie.

"Are you sure you're doing the right thing?" Laurie asked unhappily.

No, Zoey thought. Aloud, she said, "Yes." Then, she added, as much to herself as Laurie, "Brian loves me. That's reality. Anything else is a fantasy that can never come true. You do know that, don't you?"

Laurie might know it, but she didn't want to accept it. "It's just that I thought maybe you and Tyler—"

"No," Zoey insisted in a voice that was harder than she'd intended it to be.

Laurie sighed heavily. "I do want you to be happy, Zoey."

Zoey smiled with real warmth. "I know. I think I will be. I've known Brian a long time, and we're very much alike. We're right for each other, in a way that Tyler and I would never be."

Laurie didn't argue. But she didn't look entirely convinced, either.

Zoey went on in a rush, "Look, I meant what I said about you staying with me in New York. Please come. As soon as possible. I'll show you around, and we'll have a wonderful time."

Laurie said hesitantly, "Maybe . . . some time. Anyway, thanks for inviting me."

Zoey knew Laurie wouldn't come. Making one last

attempt to reach her, she said urgently, "It isn't too late. Please believe that."

Laurie merely shook her head helplessly.

Impulsively, Zoey reached out and hugged her. "Thanks for making me feel welcome," she whispered.

"I'll miss you," Laurie responded in a voice choked with emotion.

Knowing that she would burst into tears if she didn't get away from there quickly, Zoey turned and hurried toward the car. As she and Brian pulled away, she waved good-bye to Laurie, who stood watching from the porch.

Zoey turned her gaze toward the direction that Tyler would come riding in from, but there was only empty pastureland and, in the distance, the mountains. No rider appeared. She craned her neck to get a final, wistful glimpse of the ranch house, then they rounded a bend in the road, and it was gone.

Zoey had been gone scant minutes when Tyler and Jesse came riding in. Tyler's expression was grim and he was utterly silent. He hadn't said one word to Jesse on the ride back. Jesse knew better than to try to bridge the silence. When they reached the barn and dismounted, he automatically took their horses' reins and led them into the barn.

As Tyler started across the yard toward the house, Laurie, who'd been watching for him from the front porch, came running up to him. As soon as she saw his drawn expression, she knew something terrible had happened.

"What is it? What happened?" she asked, as she'd done so many times when Tyler was growing up and there had been mishaps, both large and small.

He stared at her for a moment as if unsure of how to answer the question. Finally, he murmured in an exhausted voice, "We got the herd onto our land. But the stallion went down. Broken leg. I had to shoot him."

"Oh, Ty, I'm so sorry," Laurie breathed. She knew what this meant to him, how devastating the loss must be. She longed to comfort him as she'd done when he was a little boy. But he was a grown man now, and stubbornly determined to act as if he didn't need comforting.

So, instead of embracing him, she merely reached out and lightly touched his shoulder, hoping the brief physical contact would make him feel less alone in his unhappiness.

Tyler went on dully, "I came back to get some equipment so I can bury him."

Laurie understood the implications of this terse statement. Tyler didn't want vultures and others to get at the horse.

Sad as the situation was, there was something more urgent. Laurie said quickly, "Zoey's gone."

Tyler glanced around quickly and saw that both pickups were in the driveway. Turning back to Laurie, he looked at her quizzically. "What do you mean? How did she leave?"

This was the hard part. Swallowing her nervousness, Laurie answered bluntly, "Her boyfriend came to get her."

Before Tyler could explode, Laurie went on in a rush, "But they just left a few minutes ago. If you hurry, you could catch them at the airport before their plane leaves."

"No."

"But, Ty, she didn't want to go, I know she didn't, and if you'd just go after her and tell her how you feel—"

For the first time in his life Tyler spoke harshly to Laurie. "Damn it, I'm not going after her! And I don't feel anything for her! You got that?!"

Laurie was stunned. Even when Sarah and the baby had died, and Tyler was shattered, he hadn't taken his rage out on Laurie. She knew this meant his feelings for Zoey went even deeper than she had imagined.

Laurie said calmly, "She loves you, Ty. And you love her. Any fool can see it."

"She was just using me, Laurie!" Tyler snapped. "She wanted to make her boyfriend jealous, and apparently it worked!"

"Maybe that's how it was in the beginning," Laurie conceded. "But everything changed when she got to know you. Just as it changed for you. You were only using her, too, remember? But I know that's not how you feel about her now."

"If she went off with that guy, then he's obviously who she wants. She was just amusing herself with me."

"Damn it, Ty!" Laurie shouted, infuriated by his stubbornness. "You know she's not like that! She's a good person. Smart and kind."

He interrupted, "She doesn't belong here. She'd never fit in."

"She would if you'd give her a chance," Laurie pleaded. "Zoey loved it here. She didn't want to leave. You turned your back on her out there, I'll bet. That's the only reason she would've run off with that poor excuse for a boyfriend. Zoey's the kind of woman who needs to be shown how much you love her. Hell, we're all that kind of woman! But men like you and Pete just don't get it!"

"Wait a minute, I'm not like Pete! I made a commitment in my marriage that he's never been able to make!"

"A commitment to Sarah," Laurie said gently, her anger gone. "But Sarah's gone, Tyler. Zoey's alive and she loves you. Unless I'm very much mistaken, she needs you every bit as much as you need her."

He shook his head stubbornly. "You're wrong, Laurie. I don't need her. And I sure as hell don't love her."

Laurie recognized defeat when she faced it. Tyler wasn't known as one of the most stubborn men in the county for nothing. She looked at her little brother with infinite sadness. "I kept hoping that some day you'd realize you didn't die along with Sarah and the baby. But I was wrong. You did."

She turned and walked slowly back toward the house, her shoulders sagging and her head bowed.

Watching her go, Tyler told himself Laurie was just behaving like a damn fool woman. Then why, he wondered, did *he* feel so foolish?

15

Brian chose the Hudson River Club as the site of their engagement party. Zoey would have preferred her own comfortable loft, or even Brian's fancier, less comfortable Park Avenue condo—any place where they could relax, laugh as loudly as they wished, and generally let their hair down. But Brian insisted he wanted to do this right. After all, it was the first and last time he ever intended to become engaged. And his bosses, the partners in the law firm where he worked, would be there. He had to make an impression.

The club was certainly the right choice to do that. With its magnificent views of the New York harbor and its location in the World Trade Center, it had just the right atmosphere of power and prestige. The fact that the food, regional American fare, was very good, was beside the point.

Thirty people, most of them Brian's coworkers and immediate family, were packed into a small, private banquet room. The party had been thrown together on such short notice there wasn't time for Zoey's family in upstate New York to come. Her mother had suggested a second engagement party in her hometown in a few weeks, and Zoey had eagerly agreed. Unlike this fancy affair, it would be held at her mother's house, and her mother and sisters-in-law would do all the cooking.

Zoey didn't want to admit it, but she was glad her family wasn't here. They would have felt uncomfortable in such a toney environment and would have had nothing in common with Brian's high-powered colleagues and upper-class family. She was extremely proud of her mother, a nurse, and her brothers, who were partners in a plumbing business. But she sensed, even though he'd never admitted it, that Brian preferred to keep Zoey's blue-collar background a secret.

Despite Brian and Zoey's long relationship, somehow their families had never met. It had been a conscious decision on Brian's part, and a less conscious, rather more cowardly one on Zoey's. She was frankly intimidated by Brian's wealthy, sophisticated parents, ambitious brother, and well-married sister. And she knew her unpretentious family would be even more intimidated.

Zoey wondered how they would get along when they all finally met. Her family had accepted Brian, and Brian's family had seemed to accept her. But there hadn't been a great deal of warmth expressed by either group toward their child's choice of partner.

While waiters circulated with platters of hors d'oeuvres and glasses of champagne, Zoey stood next to Brian, accepting the congratulations and good wishes of the guests. She felt uncomfortable in the designer cocktail dress, pearls, and high heels Brian had selected for her. But he had insisted that, on this one night, she needed to make a good impression so everyone would realize what a lucky man he was. Afterward, he told her, she could go back to her more bohemian look.

But she suspected her transformation wouldn't end here. He would expect her to entertain his colleagues, and he wouldn't want her to do it in jeans and T-shirts. And when they visited his family in Connecticut, she would undoubtedly be expected to dress as they did.

Suddenly, she had a vision of herself in tweed skirts and twinsets, her unruly mop of hair carefully straightened and pulled back by a velvet hairband. It was a frightening thought.

She was pulled out of her unhappy reverie when Brian's mother, Elisabeth, joined them. Elisabeth was a still-beautiful woman in her late fifties, and so impeccably groomed as to make Zoey feel vaguely unkempt. The woman had never been anything other than perfectly polite to Zoey, yet somehow Zoey never felt comfortable in her presence.

Now Elisabeth said with a pleased smile, "What a charming party. You've really done well, Zoey."

"Brian deserves the credit," Zoey responded with more truth than modesty. "He made the arrangements. All I had to do was show up. Which is just as well, since I haven't had a lot of experience at this sort of thing."

"Well, I'm sure once you're married you'll learn how to be a wonderful hostess. You'll certainly have plenty of opportunity to entertain. The social side of business is much bigger than you might imagine. When Brian's father and I were married, I knew that as his wife I could be either an asset to his career or a burden. I was determined to be an asset, and I like to think I've succeeded."

"Certainly," Zoey murmured in agreement. She couldn't resist adding, "But you know, Elisabeth, I have a career, too. It takes up a lot of my time."

"Oh, of course, my dear. I love your little pictures."

"Thank you," Zoey said in a tight voice. Little pictures indeed.

Elisabeth went on, "I'm well aware that, nowadays, two-career couples are quite the thing. In many ways I think that's an improvement over my day, when women were expected to fulfill only one role. That worked out well for most of us, but there were some women who weren't quite so fortunate in their marriages."

For a moment, Zoey had an image of Elisabeth's peer group—the lucky women who married well and whose husbands didn't die young, go broke, or leave them for younger, more exciting women, and the unlucky ones, who found themselves on their own, without the financial security and social status that a husband conferred.

For the first time, Zoey found herself feeling an emotional connection to this woman who would soon be her mother-in-law. But the moment was shattered when Elisabeth went on blithely, "But even nowadays, we know that the man's career is the really important one. After all, he'll be the main support of the family."

Zoey bit her tongue and didn't retort that for many women that wasn't necessarily the case, either out of choice or necessity. She had to remind herself that she was, after all, marrying a man who earned a great deal more than she did, a man who came from a family where women were not expected to have careers.

Brian had stood silently by during this exchange. Now, sensing that his mother was testing Zoey's patience, he stepped in. "Zoey's an award-winning photographer, Mother. I'm very proud of her success, and I don't want her to stop doing what she does so well."

Zoey gave Brian a grateful smile and, for the first time in a long while, she felt deep affection for him. That little speech meant far more to her than he would ever know.

His mother responded in her best smooth-over-differences-at-all-costs tone, "Of course, dear. I've been telling everyone you're very lucky to have such an accomplished fiancée. I'm merely pointing out that when you have children, Zoey will undoubtedly want to spend less time on her career and more time on her family."

Zoey silently agreed with her. Of course she was eagerly looking forward to being a mother. Yet, for the first time, she wondered why, if Brian's family life had been as perfect as it had always appeared to be, he didn't want to have children. She was under no illusions about his reluctant agreement to have *one* child. That was simply a concession to Zoey, not something he wanted.

Zoey looked at Elisabeth, so lovely and poised, an asset to her husband, yet with a tightness around her mouth that suggested feelings firmly repressed. Edward, Brian's father, was the very image of a successful businessman, but wasn't that his fourth drink of the evening? Zoey asked herself. Brian's younger brother, Blaine, was even handsomer than Brian, yet with a tense air about him, and Brian's older sister, Margaret, was too thin and too emotionally brittle to be as happy as she tried to appear.

Zoey wondered why she'd never noticed any of this before. Perhaps, she realized unhappily, because she and Brian never really talked about the intimate aspects of their lives. And here they were, getting married.

In one week with Tyler, Zoey felt she'd gotten to know him far better than she'd come to know Brian over five years.

But thinking of Tyler was too depressing. In the two weeks that she'd been back in New York, Zoey had forced him from her thoughts, and she wasn't about to let him intrude in them now. That brief interlude in Jackson Hole was over. It had never held the potential to be anything other than an interlude in the normal course of her life. Tyler was history. Brian was the present and the future.

Squeezing his arm affectionately, Zoey murmured, "I'm going to get something a little less bubbly than champagne to drink." She nodded at Elisabeth, who smiled politely in return.

Zoey made her way across the room toward the small bar set up there, but before she could reach it, she was waylaid. Denise, Carla, and Karen all converged on her at once.

"Come on," Carla said sotto voce, "we're blowing this joint."

Before Zoey could protest, they had hustled her out of the private room and into the restaurant's main bar. They collapsed into chairs at a dark corner table, and Carla said dryly, "That's the stiffest bunch of people I've ever encountered outside a funeral parlor."

"Carla!" Zoey exclaimed. "Those are Brian's friends and coworkers and family."

"Carla's right," Karen said with mock seriousness. "Think about it, Zoey—do you want to spend the rest of your life with that bunch of stiffs?"

"I want to spend the rest of my life with Brian," Zoey insisted. "Unfortunately, it's a package deal." She added in fairness, "And he'll have to put up with my friends and family, too."

"But we're *fun*," Denise insisted.

"A regular laugh riot compared to them," Carla said.

"And your family's nice," Karen added. "Not like Brian's. His mother could freeze water with a look."

"She's not bad," Zoey insisted, but without much conviction.

The waiter came to take their order and, when Denise asked for a glass of milk, he gave her a startled look. She explained proudly, "I'm pregnant." Unsure of how to respond to that, the young waiter simply wrote down the order and left.

"So let's see the ring," Karen said.

Zoey held up her left hand, where a two-carat, round sapphire glittered in the soft light of the bar. It was truly impressive, and her friends ooh'd and aah'd over it with suitable degrees of envy.

"Did you pick it out?" Karen asked.

Zoey shook her head. "Nope. Brian did it all by himself. He remembered that I like sapphires and prefer solitaire settings."

"I'll say this for Brian," Carla admitted reluctantly, "he's got great taste."

"And the money to indulge it," Denise added. Smiling at Zoey, she said, "I don't care what Carla says, I think Brian's a great catch and you're a lucky girl. I'm sure you're going to be wonderfully happy together."

"I hope so," Zoey murmured.

"So how did he propose? Tell us every delicious word," Karen insisted.

Zoey hesitated. In the two weeks since she'd been back in New York, she'd hardly seen her friends. She and Brian were spending much more time together than usual, planning the wedding. She was also working hard to get the photographs ready for her one-woman show coming up in only a month, and at the same time developing Cheryl's wedding pictures. She wanted to get those to Cheryl and Chuck as soon as possible. They must be eagerly and impatiently waiting for them, she knew.

She had told her friends nothing of her experiences in Jackson Hole, and they hadn't pressed her for details, though it was obvious they were dying of curiosity.

But now, there was no way to tell them of Brian's proposal without mentioning Jackson Hole. And Tyler.

She began hesitantly, "Well, you see, he flew out to Jackson Hole and proposed, and then we came back together—"

"Wait a minute," Karen interrupted. "He proposed in Jackson Hole?"

Zoey nodded.

"While you were out there meeting that cowboy?"

"Tyler Ross," Carla explained to Karen, but she was looking at Zoey. "Who, I understand, is major cute."

Karen and Denise stared at Zoey curiously.

"So," Denise said with a sly grin, "forget the proposal. Tell us about this Tyler person."

"There's *nothing* to tell," Zoey insisted.

"Yeah, right," Carla said raising an eyebrow suggestively. "Then why did you stay out there so long? Remember the S. S. *Minnow* and the three-hour tour on 'Gilligan's Island'? This reminds me of that. You were supposed to be back in two days. You stayed for a *week*."

"I told you, Carla, I was photographing wild mustangs."

"Uh-huh. And what other wild things were you photographing?"

"Seriously," Denise asked, "what's this Tyler Ross like?"

"Well," Zoey began haltingly, "he's a widower. His wife died a few years ago, and he lives with his sister, Laurie, and, until recently, her daughter, Cheryl. Cheryl got married while I was out there, and I photographed the wedding."

"You're kidding!" Karen exclaimed. "I thought you didn't do that sort of job."

"I don't, normally. But they needed a photographer and, well, they're a very nice family."

"Sounds like they're nicer than Brian's family," Carla said pointedly.

Zoey merely glared at her.

Denise asked, "Well, *is* he attractive?"

"Y-yes, I suppose so," Zoey admitted.

"As attractive as Brian?" Denise pressed.

"They're very different," Zoey said diplomatically. "Tyler's very rugged. But not stupid," she hastened to add, concerned that her friends might get the wrong impression of him—as she had done before she'd met him.

"Hmm. Sounds like I should respond to one of those ads," Denise said teasingly. "Do you think there's a cowboy out there who would want a single, pregnant literary agent with two cats and a depressing romantic history?"

"How *is* your pregnancy going?" Zoey asked in a blatant attempt to change the subject.

"Twenty-four-hour morning sickness," Denise responded ruefully. "But my doctor says it should end when the second trimester begins in a couple of weeks."

Zoey assumed the discussion of Tyler had ended, but she hadn't reckoned on Carla's persistence. Ever since her return, Carla had been trying to get the truth out of her, and she wasn't about to give up now.

Carla asked, "So what did you and this Tyler do while you were out there in Jackson Hole? Go for long rides in the moonlight? Maybe go skinny-dipping in a mountain stream?"

That last comment was too close to the truth to be comfortable. To her embarrassment, Zoey blushed.

"I *knew* it!" Carla whooped, startling the waiter, who had just come back with their drinks. After he'd set them down on the table and left, Carla went on, "A lot more went on out there than you're willing to admit. You liked that guy, didn't you?"

It was no use, Zoey realized. These were her best friends, and they could read her like a book. Especially Carla, who would stubbornly persist until she got the whole truth.

Sighing heavily, she whispered, "Yeah, I liked him." She stopped, then muttered, "Oh, hell. I fell in love with him."

For once, her friends were speechless. They stared at her in amazement. Even Carla didn't have a snappy comeback.

Denise reached out to squeeze her hand reassuringly. "It's all right, Zoey. We're here."

Zoey gave her a smile of gratitude. Whatever would she do without these women, who were such faithful, caring friends? she wondered. She hoped she would never have to find out.

Suddenly, she wanted desperately to talk about Tyler, to tell them all about him. She'd kept it all to herself, and she felt as if she would burst with the intense feelings she had for him. She had thought it would be too painful to talk about him. Now, she knew she had to talk about him or burst.

"He isn't like any man I've ever known," Zoey said, an expression of wonderment lighting her face. "He's strong, physically and emotionally. But incredibly gentle, too. I never knew a man could be so gentle. He loves horses and poetry and his values are very clear and strong."

She hesitated, searching for just the right words to explain the inexplicable. "He's someone I could really look up to and depend on. He's like the fantasy I had of the kind of man my father was."

She stopped, embarrassed. Forcing herself to meet her friends' eyes, she was surprised to see that they didn't appear skeptical. Instead, they were clearly moved. Even Carla.

Denise had tears in her eyes. She whispered in a quavery voice, "He sounds wonderful. How could you have left him?"

Remembering what Laurie had told her, Zoey said slowly, "Since his wife and baby died he doesn't believe in anything. Including love. At least not with me."

Karen said with surprising vehemence, "He needs to put the past behind him. Until he can do that, he won't be able to love anyone. That's a tragedy for both of you, but especially for him. You'll go on to love Brian and have a happy enough life with him. But Tyler Ross will be alone forever because he keeps trying to hold on to something he lost a long time ago."

The conviction in Karen's tone told Zoey that she wasn't just speaking in vague generalities. "You know how he feels, don't you?" Zoey asked slowly.

Karen, normally sweet-natured and cheerful, the stereotype of the jolly overweight person, met her look. She nodded soberly. "Oh, yes, I know how he feels. Before I married Alan, I was in love with someone else. Passionately in love."

Seeing her friends' surprised looks, she said with an uncharacteristic edge to her voice, "You don't have to be beautiful to experience a grand passion, you know." Before they could respond, she hurried on, "Anyway, he went on to become a very successful actor. If I told you his name, you'd certainly recognize it."

Carla opened her mouth, but Karen said firmly, "Forget it, I'm not naming names. The point is, I was just another notch on the bedpost for him. For me, he was the love of my life. When he dumped me, I wanted to die. I wanted to lose twenty pounds—hell, forty pounds—and be skinny and gorgeous and make him eat his heart out. I was obsessed with him. He was all I could think about."

"But Alan—" Denise began.

"Yes, *Alan*," Karen replied dryly. "He asked me out for a

year before I finally went, just to get it over with. We dated for six months, and the whole time I thought of my first love and tried to figure out some way of getting him back. When Alan asked me to marry him, I turned him down. Do you know what he said?"

They shook their heads. This story was nothing like the image the three friends had of Karen's relationship with Alan. They hadn't known her before her marriage, and couldn't imagine her behaving as she was describing.

Karen leaned back in the chair, closed her eyes, and said in a voice tight with remembered pain, "He told me that he knew all about the other guy. It hadn't bothered him at first. After all, I wasn't the first person he'd ever loved, either. But he wanted me to be the last. And he wanted to be the last for me. But he said if I couldn't put the past behind me, I couldn't have a future with him. He left. Walked out. I didn't see him or hear from him for a month. And the more time passed, the more I realized what a fool I'd been. I'd just lost the most wonderful man in the world, and a chance at real happiness, because I wasn't willing to let go of something I could never have."

"But how did you and Alan get together again?" Carla asked.

Karen smiled, once again her old self. "I went to him. I knew he wouldn't come to me again. I was willing to grovel, but he wouldn't let me. He said if I could honestly say that I loved him, that was enough. By then, I could say it with complete conviction. Six weeks later, we were married. Every single day I thank God I was strong enough to accept that a dream had died—and to know there could be a new dream to replace it, if only I would let it happen."

Zoey was deeply touched by Karen's revealing story. "I think I understand why you told us about that."

Karen leaned forward and looked at Zoey intently. "I wish this Tyler Ross could put the past behind him and let himself love you. He'd be a very lucky man to have you. But if he can't do that, then you've got to let go of wanting something you can't have. Make a good life with Brian. *If* you love him."

"Of course I love him," Zoey insisted. When they stared at her silently, she repeated, "Of course I do. I wouldn't be marrying him otherwise."

But she wasn't sure if she was trying to convince them—or herself.

Later that night, Zoey sat on the sofa in Brian's apartment, making notes about wedding plans. Brian's apartment was the opposite of Zoey's colorful, free-spirited one. Decorated in muted tones of gray and beige, with Japanese art on the walls, it had an atmosphere of pristine perfection. Not the kind of place to put your feet on the coffee table and leave the Sunday newspaper lying in piles all over the floor.

Glancing around, it occurred to Zoey that Brian would undoubtedly expect her to move into his place. He certainly wouldn't move into hers. Maybe, she thought, she could keep her loft as a studio. After all, her darkroom was there. And there was no place in Brian's small, two-bedroom condo for a darkroom.

Maybe, she continued to herself, Brian would let her change the decor a bit here. A few bright pillows and some of Carla's flamboyant artwork on the walls would make all the difference. She decided she'd better ask.

"If we have the wedding in mid-December," Brian was saying, "it would fit in well with my vacation schedule, since I get two weeks off at Christmas time anyway. That way I won't have to take off any extra time. That wouldn't look good, you know, just when they're thinking of making me a partner."

"Brian," Zoey interrupted, "would you mind if I did a little redecorating around here?"

He didn't answer immediately. Finally, he asked carefully, "What exactly did you have in mind? Not stars on the ceiling, like in your place."

"No," she laughed, "of course not. I know you wouldn't like that. I was just thinking of brightening it up a bit."

"But I paid a designer a fortune to get everything just right," he insisted. "He said this place could be in *Architectural Digest*."

"That's the problem," Zoey said frankly, "it looks like it belongs in a magazine. It doesn't feel like a home."

Brian had been pacing, thinking out loud about the wedding plans. Now, he sat down next to Zoey and kissed her forehead lightly. "All right. Marriage is compromise, I suppose. Go ahead and brighten it up a bit. Just don't put any of Carla's work in here. I can't stand her stuff."

"But she's my best friend. She'd be hurt if I didn't have one or two of her paintings up."

"You worry too much about being polite and not hurting people's feelings," Brian insisted. He added as he nuzzled her neck, "I suppose, in fairness, I must admit that's one of the things I love about you."

"I'm not just being polite," Zoey insisted, pulling away slightly. "I *love* her work. I think she's very good, and some day she'll be tremendously successful."

"When pigs fly," Brian said with a dry chuckle.

"Brian!"

"Oh, all right," he conceded. "You can put up one or two of her things, but no more. Just don't put them where I have to look at them all the time."

"This is a small place. There's only the living room and the bedroom," Zoey pointed out.

"Put them in the guest room. There's hardly ever anyone in there."

Before she could argue further, he went on, "Now, let's talk about the really serious matters."

Money, Zoey thought.

"Money," Brian echoed. "We've both got healthy incomes, though mine is a bit more robust than yours," he said with a smug grin. "For that reason, I think a prenuptial agreement is in order. We both have financial assets to protect."

As if anticipating an argument from Zoey, he hastened to add, "It's what I advise all my clients who are getting married. I could hardly do less for myself."

"I don't have a problem with that," Zoey assured him. The truth was she didn't care about Brian's money. She never had. She wondered if he would believe her if she told him that.

"Good," he said, relieved. "I'll have it drawn up in the next couple of weeks, and you can hire an attorney to go over it."

"I don't need to hire an attorney, Brian," Zoey said tiredly, suddenly exhausted with the whole subject.

"Well, do as you think best, of course. But I do think you should consult someone." Moving on, he said, "We might as well continue to keep separate bank accounts for our personal expenses, and a joint account for household expenses. All right?"

"Sure," Zoey's voice was flat.

"And I want you to know, I don't expect you to take my name."

That got her attention. She'd been leaning back against the sofa. Now, she sat up straight and said, "What?"

"Not unless you want to, of course. I understand that you're established professionally under your own name, and you may well want to keep it."

She hadn't thought about keeping her name. She had simply assumed that when she married she would take her husband's name. Rather traditional of her, she knew, but then she was pretty traditional at heart.

"I assumed I'd take your name," she said slowly, wondering if he wanted her to do so.

"Good," he responded with a smile. "I just didn't want you to think I would expect it."

Zoey understood the dangers of having expectations that were too high, but she was beginning to wonder if it was possible to have expectations that were too low.

"Finally," Brian finished, "there's the matter of the wedding gifts."

"Wedding gifts? What do you mean?"

"I think it's only fair to agree that in the event of divorce, we each keep the gifts our respective friends and families have given us. That way there's no wrangling over the Chinese vase Uncle Tim gave us and the crystal candlesticks Cousin Clara gave us."

"We don't have an Uncle Tim or Cousin Clara," Zoey pointed out, a little confused.

"You know what I mean. Agreed?"

Zoey sighed. "Agreed."

"I think that's enough for now," Brian said stifling a yawn. "We can start making a list of wedding preparations tomorrow night over dinner." He caught himself, "Oh, sorry, I have a dinner meeting tomorrow. Well, maybe the next night. Anyway, I'm exhausted. How about if we go to bed?"

"You go ahead," Zoey said. "I want to stay up for awhile."

He kissed her lightly on the lips. "All right. But don't be long or I'll be asleep," he finished with a suggestive wink.

When he had disappeared into the bedroom, Zoey sat there for awhile, her mind racing with thoughts she wished she could stifle. It was becoming terribly clear exactly what her married life with Brian would be like. A life of different last names and separate bank accounts. They would spend at least sixty-five hours a week apart as each obsessively pursued demanding careers. They would be less like a married couple than two single people with duplicate house keys.

And when the baby came—the one child they would have together—Zoey was under no illusions that things would change. Brian would provide financially for his child, but he wouldn't be an involved father—any more than Zoey suspected his own father had been.

Getting up, Zoey walked over to the window and looked out at the dark night sky. She could barely make out the moon, dimly visible through layers of smog. She remembered the Wyoming sky—clear and vast, with more stars than Zoey had ever dreamed existed. She wondered if Tyler was looking up at the moon at that moment and, if so, if he was thinking of her.

Shaking herself, she told herself it didn't matter. Karen was right. There was no use in wanting something she couldn't have.

16

Tyler took the empty bottle from the foal and set it aside. In only two weeks, the foal had noticeably gained weight and was stronger. Now, instead of collapsing as soon as he was fed, he shoved his nose against Tyler, wanting to play. Tyler chuckled and stroked his velvety muzzle. "You're a tough little guy," he murmured.

"And you're a dang fool, talkin' to a horse like that."

Looking up, Tyler saw Jesse watching him over the gate of the stall. He responded goodnaturedly, "I've heard you say a thing or two to a horse in your time."

"Cussin' 'em out, as all," Jesse said. "Ornery beasts."

"But you've got to admit they're magnificent creatures," Tyler insisted.

"I ain't got to admit no such thing. Horses are useful, when they're not givin' you trouble. An' that's all they are."

Tyler smiled to himself. He knew that Jesse was a good deal more fond of all animals, including horses, than he would admit.

Jesse went on, "What're we gonna do with this one, when

he gets bigger? We don't need no more saddle horses around here."

"Cheryl and Chuck have a small piece of land they're going to build on next year. Chuck has always wanted a horse. I thought we'd give him to them."

Jesse snorted. "The boy won't know what to do with him. His daddy never taught him about horses."

"Then you teach him," Tyler suggested.

Jesse frowned. "Like that's all I got to do with my time."

"He'd make a good mount for their children some day—if he's trained right," Tyler said pointedly. He knew that Jesse prided himself on being the best horse trainer in the county.

"I don't know," Jesse said, his tone negative.

But Tyler knew he'd be over at Chuck and Cheryl's training the horse whether they wanted him to or not.

"So what're we gonna call him?" Jesse asked.

"Red."

"Red? How'd you come up with a name like that? Sounds like a dog or somethin'."

Tyler explained reluctantly, "Ms. Donovan named him. Before she left."

"Ah," Jesse said simply, but with a world of meaning in that short syllable. Silence stretched out between the two men. Finally, Jesse asked tersely, "She gone for good?"

Tyler nodded, trying hard to ignore the tightness that seemed to grip his throat every time he thought of Zoey.

Carefully avoiding Tyler's look, Jesse went on, "Didn't think much of her at first. City girl. Downright stupid, when it come to that bull. But I gotta admit, she did all right the day we rounded up the mustangs. Didn't fall off her horse or nothin'."

"No," Tyler agreed, "she didn't fall off her horse."

"Gotta give her credit for that," Jesse went on equably. He added with a sideways glance at Tyler, "Pretty, too, if you like redheads."

"Do you like redheads, Jesse?" Tyler asked teasingly, trying to lighten the conversation.

"I gotta admit, I'm kinda partial to 'em. Thing is, they're never dull. Know what I mean?"

"Yeah," Tyler answered. "I know what you mean."

Jesse sighed. "Too bad she ain't comin' back." Before Tyler could respond, he turned and walked away, muttering to himself, "*Red.* Damn fool name."

Tyler wondered what on earth *that* had been about. Jesse, of all people, missing Zoey.

Why not? a voice deep inside him seemed to ask. *You miss her.*

But that was something Tyler definitely didn't want to think about. Leaving the stall, he closed the gate firmly behind him. As he left the barn, he paused to look up at the night sky. As always, it was studded with a billion stars and seemed to stretch into infinity. He found the Pleiades constellation, the seven little girls, as he'd told Zoey. He could still picture her as she'd listened, entranced, to the fable, the way her red-gold hair had shone in the light from the campfire, her gray eyes, so soft and guileless, looking at him with a mixture of curiosity and shyness.

Somehow, he felt that she'd sensed the personal significance for him of the fable, his hope that his own little girl lived on in spirit.

Zoey. An odd name, he'd thought at first. Then, after he got to know her, it seemed absolutely perfect for her. An unusual name for an unusual woman.

She'd only been there a week, but she'd left an indelible impression. Even on Jesse, of all people. Now, she was gone, back to New York, where, Tyler told himself, she belonged. Back to the boyfriend who was undoubtedly better for her than Tyler ever would have been.

He couldn't think of Zoey without remembering what it had felt like to make love to her. God, it had been so incredibly sweet. He'd wanted that feeling of profound connection to go on forever. Physically withdrawing from her afterward had been one of the hardest things he'd ever had to do, because he'd wanted desperately to remain a part of her forever.

When he thought of the harsh things he'd said to her after they'd made love, and the cruel way he'd rejected her the following day when the stallion died, he felt guilt overwhelm him. He knew he had no business accusing her of being dishonest, when he'd done pretty much the same thing. When the stallion died and she reached out to him, he shouldn't have rejected her so coldly. She was just trying to comfort him.

But he didn't want comfort. There was no way in hell he could've explained that to her. He didn't want what she offered—love and passion and a chance to be fully alive again. He wanted to hold on to the pain of loving Sarah and feeling guilty over her death. In a way, that kept her alive for him.

Tyler had a self-imposed lifetime sentence of feeling bad, as if that could pay for what he perceived to be his failure toward Sarah. Carrying around a complicated load of guilt and loneliness was his penance. He couldn't give it up now. Even if he wanted to.

Zoey was in her dark room developing the two dozen negatives she'd chosen from among the nearly one hundred shots she'd taken at Chuck and Cheryl's wedding. Looking at them took her back to that place and time, and she felt again the dizzying escalation of feelings that had flooded through her then: the pre-wedding excitement as Cheryl, the bridesmaids, and Laurie got ready; Cheryl walking down the aisle on her father's arm, looking a little bit self-conscious, but thrilled; Chuck and Cheryl, now husband and wife, walking arm in arm down the aisle, their faces beaming with pure happiness.

But, what really got to Zoey were the candid shots she'd taken afterward at the reception, especially one of Tyler standing off by himself, staring at nothing in particular, his expression, as always, unreadable. But now Zoey knew what he must have been thinking about—his wedding to

Sarah in that chapel and, much too soon, her funeral in the same place.

Looking at the shots of Tyler, Zoey felt her heart constrict. She wondered if she would ever be able to look at photos of him and not feel as if someone had knocked all the breath from her body.

Suddenly, she was eager to get away from all this. She was engaged to be married, and she needed to think about Brian, not Tyler. Putting the prints up to dry, she went into the living room and called Brian. It was seven o'clock; he was probably home from work by now. Perhaps they could meet somewhere for dinner. Or Zoey could pick up some take-out food and bring it to his place. She didn't care, she just wanted to see him, to remind herself that she loved him and was excited about marrying him.

But Brian wasn't home, and his machine answered. She left a brief message, remembering at the last second to add, "I love you," and hung up.

Getting up, she paced around the apartment feeling like a caged animal, unable to sit still. When the phone rang ten minutes later, she grabbed at it.

"Brian!"

"Nope. Sorry." It was Denise.

Zoey sighed in disappointment but forced herself to sound as if she were happy to hear from her friend. "Denise, hi. What's up?"

"I'm at F.A.O. Schwartz looking for a present for Megan."

Zoey had completely forgotten about the upcoming fourth birthday of Megan, Karen's youngest daughter. She groaned. "Oh, my God, I forgot. Is her party tomorrow?"

"Yeah. I can't decide what to give her. I thought I'd check and see what you got."

"Nothing. I forgot all about it."

"Well, that makes me feel less guilty for waiting till the last minute. Why don't you join me, and we can grab a late dinner afterward."

Zoey wanted to wait for Brian's call, but she knew from

bitter experience that it might not come until very late that night—much too late to get together. And somehow she couldn't stand the thought of being cooped up in her apartment all evening—alone.

"Okay," she agreed. "I'll catch a cab and be there in fifteen minutes. Where will you be?"

"On the ground floor somewhere."

"Okay. See ya," and she hung up.

A half-hour later Zoey and Denise were walking around F.A.O. Schwartz, the famous Manhattan toy store that was a child's fantasy come to life. They were supposed to be looking for gifts for a four-year-old, but Denise kept getting sidetracked by toys for babies.

"Ooh, look at this," she said picking up an animal mobile with colorful and charming tigers, giraffes, zebras, and elephants. "Wouldn't this be great over the crib?"

"Do you have a crib?" Zoey asked.

"Not yet. But now that I'm officially into my second trimester I'm getting closer to the time when I'll feel confident enough to start thinking about decorating a nursery."

"Have you gotten anything else besides the blue donkey?"

Denise smiled shyly. "No. It was silly of me to get that, but, I don't know, I really wanted it."

They were distracted by a little boy, hardly more than a toddler, who went running past them, closely followed by a harried-looking young mother. "Carlisle, come back here this minute!" she shouted.

As the mother and child disappeared into the crowd, Zoey and Denise turned to each other and grinned wickedly. *"Carlisle?"* they both said in unison, then burst out laughing.

"That sounds like the name of a hotel. Why do parents do that to their kids?" Zoey asked shaking her head in amazement.

"I don't know," Denise responded, "but I'll bet that little guy's gonna need a lot of therapy when he gets older."

"I always hated my name when I was a kid," Zoey said frankly.

"But it's pretty," Denise insisted. "Different."

"It's different, all right," Zoey said ruefully. "I really got teased about it. I would've given anything to be named something common, like Jane or Jennifer."

As they continued on down the aisle, Zoey asked, "So have you picked out any names? Like Plaza or Sheraton?"

Denise smiled. "Nothing quite so unusual. I've always liked the name Christopher. When I was growing up, I really wanted to have a baby brother, and for some reason I imagined him being named Christopher. So that's what he'll be if it's a boy."

"And if it's a girl?"

Denise furrowed her brow. "I don't know. I haven't found any particular girl's name that really appeals to me."

Zoey eyed her thoughtfully. "You think this is going to be a boy, don't you?"

Denise started to argue, "Not really . . ." Then she stopped and gave Zoey a rueful look. "Yes, I do think it's going to be a boy. It will be interesting to see if I'm right or not."

"Well, if you are, that will make me a believer in motherly intuition."

"You know," Denise said, "Karen told me—"

Suddenly, she stopped, and a stricken expression contorted her face.

"What is it?" Zoey asked in concern.

In an instant, the color seemed to have drained from Denise's face. Her hands went to her stomach. "A cramp—a bad one. But—"

Before she could finish the sentence, she was doubled over in pain and biting her lip to keep from crying out.

"Denise!" Zoey cried.

"Oh, God," Denise moaned in a ragged voice, "get me to the hospital. Now!"

The three women sat in the waiting room outside the emergency room in Manhattan General Hospital. Carla was pacing nervously, Karen was trying unsuccessfully to read a magazine, and Zoey sat curled up in a corner of the hard, Naugahyde sofa, hugging herself tightly, staring out at nothing. When a doctor came out of the emergency room, all three women stared at him hopefully, but he passed by them and went to an elderly woman on the other side of the room. He murmured something to her in a low voice, and she burst into tears.

After a moment, the woman pulled herself together, and the doctor led her back into the emergency room. Through the open door, they could hear her sobbing out her grief.

Carla threw up her hands. "When are we going to hear something, for Chrissakes?! It's been two hours!"

Karen sighed tiredly, "I'm sure they'll tell us when they know something."

"Look," Zoey began, "it's late and you guys both have to work tomorrow. Why don't you go home and I'll call you."

Both women shook their heads. "No way," Carla said firmly.

"We're not leaving you here to wait alone," Karen added. "And besides, we want to be here for Denise when she, well, when this is over."

"You think she's having a miscarriage, don't you?" Zoey asked bluntly, for the first time voicing out loud the fear that all of them shared.

"I don't know," Karen responded too quickly. "Look, just because I've had kids doesn't make me an expert on pregnancy."

But both Zoey and Carla were staring at her intently, unwilling to let her off the hook.

Karen looked away, unable to meet their gaze. "Yeah," she whispered, "I'm afraid it looks that way."

"She's been so afraid that might happen," Zoey said slowly, fighting back tears. "Being pregnant for the first time at her age—" Her voice broke, and she couldn't go on.

Karen said with determined optimism, "Look, even if that's what's happened, it doesn't mean Denise can't try again, after awhile."

Carla frowned. "I don't know why it means so much to her to have a kid. That's something I'll never understand. I would be miserable if I got pregnant. But it's what she wants, more than anything." She sighed heavily. "This will devastate her."

Suddenly, Carla slammed her hand against the wall. "Damn it, it's so unfair! Women get pregnant all the time, women who don't want kids and can't take care of them! Hell, teenage girls who have no business getting pregnant do it! Denise would be a *terrific* mother, and look at what's happening to her!"

Zoey got up and went to Carla. Putting her arms around her, she hugged her tightly and murmured, "It's all right. No matter how bad this is, Denise will get through it."

Carla wiped tears from her eyes. "I don't know why I'm so upset about this. I don't even like kids."

Zoey smiled through her own tears. "You're upset for the same reason we all are. Because we love her, and we don't want to see her hurt. And this is going to hurt big-time."

She subsided back onto the sofa and went back to waiting in tense silence. More time passed. Routine traffic continued along the corridor outside the small waiting room. The bloody victim of a brawl was hustled along by a policeman, and an elderly man in a wheelchair was pushed along by a nurse. A few people drifted in and out.

It was past midnight when the emergency room physician came to the waiting room and addressed Zoey, whom he'd met when Denise first came in. He said in a tired voice, "Your friend will be all right. She's just been moved upstairs into a private room."

"Can we see her?" Zoey asked immediately.

The doctor shook his head. "I'm afraid not. She's heavily sedated. But if all goes well, she should be able to go home tomorrow. Will you be taking her?"

"Yes."

"Good. She should have someone with her. Call in the morning and they'll let you know what time she'll be released."

"What about the baby?" Carla asked, voicing the concern that was uppermost in their minds now that they knew Denise was all right.

The doctor's brown eyes were kind but sad. He shook his head. "I'm sorry."

Zoey felt miserable. Poor Denise. Her fragile dream was shattered.

Karen asked, "Does she know?"

"Yes," the doctor answered. He hesitated, then said awkwardly, "I noticed she isn't wearing a wedding ring. Is the baby's father around?"

"There is no father," Zoey said automatically. Then, at the doctor's look of confusion, she explained, "Denise had artificial insemination."

Somehow feeling a need to explain, to justify, she went on, "She desperately wanted a child and, well, it seemed the only answer."

The doctor said simply, "Miscarriage is always difficult, but especially so when a baby is wanted as much as your friend wanted this one." He added with real warmth in his voice, "At least she doesn't have to go through this alone. She obviously has very good friends."

Zoey smiled briefly in acknowledgment of the simple statement of truth. Denise had good friends, it was true. And a successful career and a lovely apartment. The kind of comfortable lifestyle and natural beauty that most people would envy. But none of those things mattered at the moment, because she'd just lost the one thing that mattered most to her.

The doctor excused himself to see to another patient, and Zoey, Karen, and Carla left the waiting room. As they stood outside the hospital, waiting for the cab that had been called for them, both Carla and Karen said they would come over to Denise's apartment immediately after work the next day. In a few minutes, the cab arrived and they got in. But as they drove toward their respective homes, they were silent with grief for their friend's loss.

* * *

When Zoey got home, she found a message from Brian on her answering machine. He told her to call him back if she got in before eleven; otherwise, not to bother because he would be asleep. He had an early meeting in the morning.

She wanted badly to talk to him, to tell him what had happened, to feel his arms around her, comforting her, sharing her concern for Denise. But she knew he wouldn't understand. It was just a miscarriage, he would say. It wasn't as if Denise had given birth and the baby had died.

But Zoey knew that, to Denise, it was exactly like that. A miscarriage was a death. And an especially tragic one, because it was the premature end of a life that had never even had a chance to begin.

But Brian wouldn't see it that way. And he would be irritated at having his sleep interrupted when he needed to be well rested for his early meeting.

Zoey felt sick inside at the thought that, when she needed him most, she couldn't turn to Brian. But, as always when she found herself being seriously critical of him and questioning the value of their relationship, she immediately backed off. She was being unfair to him, she told herself. He was a man; he couldn't be expected to understand how Denise would feel about this, and how sad her friends would be for her.

Tyler would understand, a tiny voice inside her said. Tyler understood loss.

But that line of thinking had a dead end. Forcing thoughts of Tyler from her mind, Zoey made herself a glass of warm milk and went to bed. But, in spite of the warm milk, the late hour, and physical and emotional exhaustion, it was a long time before she fell asleep.

Early the next afternoon, Zoey brought Denise home. She had always thought Denise's apartment in an old brownstone was exquisite, with its pale-yellow walls, white molding around the ceiling, and blue-and-yellow-chintz furniture. It was a bit of English country in Manhattan, and normally it was a sunny, cheerful, comfortable place. But now, as Zoey and an unnaturally quiet Denise entered, it seemed somehow empty and lonely.

"How about if I make some tea?" Zoey suggested.

Denise merely nodded. She'd hardly said a half-dozen words since Zoey had picked her up at the hospital. She hadn't cried, either. She'd simply maintained a grim silence and rigid self-control.

However, she *had* said a heartfelt thank you to Dr. Kenneally, the emergency room physician who'd treated her the night before.

Zoey had been surprised to see Dr. Kenneally waiting in Denise's room when she arrived. And she was even more surprised when he insisted on wheeling Denise out to the waiting taxi. Normally, she knew, a nurse would have handled that minor chore. Automatically glancing at his left hand, she noted the absence of a ring. She couldn't help speculating on the situation, but knew better than to say anything to Denise.

Now, Denise sat down heavily on the chintz sofa and put her feet up on the ottoman. Zoey went into the kitchen and, in a few minutes, had put together a tray with tea and a small plate of cinnamon-flavored English biscuits. She doubted Denise would want them, but she intended to try to get her to eat. Denise looked pale and weak. She needed to begin building up her strength.

But when Zoey came into the living room, Denise was no longer sitting on the sofa. Setting down the tray on the cherrywood coffee table, Zoey went looking for her. She found her where she knew she would—sitting in the middle of the floor of the empty bedroom that would have been the nursery. In front of her was the little blue donkey, the first and only thing she'd bought for her baby. Reaching out, Denise turned the tiny crank underneath it, then set it back down again. "The Donkey Serenade" tinkled as the donkey's head nodded up and down.

Going to her friend, Zoey sat down on the floor beside her. Denise looked at her, and her eyes were great pools of unshed tears. "It was a boy," she whispered in a ragged voice. "Christopher . . . "

Finally, she cried. Zoey held her, and cried with her.

17

In the days that followed, Denise regained her strength and was able to at least appear to be dealing well with the loss of her baby. She returned to work and insisted to her friends that she was fine. Zoey didn't entirely believe her, but she knew she couldn't hover around Denise, trying to comfort her, forever. The best thing for Denise was to focus on getting on with her life. Zoey knew she needed to do the same thing herself.

So, on a hot August day, she made plans for a special, romantic dinner for her and Brian that night. She spent the morning going to several specialty stores, looking for the freshest fruits and vegetables, the choicest cuts of meat, the finest wine. She bought a bouquet of white roses for the table and new white candles for the pewter candlesticks Brian had given her the previous Christmas.

She spent the afternoon getting a manicure, a pedicure, and a facial, and having her hair styled. Brian would especially appreciate that; he often complained about her "untamed" hair. She bought a sexy, sheer white caftan, the fine fabric shot through with silver thread, and silver sandals to match. Under it, she wore a white-lace teddy from Victoria's Secret, a surprise she'd been saving for a special evening with Brian.

He didn't share her taste in music—she loved jazz, he preferred classical—so she bought a CD of Mozart's most famous pieces. Zoey didn't know much about classical music, but she assumed Mozart would pass muster with Brian.

By seven o'clock that evening, the scene was set for an intimate dinner for two. The table was set with fine china and crystal, the wine was breathing, the candles were lit, and the lovely strains of Mozart's best filled her apartment. Beef Wellington was warming in the oven, English trifle, Brian's favorite dessert, was in the fridge, and Zoey was putting the finishing touches on her appearance.

She'd just sprayed Brian's favorite perfume on her wrists and throat when the phone rang. Suddenly, Zoey's heart sank. She sensed this was Brian, and she knew what a call at this hour meant—he was either going to be late, or he wasn't coming at all.

She answered hesitantly, "Hello?"

"Hi, sweetie," Brian began easily. Before Zoey could respond, he said matter-of-factly, "I'm afraid I have to work late. A crisis with the Forbes case. We're supposed to file the motion to dismiss tomorrow. Don't hold dinner for me; go ahead and eat."

Given their history, this cancellation was hardly unexpected. Yet, somehow, this time Zoey was more disappointed than usual. She'd put so much time and effort into this dinner, and she'd so looked forward to a close, romantic evening, something she and Brian hadn't enjoyed in a long time. Ever since they had come back from Wyoming, there had been a distance between them, a distance that even the engagement and fancy engagement party hadn't seemed to bridge. She wanted to feel close to him again, this man she was going to marry in only a few short months. This evening was designed to accomplish just that.

Now, instead of automatically acquiescing as she normally did, Zoey protested, "But I've made a really special dinner—all your favorites, beef Wellington, trifle, a wine so expensive I can't pronounce it."

"Mmm, sounds delicious. Just keep dinner warming in the oven for me, and I'll have it when I get there."

"When will that be?" Zoey asked tightly.

"I'm not sure, but believe me, I'll get there as soon as possible. Gotta run."

"Brian," Zoey said quickly before he could hang up, "this evening is important. Couldn't you forget about work just this once?"

"Forget about it? Zoey, this is the *Forbes* case. You know how important it is."

"It seems they're all important. Certainly more important than I am," she responded with a sigh.

Even through the telephone she could sense Brian's impatience, "Look, are you PMSing or something?"

"Why do you assume there's got to be something wrong with me if I ask you to think about *me* for a change, instead of your work?"

"I see," he said coldly. "You want to have one of *those* talks. Well, I'm afraid I can't indulge you tonight. I've got too much work to do. Maybe it would be best if I don't come over after all."

"Maybe it would be," Zoey agreed feeling anger rise up within her. Indulge her indeed!

"I'll call you tomorrow when I get back from court," Brian said. Before she could respond, he hung up.

Zoey stood there for a moment, gripping the receiver so hard her knuckles were white. Finally, she slammed down the phone and swore loudly and passionately. Going to the dining table, she blew out the candles. Then she turned off the Mozart. In the kitchen, she took the beef Wellington out of the oven and sat it on top of the range. She seriously considered throwing it in the trash.

Suddenly, she had an idea. From the wall phone in the

kitchen, she called Karen. "Hi, it's me. Have you made dinner yet?"

"Are you kidding?" Karen laughed. "I'm a working woman with three kids and a husband who can't boil water. I'm trying to decide if this is a pizza night or a Chinese-food night."

In the background, Zoey heard Karen's young daughters groan audibly. One of them said, "Aw, Mom, we're *sick* of pizza."

"How would you like beef Wellington, hearts of palm salad, and trifle?"

"Is this a trick question?" Karen quipped.

"No, this is a dinner for a fiancé who isn't showing up."

"*Oh*," Karen replied drawing out the single syllable thoughtfully. "Well, I'm sorry Brian's a jerk, but my husband and children will appreciate anything that doesn't come out of a carton or the microwave."

"I'll drop it off in half an hour."

"You deliver, too? What a deal."

"I'm on my way out of town anyway," Zoey explained.

"Where are you going?"

"Home," Zoey answered, with all the feeling in the world wrapped up in that simple word.

It was nearly midnight when Zoey arrived at her mother's two-story, white wood-frame house with blue shutters in the middle of the small town of Chesterton on the outskirts of Adirondack Park. Nora Donovan had waited up for her daughter, but, because of the late hour, she let Zoey go straight to bed without questioning her about this sudden, unexpected visit home.

In her old bedroom, with its lavender-flower wallpaper, Zoey collapsed onto the bed. As she contemplated finding the energy to unpack, get into her nightgown, and wash her face, she thought how good it felt to be home.

When her mother got home from work at 8:15 the next

night, Zoey had dinner ready. It was a simple meal—lentil soup and corn muffins—but her mother reacted as if it were a gourmet feast.

"You have no idea how nice it is to come home from a long day at work, and not have to worry about what to make for dinner," Nora said with a grateful smile.

"It was the least I could do, Mom, after all the meals you've cooked for me," Zoey replied with a smile.

Nora joined Zoey at the small, white Formica kitchen table that bore the scars of three children. As she ate the hot, delicious soup, she went on, "It's awfully nice when your children get mature enough to start doing thoughtful things like this without being asked. When you were a teenager, I thought it would never happen."

"When I was a teenager, I was totally self-absorbed. It didn't occur to me to do anything for anyone else, because I was barely aware anyone else existed."

Nora laughed softly. "Oh, you weren't that bad. Now, your brothers on the other hand," she said with a shake of her head. "*They* were a handful."

"Little beasts," Zoey said with an affectionate grin that belied her words.

"You were very good with them, all in all," Nora said seriously. "You took on a great deal of responsibility that you shouldn't have had to take on. I don't know how I would have managed without you, Zoey."

Zoey looked away, embarrassed by her mother's rare, heartfelt compliment. She was used to her mother offering well-meant but rather bossy advice, not compliments, and didn't know how to respond. She said awkwardly, "I didn't do that much."

Then, before she lost her courage, she said something she'd been wanting to say ever since she'd met Laurie and realized how tough it was being a single mother. "I really admire you, Mom, for raising us on your own. It must have been very hard, and very scary at times. But you always seemed so . . . so brave."

Her mother was clearly pleased and embarrassed at the compliment. "It was nothing more than the courage you find in the face of desperation. You do what you have to do."

"Not everyone rises to the occasion," Zoey insisted. "You did. I didn't appreciate that until recently when I met a woman who's also had to raise a child pretty much on her own."

"Where was this?" Nora asked.

But Zoey didn't want to get into a discussion of Wyoming—and Tyler. She gave a vague answer, then changed the subject.

The rest of the meal passed in innocuous conversation. But, when dinner was over, the dishes were done, and they were sitting in the comfortable living room sipping tea, Nora asked the question Zoey knew she'd been wanting to ask ever since Zoey's arrival.

"Something's wrong between you and Brian, isn't it?"

Zoey had never been able to lie to her mother, whether it was about what time she'd gotten home from a date or whether she'd done her homework. Meeting her mother's look, she said, "I don't think we'll be happy together. I'm not happy now, and it won't be any better once we're married."

"Then why on earth are you planning to marry him?" Nora asked with perfect logic.

Zoey answered slowly, "Because I need him to love me. If I don't have that, I don't know what I'll do."

"Oh, Zoey, you're a lovely, bright, accomplished girl. Someone else will love you, someone who can make you happy."

Zoey shook her head. "I'm not so sure of that. I don't feel very lovable."

Nora said with feeling, "Why, you're the most lovable girl in the world!"

For the first time in her life, Zoey voiced her darkest doubts to her mother. "My father didn't think so."

She didn't meet her mother's look as she said the painful words. When her mother didn't immediately respond, Zoey gave her a sideways glance, and was startled to see her looking devastated.

She heard her mother murmur under her breath, "All this time, I never knew."

Realizing that she'd caused her mother pain, Zoey hastened to smooth things over. "It's all right, Mom. That was all a long time ago and doesn't matter now."

"Yes, it does matter," Nora said in a voice trembling with unhappiness. "I keep hoping the time will come when it won't matter anymore, but that never seems to happen."

"Anyway, it's not your fault, so don't feel bad, okay?" Zoey pleaded, feeling once more as she'd felt as a little girl, seeing her mother's unhappiness and wanting to make it better.

But her mother shook her head slowly and said, "In a way, it *is* my fault, for not dealing with things honestly. I thought I was doing what was best, but now I see that I just kept the wound from healing."

She looked at Zoey, her gray eyes shimmering with tears. "I just didn't want you children to be hurt any more than you already had been. And the truth was so ugly."

There was a pregnant pause, and somehow Zoey sensed that a ghost was about to be laid to rest. "What do you mean?" she asked tentatively, unsure if she wanted to know the answer.

Nora leaned forward, as if wanting to bridge the distance between herself and her daughter. "Oh, Zoey, it wasn't that you weren't lovable. The problem was your father couldn't love. He was an alcoholic, and he couldn't love anyone or anything but the bottle."

Zoey was stunned. But, immediately, it made sense—her mother's refusal to ever have liquor in the house, dimly remembered comments of aunts and uncles about her father's "problem," her mother's almost pathological concern about her sons' drinking when they became teenagers.

She looked at her mother as if seeing her clearly for the first time. What a terrible secret to have kept for so long. "What happened?" she asked, needing to know it all now, no matter how painful.

Her mother sighed heavily and leaned back in her chair. Closing her eyes, she said, as if reciting a story so familiar it had grown stale in the telling, "Your father was an alcoholic when I married him, only I didn't realize it at the time. There wasn't so much knowledge about the problem then. I just knew that he liked to drink, and sometimes when he had too much to drink he didn't behave very well."

Opening her eyes, she met Zoey's look and continued in a sad voice, "He was deeply unhappy, and he would take out that unhappiness on the people around him, telling off a boss and getting fired, accusing me of not being supportive of him when I worried about how we would survive. I don't know why he was so desperately unhappy, child, but he was. And he turned to the bottle more and more to try to deal with that unhappiness. But instead of helping, it only made everything worse."

"Why did he leave?" Zoey asked, finally voicing the question that had haunted her for twenty-seven years.

Nora explained carefully, "When I got my nursing degree and began working at the hospital, I started to learn more about alcoholism. One of the doctors, whose wife was an alcoholic, persuaded me to go to an Al-Anon meeting. I learned so much there. Enough to know that I couldn't let things continue as they were going. I told your father he had to get help for his drinking—or leave. He denied that he had a problem, and he left."

"Why didn't you tell us this?" Zoey asked, thinking of her brothers who, like her, had never known why their father left.

Her mother looked intensely guilty. "Oh, I realize now I

didn't handle it well. But I was so desperately unhappy and scared. I was afraid you and the boys would blame me for your father leaving. Even after everything that had happened, I didn't want you to think badly of him. I still loved him, you see, and I hoped that he would get well and come home. It was years before I accepted that that would never happen."

Zoey felt a raging maelstrom of emotions—shame at the knowledge that her father was an alcoholic, anger at her mother for somehow not handling things better, and, at the same time, a recognition that her mother had handled a terrible situation the best way she knew how at the time.

She forced herself to ask another hard question. "Do you know what ever happened to him? Is he still alive?"

Her mother shook her head helplessly. "I don't know. No one in his family has heard from him in years. The last anyone knew, he was living in a shelter for indigent men in Boston. But that was ten years ago."

"Then he could've died, and no one would know," Zoey said sadly.

Her mother nodded, unable to speak.

Looking at her, Zoey realized what it had cost her to reveal all this. She reminded herself that her mother had only done so out of concern for Zoey. She didn't want Zoey to continue carrying the burden of doubting that she was worth loving.

Her mother reached out to cover Zoey's hand with her own. She said with a desperate intensity, "Listen to me, Zoey. If you don't really love Brian, if you're not happy with him, don't marry him. You deserve someone who can make you feel loved."

Brian. Finally, Zoey faced the fact that she'd never really loved him. She'd clung to him because somehow he'd gotten all mixed up in her feelings about her father. She'd felt that, if she could make Brian love her, and commit to her, it would make up for her father's abandonment.

And then another realization hit her with all the force of a freight train. Until she met Tyler, she'd never really fallen in love. She couldn't allow herself to truly love someone when she'd been so badly let down by someone she'd loved so much as a child. Growing up as she had, with loss and abandonment, she'd developed certain protections to survive. The shell that enabled her to survive the loss of her father wasn't easy to shed once she was grown.

But she'd shed it with Tyler. She'd trusted him, felt safe with him, and, in only a week, had been able to open up to him in a way she'd never done in all the years she'd known Brian.

"I'm so sorry, child," Nora whispered miserably.

Zoey smiled at her gently. "It's all right, Mom. I'm glad you told me the truth. You need to tell the boys, too."

"I know," her mother agreed, clearly not looking forward to doing so.

Zoey insisted, "It's better to be honest, no matter how much it hurts. At least now I think I'll be able to deal honestly with some other things in my life."

"You mean Brian, don't you?"

"Yes. Brian."

And Tyler, she added silently to herself.

18

Brian stared in amazement at Zoey. "What do you mean you don't want to get married?!"

Zoey could understand his anger and confusion. For years she'd made her hopes clear. Now that he'd finally popped the question, she was saying, "No, thank you."

They stood facing each other in his apartment. She'd thought it best to have this final scene between them there, so that she could leave as quickly as possible after she'd said what she had to say. When she'd returned to the city the night before, there were several messages on her machine from Brian asking where the hell she was. She'd called him right away and, without explaining where she'd been for two days, asked to meet him at his place as soon as he got home from work.

He'd immediately sensed something was wrong, and, when he pressed her for an explanation, she'd told him she thought it would be best if they talked in person. She felt she owed him that.

Now, she tried to explain her feelings in a way that

wouldn't hurt him any more than was absolutely necessary. "I went home to think things over," she began carefully, "and the more I thought, the more I realized we're not really right for each other."

"Damn it, Zoey, we've been over this," he began sternly, clearly deciding his best chance was to take the offensive.

She interrupted him in a gentle but firm tone. "No, we haven't, Brian. Not really. There are so many things I couldn't share with you, because I didn't understand them myself until now. I've been very unfair to you."

That got his attention. "What do you mean? Did you have an affair with that cowboy in Wyoming?"

She shook her head. "It has nothing to do with him. I've been unfair to you because I wanted you to love me, but I wasn't really able to love you back. Not the way you deserve to be loved. I was using you for emotional security and pretending that I was happy with you, when I wasn't."

She looked at him thoughtfully. He was quite a package—handsome, successful, a real catch. The kind of guy most women would kill for. But, to her, the package was empty inside.

He looked concerned, but not shattered. Zoey knew he hadn't yet accepted that her words were final.

"Look, Zoey, we can talk things over. If there are problems, we can deal with them. I can cut down on the number of hours I work, at least a little."

"I'm not asking you to change, Brian. I don't believe you could, and, even if you were willing to try, it wouldn't be fair to you. We should both be able to be who we really are inside, not who the other person wants us to be."

"This makes no sense at all," he said, his mouth set in a grim line.

"When you've had a chance to think about it, I think you'll realize it makes a lot of sense." She couldn't resist adding pointedly, "I think if you truly loved me, you would've wanted to get married years ago. I think you've had your own doubts."

"I *did* ask you to marry me," he reminded her defensively.

She smiled softly. "Yes, you did. And I'm honored. But you must admit you didn't do it until you realized you might lose me. Be honest, Brian—you didn't *really* want to get married. At least not to me. You were just afraid of being alone—as I was."

To his credit, he didn't argue. For the first time in that difficult conversation, he seemed to accept that there was no way of talking her out of the decision she'd made. She saw his hands tightly clenched at his sides and knew it took all of his vaunted self-control not to give way to anger or recriminations.

She added frankly, "And you didn't really want children, either."

He said slowly, "Why would anyone want to bring a child into a world like this one?"

Looking at Brian—handsome, financially secure, privileged—Zoey wondered, as she had done at their engagement party, about the truth of his seemingly picture-perfect family.

She took off the sapphire ring he'd given her only weeks earlier and held it out to him. He hesitated for an instant, then accepted it.

As she turned to go, he asked, "Are you sure this isn't about Tyler Ross?"

Looking back at him, she couldn't give him a direct answer. Instead, she said honestly, "I'm never going to see him again."

Brian responded in a surprisingly tender voice, "Then it's his loss."

She smiled at him gratefully. "Thank you."

And she left.

Zoey threw herself into the thing that had always given her life a sense of purpose and meaning, even when nothing else seemed to be going well—her work. She'd finished the photos of Cheryl's wedding and mailed them off. Now she spent long hours in her darkroom, developing the photos she'd taken of the mustangs. In the photos, they were even more magnificent than she remembered. And, though she'd had very little time, she'd gotten some spectacular shots.

The more she looked at them, the less enthusiastic she was about the photos she'd chosen for her upcoming show at Emile's gallery. They were simply more of the same gritty cityscapes she'd become known for. Somehow, the photos of the mustangs seemed more positive and uplifting, more emotionally compelling and less pretentious.

Looking at them, she remembered what Tyler had said about using his ranch as a refuge for them, and the high cost of doing so—buying feed for them in the winter and cutting down on the number of head of cattle he could run on the same land he let the mustangs graze on.

Suddenly, Zoey had an idea. It was impulsive, and Emile would undoubtedly be less than enthusiastic about it, but she didn't care. Hanging the negatives to dry, she left the darkroom, went to the phone, and called him. When his assistant put Zoey through to him, she began excitedly, "Now, don't argue, just listen."

A while later, after a heated debate, Emile had given in to the inevitable. When push came to shove, his French arrogance was no match for her Irish stubbornness. Her show would now feature photographs of wild mustangs. Zoey's share of the profits would go to Tyler. She knew he would never accept the money if she offered it to him directly, but she was sure that, with Laurie's help, she could somehow get the money to him.

When she finally hung up on a frazzled Emile, Zoey felt better than she'd felt in weeks. If this show was anywhere near as successful as her previous one, she would raise a great deal of money for the mustangs.

* * *

Laurie and Cheryl sat at the kitchen table drinking tea and looking at the wedding photos Zoey had sent.

"Oh, Mom, they're gorgeous!" Cheryl exclaimed.

"They sure are," Laurie agreed beaming happily. She was enormously relieved that what had been such a source of worry for Cheryl had turned out so well, thanks to Zoey.

"I can't wait to show them to Chuck when he gets home from work."

"You'll have to send Zoey a thank-you note," Laurie said.

Cheryl gave Laurie *that* look, the one she'd been perfecting since she was a teenager. "*Mother*, I know what to do."

"All right," Laurie conceded. "It was just a reminder."

"I'm a grown-up, married woman now, and I have very good manners." She added with a wry grin, "Thanks to you."

Laurie chuckled. "And don't you forget it."

"Do you think Zoey might come back for a visit sometime?" Cheryl asked.

Laurie's smile faded. "No, I'm afraid that's not very likely."

"Even if Uncle Tyler invited her?" Cheryl asked pointedly.

Laurie stared at her daughter in amazement. "What on earth are you getting at?" she asked, though she knew the answer perfectly well. She just hadn't realized Cheryl was that observant.

Cheryl grinned suggestively. "You know. I don't think I have to spell it out."

When Laurie didn't respond, Cheryl went on, "I saw how they were looking at each other at the Fourth of July celebration. Major lust, if you asked me."

"Cheryl!" Laurie exclaimed, trying unsuccessfully to sound disapproving.

Cheryl went on blithely, "Chuck agreed with me. We were talking about them on the way home from the dance. He thought it would be just great if they'd get together. We think Uncle Tyler's been alone too long. And Zoey's awfully nice."

"She's also engaged to someone else," Laurie informed Cheryl.

Cheryl's romantic fantasy about her uncle and Zoey popped instantly, like a balloon being pricked by a sharp pin. "What? Who is this guy?"

"Someone she's known for some time. He lives in New York."

"Then why'd she come all the way out here to meet Uncle Tyler?" Cheryl demanded.

Laurie sighed. "It's a long story." Glancing at her watch, she said, "It's nearly dinner time. Would you like to call Chuck and ask him if he'd like to eat here? I'm making lasagna."

"Thanks, but I put a pot of stew on to simmer before I left."

Laurie looked at her daughter in amazement. "You're cooking now?"

Cheryl said confidently, "You bet. Chuck says the less money we spend on eating out, the more we'll have to spend on the house. So I'm learning how to cook. By the way, can I have your recipe for chicken and dumplings? That's Chuck's favorite."

Laurie just shook her head. "I never thought I'd see the day when you'd do anything in a kitchen besides eat."

"Oh, Mom, I'm not that bad."

Gathering up the photos, Cheryl said, "I'll show these to Chuck, then we'll start dividing them up among the relatives. *You* get first pick."

Laurie smiled. "Thanks."

She rose and went over to the drawer that held her tattered spiral binder of recipes. Taking it out, she returned to the table and began flipping through it. "Let's see, chicken and dumplings . . . "

To her surprise, Cheryl reached out and closed the binder. "Don't worry about that now. I can get the recipe another time. There's something I want to talk to you about before I go."

Laurie felt a jolt of concern. Were Cheryl and Chuck having problems already? She hoped not. She wanted Cheryl to be far happier in her marriage than Laurie had been in her own.

Before she could voice her concern, Cheryl gave her a reassuring smile. "Everything's fine with me and Chuck. You don't have to worry about me anymore. Chuck says it's his job now."

"Then what—" Laurie began.

Cheryl interrupted, "I want to talk about *you*."

"*Me*?" Laurie was thoroughly confused now. In all of the talks she'd had with her daughter over the years, Cheryl had always been the focus. Never Laurie.

"Something's been on my mind for awhile, and I think now's the time to say it."

"Okay," Laurie said slowly, wondering what on earth was coming.

"When was the last time you talked to Daddy?"

Whatever Laurie had expected, it wasn't that. Thinking hard, she said after a moment, "I guess it was a couple of weeks ago."

"And he hasn't been home since my wedding, has he?" Cheryl pressed.

"No," Laurie admitted, feeling the dull ache deep inside that always seemed to be there when she allowed herself to think of Pete.

Cheryl said gently, "Mom, I know how unhappy you've been. I've always known."

As always, Laurie tried to smooth over the problem. "It's true that your dad's gone a lot, but we get along okay when he's here. We don't argue."

"Yes, you do," Cheryl protested. "You just do it late at night when you think I can't hear."

Laurie was stunned. She had no idea that Cheryl was aware of those painful arguments. Immediately, she felt that she'd let her down. Somehow, she should've been better at hiding her unhappiness.

Before she could figure out what on earth to say, Cheryl went on, "I know how hard you tried to make everything look okay, for my sake. But, you know, kids aren't dumb. They always know more than their parents think they do."

"I'm so sorry," Laurie whispered unhappily. "I wanted everything to be wonderful for you."

"Mostly, it was," Cheryl responded. "You're a great mom. I always knew how much you loved me. And when Dad was around, he was good to me. But I knew he wasn't so good to you."

Laurie didn't know what to say. She didn't want to criticize Pete, who, no matter what kind of husband he might be, was still Cheryl's father. But it was obvious that there was no point in pretending things were better than they were. Her bright, perceptive daughter had seen through all that. While Laurie felt that she'd somehow let her down, she also felt an enormous relief at the knowledge that she wouldn't have to pretend any longer. Keeping up a pretense of happiness was very exhausting.

Cheryl went on, "That's one of the reasons I got married, you know. All I ever wanted was the kind of family life that you tried so hard to give me, but couldn't. Chuck and I will have that together. We want the same things—to have a bunch of kids and grow old together. We're real happy, and we're gonna stay that way. Maybe not every minute, but most of the time, and forever."

Laurie looked at her daughter and felt a surge of pride. "How did you get to be so wise?" she asked teasingly.

"I must've gotten it from you. It sure as hell didn't come from Dad," Cheryl quipped.

Laurie laughed in spite of herself. With the back of her hand, she wiped away the tears that had sprung to her eyes.

Cheryl went on, "So you can stop worrying about me and start thinking about yourself. You don't have to live a lie for me anymore. You can go out there and try to find some happiness for yourself. You sure deserve it."

Laurie felt as if an immense weight that had been crushing her was suddenly lifted. She realized that Zoey was right—for the first time in her life, she didn't have to think of anyone else. She was free to do what she wanted. It only took a moment to know what that was. But she wasn't at all sure she had the courage to do it.

Later, after Cheryl left and Laurie, Tyler, and Jesse had finished supper, Laurie asked Tyler if she could speak to him.

"Sure," he replied distractedly, his mind on ranch matters.

They went out to the front porch and sat on the same ancient, bent-willow chairs that had been there forever. It was a warm evening, and the slight breeze that rustled the pine trees at either end of the house was especially welcome. Looking out at the familiar scene—the barn in the foreground and the mountains in the distance—Laurie wondered idly how many times she and Tyler had sat out there, talking about matters both large and small; his failing grade in algebra, whether or not there was a God, should he try to persuade Sarah to go away to college with him or accept her decision to stay with her father.

Remembering her earlier conversation with Cheryl, Laurie wondered now about all the things she and Tyler hadn't talked about. She wished now they'd been able to be more honest with each other. But she'd always wanted to protect him, just as she'd wanted to protect Cheryl. And Tyler—well, he had learned from their father not to let his pain show.

Now, she looked at Tyler, sitting beside her, looking out at nothing, his mind clearly a million miles away. She said gently, "I'm afraid I have to go away, Ty."

His startled look tore at her heart. She knew this would be hard for him—another loss in a life that had seen far too many losses. But she had to do it. If she didn't take her life in her hands now, she never would.

He stared at her uncomprehendingly. "What do you mean? When? Where will you go?"

She gave him a reassuring smile. "I won't stay away forever. I'll come back as often as I can. But I can't live here anymore. I'm going to college in New York."

The moment she said the words, she realized how bold they sounded. And maybe silly. If she were eighteen and saying them, that would be acceptable. But forty-one? Then she remembered what Zoey had said—"It's never too late to become what you might have been." *I sure hope you're right,* she thought. Because otherwise she was about to make a damn fool of herself.

To her relief, Tyler didn't say it was a stupid plan. Instead, he asked slowly, "When will you leave?"

"I'm going to call my supervisor tomorrow and give two weeks' notice, then I'll write to Pete and tell him I want a divorce."

Tyler let out the breath he'd been holding. "Well, that's the smartest thing you've done in awhile."

She grinned through the tears that pricked her eyes. "You, too? Does everyone think I should've left him a long time ago?"

"Yup," Tyler responded succinctly.

Laurie actually managed to laugh, just a little.

Tyler asked with real concern, "How will you live in New York?"

She hated to bring up a delicate subject, but there was no choice. "Zoey invited me to stay with her. At least at first. I think she meant it. Anyway, I hope so."

She went on with more hope than conviction, "I'll get some kind of job and apply to some colleges. And if I get accepted, I'll try to get a student loan. Zoey said they have special programs for people like me—reentry students, she called them."

Tyler gave her a reassuring smile. "You can do it, Sis. You can do anything you put your mind to."

"Oh, Ty, do you think so? I'm so damned scared," she admitted in a shaky voice.

"I know so," he insisted. "You're my big sister. My whole life, I've always known you could do anything."

Though she knew he hated displays of affection, she reached over and hugged him tight. To her surprise, he hugged her right back.

"I'll miss you," he whispered. "But I'll be all right. Don't worry about me. It's time you had a life of your own."

Pulling back, she looked at him and wondered how the little boy she'd often wanted to strangle had grown up to be such a wonderful man. Maybe, she thought proudly, she could take a little bit of the credit for that.

Later, she called Zoey. When Zoey answered on the first ring, Laurie was taken aback. She'd hoped to get an answering machine. That way she could leave her message, and Zoey would have time to think of a polite turndown if she really didn't want Laurie to come. When Zoey realized who it was, she said with genuine pleasure, "Oh, Laurie, it's so good to hear from you! Is everything okay? Did you get the pictures?"

"Oh, yes, and they're wonderful. You're so sweet to go to all that work."

"Hey, it was my pleasure. Did Cheryl like them?"

"Are you kidding? She was thrilled. You'll be getting a thank-you letter from her."

There was a pause in the conversation, and Laurie struggled to find the courage to ask for what she felt was an enormous favor. She was used to doing things for other people, not asking other people to do things for her.

Filling in the gap in the conversation, Zoey asked with studied casualness, "So, is everyone okay, then?"

Laurie knew exactly who Zoey meant by "everyone." "Yes," she answered. "Everyone's just fine. But everyone misses you," she added.

"Oh, well, thanks," Zoey responded awkwardly.

Grabbing at any excuse she could think of to put off the inevitable difficult question, Laurie asked politely, "And how is your, um, fiancé? Brian."

There was a pregnant pause. Then Zoey said calmly,

"He's fine, I guess. I don't see him anymore. We're no longer engaged."

"You're not?" Laurie exclaimed, trying hard not to sound too happy about it. After all, it was probably a painful subject for Zoey.

"No, we agreed we just weren't right for each other."

Laurie had to admit that Zoey sounded perfectly okay with the whole thing. She was tremendously glad. She had only talked to Brian for a few minutes, but she didn't like him. Even if she hadn't wished that Zoey and Tyler could get together, she wouldn't have wanted Zoey to end up with someone like Brian, someone so dull.

There was another pause in the conversation, and Laurie knew she couldn't put off her question any longer. Gathering all her courage, she said in an embarrassed rush, "Is that invitation to visit you still open?"

"Of course!" Zoey said without hesitation. "I'd love for you to come for a visit. I'll show you all around the city. We'll have a ball."

"The thing is," Laurie explained slowly, "it's not exactly a visit. I'm moving to New York. And going to college. If I can get in."

When Zoey didn't immediately respond, Laurie went on, "But don't worry, I would only stay with you for a few days, until I can find a job and an apartment. I don't want to impose."

Zoey interrupted, "You're welcome to stay as long as you want. For weeks! Months!" she said with a laugh. "Oh, Laurie," she finished, "I'm so glad you're not giving up."

"So am I," Laurie said in a voice suddenly choked with tears.

Two weeks later, Laurie sat at Jackson Airport waiting to board a flight to New York. Tyler and Cheryl sat next to her, making a pretense of skimming the magazines she'd bought to pass the time on the long flight. She knew they weren't actually paying attention to the articles. They felt as emotional as she did about this, but they weren't about to show it for fear of making her feel guilty.

It had been a hectic two weeks. She'd given notice to her employer, hired an attorney who started divorce proceedings against Pete, sold her pickup, and donated most of her clothes to Goodwill. She would arrive in New York with one suitcase, a letter of recommendation from her previous employer, and a heart full of hopes and dreams.

In a way, she almost felt as if she were eighteen again and, this time, instead of choosing marriage to Pete, she was pursuing her dream of going to college in a big city. It was scary as hell, but also damned exciting.

She'd had one conversation with Pete. He wasn't upset about the divorce—he just wanted to make sure she wasn't going to ask him for alimony. She had to laugh at that. Considering their respective incomes, it was more likely he could get alimony from her. When she told him she didn't want anything from him, he said, "Suit yourself then," and hung up.

Worthless though he might be in many ways, Laurie hoped Pete would remain in touch with Cheryl, for both their sakes. Cheryl needed a father, even an uninvolved one, and someday Pete would realize he needed the family he'd treated so casually. As for herself, Laurie fervently hoped she would never have to see Pete again.

When they called her flight, Laurie stood up, gathering her purse and magazines. Looking at her daughter and her brother, she said in a trembling voice, "Oh, there's so much I want to say."

"We know, Mom," Cheryl said with a grin that didn't quite disguise her own quivering voice. She hugged her mother tightly, whispered, "Go get 'em," then stepped back.

Tyler hugged Laurie briefly and said, "You let me know if you need anything."

She'd been trying to find a way to tell him about Zoey's breakup with Brian. Somehow, the moment had never seemed quite right, and there was so much to do. Now, before Tyler could pull back, she whispered to him, "Zoey told me she isn't marrying that guy."

He stepped back and looked stunned, but he didn't say anything.

"You'd better hurry, Mom, the plane won't wait for you," Cheryl said.

As Laurie hurried to the doorway leading to the tarmac, she paused briefly to look back at her family. "I love you," she mouthed silently. Then she turned and walked toward the plane that would take her to New York—and a new life.

19

Zoey and Denise stood near the gate where Laurie's flight from Jackson Hole would disembark.

"Are you sure her stuff will fit in my little car?" Denise asked for the third time.

"*Yes*. I told you, she's only bringing one suitcase. We can put that in the trunk, and she can curl up in that tiny little pseudo-backseat. It'll be uncomfortable, but it isn't that long a drive back into town."

"Why isn't she bringing more stuff?" Denise asked curiously.

"Because she's starting a brand-new life and she wants to leave the old life behind. I told her I'd take her shopping and help her pick out a new wardrobe. Then we'll go down to NYU and see about getting her enrolled. I've got an idea about a job for her . . ."

Zoey's voice trailed off as she saw Denise grinning at her. "What? What's so funny?"

"You—once a big sister, always a big sister."

"Do you think I'm being too pushy, trying to organize her life?" Zoey asked with concern.

Denise laughed. "*No.* I think you're being a good friend, and this Laurie person is lucky to know you." She added with real sincerity, "But not nearly as lucky as I am. Have I thanked you recently?"

Zoey tried to sound dismissive. "For what?"

But Denise wasn't about to let her off the hook. "For being there."

"Hey, any time," Zoey responded casually. She went on in a much less casual tone, "How are you doing?"

"Taking it a day at a time," Denise answered honestly. "Some days are better than others. But none of them are as bad as they were in the beginning."

"You know I'm there if you need a shoulder to cry on, even in the middle of the night," Zoey said, meaning it.

Denise grinned. "Definitely a big sister."

"By the way," Zoey said, "I'm taking Laurie out to dinner tonight to celebrate her first night in New York. Why don't you come?"

"I'd love to, but I can't. I have plans."

Denise looked embarrassed, and Zoey wondered what on earth these mysterious plans were. Cocking her head to one side, she eyed her friend thoughtfully. "All right, out with it. What's going on?"

"Nothing."

"Denise, you may as well come clean. You know I'll find out sooner or later."

Denise sighed in mock frustration. "You're right. You're worse than the Gestapo. All right, here's the deal. I'm going out to dinner with Larry."

"Larry?"

"Larry Kenneally. You remember—the doctor who treated me in emergency."

"Oh yeah, *Dr.* Kenneally. Cute, *single* Dr. Kenneally."

"Zoey," Denise began warningly.

Zoey assumed an innocent expression. "What? I'm not suggesting anything. I'm sure you guys simply have a nice little friendship going."

"Yes."

"It doesn't have to lead to anything more."

"No."

Zoey asked, "So, is this your first date?"

Denise couldn't quite meet Zoey's look. "Well, no, not exactly."

"Exactly how many dates have you two pals had?"

"Um, well, eight or nine. Or ten."

Zoey grinned. "Sounds like the friendship is progressing very smoothly. Why on earth have you kept it a secret?"

"Because I was sure it was going to end the way all my relationships do—either with him dumping me because he doesn't want commitment or me dumping him because I discovered he was a jerk."

Giving up the pretense of being blasé about the whole thing, Denise continued with feeling, "But that hasn't happened. He's nice, Zoey. Not boring-nice, but interesting-nice. And intelligent and funny. And not into playing games. Do you know what he said to me on our first date?"

"No," Zoey responded, "because you've been keeping the whole thing a secret."

Ignoring the little dig that Denise knew perfectly well wasn't meant seriously, she went on, "He said he isn't looking for a casual affair. He wants a serious relationship and, if things work out, marriage."

Zoey squealed with delight, causing several people standing nearby to stare at her.

"Don't squeal," Denise ordered sternly.

"Sorry, I can't help it. There are some things you just have to squeal at if you're a woman, and that is definitely one of them. Denise, this is fabulous!"

"Look, just don't count on anything, okay? I'm not."

"I still say you shouldn't have kept it a secret," Zoey said.

"It's complicated."

"Uh-oh," Zoey responded. "Don't tell me. He's married."

"Divorced."

Zoey breathed a sigh of relief. "Then what's the complication?"

"He has two children, a boy and a girl, six and eight. He has full custody of them. Their mother just took off with some ski bum she met at Vail. The kids didn't fit into her new lifestyle with a young boyfriend who likes to flit from one ski resort to another."

Zoey gave Denise a long, thoughtful look. Finally, she said, "So, how do you feel about having an instant family?"

"I don't know. I haven't met the kids yet. In fact, I'm meeting them tonight. I'm having dinner with Larry at his house. It's introduce-the-girlfriend-to-the-kids night."

Zoey correctly interpreted her friend's reluctance to count on anything as nervousness over meeting the children. She said sincerely, "They'll like you, Denise. Maybe not immediately. Maybe they have issues about their mother's abandonment, and those issues will get dumped on you. But the more they get to know you, the more they'll like you. Eventually they'll accept you."

"Oh, Zoey, you can't be sure of that."

"Yes, I can. You're perfect for each other. You need someone to love, and they need to be loved. I'm not saying it will be easy. But I think it will work."

"I hope you're right. I just have visions of them hating me on sight."

Zoey started to argue, then spotted Laurie coming toward them in a crowd of disembarking passengers. Putting Denise's fears aside for the moment, she hurried to greet Laurie, who looked like she had plenty of her own fears.

"Welcome to New York," Zoey said brightly. "Welcome to your new life."

Zoey and Laurie went out to dinner at a charming restaurant in the Winter Garden in Battery Park. Laurie was suitably impressed by the 120-foot-tall, vaulted-glass roof. She was even more impressed by the colorful variety of people and the nonstop pace of the city.

"It's as different from Jackson Hole as night from day," she said in amazement.

"Are you sorry you came?" Zoey asked, aware of just how big an adjustment Laurie had to make. Zoey had made the same adjustment in moving to Manhattan from Chesterton.

Laurie seriously considered the question for a moment. Finally, she said carefully, "I'd be lying if I said I wasn't scared. It's all so different from what I'm used to. There's safety in familiarity, and none of this is familiar. But this has been my dream for as long as I can remember."

"Sometimes when a dream comes true, you discover that it wasn't the right dream after all," Zoey said thinking of her relationship with Brian.

Laurie nodded in agreement. "That's true. At one time my dream was to marry Pete, and look how that turned out. But I want to give this dream a chance. So far, I'm not disappointed. I'm just worried about getting a job, being accepted into school, and figuring out how I'm going to pay for it."

"I have some ideas about that," Zoey said reassuringly. "I'll explain it all tomorrow. In the meantime, I know this fabulous little jazz club in the village. Greenwich Village," she explained to a confused-looking Laurie. "Want to give it a try?"

Laurie grinned. "Why not? I'm up for anything now."

"I like your attitude, girl," Zoey said. "Come on, let's boogie."

They got back to Zoey's apartment at 2:00 A.M. Even though Laurie was the one with a long day of traveling behind her, it was Zoey who'd finally called it a night. Laurie seemed to have a lifetime of stored-up energy within her. She was still wide awake, while Zoey was exhausted.

The message light was blinking on Zoey's machine, and, when she punched the playback button, she heard Denise's voice. Her tone was ecstatic. "Zoey, call me when you get in, no matter how late it is! I *have* to tell you what happened!"

Leaving Laurie to brew some herbal tea, Zoey went into her bedroom to return Denise's call. Denise picked up on the first ring, and Zoey realized she must not have gone to sleep yet.

"Denise, it's me, but it's late and you'll probably want to talk tomorrow," Zoey began. Actually, *she* wanted to have this conversation the next day. Right now, all she wanted to do was have a quick cup of tea and collapse into bed.

But Denise, like Laurie, seemed to have an inexhaustible store of energy. "Oh, no, I can't wait to tell you how it went. I'm still so high I can't sleep. Thank God tomorrow's Saturday and I can sleep in."

Zoey forbore to point out that she couldn't sleep in. She had an early-morning appointment regarding a possible job for Laurie. Stifling a yawn, she asked, "So what happened with Larry and the kids?"

"Well, I was so nervous at first. I felt like I was going on a job interview or something. But they're so adorable, with incredible manners for such little kids. Larry's doing a great job raising them. I was afraid they would look at me as just the latest woman to come in and out of their dad's life. But you know what? I'm the first woman he's brought home to meet them. Can you believe that? And *they* were nervous about meeting *me.*"

Zoey was genuinely interested in what Denise was saying. But she was *so* tired. "That's nice," she said stifling another yawn.

Denise's euphoric tone grew more subdued. "The thing is, Zoey, looking at those precious little faces, seeing how eager they were for approval, I just couldn't understand, well, how their mother could have walked out on them like that. Larry told me she hardly ever sees them, or even calls.

When I left tonight, they hugged me good-bye. Having felt those little arms around you, how could you ever leave them?"

"I honestly don't know," Zoey said sadly, thinking of her father, and the way she'd thrown herself into his arms every night when he came home from work. Having felt her arms around him, how could he have walked away? But he did.

Zoey struggled to find the right words for Denise. She said carefully, "I've never really believed in miracles. I'm more of a show-me kind of person—the original cynic, for reasons that are probably obvious. But, Denise, I honestly believe that it's a miracle that Larry and his children have come into your life at this time. You have so much to give, and they need everything you have to offer."

There was a silence on the other end of the line, then Denise said slowly, "Do you remember when you made me wish on that blue moon?"

Zoey chuckled. "Oh, yeah. You thought Gran Eileen was crazy, and I was even crazier."

"Well, I don't think so anymore. Your Gran Eileen was a wise woman, Zoey. I wished for love, and I think I just may have found it. Not quite in the manner I expected, but in a way maybe even better." She finished softly, "You wished for love, too, that night. I hope your wish comes true as well."

"Maybe," Zoey said with a lump in her throat, "there's a limit as to how many wishes can come true."

"I hope not. I'll be pulling for you."

But as Zoey said a tired good night to Denise, she believed that, for her, wishing on that blue moon had been a futile exercise.

At nine o'clock the next morning, a tired Zoey and a nervous Laurie met with Emile at the art gallery he owned just down the street from the photography gallery where Zoey's show was about to be held. When Laurie had called Zoey to say she was coming to New York, Zoey had made a point of telling her to bring the painting of a storm over the Tetons. Now, Emile sat at his desk, with Zoey and Laurie sitting on the other side. He carefully examined the picture, and Zoey could tell from his restrained response that he was impressed but trying hard not to show it. A poker face was an essential quality in a successful art dealer.

"Not bad," he murmured. "I've seen worse. But I've also seen better. Much better."

"You have not," Zoey said bluntly. "It's damn good and you know it. I'd say it's worth at least twenty thousand."

Laurie nearly choked on the figure. "Wh-what?" she stammered.

Zoey frowned at her, indicating that Laurie should let her do the talking.

Emile snorted. "Pah! Don't be ridiculous. He's unknown."

"Not in Jackson Hole."

"What is Jackson Hole?" Emile asked with a dismissive wave of the hand.

"Only the latest 'in' place to live," Zoey pointed out. "With Californians and New Yorkers moving there, you know what that means. They'll discover the best local artists and their prices will skyrocket."

"At any rate," Emile replied, refusing to acknowledge the truth of Zoey's statement, "this is hardly worth more than five thousand."

"Ten," Zoey insisted. "And if you haggle any further, I'll take it to Franco's."

"That cretin!"

"He may be a cretin, but he knows what he can sell. He'll realize he can sell this for at least twenty thousand."

When Emile didn't immediately respond, Zoey turned to Laurie. "Let's go. We don't have all day."

As she started to rise, Emile put out a hand to stop her. "Don't be so hasty. Give me a moment." Glaring at Zoey, he said, "You know, I would expect more loyalty from someone whose work I have supported."

"It's more like my work has supported you, considering the profit you make from it," Zoey said dryly.

"Oh, all right," Emile gave in grudgingly. "Ten thousand. You're a hard woman, Zoey."

"Under the circumstances, I'll take that as a compliment," she responded with a grin.

Giving Laurie a sideways glance, Zoey saw that she was barely able to contain her excitement. But Zoey wasn't finished. A financial stake to get her started in college was important, but ten thousand dollars wouldn't go far. A job was even more important.

Zoey said ruminatively, "You know, Emile, Western art is very big right now. I'm surprised you don't show more of it. I hear there's quite a demand for it."

"Yes, there is," he admitted reluctantly. "I won't have any difficulty in selling this piece."

"Then why don't you buy more of it?"

"Because one has to go where the Western artists are—in the West. I don't have time for that."

"Laurie does. She knows who the really talented, up-and-coming artists are in the West. And she has a discerning eye. She bought this piece when no one else had heard of the artist."

Emile studied Laurie critically, as if finding it difficult to believe this nondescript-looking woman could be an art connoisseur. "Mmm, I don't know."

"You could hire her for a minimal salary and a commission. She could be your expert on Western art. If it doesn't work out, what do you have to lose but a small outlay for her meager salary and travel expenses? If she finds more paintings like this one, she'll make a fortune for you."

Zoey hadn't warned Laurie of what she was going to do. She was afraid Laurie would be too nervous if she went into this meeting knowing a job might be at stake. Now, Laurie stared at her in amazement.

Emile frowned at Laurie. "What's your art background?"

"She has studied art history in college and is a respected

local expert in Western art in Wyoming," Zoey answered for her, embellishing Laurie's credentials more than a little.

"Is this true?" Emile asked.

Laurie looked to Zoey for direction. Zoey nodded almost imperceptibly. Gathering her rather frazzled wits about her, Laurie managed to answer in a surprisingly confident voice, "Absolutely."

As Zoey well knew, Emile wasn't one to hesitate when he saw an opportunity to make money. "Very well," he said, "I'll try you out. You may start a week from Monday. One month's trial. We'll see how you do."

Five minutes later, Zoey and Laurie were standing on the street outside the gallery. Laurie had a check for ten thousand dollars in her purse—and a job.

"I don't believe it!" she exclaimed. "But what if I can't do it? Oh, Zoey, I'm no art expert."

"Yes, you are. I told you the first day we met you have a good eye, and that's all it takes. Now then, how about if we go shopping and spend some of that money? If you're going to be a buyer for an exclusive gallery, you need to dress the part. Then on Monday morning we'll go to NYU and see about getting you enrolled through the reentry program."

As they set off down the street, Laurie looked like Cinderella at the exact moment when the fairy godmother waved her magic wand and transformed her into a whole new person.

Tyler finished the dinner dishes, then took a cup of coffee out to the front porch. Jesse was in town at a pool hall with some of his buddies, and, for the first time in Tyler's memory, he was completely alone at the ranch. It seemed strange to know that Laurie wasn't back in her office working and Cheryl wasn't running around getting ready for a date with Chuck. Normally, Tyler found the silence of the countryside soothing. Tonight, it seemed too silent. Downright lonely, in fact.

He told himself that he couldn't sit around feeling sorry for himself. He would just have to get used to it. Maybe, he grudgingly admitted, he should think about finding someone to go out with just on a casual basis. After all, he didn't want to turn into a hermit, stuck out here at the ranch, never going into town or seeing anyone. They'd start gossiping about him. "Tyler Ross has turned strange, you know, never sees anybody. They say he hasn't talked to anyone but that old ranch hand of his in years."

He smiled ruefully at this exaggerated image of himself. But, in a way, it was a real possibility, he knew. It was easy to lose the knack of interacting with people. He decided he definitely needed to find someone to date. But who?

Immediately, Amy Fleming came to mind. She worked as a receptionist at the Snow King Lodge, where he'd tried unsuccessfully to get a room for Zoey the first day she'd arrived in Jackson Hole. Tyler had noticed Amy's thinly disguised jealousy of Zoey. Even before that, he'd sensed Amy's interest in him, but he hadn't returned that interest. Now, he told himself Amy was an attractive woman with a pleasant personality. She'd be perfect for a casual relationship.

Going inside, Tyler called information and got Amy's number.

The next night, Saturday, Tyler and Amy had dinner at a local steakhouse. Over dinner, Amy kept up a running commentary on everything, from the interesting people she met in her job, to her family, who had been in Jackson for generations. Tyler was relieved that Amy liked to talk. It took the pressure off him to make small talk, something he wasn't good at.

When Tyler did make a comment, Amy was quick to agree with it—unlike Zoey, he couldn't help thinking, who would argue with him at the drop of a hat, and was so damned opinionated. Amy didn't seem to have an opinion, at least not a controversial one, on anything.

After dinner, they went to a popular club that featured country-and-western dancing. Amy was a terrific dancer, and Tyler told himself he was lucky to be her partner.

Then why, that same irritating little voice asked, didn't she feel right in his arms, as Zoey had done?

Finally, they wound up at Amy's apartment on the outskirts of town. As Tyler had expected, she invited him in for coffee. But they both knew that coffee was the last thing on their minds. On the sofa in her small living room, Amy turned her face toward Tyler to be kissed. He obliged. Her lips were soft and sweet, and she was oh so willing.

But, when he pulled back and looked at her, he knew he couldn't go through with it, because when their lips touched he felt absolutely nothing at all.

He shook his head regretfully. "I'm sorry, Amy," he whispered. "I have to go."

"It's all right," she said putting a hand on his arm to stop him. "It doesn't have to last forever. It doesn't even have to last all night."

She was offering exactly what he'd told himself he wanted. A casual relationship, no strings attached. No commitment and no real intimacy.

No love.

But what had sounded so perfect in the abstract was far less appealing in reality. Whatever temporary pleasure he would take in having sex with Amy would dissolve in the inevitable return of loneliness afterward. After what he had experienced in making love to Zoey, he couldn't go back to empty, meaningless sex.

Looking at Amy, who sat there watching him expectantly, he knew what he had to do.

"I'm sorry," he whispered. "You're a lovely woman, with a lot to offer, and you deserve more than I have to give."

"But I'm not asking for more," Amy insisted, a hint of desperation in her voice.

"Maybe I am," Tyler said slowly, surprising himself with the unexpected revelation.

"I'm sorry," he repeated, and left.

20

By noon on Monday, Zoey and Laurie had left the reentry office at New York University. Laurie had an armful of forms to fill out for everything from admission to the university to student aid, and a head full of hopes and dreams that she was beginning to believe might actually come true. As they headed for Zoey's favorite deli for lunch, Zoey felt that she'd done everything she could to help launch Laurie into her challenging but exciting new life.

They'd had a full weekend, shopping for clothes on Saturday, then exploring Central Park on Sunday. In her New York duds, and with her hair newly styled by Zoey's hairdresser, Laurie looked ten years younger—and infinitely happier.

After lunch, Zoey decided it was time to slow down the pace a bit and let Laurie relax. She took her to one of her favorite places in the city, the Museum of Modern Art's sculpture garden. On this hot August afternoon, it was covered with leaves and looked at once casual and stunning. Calming and restful, with its fountains, ivy-planted terraces, and trees, the garden had works by Pablo Picasso and Auguste Rodin, among others.

Zoey always felt at peace when she came here, and now, sitting on a shady bench with Laurie, she saw the same feeling of calm steal over Laurie's face. They sat in silence for a long moment, then Laurie turned and gave Zoey a grateful smile. "Thank you. I seem to keep saying that over and over, but I mean it. You've turned my life around."

"*You've* turned your life around," Zoey corrected her gently. "All I did was provide a little support. You're the one who had to let go of the trapeze and go flying through the air."

Laurie laughed. "It's an exhilarating feeling. I'm still not sure if I'll come crashing down. I just hope if I do there's a safety net down there."

"There is," Zoey assured her. "Your friends and family."

Laurie admitted ruefully, "You know, when we drove in from the airport and I got my first look at the Manhattan skyline, I felt enchanted and terrified at the same time. Here I was, this forty-something woman from Jackson Hole coming to a place I'd always dreamed about. It was just like—pow! I felt like I was entering Oz."

Zoey nodded empathetically. "I know. I felt the same way when I first came here from Chesterton. The city represented everything I yearned for growing up in that small town—excitement, success, fame and fortune. It was tough for a long time. I really struggled and was filled with self-doubt. But eventually my tenacity was rewarded, and I got everything I ever thought I wanted."

"And now?" Laurie asked eyeing Zoey thoughtfully.

"Now, well, it's definitely nice to be a success. I'm looking forward to sharing my photos of the mustangs with as many people as possible."

"But . . ." Laurie prompted.

"But . . ." Zoey shook her head in frustration. "It's not enough. Some important things are missing."

"Some things you found in Jackson Hole?" Laurie asked pointedly.

They'd avoided any discussion of Jackson Hole until now. Laurie hadn't mentioned Tyler, and Zoey hadn't asked about him. But it was always there, just under the surface of every conversation they had. Finally, it was out in the open, and, while it was painful, Zoey knew it was best to face it. She'd learned a lot lately about facing painful truths instead of trying to keep them hidden.

She met Laurie's concerned look and admitted, "I fell in love with Tyler. There's no point in denying it. And I think he fell in love with me, too."

"He *did*," Laurie assured her. "I know my little brother, and I know he's only been in love twice in his life. You were the second time—and I believe the last. I don't think he'll ever fall in love again."

"I don't believe I will, either," Zoey whispered unhappily.

Laurie said helplessly, "Oh, Zoey, you've done so much for me, I wish I could do something for you. I'd like to shake Tyler and make him realize what a fool he's being."

"If I thought it would do any good, I'd buy you a plane ticket back to Jackson Hole so you could do it," Zoey said attempting to smile.

Giving up the ineffectual effort at humor, Zoey's pathetic little smile faded. "It's no use, Laurie. It's over. Tyler wants to hold on to the past. He doesn't want a future. At least not with me."

Laurie put her arm around Zoey and hugged her briefly. "Who knows, maybe someday—"

But Zoey said with infinite regret in her voice, "I'm afraid there are some dreams that don't come true."

The cemetery was a small one just outside Jackson. It was also old, and there were names of families stretching back to the early days of white settlers in the 1800s. Tyler couldn't bear to visit the place often. But, once a year, on the anniversary of the deaths of Sarah and their baby, he placed flowers on their graves. Yellow roses. Sarah's favorite.

On this typically hot, early-September day, he knew the roses wouldn't last long in the heat of the blazing Wyoming sun. But it didn't matter. What really mattered was thinking of Sarah, reinforcing his memories of her, so that he would never forget what she had been like and how deeply he had loved her.

He knelt by the side-by-side graves in silence, not one to voice his grief out loud or to speak to Sarah. He had no illusion that she could somehow hear him. She was gone and he could do nothing about it except hurt forever.

Finally, he stood up and turned to leave. To his chagrin, he saw Hank Jamison standing nearby holding his own bouquet of yellow roses, watching with a grim expression. In the four years since Sarah's death, Tyler and his ex-father-in-law had managed to avoid running into each other here. Now, remembering their conflict over the mustangs and the death of the stallion, Tyler clenched his teeth in anger. His hands, hanging at his sides, balled into tight fists. But he wouldn't say or do anything to Jamison. Not here.

He started to walk past Jamison in stony silence and was stunned when Jamison spoke. "Tyler."

Tyler looked at the older man, wondering if he actually intended to have a confrontation here, in the cemetery where his only child was buried. Instead, when Jamison spoke, he said something Tyler had never expected to hear. "I've been thinking it over, and I guess I owe you an apology."

Tyler was stunned. "What?"

"I blamed you for Sarah's death, because I had to blame *someone*. I think maybe I was wrong. Wasn't your fault." He let out a sigh. "Wasn't anyone's fault. It just happened."

Then, without saying another word, he walked past Tyler and went to Sarah's grave.

Tyler stood there for a moment, filled with conflicting

emotions—confusion over Jamison's sudden about-face, anger at the man for reinforcing Tyler's own feeling of guilt, and a fragile, dawning realization that Jamison might be right. Maybe it hadn't been anyone's fault. It just happened, the way tragedies occur with random viciousness, devastating some people's lives, and passing by other people entirely.

Hardly conscious of what he was doing, Tyler went to his pickup and drove back to the ranch. He felt profoundly unsettled, and he paced around the house, unable to sit still, to concentrate on anything. He kept coming back to Jamison's words: "Wasn't your fault." Tyler had never expected to receive Jamison's forgiveness, let alone an acknowledgment that Tyler wasn't to blame. Why had the man done so? And why now?

There was something Tyler wanted to do, something he hadn't been able to bring himself to do for four years. He went upstairs to his bedroom and opened the top drawer of the dresser. Taking out a photo album, he sat down on the edge of the bed and stared at it. It was covered with a thin film of dust, and the plastic pages stuck slightly after not being opened for four years.

Slowly, Tyler turned each page and, to his surprise, found himself smiling at pictures of Sarah playfully mugging for the camera . . . the two of them all dressed up for the senior prom . . . on horseback. He felt a lump in his throat as he looked at their formal wedding portrait. She had looked so beautiful that day. He remembered exactly how he had felt as that picture was taken. He had felt like the luckiest man in the world.

Then came the hardest part of all, looking at the last photo in the album—Sarah at seven months pregnant, only days before her death, standing on the front porch. She glowed with happiness.

Suddenly, he remembered something he'd shoved to the back of his mind. When he'd taken that picture of her, she'd asked him if he found her unattractive now that she was getting so big. He had told her in all sincerity that she was more beautiful to him than she'd ever been.

Three days later, she was dead. And the baby they'd both wanted so badly was dead. And Tyler's life was over.

Finally, the tears that he couldn't shed when she died trailed down his rough cheeks. He had become an expert at not feeling, at numbing himself in order to survive the loss of his wife and child. He had forced himself to put one foot in front of the other and get through every day. But, in killing his ability to feel pain and loss and grief, he had also killed his ability to feel joy and love.

He had been walking around in a state of secret despair, his heart full of frozen feelings that he couldn't acknowledge.

Until Zoey.

She had touched him as no one else since Sarah had done, and he had responded. For one shining moment, he had let himself connect with her, to feel with her all the things he hadn't allowed himself to feel for so long.

But thawing out his frozen heart required far more than a brief connection. He needed to cry all the tears he had never shed and release the old guilt that tormented him. He needed to forgive himself for Sarah's death. And to be willing to let go of her.

He sat there for a long, long time, looking at the last picture of Sarah, remembering the future they'd planned together. Finally, he slowly closed the album—and accepted that what might have been could never be.

He took the album, and the photo of himself and Sarah that sat on his nightstand, and went up to the attic. The dimly-lit, dusty room was filled with all the things generations of Rosses couldn't bear to throw out. Opening an old trunk, Tyler carefully placed the picture and the album inside. Then he closed the lid.

He would never forget Sarah. She would always have a special place in his heart. But he knew now there was room in his heart for another love—if only he had the courage to seize it.

A few minutes later, after throwing some clothes in a suitcase, he went outside and hitched the horse trailer to the pickup. Then he went to the corral where the colt was and loaded it into the trailer.

Coming out of the barn, Jesse looked at him curiously. "What're ya doin'?" he asked.

"Taking the colt to New York. Be back in a few days."

Jesse stared at him as if he'd lost his wits.

"Take care of things, okay?" Tyler asked throwing the suitcase into the cab of the pickup.

"Sure, but—" Jesse began.

But Tyler had turned on the engine and was pulling away.

Jesse stood there staring after him in utter confusion. Then, his eyes opened wide in sudden understanding. "Of course," he murmured to himself. "A bride price."

And his grizzled old face split into a wide grin.

As she had done two months earlier, Zoey crossed Washington Square Park on a warm, clear evening. This time, she was heading toward Emile's gallery instead of away from it. Her show was tonight, and she was both nervous and hopeful, as she always was before these things. She hoped people would respond to the photos of the mustangs as she had done. There was every reason to be optimistic. Even Emile, who had been so irate when she told him she was changing the show, had been blown away by the pictures when he finally saw them.

Of course, his response was primarily a mercenary one; he was confident he could sell the photos for a great deal of money. He had made a final attempt to talk Zoey out of donating her share of the profits to saving the mustangs. Didn't she realize she was giving away a small fortune? Why, the profits from posters and cards alone would amount to thousands, perhaps hundreds of thousands of dollars.

Zoey had replied with infuriating calm, "I hope so," and that was the end of the discussion.

Now, as she hurried across the park, she glanced up at the sky and saw a full moon shining down. She remembered another full moon—a blue moon.

You were wrong, Gran Eileen, Zoey thought sadly. *Wishing on a blue moon didn't bring me love.*

But there was no point in dwelling on that. This was going to be a triumphant night, and all her friends would be there to share it with her. Denise was coming with Larry, and Carla, Karen, and Laurie would be there as well. It would be wonderful, she told herself. Even if it wasn't, she would act as if it was. And maybe, if she put up a good enough act, eventually she would believe it herself.

She entered the gallery moments before the official start of the show. It quickly filled with clients of Emile, art critics, and fellow photographers. Zoey stood at the back of the gallery accepting effusive compliments, while Emile worked the crowd. It was every bit the success she'd hoped it would be, and she was gratified to know it would help ensure a safe future for at least some of the mustangs.

Denise and Larry had arrived, followed by Carla and Karen. Shortly, Zoey knew, Laurie would be there. Afterward, they would all go out to dinner together to celebrate her success. She would force herself to appear excited, and wouldn't let them see how empty her success was.

A few blocks away, a tall, lean man dressed incongruously in Western garb strode down the sidewalk leading a small, reddish-brown colt behind him. He was oblivious to the curious stares of the people passing by. When he had arrived in Manhattan, he'd managed to call a delighted Laurie before she left Zoey's apartment and had gotten the address of the gallery from her. It had been frustratingly hard to find a parking place for his pickup and trailer, but now he knew exactly where he was going, and he was in a hurry to get there.

At the gallery, Zoey chatted easily with Denise and Larry. They made such a perfect couple. They were so obviously in love with each other that Zoey knew a wedding would be happening in the not-too-distant future. She was thrilled for her friend. Denise deserved the happiness she'd waited so long to find.

"We're going into family counseling," Denise was saying to Zoey. "We want to be a happy, healthy family, and there are a lot of issues to be resolved."

But Zoey was only half-listening. She noticed Karen talking to Emile and Carla flirting outrageously with a cute young photographer. He was clearly quite taken with her. Another conquest, Zoey thought ruefully, and wondered how long this fling would last.

Zoey had worked long, hard hours to get the show together on such short notice, and she felt herself growing more and more tired as the evening wore on. As soon as Laurie came and had a chance to look at the photos, Zoey would suggest they all leave. She wanted to have dinner, then go home and collapse.

She was relieved when she saw Laurie come hurrying in. Before Zoey could greet her, Laurie asked, "Did he come?"

"Who?" Zoey asked wondering why Laurie looked so excited.

At that moment, Zoey's attention was drawn to the crowd surrounding her. They seemed to be parting like the Red Sea and staring at whoever they were making way for.

Suddenly, Zoey was stunned by what she saw—Tyler, striding purposefully toward her, leading the colt. She watched in utter amazement as he crossed the distance between them and stopped before her.

Gesturing toward the colt, he said with that wry, heart-stopping smile, "Will this do for a bride price?" And he held out the reins to her.

She knew he was offering far more than words could express. But she was filled with doubts. Had he really put the past behind him? Could he love again? She wanted desperately to believe so, but was afraid.

And then she looked into his eyes and, as Gran Eileen had done when she looked into Michael Donovan's eyes, what Zoey saw there took her breath away. She saw all the love in the world.

Tears of joy spilled from her eyes as she accepted the reins—and Tyler. Ignoring the gawking crowd and the knowing smiles of her friends, he pulled her into a deep kiss.

What happens when you get everything you ever wanted? Zoey thought as she lost herself in Tyler's embrace. *You live happily ever after.*

The winner of an Academy Award for cowriting the screenplay for the motion picture *Witness*, Pamela Wallace has published twenty-three novels and is the recipient of a Writers Guild Award, a Mystery Writers of America Award, and a *Romantic Times* Reviewer's Choice Award. Several of her novels have been made into cable television movies and network television miniseries. She lives in Fresno, California.

Home Fires by Susan Kay Law

Golden Heart Award-Winning Author. Escaping with her young son from an unhappy marriage, lovely Amanda Sellington finds peace in a small Minnesota town—and the handsome Jakob Hall. Amanda longs to give in to happiness, but the past threatens to destroy the love she has so recently found.

The Bandit's Lady by Maureen Child

Schoolmarm Winifred Matthews is delighted when bank robber Quinn Hawkins takes her on a flight of fancy across Texas. They're running from the law, but already captured in love's sweet embrace.

When Midnight Comes by Robin Burcell

Time Travel Romance. A boating accident sends detective Kendra Browning sailing back to the year 1830, and into the arms of Captain Brice Montgomery. The ecstasy she feels at his touch beckons to Kendra like a siren's song, but murder threatens to steer their love off course.

Buy 4 or more and receive FREE postage & handling

MAIL TO: HarperCollins Publishers
P.O. Box 588 Dunmore, PA 18512–0588
OR CALL: 1-800-331-3761 (Visa/MasterCard)

YES! Please send me the books I have checked:

- ❑ **DANCING ON AIR** 108145-0 .... $5.99 U.S./$6.99 CAN.
- ❑ **STRAIGHT FROM THE HEART** 108289-9 .... $5.50 U.S./$6.50 CAN.
- ❑ **TREASURED VOWS** 108415-8 .... $4.99 U.S./$5.99 CAN.
- ❑ **TEXAS LONESOME** 108414-X .... $4.99 U.S./$5.99 CAN.
- ❑ **SIMPLY HEAVEN** 108221-X .... $5.99 U.S./$6.99 CAN.
- ❑ **HOME FIRES** 108305-4 .... $5.50 U.S./$6.50 CAN.
- ❑ **THE BANDIT'S LADY** 108340-2 .... $4.99 U.S./$5.99 CAN.
- ❑ **WHEN MIDNIGHT COMES** 108393-3 .... $4.99 U.S./$5.99 CAN.

SUBTOTAL .... $________

POSTAGE & HANDLING .... $ 2.00

SALES TAX (Add applicable sales tax) .... $________

TOTAL .... $________

Name________________________

Address________________________

City____________ State____ Zip Code________

Order 4 or more titles and postage & handling is **FREE!** Orders of less than 4 books, please include $2.00 p/h. Remit in U.S. funds. Do not send cash. Allow up to 6 weeks for delivery. Prices subject to change. Valid only in U.S. and Canada.

M015

Visa & Mastercard holders—call 1-800-331-3761